University of St. Francis
GEN 808.838 K274
Kellev. Leo P.,

W9-BBI-854

1978

Themes in Science Fiction

A Journey into Wonder

Edited by
Leo P. Kelly

LIBRARY
College of St. Francis
JOLIET, ILL.

WEBSTER DIVISION
McGRAW-HILL BOOK COMPANY

New York St. Louis San Francisco
Dallas Atlanta

ACKNOWLEDGEMENTS

Isaac Asimov for permission to reprint "Founding Father" by Isaac Asimov. Copyright 1965, Galaxy Publishing Corp.

Collins-Knowlton-Wing, Inc. for permission to reprint "Far From This Earth" by Chad Oliver. Copyright © 1970 by Harry Harrison.

Harlan Ellison for permission to reprint "Soldier." Copyright, ©, 1957, by King-Size Publications, Inc. Originally published in *Fantastic Universe Science Fiction* (under title "Soldier From Tomorrow"), October, 1957, by King-Size Publications, Inc.

Barthold Fles, Literary Agent, for permission to reprint "The Good Provider" by Marion Gross.

Virginia Kidd, Literary Agent, for permission to reprint "Look, You Think You've Got Troubles" by Carol Carr, copyright © 1969 by Damon Knight, reprinted from *Orbit 5*, edited by Damon Knight, originally published by G. P. Putnam's Sons. And for permission to reprint "Short-stack" by Walt and Leigh Richmond, copyright © 1964 by The Conde Nast Publications, Inc., and © 1970 by Walt and Leigh Richmond, reprinted from *Analog*, December, 1964, or POSITIVE CHARGE (Ace collection of Richmond stories). And for permission to reprint "The Post-mortem People" by Peter Tate. Copyright © 1966 by Peter Tate. Originally published in *New Worlds* (London) by Roberts and Vinte. All Rights released to the author. All stories are reprinted by permission of the authors.

Keith Laumer for permission to reprint "The Last Command," copyright © 1966 by Keith Laumer, originally published in *Analog*, January, 1967, by Conde Nast Publications, Inc.

Seymour Lawrence Book/Delacorte Press for permission to reprint "EPICAC" from WELCOME TO THE MONKEY HOUSE by Kurt Vonnegut, Jr. Copyright 1950 by Kurt Vonnegut, Jr., originally published in *Collier's*.

William M. Lee for permission to reprint "A Message From Charity," copyright © November 1947, 1967, by William M. Lee, originally published in *Fantasy and Science Fiction Magazine* by Mercury Press.

Fritz Leiber for permission to reprint "X Marks the Pedwalk," copyright © 1963 by Fritz Leiber, originally published in *Worlds of Tomorrow*, April, 1963.

The Harold Matson Company, Inc. for permission to reprint "Holdout" by Robert Sheckley, copyright 1957 by Mercury Press, Inc. And to reprint "Witch War" by Richard Matheson, copyright 1951 by Better Publications.

Scott Meredith Literary Agency for permission to reprint "The Silk and the Song" by Charles L. Fontenay, "The Last of the Romany" by Norman Spinrad, "Puppet Show" by Fredric Brown, "The Man Who Came Early" by Poul Anderson, "Muse" by Dean R. Koontz, "The Cold Equations" by Tom Godwin, "The Father-thing" by Philip K. Dick, "Maelstrom II" by Arthur C. Clarke, "Who Shall Dwell" by H. C. Neal, and "Lost Memory" by Peter Phillips, Scott Meredith Literary Agency, Inc., 580 Fifth Avenue, New York, New York 10036. All stories are reprinted by permission of the authors.

Robert P. Mills, agent for the author's estate, for permission to reprint "Gomez" by Cyril Kornbluth.

Walter F. Moudy for permission to reprint "The Survivor," copyright © 1965 by Walter F. Moudy, originally published in *Amazing* by Ziff-Davis Publishing Company.

Charles Platt for permission to reprint "The Total Experience Kick," copyright © 1965 by Charles Platt, originally published in *New Worlds Magazine* by New Worlds Publishing.

Frederik Pohl for permission to reprint "The World of Myrion Flowers" by Frederik Pohl and Cyril Kornbluth, copyright 1961 by Mercury Press, Inc., originally published in *The Magazine of Fantasy and Science Fiction*.

Fred Saberhagen for permission to reprint "Young Girl at an Open Half-door," copyright © November 1968 by Fred Saberhagen, originally published in *The Magazine of Fantasy and Science Fiction* by Mercury Press, Inc.

Gene Wolfe for permission to reprint "Eyebem." Copyright © 1970 by Gene Wolfe, originally published in *Orbit 7* by G. P. Putnam's Sons.

Robert F. Young for permission to reprint "One Love Have I." Copyright © 1955 by Robert F. Young. Originally published by Quinn Publishing Company, Buffalo, N. Y.

Copyright © 1972 by McGraw-Hill, Inc. All Rights Reserved. Printed in the United States of America. No part of this publication may be reproduced, stored in a retrieval system, or transmitted, in any form or by any means, electronic, mechanical, photocopying, recording, or otherwise, without the prior written permission of the publisher. *Library of Congress Catalog Card No. 73–160714*

ISBN 07-033504-4

Editorial Development, Jack Dyer; *Editing and Styling*, Linda Epstein and Dan Zinkus; *Design*, John Keithley; *Production*, Dick Shaw.

808.838
K274

CONTENTS

80770

Tomorrow

CHAPTER ONE

Everyone makes plans. The very act of planning presupposes the existence of a tomorrow to come. What was done yesterday determines to some extent what occurs today. It follows that what is done today will in turn affect the events that occur tomorrow.

Science-fiction authors have always been very much concerned with tomorrow. But, as authors, their concern encompasses an additional dimension not always shared by everyone, at least not to the same degree. They are deeply concerned with the events that may result from actions taken by men today. Such authors observe the behavior of men in the world today and they speculate on how that behavior may determine the nature and character of the not too distant future which here is referred to figuratively as "tomorrow."

Science-fiction authors may be called dreamers. They look about them and they see that we are and have been polluting our air, to use one example of a pressing problem facing mankind today. They ask themselves what might happen in our world as a result. One writer may decide to deal with the subject in fictional terms by depicting a world in which the uncontrolled growth of cities has so thoroughly destroyed all oxygen-emitting plants that men and other species are rapidly dying. Another writer may postulate a future criminal justice system in which the destruction of a tree or living plant by a human being is a capital crime.

Both authors in this hypothetical example have considered the problem of air pollution. Both have focused on the same aspect of the problem—the need for sufficient oxygen in the air to maintain life. But each has created a different story although both have started from the same premise after thinking about the same problem.

The possibilities for such stories are almost infinite. What is important is the fact that science-fiction stories are stories written by men and women who are concerned not only about conditions as they currently exist but also about what those conditions may imply about future conditions.

A computer, for example, may someday be constructed that possesses what could literally be called a mind. It may eventually be possible for people to travel in time as well as in space. It might be commonplace at some future date to vacation on Venus.

Such subjects are the province of the science-fiction author. The fact that the events and beings he portrays may not now exist in no way negates the value of his stories. The principal value of such stories as literature lies in the insight into the human condition which the authors display and the skill with which they express that insight. In this regard, science fiction does not differ from general fiction. Science-fiction writers, like other serious writers, are interested in basic questions that affect mankind. What is a man? How should life be lived? These are but two of the questions writers—science-fiction writers definitely included— ask themselves.

Their stories are their answers.

Science-fiction stories are not necessarily written to predict the future although many such stories have predicted it with surprising accuracy. Instead, the science-fiction story attempts to portray the writer's vision of such subjects as interstellar travel or war in the future. *Vision* is the key word here.

In this chapter, the reader will be helped to envision cities of the future and share one writer's vision of what might one day happen to the gypsies. He will be able to visualize a fictional Africa of the future. He will also discover a unique vision of the future's popular music and of some of the people who inhabit the world in which that music is made.

INTRODUCTION: The Last of the Romany

In our society, we have reaped the benefits of technological progress. The products of technology wash our clothes, condition the air in our buildings, allow us to talk to people a continent away within seconds, and perform other functions to make our life more enjoyable and less laborious.

The author of this story questions the degree to which technological progress can go before it effectively destroys the yearning for romance in man. He focuses his story on a search for the last of the Romany, a name for the people commonly called gypsies. Where, he wonders, would a romantic, nomadic people like the Romany flee when technological civilization threatens their existence.

The Last of the Romany
by Norman Spinrad

"It's been a long, hot journey," said the man with the waxed mustache. "A Collins please, bartender."

The fat bartender reached over to the console, punched the "Collins" button, and asked, "Gin, rum, vodka or grahooey?"

"Gin, of course," said the man with the waxed mustache. "A grahooey Collins indeed!" He lit up a large olive-green cigar.

The bartender punched the "gin" button, and tapped the serve bar. The clear plastic container of cloudy liquid popped up through the serving hole in the bar.

The man with the waxed, black mustache looked at the drink, and then at the console, and then at the bartender. "Do not think me rude, my friend," he said, "but I've always wondered why there are still bartenders, when anyone could press those silly buttons."

The bartender laughed, a fat good-natured laugh. "Why are there bus drivers on robot buses? Why are there brewers when the beer practically brews itself? I guess the government figures that if everyone who was unnecessary was fired, they'd have a hundred million unemployed on their hands."

The man with the mustache, who called himself Miklos, toyed with the battered guitar, which leaned against the bar. "I'm sorry my friend, for my remark," he said. "Actually, bartenders are still useful. Could I talk to that machine? And they still don't have an automatic bouncer."

"Oh?" said the bartender, leaning close to Miklos. "I was in Tokyo last year, and there they have a great padded hook that drops from the ceiling, grabs a drunk, and heaves him out the door. All untouched by human hands. Ah, science!"

Miklos scowled, and then brightened. "Ah, but the bartender still must decide who to bounce! A very delicate task, not to be trusted to a machine. Therefore, a bartender will always be necessary. Another Collins, please."

"Why are you so concerned with my usefulness?" asked the bartender, punching out another Collins.

The man with the waxed, black mustache and the weather-tanned face became very serious. "It is one of the things I search for in my travels," he said. "It is very important."

"What is?"

"Men who are still useful," said Miklos. "They are like rare birds. When I spot one, it makes my whole day. I'm sort of a people watcher."

"You travel a lot?" asked the bartender, with a little laugh. "You must be one of the idle rich."

"No," said Miklos without smiling. "It's part of my job to travel."

"Job? What kind of job? There are no more traveling salesmen, and you hardly look like a pilot—"

Miklos puffed thoughtfully on his cigar. "It is a hard thing to explain," he said. "Actually, there are two jobs. But if I succeed in one, the other is unnecessary. The first job is to search."

"To search for what?"

The man with the waxed mustache picked up his guitar and fiddled with the strings. "To search," he said, "for the Romany."

"The what?"

"The Romany, man! Gypsies."

The bartender gave him a queer look. "Gypsies? There aren't any Gypsies left. It wouldn't be permitted."

"You're telling me?" said Miklos, sighing. "For fourteen years I have searched for the Romany. I've hitched when nobody hitches, I've bummed when nobody bums. I've looked in fifty states and six continents. I even went to the Spanish caves, and do you know what? They have a big mechanical display there now. Robot Romany! Flamenco machines. The things even pass a metal hat around. But the Romany are gone. And yet, some day, somewhere . . . Maybe you could . . . perhaps you would . . . ?"

4

"Me?" said the bartender, drawing away from the man with the mustache.

"Ah, but of course not. Nobody knows. And of course, everyone thinks I'm crazy. But let me tell you, my friend, crazy is strictly relative. I think you're all crazy. Nothing personal, you understand. It's this dry, clean, shiny, Romany-killing world that's crazy. But come close, and I'll let you in on a secret."

Miklos stuck his face in the bartender's ear. "They have not killed the Romany," he whispered. Then louder: "I am the last Romany. That's the other job, to keep it all alive until I can find them. It's a good joke on the world. They try to kill the Romany, and when they fail, they try harder. But it is good for them that they do not succeed, for it is the Romany that keeps them alive. They don't know it, but when I am gone, they will die. Oh, they'll walk around in their nice, antiseptic cities for a few hundred years before they realize it, but for all practical purposes, they'll be dead."

"Sure," said the bartender. "Sure."

The man with the waxed, black mustache frowned heavily. "I'm sorry," he said. "Sometimes I forget that I'm crazy, and then I become crazier. A neat paradox, no?"

"You sound like an educated man," said the bartender, "a not-stupid man. How come you can't get a job?"

Miklos raised his head proudly. "Can't get a job! Sir, before I became Miklos, the Last Romany, I was assistant vice president in charge of sales for General Airconditioning. I am a moderately wealthy man. I know what success in this boring world is. You can have it."

"But with your money . . ."

"Bah! I wanted to see the exotic Orient, for example, so what was there? Tokyo was New York, Hong Kong was Chicago, Macao was Philadelphia. Far Samarkand is now a Russian rocket port. It's all gone. The Baghdad of the Caliphs, the China of Kubla Khan, Far Samarkand, Cairo . . . Oh, the cities are still there, but so what? They're all the same, all neat and clean and shiny."

"You ought to be glad," said the bartender. "They cleaned up the opium traffic and the prostitution. They licked malaria and yellow fever —even dysentery. They got the beggars off the streets, and built sanitary markets for the street vendors. I was in Tokyo, as I said, and it's every bit as modern as New York."

Miklos snorted cigar smoke. "And while they were at it, they replaced the Caliphs and Sultans and Khans with City Managers. Feh!"

"Well," said the bartender, "you can't please everybody. Most folks like things the way they are."

"They think they do. Ah well, I've got things to do. Can you tell me where there's a playground?"

"A playground? You wanna play golf or something?"

"No, no, a *children's* playground."

"There's one three blocks west of here," said the bartender, "But what do you want there?"

"It's part of the job, my friend," said Miklos, getting up and hoisting his guitar to his shoulder. "It keeps me from thinking too much and doing too little, and besides, who knows, maybe it does some little good. Good-by." He left the bar whistling a *chardash*.

"A nut," mumbled the bartender, tossing the used containers into the disposal. "Seems harmless enough, though."

The playground was the standard model, one block square, surrounded by a six-foot force-fence, with one entrance on each side. In addition to the usual exponential hopscotch board, force-slides and basketball grid, there was some newer equipment, including a large tri-D, and a robot watchman. Most of the children were seated on benches in front of the tri-D watching "Modern Lives," the playground educational series. They seemed quite bored, except when, as a sop to their frivolity, someone was hit over the head.

The man with the waxed, black mustache and the battered guitar walked through the gate. He was noticed only by the robot watchman.

"Sir," rasped the robot, "are you the parent or guardian of any of these children?"

Miklos blew a smoke ring at the robot. "No!"

"Peddlers, beggars, salesmen, roller skates, pets and children over twelve years of age are forbidden in the playground," said the robot.

"I am not a peddler, beggar, salesman, roller skate, bicycle, pet or child over twelve," said Miklos, who knew the routine.

"Are you a sexual deviate?" asked the robot. "Sexual deviates are prohibited from the playground by law, and may be forceably removed."

"I am not a sexual deviate," said the man with the mustache. Predictably, the robot stood there for a moment, relays clicking confusedly, and then rolled away. Miklos entered the playground, threw away his half-smoked cigar, and sprawled himself on the last bench in front of the tri-D.

He strummed a few random chords on the guitar, and then sang a staccato song in Spanish. His voice was harsh, and his playing, at best, passable, but both were loud and enthusiastic, so the total effect was not unpleasing.

A few of the younger children detached themselves from the group around the tri-D and grouped themselves around Miklos' bench. He went through "Santa Anna," some very amateurish flamenco, and an old Israeli marching song. By the end of the marching song, all but the oldest children had gathered around him. He spoke for the first time. "My name is Miklos. Now my friends, I will sing for you a very nice little song about a rather nasty fellow. It is called 'Sam Hall.'"

When he got to the part of the chorus which goes: "You're a buncha bastards all, damn your eyes," the robot came rolling over at top speed, screeching "Obscenity is forbidden in the playground. Forbidden. No child must say naughty words. No obscenity. Will the child who said the bad words please stop."

"I said the bad words, you pile of tin," laughed Miklos.

"Please stop using obscenity," croaked the robot. "Obscenity is forbidden to children."

Miklos lit a cigar and blew a huge puff of smoke at the robot. "I am not a child, you monstrosity. I can say what I please." He grinned at his appreciative audience.

Relays clicked frantically. "Are you a sexual deviate? Are you a beggar, saleman or peddler? Are you a child over twelve?"

"We went through this already. I am none of those things. Get out of here, before I report you for interferring with the civil rights of an adult human."

More relays clicked frantically. There was a slight smell of burning insulation. The robot wheeled off, careening crazily. It stopped about a hundred yards away, and began to mumble to itself.

Miklos laughed, and the children, all of whom were now clustered about him, roared with him.

"And now, my friends," he said, "let us talk of better things: Of pirates and khans and Indians. Of the thousand and three white elephants of the King of Siam. Of the Seven Cities of Gold, and the great Caliph Haroun-al-Rashid."

"Have you been to all those, mister?"

"Are you a pirate?"

"What's a caliph?"

Miklos spread his large hands. "Wait, wait, one at a time." He smiled. "No, I am not a pirate. I am a Romany."

"What's a Ro . . . ?"

"Romany! A gypsy, my young friend. Not so long ago, there were thousands of us, rolling all over the world in bright red and yellow wagons, singing and playing and stealing chickens. Now I am the only one left, but I know all the stories, I know all the places—"

"You ever steal a chicken, mister?"

"Well . . . No, but I've stowed away on planes, even on a ship once. Do you know what that would have meant in the days of the pirates? Sir Henry Morgan would have made me walk the plank!"

"Walk the . . . plank?"

"Yes, he would've stroked his dirty, black beard, and said: 'Miklos, ye scurvy bilge-rat, ye'll jump into the drink, and be ate by the sharks, or I'll run ye through with me cutlass!'"

"Couldn't you call a cop?"

Miklos grimaced and twirled the ends of his mustache. "A cop! Sir Henry would've ate one of your cops for breakfast. And at that, he'd be getting off easy. You know what Haroun-al-Rashid would've done? He'd have his Grand Vizier turn him into a camel!"

An older boy snickered loudly. "Aw, come on, ya can't turn a cop into a camel."

"I can't, and you can't, and maybe nobody today can. But in those days, in Baghdad! Why, anyone could!"

Most of the older children wandered away, but a hard core of six- and seven- and eight-year-olds remained.

"You must believe," said Miklos, "and then you can do these things. Fifty years ago, you could cross the world with your thumb. Now they say it's impossible. But, my little friends, I know better. I have done it. How? Because I am a Romany. I believe, even if they say I'm crazy."

"Wow mister, Romanies is smart, huh?"

"No smarter than you. In fact, you can only do these things if you're a little stupid. Stupid enough to believe that somewhere, sometime, there still is a Baghdad, and Samarkand is still Far. You must be stupid enough not to care when the police and the Chairmen of the Board say you're crazy. And if you believe hard enough, and are crazy enough . . ."

"What, mister?"

The man with the waxed, black mustache sighed, and then he leaned close to the circle of small heads and whispered: "If you believe hard enough, and care long enough, and are crazy enough, and become nice and wicked, then some day you will get to the Spanish Main, and the Seven Cities of Gold, and the magic city of Baghdad, where there are no robots or schools, only magicians and wild, black horses. And some day, you will see Far Samarkand, shining white and gold and red above the sands of the desert. And, little friends, if you are especially dirty, and never, never wash behind your ears, and only brush your teeth once a day, and don't watch the tri-D, and say four bad words a day for a month, and dream always of the lost far magic places, some day you will wake up, early on a cool autumn morning, and you will be a Romany!"

Miklos picked up the guitar. "And now, my little Romany, we will sing."

And he played the old songs, and sang of the far places until the sweat dripped onto his mustache. Then he pulled out a red bandanna, wiped his face, and played some more.

For two hours, he played and sang, and told the old tales.

He was just finishing the story of Atlantis, when the cop arrived. The cop was dressed in the usual blue tunic and shorts, and the usual scowl. "What the hell's going on here?" he said.

The robot came wheeling over, moaning, "Obscenity is forbidden in the playground. Obscenity is—"

"Shaddap!" said the cop.

The robot shut up.

"All right, bud," said the cop, "what do you think you're doing?"

"Just singing a few songs, and telling a few stories," said the man with the waxed mustache meekly.

"You're disturbing a public playground," said the cop. "I think I'll run you in."

A little sparkle returned to the man with the mustache. "Is that a crime, officer?" he said.

"No, but . . ."

Miklos chewed on his cigar. "Then I guess you'll be on your way," he said.

"No so fast," said the cop. "I can still run you in for vagrancy."

The man with the mustache grinned, and then permitted himself a large laugh. "I'm afraid not, my friend. No indeed, I'm afraid not." He reached into his pocket and pulled out a role of wet, soiled bills. He counted out two hundred dollars, and shoved them under the cop's nose. "See, my friend? I am hardly a vagrant. Well, my little friends," he said, turning his back to the cop, "I must be going, before there is any more trouble, and I am tempted to turn this worthy officer of the law into a you-know-what. Good-by, my friends. Remember the Romany."

The children grinned. The cop stood there. The man with the waxed, black mustache hoisted his guitar to his shoulder, and slowly walked out of the playground, whistling loudly.

The early morning sun shone in through the large picture window, bathing the bar in bright yellow light. The bar was empty, except for the bartender and a young man with a detached, faraway look. The young man, who was wearing the gold and black uniform of the Space Corps, sat at one end of the bar staring out the window and sipping a beer.

Miklos stepped in, the open door admitting a blast of hot air into the air-conditioned room. "Hello, my friend," he said, sitting down two seats away from the young Spaceman. "A beer, please."

The bartender pressed beer, and the plastic stein appeared in front of Miklos. Miklos took a long drink. "The morning is the best time for a good, cold beer," he said. "Too bad so few people recognize its beauties." He glanced at the young man. The Spaceman gave Miklos a funny look, but not one of distaste. He said nothing, and continued to stare out the window.

"Did you find the playground?" asked the bartender. The Spaceman smiled a twisted smile.

"Of course," said Miklos, lighting a cigar. "No trouble at all. That is, except for a cop that tried to chase me away. But he was little trouble." He pointed to his head. "Not too bright, you know."

The Spaceman chuckled softly.

"You still haven't told me what you did there," said the bartender.

The man with the mustache thumped his guitar. "I played this thing, I sang, I told the kids a few stories."

"What for?" asked the bartender.

The young man got up, and sat down next to Miklos. "I know what for, don't I?" he said, smiling.

Miklos laughed. "If you say you do."

"Say," said the bartender, "you're a Spaceman. You been around, no?"

"I suppose I have."

"Well, then," said the bartender, "maybe you can help our guitar friend here. He's looking for something."

"Oh?" said the young man with the faraway stare. He seemed to be suppressing something between a snicker and a grin.

"Yeah," said the bartender, laughing, "Gypsies!"

The Spaceman did not laugh. He ignored the bartender, and turned to Miklos. "You are looking for Gypsies?"

"Yes," said Miklos soberly. "Yes, I am looking for Gypsies."

"For the Romany?"

Miklos stared hard at him. "Yes, the Romany."

The Spaceman drank the last of his beer. "It is a hard thing," he said, "to find Romany these days."

10

"I know, I know," said Miklos, resting his head in his hands. "For fourteen years I have looked. Fourteen years, six continents, and God knows how many countries. It's a long time—a long sweaty time. Perhaps too long, perhaps I am crazy, and there are no more Romany, and perhaps there never will be. Perhaps I should give up, and go back to being a vice president in charge of sales, or go to a psychiatrist, or—"

"I know a place," said the young man.

"A place?"

"A far place," said the Spaceman. "A place that no one has yet seen. Alpha Centauri. Or perhaps Sirus. Or Rigel."

"The stars?" said Miklos. "Nobody's ever been to the stars."

"Indeed," said the young man, smiling, "no one has ever been to the stars. What better place to find the Romany? Out there, in a land that is not yet in the travel tours, a land that no one has ever seen, the kind of land where the Romany have always gone. Somewhere out there, there are cities that put all the legends to shame. And magic, and wonder . . . The Universe has a billion worlds. Surely, on one of them there are Gypsies, on another Khans, on another ancient Baghdad."

"A very pleasant picture," said Miklos, lighting a cigar, "and probably true. But unfortunately, it's as possible to go to those worlds as it is to visit ancient Baghdad."

"Not quite," said the Spaceman. "On the Moon, they are building a faster-than-light starship. First stop Alpha Centauri. There will be others. Many others."

Miklos stood up. "A starship! Yes! I'll book passage right away. You wouldn't think it, to look at me, but I'm moderately rich." He stared out the window at the sky. "Perhaps I'll find them yet, out there."

"Of course," said the young man, "It's a government project, like the Moon and Mars and Venus. As they say, there's only room for 'trained experts.'"

"Of course," said Miklos, "of course . . . it's always that way. Always machines, or men like machines, always. But no matter! If those ships exist, there is a way on them. If the stars are there, there's a way to bum your way. If the Romany exist, some day, somewhere, I'll find them." He stood up, and slung his guitar over his shoulder. "I'm off for Cape Kennedy," he said. "And then to the Moon, and then . . . Well, good-by and thanks."

The man with the waxed, black mustache strode out into the sunny street.

"Thanks, pal," said the bartender. "You really got rid of that screwball. He was starting to worry me. You really knew what made him tick."

"I ought to," said the Spaceman.

"Whaddaya mean?"

"Well, once there was a kid in Springfield, Ohio, in fact, the kid was me. And this kid was like all the other kids in this world, a nice, packaged, future member of a nice, packaged society. And then one day, maybe eleven years ago, a crazy guy with a mustache blew into town and told that kid a lot of tall tales about a lot of far places. Something changed in that kid that day—a very small change. But it got bigger and bigger every year, until now that little change is the whole person. And here I am, on my way to Centaurus."

"You mean there really is a starship?"

"There sure is, and you know something? Somehow, someday, in some highly illegal manner, that guy is going to get on it." The Spaceman looked out the window as if he were already on his way to Centaurus.

"What'll they do to him when they find him?" asked the bartender.

The Spaceman looked at him, a strange softness in his eyes.

"Only a certain rare kind of man can go somewhere no one's ever seen. You can't package that kind of man. You can't grow him in controlled schools and mold him on canned dreams. You've got to beat him and kick him and laugh at him and call him crazy. And if someone has whispered certain things in his ear at a critical time, you have a man who will go to the stars."

The young man glared at the bartender.

"What will we say to him, when we find him on the ship? What else, but 'Welcome, Miklos. Welcome home.'"

FOR DISCUSSION: The Last of the Romany

1. The very first sentence in this story sets the tone of what is to come in the conclusion. In what way does it do so? What does the author suggest is the larger meaning of Miklos' remark, "It's been a long, hot journey."?

2. Compare the attitudes of the bartender and the Spaceman toward Miklos. What can be deduced about their sets of values from their differing attitudes toward Miklos?

3. What is the significance of Miklos' statement to the bartender, "It's this dry, clean, shiny, Romany-killing world that's crazy." What kind of a world is the "Romany-killing world" of the story? Is it a world which kills Romanies as people, or is something else meant by the author?

4. Can you detect any similarities between Miklos and Cervantes' celebrated character, Don Quixote? If so, what are they?
5. Can you quote specific lines from the story that indicate that the author has carefully presented the image of the Romany as one that is not entirely unblemished? What is the purpose of noting such blemishes? How do they serve to highlight certain aspects of the society described in the story?
6. How does the Spaceman's remarks near the conclusion of the story concerning his childhood in Springfield, Ohio, relate to Miklos' visit to the playground earlier in the story?

INTRODUCTION: The Total Experience Kick

Science-fiction stories have long dealt with the subject of thought control. They have also speculated on the possibilities of controlling human emotions. Some of these stories have discussed in fictional terms the philosophical question of whether the end achieved justifies the means used to achieve it.

This story deals with matters of equal importance. It suggests that the manipulation of human emotions may one day be an economically profitable venture. It points out that certain types of individuals may manipulate the emotions of other individuals for personal gain without concerning themselves with those other individuals' personal welfare.

Although this story takes place in London in the year 1982, the musical performance techniques and methods outlined have their genesis in techniques and methods developed yesterday and in use today. This story exemplifies the way science-fiction authors examine what exists in the present and then speculate on what might exist in the future as a direct result.

The Total Experience Kick
by Charles Platt

It all happened back in that wild winter of '82, when Total Experience was sweeping through the music business and knocking the small agencies over right and left. Half of them went bankrupt buying the new T.E. equipment; the other half were left behind by the trend, unable to afford it.

At that time, I was fairly new on the staff of Sound Trends—an outfit as cheap as its name. They couldn't afford the T.E. equipment, and they were worried, not partial to the idea of going bankrupt because they couldn't get on to the latest music kick.

I was leafing through the small ads section of *Discord Weekly* when I caught sight of a paragraph that really started me thinking and scheming. "Urgently wanted by major Total Experience music company," the ad read. "Grade III computer programmer with tone generator experience and wide knowledge of musical instrument modification. Must be trendy, go-ahead, able to sight-read Fortran."

My first thought was one of disappointment. The job was ideal for me, but I was stuck in Sound Trends, sinking fast, tied to them by a pretty strong contract.

Then I began to see glimmerings of an idea. I checked with a contact I had on the staff of *Discord Weekly* and found that the small ad in question had been placed by Harry King, biggest firm in the business. They wouldn't be using a discreet small ad, I reasoned, unless trying to do some fast recruitment on the quiet. And *that* could only be because they'd caught on to something new and suddenly needed staff to develop it.

So this was our chance (I put it to Sound Trends' director) to get inside the Harry King organization, scrap the Total Experience kick, and steal the idea King was working on to supersede T.E. Send me in as a spy, I reasoned, and Sound Trends doesn't go bust after all—it gets one jump ahead of everyone else.

They were desperate enough to try it out. And that's how it was that, the next day, I was sitting in Harry King's own office overlooking the old Shell Center and the Thames, beginning to wonder if my idea of amateur spies was quite as foolproof as it had first seemed. At that time, King was by far the biggest man in the business; somehow he'd come up with the right ideas at the right time, and within twelve months his empire was made.

I presented a hastily assembled file of false information about my free-lance status and previous experience, which he glanced at. He gave me a lot of talk about fantastic prospects and salary increases, which was obviously phoney. After these preliminaries we got down to business.

He strode up and down, gesticulating, creasing up his pastel pink one-nighter suit. (Its style just wasn't right for his age or waistline, but he had to maintain the trendy-young-man image.)

"You think Total Experience is just another gimmick?" he said loudly. "It's not. Never was. It's an in-no-vation." He spoke the word slowly, as though only having learned it recently. "A genuine in-no-vation. Total musical appeal to all the senses. Lemme show you something. What we've pushed the kids so far is nothing, nothing at all." He pressed desk buttons and the windows opaqued, indirect lighting glowed, and two wall panels retracted to expose a pair of T.E. projectors. A Diacora screen lowered. He looked around, grunted. "Sit in that chair over there, and get this." He pressed another contact and the lights dimmed.

The screen lit up in a whirl of colors, and a jangling screech totally unlike anything I had experienced before blasted out from giant acoustic panels in the ceiling. The screen cleared, and suddenly there was a giant-size image of Marc Nova in shatteringly intimate close-up, all in depth-effect color, singing (somewhere behind the rest of the noise) his latest number. Bass notes of slightly different frequency produced stomach-churning beats. The two T.E. projectors focused on me and flickered in a subliminal pattern. Blasts of hot air, scented with a smooth, moist perfume mixed with acrid body odor, wafted over me—it matched Marc Nova's image perfectly, I noted with admiration.

The effect was cataclysmic; as the bass bleats speeded up and the pitch rose, colors flashed across the screen faster and a high-pitched whistling, hissing noise filled my ears. The sequence ended just when I felt more of it would be unbearable and I sat weakly, sweating, as if I'd awakened from a nightmare. King pressed the desk buttons and the room restored itself to its former state. "Make no mistake, fella," he was saying, pounding his desk, "that may look great now, but we gotta think ahead past it, past T.E. even, to what the trend's gonna be in six months' time." He shuffled papers on his desk, almost like an actor who's forgotten his next line. The awkward moment was broken when a girl walked in.

She dropped some folders on King's desk, then looked round and saw me. "I'm sorry," she said. "I didn't realize you had someone in here..."

When I say she looked round and saw me, this isn't really an accurate description. My image may have registered in her brain, vaguely, as a person, a visitor; but her glance went right through me, passing over me as if I was a piece of furniture. I looked down from her cold green eyes and saw a face that was beautiful, perfectly formed, yet equally cold. Then she turned back to King. "Is there anything else?"

"No thanks, honey," he said, getting up from his chair behind the desk. She went out of the room. King walked over to the window, stared out a moment. "Right," he said. "Let's make a little trip, O.K.? Go see the boy you'll work with if you join our organization." We walked up to the roof and soon were jetting over the Thames in his private 'copter.

He steered with one hand and gestured with the other. "I keep my boys split up, see? Find it works out better. They like their familiar surroundings, and this way there's less chance of any ideas leaking out. Get what I mean?"

I nodded uneasily, reminded of my role as a spy. I glanced at King's fat face; his eyes were invisible behind pola grey shades stretched across his forehead.

The 'copter began to lose height as we came down over a shabby area in Camden, east side.

"This boy," said King, "he's a creep, know what I mean? But he's a genius as well. Lemme handle him. True creative genius."

We touched down on a makeshift platform built over one of a line of

Camden back-to-backs, and walked down a rusty fire escape to the front door. King rang the obsolescent mechanical doorbell.

After some time a thin, stooping, pasty-faced figure dressed in pajamas opened the door.

"Hi there, Gerry boy," King exclaimed, stamping into the place.

"Careful, Mr. King. Damp rot in the floor, you know."

King's high spirits faded a little, but he forced a broad smile all the same. We went into the back room.

"I been working on the feedback unit, like you said, but I can't demonstrate it properly until . . ."

"Yeah, all right, so long as it's ready for the Trafalgar Square bit next week. Right now, this is the man who'll be working with you in the future, if he likes the set up." "Gerry boy" smiled nervously and we shook hands.

"My name's Joe Forrest," I said. "Glad to know you." For the first time, I really noticed the surroundings. A broken-down bed was in one corner of the shabby little room, two cats curled up on it. An '82 Descomp unit stood by the window, case shining, only a few months old. There was a dirty dinner plate on top of it and another cat sleeping on the keyboard. Adjacent to the Descomp, three obsolete, battered, quarter-track stereo tape decks and two oscilloscopes so old that the tubes were faded yellow stood on a rough bench covered with odd electrical components. There were signal generators and tone benders, boxes of second-hand parts and incomplete assemblies. It seemed impossible that such a cheap set-up could produce anything of remote value.

"What was the, ah, feedback unit you mentioned?" I asked, fishing for information. This could be what we were after.

"It's upstairs," "Gerry boy" said, shuffling to the door in his carpet slippers. "Come on, and I'll show you . . ."

"Just hold on a moment," said King. "I'm thinking that if Mr. . . . uh . . . Forrest is . . . uh . . . interested in our organization, some kind of routine . . . uh . . . loyalty test, is required. And if not, he'd best not see all our little secrets, right?" I saw King could be tough if the occasion arose.

"Gerry boy" looked confused, as if the politics of big business were beyond him. King smiled blandly at me. "Well, what's your answer, Forrest? Subject to, ah, formal agreement, you interested in joining up with the big family of Harry King?" He laughed heavily.

I swallowed uncomfortably. How could I back out? "Yes, of course I am," I said. "Only . . ."

"Fine, fine. Got a meter, Gerry boy?"

"I think so, Mr. King." He found a battered Verilyser under a pile of junk on the bench, and I watched with dumb fascination as he strapped it on my wrist, plugging the lead into an oscilloscope. My mind acted as if overloaded: it seemed impossible to find a way out of the situation, and all I could do was think around in circles, fascinated by the unstoppable sequence of events.

"I must apologize for this, ah, inconvenience," King said, looking just a tiny bit uncomfortable. "But in our business, you know, we can't afford to take any chances over personnel loyalty." He dragged out a sheet of standard questions from his pocket.

"Gerry boy" adjusted the equipment and we went ahead. "Are you, Joseph A. Forrest, presently in the employment of any rival company or engaged in any work which could be construed as competitive and contrary to the interests of the Harry King organization?"

I tried to stay calm, watching the oscilloscope trace. "No," I said firmly. The trace kinked in the characteristic sine curve that Harry King, "Gerry boy," myself and anyone else knows only too well as signifying "untruth." I started to sweat heavily.

"Hold it a moment," said "Gerry boy." He turned to me, displaying two fingers of his hand. "How many fingers am I holding up?" he said.

"Two," I replied. Again the "untruth" sine curve resulted.

"I bungled it. Wrong polarity. Truths registered as untruths." He reversed the leads. "Go ahead now." I met his eyes briefly, and the hard look he gave me only confirmed my suspicion that, for some reason, he'd fixed the test for me.

King went through the whole list of questions and my answers flashed up "truthful" every time. By the end of it he was overflowing with good spirits. "First thing tomorrow, you get down to my office, we fix the contract. Then straight along to the main studio, see how we make the recordings. We'll be starting Marc Nova's new tape. How about that, hey?"

I smiled weakly, still a bit shaken. "Terrific."

King turned to "Gerry boy." "You got room for Joe to live upstairs? Be better if you two were working as closely as possible." Gerry nodded. "Fine, fine." King pounded him heartily on the shoulder.

"Please, Mr. King, my asthma . . ." he crumpled up, coughing and gasping for breath. King ceased his pounding, looked a bit put out.

"You oughta get this dump cleaned up."

"I can't afford it right now, with mother at the clinic . . ."

"Well, you get our new gimmick working, we see what we can do." I followed him out of the house turning once to glance back at Gerry standing in the doorway, watching us leave. His normally impassive face looked faintly, cynically, amused.

The studio was, undeniably, impressive. Vast banks of unitized equipment—the T.E. recording gear—were attended by technicians, monitor-transceivers clipped to their ears. In one corner, Gerry shuffled around a piece of hardware, making adjustments, still wearing carpet slippers. It was basically a tone synthesizer, but heavily modified.

On the other side of the double-glass wall that divided the studio in two, Marc Nova, Britain's leading subvocalist, confronted the T.E. cameras, standing on a platform as spotless white as the backdrop. Above and around him, polychrome projectors stood ready to beam down the effects that were so much a part of T.E. To one side, session musicians, mostly unemployed jazzmen, sat holding their outdated, physically blown instruments, almost protectively.

Harry King and myself and a number of others observed the scene from a gallery fifteen feet above. "None of the old methods, here," King was saying. "This studio layout was designed specially for T.E.—none of the old makeshift mods and breadboard electronics. See the white goo they're pasting on Nova's face? Symbolic of our methods. Blank it out, then build up what you want. The correct skin-pigment tint will be added when the film is processed. And using that goo we can fix his face up, too. More aggressive, more sexy . . . sculpt a bit on here and there and the stuff dries to a homogeneous plastic texture in ten minutes. It's the only way to get just what you want." He peered down at the electronics section. "Same thing goes for the sound. Each component synthesized separately, harmonics and overtones meshed separately, one at a time. Hold it, I think they're gonna make the subvocal tape now. It's the first step."

Marc Nova strapped an S mike around his neck and sat down in a comfortable chair. The session musicians started to play the intro to the new number. He began silently mouthing the words.

"See, the days when you had to compromise are over," King said quietly to me. "Used to be that you often found a kid with a great image, but he couldn't get anywhere near the singing voice you needed. Or you found the right voice, but the guy was a monster. This way, we choose the face, and as long as we got the throat movements and vowel forms for the timing and sound shapes, it don't matter if he can sing or not. 'Gerry boy's' equipment puts together whatever kind of voice you want."

The recording ended and the musicians packed up, having provided the mime-backing. Their job was over; nothing as imperfect or uncontrollable as the noise of a wind-blown instrument could be allowed to form part of the finished recording. The technicians rewound and played the tape over the studio sound system. The voice was hard, harsh and demanding, wonderfully sexual. The lyrics were bare and blunt, yet suggestive in a curiously subtle way.

"What do you think, Sam?" said King, addressing a man I hadn't noticed before. He wore clothes that were modern, yet not immediate; he had a clean, but not slick, haircut. His face was kind of dull. He stared down at the studio, looking bored.

"It's O.K.," he said, after a while.

"As great as the last Marc Nova smash?"

"Dunno, really. This one could be a bit bigger."

King slapped him on the shoulder. "We done it again, boys," he called down to the technicians. "Sure hit. Keep it moving."

I drew King aside. "Who's the fellow called Sam that you just spoke to?"

"Our special king. Statistically Average Man. We used a census, found a guy typical of the music buyers. Looks like them, thinks like them, wears the same clothes, and most important, he's *got the same tastes*. Get the picture? His word is ultimate. What he says will sell, sells. If he says no, we scrap it."

I stared at Sam's blank face, fascinated. Suddenly I realized just how totally ordinary the man was. No distinguishing features at all.

King looked round as a girl came in, carrying papers. He took them, started to look through them. I stared at her, unable to look away. Our eyes met briefly; I saw she was the one—Jane—who'd come into King's office during my interview. Once again it was as though she looked straight through me. Despite the stunning appearance, there was little, if any, warmth. Her face was hard, and though her lips weren't thin, they were firmly set. Hers was a cold, self-contained kind of beauty.

I moved some of my essentials into Gerry's house that night, not looking forward to it. He'd cleared up a lot of the mess, but the place was still shabby and smelled of cats and Gerry's feet. He greeted me very amiably, sitting on the bed in my room while I put away the stuff I'd brought with me.

"How was it at the studio this morning?" he asked.

"Instructive. I hadn't realized the scale of the organization."

Gerry shook his head. "Don't be deceived. If Harry King can cut a corner, he will. Why do you think I'm working in this dump? Because it's good security, cheap and convenient. I wouldn't be surprised if the organization's nearly bankrupt."

"For a bankrupt firm, it's doing pretty well."

20

"You're misled by the surface effect. Sure it's got the best studio facilities, the best equipment. But it's more than King can afford, yet. He's already spent next year's profits."

"How come?"

"He was nothing twelve months ago, remember that. And he won't use accountants. *I* don't think he ever adapted to decimal currency properly, when Sterling was discontinued. Still treats cents like pennies, dollars like pounds. That's partly guesswork, you understand."

I shrugged, sat down carefully on a fragile-looking chair. "I've got something to ask you," I said, changing the subject. "Why did you fake that Verilyser test? Don't pretend you didn't; I know as well as you do that you can't reverse a truth reading simply by swapping over the output wires."

Gerry's face creased into a faint, cynical smile. "I fixed it because I'm sick of Harry King. You're the fourth one who's seen this enterprise; the other three were scared off by it. I'm not interested in your loyalty, and I need an assistant. It seemed the logical thing to do. For all I care, you could be an industrial spy."

I breathed in sharply; the casual way he'd touched on my secret was unsetting, though his attitude was reassuring.

Gerry blew his nose loudly, on a dirty handkerchief. I saw, with distaste, that it wasn't even disposable. He shoved it back in his pocket.

"Since you haven't seen it yet, you might as well get familiarized with the new gimmick." Gerry stood up and I followed him into another room. It was completely bare, except for a large modified Hammond organ in the center of the floor. This had been extensively remodelled and enlarged, but the dual keyboard remained.

"Emotion detector, amplifier and feedback unit," Gerry said. "Styling people haven't cleaned up the appearance of it yet, but it's otherwise complete." He opened an inspection panel; I looked in and saw there was a little padded seat and control panel inside the unit.

"New gimmick. Marc Nova pretends to play this thing—that's why we left the old Hammond keyboard on the outside—while I sit in there and press the buttons that really control it. Harry King's got the idea that groups may be coming back, replacing the solo singer. In a way this is the first step in the trend."

"How's this unit different from T.E.?" I asked.

"I'll show you." He turned on power switches, then climbed inside the machine. Music came from a loudspeaker somewhere. "That's the monosensory version of Nova's latest tape," Gerry said. "I don't know what it does for you, but for me it's just boring." As he spoke he made adjustments on the control panel. I began to feel vaguely lethargic; the music suddenly seemed more banal, as if the nature of it had changed slightly, becoming duller. Involuntarily I yawned, as the feeling increased in intensity.

"Alternatively, some people reckon the music gives you a kick." His voice seemed to come from a long way off.

The feeling of the music changed. I became aware of aspects of the melody line that were exciting. The beat was uplifting. Soon I felt like dancing; I was almost deliriously happy, as if on a drug.

The music ended and the sensation vanished. "You see," said Gerry, getting out of the unit, "music is basically emotional. Pop music is both very simple in construction, and yet complicated in appeal; it carries a lot of emotional punches to the listener. In the past, songwriters used to feel this instinctively; Lennon-McCartney songs, for instance, were early examples of how adolescent happiness, with an underlying miserable sadness, could be implied in the same melody line. The last three chords in "She Loves You" are the best example."

"Well, as you know, now songwriting is computerized, the emotional content of a melody can be evaluated and controlled. Inevitably, the sex-appeal component is usually played up. This unit takes the system a stage further; it selects an individual emotional component in the general response that the music is invoking in each member of the audience. It detects it, rebroadcasts it. The stimulus is received by the brain it was drawn from, but in a much amplified form. The unit then redetects it, amplifies it again, and re-broadcasts. Positive feedback effect. The trick is to key into natural cortical frequencies."

I thought it over. "Does King know what you have here?"

Gerry shrugged. "He knows what it does. If someone gave him an atomic warhead in a matchbox he wouldn't be impressed—he'd just accept it as another marvel of science. That's how he looks at this."

"But the implications . . . T.E. used existing audio-visual-sensory techniques, just combining them. This is something entirely new. There's a difference."

Gerry shook his head, "No difference. This gadget uses techniques already applied now in brain surgery, cortical analysis, EEG developments. They're slightly modified, but not very greatly."

I followed him out of the room, back into my bedroom. In spite of the impact of the experience, I was already thinking ahead. My company, Sound Trends, would find it difficult to get staff to manufacture such a piece of equipment; it would be more costly than T.E., and they couldn't even afford that. And I doubted my ability to reconstruct a unit, even after lengthy study of the one I had seen.

"I've a proposition, Gerry," I said slowly. He sat on the bed, stroking a tabby cat on his lap. "You don't admire the Harry King empire very much, do you?"

Gerry shook his head. "To some extent that's true."

I took the plunge. "I know of an organization that would pay you 50 percent more, provide proper facilities, guaranteed conditions, what you wanted—if you'd leave the King organization."

"I'm under contract, Joe."

"There's bound to be a loophole."

He sat there, silent, for some time. He pushed the cat off his lap and stood up, walking to the window, a kind of tragic-comic figure. "There's another reason," he said, in a rather small voice. "I don't dare antagonize Harry King. Look, this may sound ridiculous to you. It *is* ridiculous. But ever since I met her, I've just been crazy about his daughter. I love her. I can't help it."

"Have I ever met the girl?" I said.

"She came into the studio today. In the gallery, where you were."

Suddenly it clicked. The frigid blonde, the one I'd thought was King's secretary. The one called Jane.

"It's funny," Gerry went on, "but all my life I've had a kind of a vision of a perfect girl. When I saw her the vision came alive; it was unbelievable. She's the only reason for my coming to work here in the first place. I just *know* that, sooner or later, something will happen. . . ."

Inwardly, I groaned. The situation was doubly ridiculous; Gerry disliked the organization, but the only reason he wouldn't leave was based on a piece of hopeless romanticism. What could I do? I couldn't tell him he'd got no chance with the girl—him, a stooped, asthmatic, penniless electronics expert; her a frigid, untouchable beauty, the boss's daughter. He must be aware of the facts. Throwing them in his face wouldn't help.

"Well," I said lamely, "think it over, Gerry."

He walked to the doorway. "I suspected you were from a rival firm, when we first met, and when I fixed that test. So this is no surprise to me. I'm just sorry to mess up your plans, Joe. My motives must look pretty hopeless. But somehow, I just feel that if I wait long enough, things will turn out all right. . . ." He lapsed into silence for a moment, then pulled himself together. "Good-night, then."

I stayed up quite late, thinking the problem through. There had to be a solution somewhere; but right then, I couldn't see it. Even if Gerry were more glamorous, from what I'd seen of the girl, she had little interest in men. Although Gerry would be in a position to join Sound Trends if he somehow managed to marry the girl, there was just no way I could see of arranging it.

I fell into a restless sleep and dreamed of emotional feedback units governing the entire world. Teen-agers, old men and newly born children were moving in the same relentless rhythm of beat music; the earth's crust gave way and I woke up shouting for help. . . .

A week later, I was in Trafalgar Square under Nelson's column with the rest of the studio crew, hoisting great banks of acoustic panels into place, positioning T.E. projectors, cursing the cold wind and trying to coax generators and mixer units into life. A vast Diacora screen, suspended above the stage that had been erected yesterday, rippled and snapped in the brisk wind. It was Easter Monday; but the warmth of Spring had yet to arrive.

By three-thirty, teen-agers were already crowding the square, some of them in the period costume fitting to the occasion, carrying placards and the tripod-symbols reminiscent of the old pageantry of disarmament campaigns. I even saw a few shaggy false beards.

The event had been plugged for the past few days in all the media as something really new; not just another Total Experience Marc Nova concert. But few people realized that the new gimmick lay within the re-styled Hammond organ standing to one side of the stage.

Gerry was there, making final adjustments. It had been a surprisingly busy week with him, eliminating bugs in the circuits, familiarizing me with the principles involved. Harry King stood to one side, a little nervous because this was the first time the feedback unit had been used with a large audience, in public.

By four, the massive generators were roaring away, the projectors were all live, the sound system tested out O.K. The show started, the music blasting out in great waves of sound, the audience shouting and chanting, the artistes raving through their acts. It was just the usual Easter concert; the feedback unit wasn't to be employed until Marc Nova came on at the end. I monitored the cameras that were being used for the projection of a vastly enlarged image of each performer on the screen over the stage, and time passed surprisingly quickly. I realized suddenly that the hysterical compère was announcing the last act; Gerry was climbing into the feedback unit; Marc Nova stood ready, offstage, impassive and bored as always. I tensed, afraid that somehow there would be a mistake, that the unit would be a failure. But then Marc Nova was out there pounding away on the dummy Hammond keyboard, miming his guts out; the earthy, vital music screamed through the speakers; his sensual features moved, magnified in a riot of color, over the screen behind him; and I knew everything was going to work out fine.

By the end of the first verse, I could feel excitement building up slowly, subtly. Gerry was keeping the feedback damped heavily at first, letting the emotions gradually mount. The dancing and screaming in the crowd below me became more frantic and excited, and though I knew the emotion was artificially amplified, I couldn't fight it myself. The sea of moving people, bathed in the flickering of the T.E. projectors, became blurred by sheer happiness.

The number ended, and the sensation cut off. I came back to reality with a jolt, mopped sweat off my forehead. Even Marc Nova seemed to have been slightly affected; he rested against the feedback unit for a moment, before announcing the next number. And then it started again.

Except that this time it was different. The distinction was hard to see, at first, but then it became clear: Gerry had switched the selectivity of the unit. He was no longer detecting and amplifying the happiness component of the emotional response. This time, it was love that swelled up inside the audience, and inside me; a meaningless, overwhelming feeling of helpless romantic love. And as I looked down near the foot of the stage, I saw why. In the crowd was Harry King's daughter Jane, conspicuous by the fact that she was standing cold and motionless, unlike the dancing, screaming kids either side of her. Gerry must have seen her there, near the front of the audience, and as I felt the helpless awakening of sheer joy and affection within me, I couldn't help admiring Gerry, feeling sorry for him, and hoping his desperate scheme would pay off. Then further thought became difficult; vision blurred, the mind slowed down. All I could contemplate was love, for the world around me, for all people, for everything. The intensity increased, and increased again. With a kind of detached concern I saw Marc Nova falter and then slump against the unit, overcome. People were fainting in the audience. I could hardly stand up.

From my position near the stage I saw faint trails of smoke creeping out of one side of the feedback unit. Insulation burning? Components overloading? Suddenly the cover at the back swung open and Gerry staggered out, wiping his eyes. And still the emotion of love thundered over me and over everyone else.

Somehow I got down on to the stage, amidst the shouting and pandemonium, and staggered over to Gerry and the unit. Inside I could see coils glowing with heat. Desperately, I lunged at the power cable and pulled it free.

The vast feeling of emptiness that descended on me was overpowering, as the love emotion was suddenly turned off. But recovery came fairly quickly; I barely managed to drag the unconscious figure of Gerry out of Trafalgar Square before the confused, bewildered audience became a destructive mob.

Back at Gerry's house, that evening, we talked about what had happened.

80770

LIBRARY
College of St. Francis
JOLIET, ILL.

"I saw what you tried to do," I said. "In fact I think I'd more or less guessed your intentions beforehand. Your inclusion of a 'love' selectivity circuit in the unit was, really, a give-away."

Gerry smiled half-heartedly.

"But did it work?" I went on. "Did it have any effect on the girl?"

Gerry sighed, and shook his head. "I'd planned on using the unit as a kind of twentieth century love potion. It was just a vague idea, you understand; just a hope. If she was there—and Harry King usually gets her a position in the audience of an important show; he values her reactions—if she was there, I thought the least I could do was, perhaps, awaken her interest in some way."

"And did you?"

"No." The reply was bare, defeated, an empty sound in the drab room. "Even as I increased the intensity I could see it was ineffective. Her eyes never changed, Joe. She just stood there, bored. And I know why; it's in the principles of the unit. It doesn't *implant* emotions, it *intensifies* them. If there's no love response at all in a person, there's nothing there to intensify. There was no love in Jane, none at all."

I surveyed the workroom, the junk and the equipment, Gerry sitting on his bed surrounded by it all. It was a depressing scene.

"I suppose you feel pretty bad about it," I said.

He looked up. "There's a sense of loss, of disappointment. But it's a funny thing, Joe. It must be the defeat of the situation, or something. But . . . somehow, I just don't feel I love the girl any more."

I felt a little uncomfortable, meeting his eyes, and looked away. "See how you feel tomorrow, Gerry," I said, and went out of the room and up to bed.

That's all past history, of course; three months in the past. And in this business, three months is a hell of a long time. It's time enough for the Harry King empire to go bust, deep in debt, and for Gerry to desert the organization and the girl, and come over to Sound Trends as we'd originally planned.

Our company's rushing ahead, now; emotional feedback has swept the country. Gerry and I are still working together and we get on well. We have a great new kick lined up for when the feedback gimmick gets that tarnished, outdated feel to it.

I know Gerry thinks back about the past sometimes, and I still feel guilty, in a way, about the method I used for getting him free from the Harry King organization. Perhaps one day, when I know him better, I'll tell him what really happened—how, suspecting his plans for using the unit to try and awaken love in the girl, I made some hasty modifications to it the night before. How I fixed it, so that a field of opposite polarity to that of the emotion broadcast would, instead of being converted and dissipated electrically, be set up within the unit.

I fixed it so that, when the love-intensification component was selected, the field broadcast outside would be balanced by a negative field *inside* the machine. So that when, on that Easter Monday, Gerry boosted the love-emotion intensification, he felt the exact opposite himself; not hate, but a negation of love.

It was a hamfisted, desperate kind of scheme, and as it was, my modifications sent several circuits out of adjustment and brought the unit near complete overloading.

But it worked. One day when Gerry thinks back and tries to understand how his helpless romantic attachment for the girl suddenly vanished, I'll tell him the true story.

FOR DISCUSSION: The Total Experience Kick

1. What elements in this story are currently in use and how have they changed in the story's fictional future?
2. The narrator of the story, Joseph A. Forrest, and Harry King may be said to be birds of a feather. What characteristics does the author give each of them in common? What major characteristic do they share in relation to Gerry?
3. What point is the author making about human nature through the character of Jane? In this connection, what is the significance of the fact that the emotional feedback machine in the story does not implant, but intensifies already existing emotions?
4. When Marc Nova is being made up for a performance, his face is covered with a material which can be sculpted to create any desired image. To what extent, therefore, can Marc Nova be said to exist as an actual person during his performances?
5. In *The Last of the Romany*, the author postulated the death of romanticism in his fictional society. Does this story touch on the same subject? Explain.

INTRODUCTION: Shortstack

In the early days of science fiction, the eccentric inventor was a commonly met character. Modeled on such inventors and experimenters as Benjamin Franklin and Thomas A. Edison, he built his contraptions in basements and attics and was far from obsolete as a fictional creation. In more recent years, such a figure has appeared less often in science-fiction stories.

Here, however, is the homespun inventor going about his business while an interfering and insensitive world intrudes upon his fancies and misunderstands his dreams. This is a story which contains humor, subtle social satire, cleverly extrapolated scientific principles, and a warm humanity.

Shortstack
by Walt and Leigh Richmond

"Dad," the boy was gazing up at the dome over Los Angeles, and the stacks that held it, "why do they call them Shortstacks when they're so tall?"

His father gazed at the dome. "Well, Son," he said, "it was this way..."

Willy Shorts was a man of decision—flexible, haphazard decision to be sure, but nevertheless, decision.

This decision had been easily reached. He had been offered what he considered something of a fantastic price for his farm laboratory in the Carolina mountains, and at the same time his friend Joe had written from California describing the wonderful climate and the opportunities.

So Willy was off to California and, being Willy, headed for trouble.

The first trouble was that Willy had bought, sight unseen, from Joe "Twenty Golden Acres in the San Bernardino Valley—only a few minutes from Los Angeles," Joe had assured him. That this was assuming you operated a jet plane, Willy didn't realize. A creek wound through the center, Joe had said. That the creek was a dry wash eleven months of the year had not been included in the description. That the nearest water of year-round duration was some twenty-eight hundred feet straight down, at four-eighty-a-foot drilling expense, also hadn't been explained.

Joe hadn't meant to rook his friend. It was just that Joe was a salesman. He couldn't help selling. He sold things with the automaticity with which most people breathe, and his automaticities had got the better of him. Also, Joe was one of the few that considered Willy a genius—an impractical one, he admitted even to himself, but one that his own "practicality" would nurture. He was convinced that Willy would invent something to make the description come true.

Even when Joe took Willy out to the Twenty Golden Acres—the capitals were Joe's—blistering under the desert sun, Willy remained undaunted. It was only when he contacted the local power company to inquire about a line to the new property that he began to realize the extent of the disaster.

It wasn't that they wouldn't. It was just that the miles and miles of empty desert surrounding the twenty acres had never seen a power line. They would have to have so much a mile, in cash. Fine if it were only a mile or two. But it was far more than Willy's—as he was thinking of them—meager resources could hope to cope with right now.

The temporary house was no problem. Willy simply ordered in a bulldozer and put it to pushing up dunes. Fifteen feet wide at the base, and some twelve-point-five feet high at the crest, in two parallel rows—and then a couple of shorter cross-rows at the ends. The forty-foot distance, crest-to-crest, was easily spanned by telephone poles that Willy found to be surprisingly inexpensive for all their monster length. Of course the walls proved a bit slippery until Willy had the bright idea of spraying them with a mixture of plastic that firmed them up nicely.

To cover his telephone-pole roof, Willy first tried eight-mill sheet plastic—forty-foot wide and one hundred-foot long sheets, that stretched nicely over the poles; but on the first day the problem *that* created showed up. Willy was in a bakeoven. What he needed, he decided, was insulation. So he covered the plastic with sand, firmed with the plastic spray, leaving areas for skylights.

A bit unconventional, but it would do for a lab.

Still, no power. But that shouldn't be too difficult to solve, Willy decided, not when you had such a differential between day and night temperatures as there was here.

The solution came to Willy in a flash of cognition such as that defined by the patent office as being the requisite for a new invention. He had been unrolling another of the plastic films when he came to the surprising conclusion that it had no outer edge. A goof at the factory had permitted this particular roll to come through unslit, in its original hollow-tube form. Presumably a sheet forty feet wide, it was in fact a tube with a forty-foot circumference; and this particular piece was over two thousand feet long, since when Willy bought plastic he bought it in a big way.

His original intention had been to build a sort of heat engine, using the plastic as a heat trap in much the same manner as his original building had been. But now Willy had a better idea.

A chimney. A thousand feet of chimney in this climate should act, Willy decided, to create a really terrific draught. A windmill at the bottom, and he would have it made. And just maybe, Willy thought, up near the top it would be cold enough to act as a water trap as well. And that was a problem worth solving, because Willy was getting tired of hauling drinking water over the dusty back road that led from Pasco, the nearest point of civilization.

While Willy stood dreaming of the power song that would be played by this beautiful contraption—perhaps a few organ pipes would help that song, he decided—a rattle-trap pickup was creeping across the desert towards him. Willy, absorbed in his dream, didn't notice it, and so he was doubly startled by the bright, young, smiling voice that issued from it.

"Halloo, there! Are you the owner or the caretaker?"

"I—Willy stood with his mouth open. Left to his scientific devices, Willy made good sense or no sense or eccentric sense, depending on your attitude. But asked one personal question, he became a moron in anybody's language, squirming on some sort of internal hook.

A young girl hopped out of the pickup, her jeans-clad legs agile, her freckled face boyish. "What a lot of plastic!" she said, not noticing his confusion. "And is that your house there? It's a helluva swell fallout shelter. Have you registered it with Civil Defense? Would you mind if I registered it? How'd you build it? How many will it accommodate? May I see the inside?"

Willy was still struggling with his first words, but he gave up the struggle, and merely nodded mutely.

Happily the girl preceded him towards the building. "I'm Cynthia Stafford," she said over her shoulder. "I came out to count you for the census. But my father's CD director, and CD's a lot more important than a census these days. A census would be completely wrong if one bomb dropped, and if we get enough shelters we can take a census afterwards. Have you ever thought what you'd do if a bomb dropped right now on Los Angeles? Yes," she continued, opening the door that was set into the forward dune, "you have."

Actually, Willy hadn't, but he couldn't have interrupted even if he'd been a normal conversationalist, which he wasn't.

"Why!" The flow of words stopped for a full minute, as Cynthia contemplated with awe the barren, one hundred twenty-foot long, forty-foot wide laboratory, completely surrounded with its sand-cum-plastic walls. "Why," she said, "you'd be able to hold the entire population of Pasco here! If you'll let us list you, we can get Federal Aid because we'll have proved we've got a fallout shelter, and you have to prove you've got a fallout shelter before you can get Federal Aid. That's the new ruling," she added as an afterthought.

"Why, we can put the communications system in that corner, and the fire control unit over there, and the—" she stopped, breathless.

"Mr. . . . Mr. . . . I don't know your name. But we *can* list you, can't we? Then we can stock the place and hold a few practice alarms, and otherwise we won't bother you much. You wouldn't mind if we held our meetings here, too, would you, just so the unit can get familiar with the roads and the problems?"

"No!" said Willy in a reaction of horror. "No! This," he said, and his voice was firm with decision, "this is a laboratory. A research laboratory." He ran out of words, looking at her upturned freckled face; and the consternation that registered on it.

"Well . . ." he said hesitantly, "well. It's a research laboratory, of course. And I'm a reseracher. But . . . well, maybe—"

Cynthia's face brightened to what was to Willy an intolerable degree. He couldn't—

"Well," said Willy, choking on the words, "I guess CD's sort of a research organization too, isn't it?"

"Oh, yes!" breathed Cynthia. "It's terribly researchish. Why, we've never had an atomic war before."

"Well, then," said Willy, "I guess—"

To his complete consternation, Cynthia rushed over and gave him a bearhug. "You're wonderful!" she said breathlessly. "We . . . we won't bother you before tomorrow. We'll be out tomorrow with equipment and stuff. There's a meeting tomorrow evening. Would . . . well . . . would that be too soon to hold our first meeting here? I mean, we don't want to get in your way or anything, and we won't bring all the equipment, because we don't want it to get in your way. But I'd better tell the people of Pasco that we've got a shelter big enough for all of them. We'll bring out the mimeograph and I'll get Larry—he's the artist of the unit—to draw a map on a stencil, and we'll mimeograph maps to post around town, and tell people they can start driving out to familiarize themselves with the way, but not to get too near because they might bother you."

"See you tomorrow," she said brightly. "Oh, by the way, what's your name? And is there only one of you. For the census, I mean."

"Willy, uh, Shorts."

"Shorts for what?"

"Uh, that's . . . I mean, uh, Willy Shorts," Willy repeated.

"You're kidding!"

"No! Honest! I'm named Willy Shorts."

"For the government? I mean, it's got to be accurate."

"My name," he said, "is Willy—not William, Willy—Shorts. I'm a—researcher."

"You're a lamb," she said. "Are you married?"

Willy blushed a bright red. "Yes," he said. "She'll be here . . . uh . . . tomorrow." Molly wasn't expected for at least a week yet, but Willy felt he needed a defense mechanism of some sort. He wasn't sure, because certainly nobody in their right mind—not him! But anyhow . . .

It was late the next afternoon, and despite the vents that Willy had left near the roof of his lab, it was reeking with thick fumes from an automobile engine, and a blue haze of machine oil smoke, when the Civil Defense group arrived.

The car was sitting on jacks, and one of the fenders had been ripped to provide belt contact with the back wheel. The belting was strung haphazardly across the floor to make further contact with the lathe over which Willy was sweating.

Behind him was a framework, some thirteen feet in diameter, and evenly spaced around the framework were bright, shiny, new rollers which Willy was mounting as he turned them from his lathe.

Over the roar of the throttled-down motor, Willy had not noticed the intrusion, so it was with startled surprise that he looked up to discover himself and his project being admired by three old men, and five youths—with Cynthia, finger to lips, holding them at a respectful distance.

The lathe emitted an ungodly shriek as Willy's fingers twitched on the feed, and there was a snapping *ping* as a tool tip flew off into left field. Willy stared, aghast, at the ragged groove that he had gouged into his work piece, and then in consternation at the group behind him.

"Oh!" cried Cynthia. "We startled you after all! We were staying quiet until you'd finished! Oh, I'm so sorry! I—"

Willy blushed a deep red. "It's—" he stammered and came to a stop.

"This is Mr. Shorts, people," Cynthia shouted over the roar of the automobile motor that continued to turn the lathe. "This is . . . Hadn't you better turn off that motor a minute, Mr. Shorts?" she shouted.

Willy obediently disengaged the lathe and made his way through the group to the old car, reached in and turned the key. The silence was abrupt, but short. Cynthia's own mile-a-minute chatter managed to supplant it with great ease.

"Mr. Shorts," she informed the group, "is the benefactor of the entire town of Pasco, but especially of our CD unit, and I think we should show our gratitude by offering to help in ... whatever it is you're doing, Willy," she said, becoming informal as she addressed him.

"Uh ... I'm ... that is, I'm not sure ... I'm not doing anything particularly. Right now," he added as a sop to his truthfulness, for he told himself the lathe was now off and the project in suspension. "Uh ... you all going to have a meeting?"

It was one of the older men who took over. "I'm Cynthia's father, Cliff Stafford," he said, holding out his hand and shaking hands formally with Willy. "Cynthia tells us that you have offered us your laboratory as a CD shelter. So long as we don't get in your way," he added. "It is certainly," he continued, "magnificent as a shelter. I don't understand why no one thought of this type of construction before! Meantime, Cynthia tells me that we may store our equipment here, and we *did* bring it along if it's not too much—"

Willy was immediately interested. "What sort of equipment?" he asked.

"Well," Stafford began itemizing on his fingers, "we have one hundred blankets, and twenty lister bags each with four spouts, and five generators—"

"Five generators?" Willy tried to conceal the delight he felt. "What voltage?"

"They're ... Ray, you're our expert. What is it?"

"Well, they're none of them of much use," Ray answered, "but they were the only ones we could get at the Camp. They're all one and a half kilowatt, 400 cycle, 115 volt."

"The voltage," Stafford interpolated, "I understand, is fine, but the rest of it doesn't work, somehow."

Ray, as the expert, broke in. "Of course they don't work. I told you guys not to get 'em. If I hook 'em into my transmitter, they'll burn up the transformers. And you can't run refrigerators or anything else off 'em."

Willy spoke diffidently. "That can be fixed. They'll run a light bulb as is, and—"

"Well, sure," the expert agreed, "but who needs that many lights?"

By this time it was growing quite dim inside the shelter-lab. Cynthia looked around. "We could use a few in here, couldn't we? Where's your light switch, Willy?"

Willy walked over to the lathe and picked up a beat-up kerosene lantern. "Anybody got a match?" he asked. "I have several lamps, too," he said, "there beside the wall."

"But lights, Willy. Don't you have any lights?"

"Oh sure." Willy thumbed over his shoulder. "Whole case of 'em over there. But no juice. You see, the power company . . . well, that is, that's what I was building when you came in. A sort of generator."

"Well, you won't need to now. We've found a way we can repay you in part for the use of your lab!" Cynthia's voice was delighted. "Ray, you and the others go get those generators and hook 'em up. Right now!"

"But . . . but, they're supposed to be for CD use only! That's the agreement on which the government let us buy 'em. Anyhow, we haven't got anything to run 'em with."

"Bring them in!" Cynthia's tone was final. "I'm sure Willy can *do* anything. We're not a very efficient unit, as far as equipment goes," she added apologetically to Willy. "You see, we've got lots of equipment, but somehow none of it . . . well, none of it works as is. All of it needs something else to make it work. Even the lister bags," she added mournfully. "They need water."

"Well, couldn't you put water in them?" asked Willy reasonably.

"But then, you see, they couldn't be taken to where they were needed when they were needed, because they'd be too big and awkward. We'll fill 'em here and have 'em ready, though, now that we've got . . . now that you've given us a shelter."

"Uh . . . I'm . . . that is, I don't *have* any water," said Willy. "You see, that's part of what I was building."

"Oh!" said Cynthia. "And I thought we had everything solved now. Well," she added brightly, "you'll get water. You'll have to, of course, to live here."

There were the sounds of struggling at the entrance, and two of the young members of the CD unit came awkwardly in with a small but obviously heavy wooden crate, which was stamped with various Army-Navy numerals and designations, and labeled in a small corner "Aircraft Generator. Handle with Care." Over the whole was boldly painted in red "Surplus."

The two stood, panting, indeterminately, half-way between the car and the lathe. "Where," one gunted, "ya—want—'em?"

Willy waved them over towards the car, and picking up a hammer and the lantern came purposefully behind. He motioned them to set the crate near the jacked-up rear wheel.

As he approached, a voice behind him said, "Let me, sir," and the hammer was taken unceremoniously from his hand and one of the youngsters began a mighty, claws-first swing at the wooden crate. But in this instance, Willy proved fast, and the young man found himself sprawling on the ground.

"Fragile," Willy said. "It says."

Cautiously Willy began to pry loose the top of the packing crate. Inside he was confronted by silver foil wrapping, which proved to be backed up by something like kapok, which in turn was backed up by a steel box which defied everyone's imagination as to how it was supposed to be opened.

Eventually, having gotten the steel box out of its other crating and wrappings and turned over, they found a strip wire and key, somewhat on the order of a can of corned beef. After much labor, the strip wire gave slightly and the key began to turn, and Willy began to feel that he might be getting somewhere. But he hadn't reckoned with Service experts who design packages for overseas shipment.

Inside the oversize corned-beef can, there was more packaging—silver foil, tar paper, and then—cosmoline.

Eventually, beyond the cosmoline, they found the plastic sack that contained the generator itself—a full six inches in each direction smaller than the crate that had contained it. And the weight? Well, now one man could almost pick it up.

Experimentally, Willy twirled the shaft. It twirled easily.

Willy got up and walked to a corner where he began rummaging in a pile of junk. Then he came triumphantly back, bearing three rubber-faced drive pulleys, once part of a washing machine, which fit snugly onto the shaft and provided a surface that a wheel might turn without undue difficulty.

Willy wandered away again, noticing as he went that there were struggling figures at the entrance way, busily transporting in, in the darkness, huge awkward bundles and packages. This time, Willy came back with wire, sockets, and light bulbs, and began unmounting the panel of a little black box on top of the generator labeled "Caution. Not to be opened except by . . ." The rest was hard to read, because of a greasy thumb smear that Willy had left.

With the panel off, Willy busied himself snipping wires and making connections, and in the panel's place there was soon a haphazard array of regulation wall plug units, sans box and cover plates, but serviceably mounted. The entire time the CD "expert" had been standing back with his mouth slightly open as though ready to admonish Willy any second, if he could only think of a polite way of doing so.

Willy slipped the generator into place in contact with the wheel, plugged in a few extension cords, and walked purposefully to the driver's seat of the automobile.

The roar of the motor echoed through the laboratory—and there was light. Fifteen one hundred watt light bulbs at the ends of the mass of extension cords sprang brightly to life, as Willy throttled the motor back and set it to a good fast idle.

A concerted shout went up from the members of the unit. "Hooray for

Willy! We got lights!" chanted Cynthia over the rest, though it was rather hard to hear any of them over the roar of the motor.

Cliff Stafford, though, made his way to Willy's side and shouted in his ear. "What about the exhaust? Won't that suffocate us? Maybe we'd better just use the lantern for now?"

Willy looked unperturbed, and pointed towards the vents just under the roof timbers and over the walls. "Ventilation," he shouted. "Enough for now, anyhow." But, he thought to himself, I'll have to do something about it pretty soon.

The CD meeting as such never did materialize, and the members of the unit departed at what was probably an abnormally early hour for their meeting nights. There was light, but the roar made normal conversation impossible.

When the group had finally gone, Willy contemplated with great satisfaction the pile of blankets, lister bags, crates and oddments in the corner of his lab. There were most of the parts of a communications system there, he'd been assured; and what other equipment of what variety he'd find he had no idea. As far as he was concerned he had fallen heir to a treasure trove of only slightly dubious content.

The next meeting, he had been informed, was not due for a week, so he was totally unprepared for the interruption two days later.

He was busy setting up a ring of spare telephone poles and some equipment in the center, when he was interrupted by a bright flash that nearly blinded him, and Cynthia's indignant "I told you not to interrupt him!"

Gropingly, Willy looked towards the sound of the voice, and dimly in the desert brightness he made out two nattily dressed strangers and a vague form that might have been Cynthia. As the glaring halo of the flashbulb's after-image dimmed from his vision, the figures before him cleared.

The interview was brief, and so far as Willy could recall, he hadn't been allowed to complete a single consecutive sentence. But the headlines were fantastic. "Eccentric Inventor Creates Desert Fallout Shelter," they read. "Dedicated to the preservation of postatomic mankind, this huge, awkward-looking building. . . ." The story went on and on in that vein, half-humorous, half-serious. And not in the least, Willy decided, factual.

The figures given for the construction costs of the building ran to more than Willy had paid for the entire twenty acres, building and all, although they were cautiously labeled only "an expert estimate."

An editorial quoted the vast sums of money that it seemed to think the Federal Government should supply for the purpose of erecting Shorts

Shelters for the entire populace. But another editorial laughed at it as a silly—and rather vicious—publicity gimmick. "Who wants to live in a Shorts Fox Hole?" the editorial asked, and described what it called the "Shortscomings" of the whole idea with a whimsical satire that made the reading highly entertaining.

There were figures to prove that such a structure could or couldn't withstand this or that type of weather condition; but Willy had long since quit reading the papers, and was once again busy with his project.

The ring of telephone poles outside the lab had grown to completion, and within it sat the thirteen foot diameter strip sealer that Willy had been working on when he was interrupted by the CD meeting.

The plastic tube for his chimney would be fed through this sealer as a double tube, one inside the other, and sealed lengthwise every foot around its circumference into continuous long, slender air tubes as the chimney itself rose from the ground, supported by hot air forced into the air tubes thus created between its two walls.

As it reached its full height, the air pressure would be increased until the air-stiffened tubes were self-supporting, with the minor aid of a few guy-lines stretched down to tie points in a thousand-foot circle around the chimney's base.

Beneath the sealing unit was a large squirrel cage fan; and connected to the fan were four of the surplus generators which CD had so trustingly stored with him.

It was late in the afternoon as the plastic chimney began to rise, and it had already reached the five-hundred-foot mark before Willy was interrupted by the approaching cloud of automobile dust, as the CD unit descended upon him in increased numbers.

The publicity might not have been the best, but it had served to swell the ranks of the local unit by nearly twenty-five members, who might have been only curiosity seekers, but quite possibly *were* concerned for the safety of themselves and their fellowmen.

Quietly they began to gather around the base of the machine, staring up at the awe-inspiring sight of the now six-hundred-foot tall filmy column of clear plastic, with its catenary traces of guy-line sweeping down to the distant anchor points, and its somewhat awkward tilt that was being caused by the stiff desert breeze.

The plastic continued to climb, and Willy continued to ignore the on-lookers. And eventually, a half hour later, it had reached its glorious thousand feet of height.

As it neared its final few feet, the onlookers could see that it seemed to be strangely kneaded at the base in a constricting movement, as though mighty, unseen fingers were attempting to crush it inward. And as the final foot of plastic snapped off the reel and came to a halt in the sealing machine, there was a mighty roar as the air around them found escape up the suddenly opened chimney.

The squirrel cage at the base quivered and began to turn. Rapidly it picked up speed to the accompanying whine of its attached generators. In the laboratory behind them, and in several places on the ring of telephone poles about the chimney, lights sprang brightly into being to compete with the waning sunlight casting its final golden glow across the desert surface around them.

Most prominent of all was the ruby-red glare of a spotlight mounted in the center of the chimney and aimed upwards so that its illumination was spread along the interior of the plastic tube, and as the sun sank below the horizon, the plastic tube became a glowing red column stretching endlessly into the heavens above.

Still ignoring the staring onlookers, Willy checked the anchors of the chimney at the telephone poles and then took off in a thousand-foot circle, checking each of the guy-lines to his mammoth pole. Satisfied, he returned at last to the group.

"All those generators needed was something to run 'em," he said cordially. "Come on in. You can hear for your meeting this time."

"But . . ." For once, Cynthia seemed lost for words. "But, Willy! What is it?"

"Just a chimney." Willy glanced casually back at the structure and the squirrel cage, which was now emitting a low moan. "Air . . . hot air, that is . . . rises." Willy gestured awkwardly. "The, uh, the . . . temperature difference." He waved towards the top of the chimney. "Up there"—his fingers seemed to encompass the plume of cloud forming around the top of the chimney—"it's blessedly cold," he muttered. "And the air down here. Well, it's hotter. So it'd like to be up there. See?"

"Yes, Willy."

"Molly said she'd be out as soon as I got some power going for her washing machine. I didn't tell her I haven't got water. But maybe I will have," he said hopefully, looking back at the top of the chimney stack where the cloud wavered uncertainly. "Matter of fact, we'd ought to be getting water down from there almost any time now," he said. "You can fill your lister bags," he added.

"But, Willy—" Cliff Stafford's big, booming voice spoke almost gruffly. "Shouldn't you patent it? I mean, before you put it up where everybody can copy it if they want to? It's just not good business sense . . . I mean, if it works, and it obviously does . . . shucks, you could get a million dollars for something like that!"

"Well," said Willy, "well, I never did have much luck with patents. They'd just say what's new in a chimney, anyhow."

"Well, sell it to a company." Stafford's voice was almost horrified at the waste. "A power and light company. Willy, you take that thing down right now before anybody else sees it. You could use a batch of money, I'll bet, and there must be some way to really make a pile out of this!"

"You know," said Willy, "I really don't think I could. Make money out of it, that is. I . . . well, I guess I'm just not the money-making type. And, well . . . I just want a chimney to run my traps and calamities so I can do some research in hydroponics," he added lamely.

A garden hose, stretching from above the squirrel cage fan down to a nearby pole, suddenly gurgled and spat forth a driblet of water. The driblet grew, and was soon flowing a nice stream. Not large, but merging with a good velocity.

"Have a drink, anybody? It's pure—it's distilled," said Willy, pride edging into his voice. "I sort of thought I'd get water."

"But Willy—how? Where?" Cynthia's voice was awed.

"Oh," Willy shrugged. "Condensation. Helped along, of course, by a Cotterell precipitator. I'm not getting it all," he muttered, looking up at the pink wisp of cloud that was breezing away from the top of the chimney. "But," he added, "I guess this'll be enough for now."

"And that light at the bottom, Willy?" Willy recognized the speaker as the CD's "expert." "That provides the heat to make it work?"

"Nanh-nh." Willy shrugged. "That's just an aircraft warning light. Any structure over one hundred fifty feet tall," Willy quoted, "is required to be lit with red indicator lights. To prevent aircraft collision. I couldn't see running wires all the way to the top, so I decided one good floodlight in the bottom would do it. Think they'll be able to see it all right?"

The group, chattering excitedly, moved inside to the newly well-lighted laboratory-shelter, leaving the tall, red chimney-beacon alone beneath the sudden dark of the desert night, the whir of its squirrel cage and the gurgle of the small stream of water flowing from its garden hose a new sound in the desert.

The meeting had progressed for some time when Willy's wandering attention was caught by a sentence from one of the younger members of the group.

"What about surplus machine guns?" he was asking. "Can we get them?"

"Whatever for?" one of the other members wanted to know.

"Well, with all this publicity, everybody in the state knows we've got the best bomb shelter there is, and so far the only one. That is, that's really well known. And—well, we could easily put all the people from Pasco in here. But when you start getting those refugees from Los Angeles—well, hell man, what else can we do?"

"NO!" The horrified sound burst from Willy as an explosive roar that crashed frighteningly against even his own eardrums. It was nearly a minute before he found more words, but nobody else spoke.

"You can't," he said miserably, finally. "Not people!"

"Anyhow," he said finally, "we can build a big one. Big enough for anybody. Look," and his voice took on a firmness that surprised even himself. "Look," he said. "Fallout—this is a fallout problem, not a bomb shelter, you know—fallout is just metallic dust that happens to be radioactive. It's not heavy or anything. Very little of it is, anyhow. All you need is something to keep it far enough away from you—the metallic dust, that is. All you really need is a big enough tent that will keep it"—he reached back into the scrap-box file of information in the back of his head and came up with figures—"keep that fallout dust seven hundred feet of air away from you. Three feet of sand, seven hundred feet of air. Same thing. It's the equivalent. Say seven hundred fifty feet of air to be on the safe side.

"All you need is a tent big enough so that fallout is seven hundred fifty feet away from you. And that chimney's one thousand feet tall. That would keep it high enough. And the guy-ropes stretch out one thousand feet. That would give you a three hundred-foot circle in the middle, even from this chimney. And you could have several.

"Now you take plastic—you wouldn't need to have plastic as heavy as the tower—just film plastic like you can get in a roll at the grocery store— and you make a tent of it, and use a batch of those chimneys for tent poles, and you put up a tent one thousand feet tall, and just as wide as you want to make it—you could make a shelter for as many people as you needed. Put it up right over a town, so people could stay at home.

"You'd hold it up by air pressure, of course." He was thinking out loud now. He'd forgotten his audience and could go on talking. "It wouldn't take much air pressure. Say half a pound differential from the air outside." Suddenly he remembered his audience and sat down, red-faced and tongue-tied.

Then he remembered, and he stood up again, slowly. And his voice was hesitant but very firm.

"But," he said, "no machine guns. Not here. No guns of any kind. None at all, sir," he said addressing Mr. Stafford. "I . . . well, I just won't have it, and if CD doesn't like it I guess they'll just have to try somebody else's property."

"Well," said Stafford. "Well." Then he added, "Just as you say, Willy. No guns, if you say so. But you realize that people will be panicked, and—"

"Then get shelters ready for 'em." Willy's voice was still stubborn. The idea, people shooting people—

Ray, the expert, spoke up. "Wouldn't work," he said. "You could never get it up. And if you did, the first wind would blow it down."

"I was going to put just a low one up for my hydroponics farm," said Willy, "but I can make it bigger and show you."

"Better write to CD headquarters and get their permission first," said Ray, firmly. "They've gotta approve it first, you know."

"Better see if you can't get the government to evaluate the suggestion," said Stafford kindly. "They have experts who evaluate these things, and they'll let you know whether it will work or not."

"Well," said Willy, "I already know whether it'll work, so why wait? But it would be nicer to let other people know, so I'll write 'em like you say. Do you have their address?"

"Just write National Civil Defense, Washington, D.C. It'll get to them," said the director still with the kindly tolerant note in his voice. "Now, men, to other subjects—"

"But no guns," said Willy. "No guns."

Molly arrived next day, and Willy drew a breath of relief. Molly would know how to handle all these people. CDs and another batch of newsmen had come that morning. He'd asked 'em to please go away until Molly got there this afternoon.

Also, Molly would write that letter to the government for him. It really was just and right that when you know how to build a shelter that would work for a whole town full of people—let 'em stay right home where they already had water and groceries and things—you should tell the right people about it. But he just wasn't much at letter writing, "and that's a fact" he told himself. But Molly would take care of that.

Molly was one of those who thought Willy was a genius, so when he told her about his idea, on the way home from the train, Molly knew it would work.

When they got back to the Twenty Golden Acres, with the laboratory and the chimney, there were all those reporters back and waiting, so Molly told the reporters about the idea.

One of the reporters laughed and made fun of it, and Molly lit into him like a cat with all claws out, so he shut up and after that the whole gang of them listened quite politely, both to her explanations of the new Shorts Shelters and to Willy's rather halting explanation of the chimney, which they promptly dubbed the Shortstack, and how it generated the electricity for the lights and gave water, too. They could see that that worked, and they seemed quite impressed.

Flashbulbs were popping all over the place, and Willy wished they would go away, but it was hours before they did. Then Molly wrote the letter, while it was fresh in her mind.

But the headlines weren't as concise as Willy's explanations had been. Nor were the stories that followed them. One paper carried a picture of an atom bomb exploding harmlessly over a domed city, and the head read "California Desert Genius Will Save Cities with Bombproof Plastic."

"Ridiculous!" Willy snorted. "I never said a word about this stuff standing up to a bomb. Never even thought it would." And he had *carefully* explained that it was only a fallout shelter.

Other, more sober papers had followed the explanation a bit more carefully. But only a bit. There seemed to be a strong current of misunderstanding flowing beneath their words. In some editorials he was a genius. In others, he was a crackpot. And all of them seemed to find it easier to poke holes in his plastic bubble than to look at what it would and could do.

In the hullabaloo over the shelter question, the story of his generating chimney was lost.

"Oh, well, we tried," said Molly brightly.

It was weeks later that the long white envelope with the Civil Defense imprint arrived. The letter itself was not long. It thanked Willy kindly for his suggestion about shelters, and after stating that the government was already aware of the air-supported type of structure that Willy had outlined, it went off at a tangent to say that the acquisition of right-of-way for the base line of such a structure would be an appalling problem which, the assistant to the Secretary of CD seemed to think, was the end of that.

Willy snorted over the breakfast table to a complacent Molly. "One to five million bucks a mile for super highways, and they think the right-of-way around a town for this thing would be expensive!" But Molly soothed him and poured him some more coffee.

"Never mind," she said. "After you have your hydroponics going well, you can build one for here. And make it big enough, if we have enough money for plastic, to hold quite a number of people."

Joe didn't announce his arrival; he just drove up in a white convertible, for currently Joe was not only out of jail, he was in the money. "And in Hollywood," he said grandly, "you dress the part or you're just not anybody."

42

Joe had read about Willy's "bomb"—fallout—shelter. Who hadn't? And though he had come ostensibly to see how his friends were faring on their Twenty Golden Acres—which he assured them he had known all along Willy could make Golden—his motivations were somewhat more devious. He wasn't sure quite what it was that Willy had been outlining for the various news agencies, but he thought it might have commercial possibilties. Anyhow, he ought to go see his old friends, Willy and Molly.

His first sight of the Shortstack convinced him he'd been right. "What a gimmick!" he declared in awed respect. "What a gimmick!"

"It generates twenty-five horsepower of electricity, and gives us about a gallon of water a minute," Willy told him proudly. "Should do a good deal for agriculture around here!"

"Agriculture is for hicks, and hicks don't have money," said Joe, firmly. "But boy, that's the best gimmick I've seen in a long number of years. Boy, oh boy, Willy, you just leave the hicks alone and let me do the selling. If we can't make a pile out of this one, why—" He didn't even bother to finish the sentence.

"Now you just lay in the stuff to make me just one like this one," he told Willy solemnly. "And you pack your suitcase and get ready to come when I whistle. Where do I whistle to?" he asked dubiously, looking around for a phone. "How do I reach you?"

"Well," said Willy, "we get our mail at Pasco when we go in every week to shop, and—"

"Now, Willy," said Joe, "no wonder you ain't rich. Nobody can even reach you! You put in a telephone, and—"

"A telephone'd cost more than electricity," said Willy. "I'd have to put in about ten miles of poles."

"Well, shucks, get a radio or something!"

"I've got a CD radio. I fixed up the stuff they left, and it works fine. But you can't call me unless you've got an official CD rating. You have to use CD frequencies."

"O.K. Who's a CD that I know? Is the sheriff in these parts in on those CD things?"

"Oh, yes. The sheriff has as CD frequency-tuned outfit. It's for Liaison—"

"O.K. I'll get you through the sheriff. So when the sheriff calls, don't get the wind up. Just pile your suitcase and the stuff to make that Shortstack into the old jalopy and get going. For Los Angeles. I'll give the sheriff the place for you to go to. Oh, and can you make it any higher?"

"The jalopy?"

"No, the Shortstack. Can you make it higher—you know—more up?"

"Oh, sure, but—"

But Joe had quit listening. "Bring the makings for one about twice that high. O.K., now, I'll be seeing you."

And that was how it happened that the Shortstack was being placed on the Magnum, Goldwich, Fox lot on the day of the premiere of "Souls in the Sun."

The plastic chimney was readied, with the title of the movie and a plastic molding of the star at the top, ready for inner lighting to bring them into relief a towering two thousand feet above Hollywood.

There was no squirrel cage at the bottom this time, for as Joe explained to Willy, "They got all the electricity they need in Hollywood." And no Cotterell precipitator. "They got water, too," said Joe. Just the chimney, closed at the bottom until it should reach its full height and begin to function.

It was a humid day in Hollywood, and the Los Angeles smog pressed down, held in the valley by the peculiar thermal inversion that its surrounding mountains create on the warmer days.

The normal complement of sidewalk watchers gathered to see what was going on, tears streaming from smog-burdened eyes, wiping runny noses; and the monstrous chimney rose on its columns of plastic-enclosed air.

The full height was reached. The bottom of the chimney was removed.

With a swish the cold air that held the blanket of smog over the city rushed down the chimney.

"Holy smoke!" cried Joe, holding himself against the sudden gust of wind. "It's upside down! Make the wind go up the chimney, Willy!"

"It's a thermal inversion!" Willy declared, quite excited. "It's working . . . the air in the chimney—that is the air that went up with the chimney—was warm and humid. But we didn't let any air in at the bottom to start an updraft. So the air in the chimney got cold, that air at the top. And when it got cold, it got heavy. The water vapor helped. Then we opened the bottom. And it all fell out."

"But it's still falling!" wailed Joe.

"I expect it will keep on falling," said Willy.

At the top, lighted now by the spotlight from below, "Souls in the Sun" and its star glowed vividly, far above Hollywood.

Beneath, the crowd of sidewalk watchers took a nearly concerted deep breath as the clean, cold air gushed out.

The gushing air swept beneath the smog and lifted it, threw it back. It whished and whirled and danced through the smog, and the atmosphere over the Magnum, Goldwich, Fox lot cleared as though by magic.

44

The eyes stopped smarting. The noses, relieved of their burdens, quit running.

The smog area was pushed farther and farther back from the chimney stack, down which rushed the clean, cold air from above the surrounding mountains.

"And that, Son, is why it's called a Shortstack, even if it is so tall," the man said, gazing up at the plastic tent above the city, and the stacks that centered its vents—vents around each stack where the air pressure created by the down-rushing air through the chimneys was allowed to relieve itself at a pressure just above that which supported the tent itself. "It didn't take people long to realize that a chimney works both ways, and that a Shortstack would blow away the smog."

"But the fallout shelters, Dad? Whatever became of them?"

"Well, Son, you know that the fact that this is a domed city makes it possible to air condition Los Angeles. It's not a Shorts Shelter, any more. It's a Shorts City Air Conditioner. But it's just like the one Willy Shorts described.

"Hardly a city or a hamlet left that doesn't have a Shorts City Air Conditioner. But it works both ways, just like the chimney. Every air conditioner is a shelter.

" 'Course, if we had a bombing war, Los Angeles would be the first hit, and he never did think it was a bomb shelter. But with every hamlet conditioned, if we got out of the bombing alive, we'd be able to get to a shelter.

"Nobody would buy the idea of making a city a fallout shelter. But once Joe told 'em you could air condition a city, they fell for it in droves."

FOR DISCUSSION: Shortstack

1. What characteristics does the author give Willy Shorts which make him a person of interest to the reader? Are all his characteristics desirable ones?

2. Looked at in a symbolic way, what might the character of Cynthia be said to represent as she arrives suddenly in Willy's quiet and thoughtful world? Both of these characters are entirely different kinds of people. What purpose does the author have in juxtaposing them?

3. Authors often poke fun at individuals and institutions to highlight one or more of the points they are making in their stories. An example of this technique is found in the way the newspapers cover the story of Willy's Shorts Shelters. What is the reason for including the reportorial misunderstandings in the story?

4. Many different techniques can be used for telling a story. This one is told long after the events described have taken place. Why do you suppose the author chose this method rather than a straightforward telling of the story which would have eliminated the conversations between the father and the son at the opening and closing of the story?
5. Willy's purchase of the California land "sight unseen" tells us something about Willy's personality. What characteristic does it define?

INTRODUCTION: Far From This Earth

Authors have written stories, plays, and poems about people who achieved their goals only to find that once achieved, the goals appear to have been not worth seeking. At such a point in a person's life, "success" can cause many emotions—despair and anger among them.

Far From This Earth is a science-fiction story set in an Africa of the future in which a man confronts the dust to which his dreams have turned. He admits his defeat but maintains a faint hope for the future —not for his future, but for the future that belongs to his son and his son's sons.

Far From This Earth
by Chad Oliver

Stephen Nzau wa Kioko dressed quietly so as not to awaken his wife and son. It was still early—the African sun shed pale light but no heat against the windows—but he felt a nagging irritation even as he tried to move without sound. In the old days, his wife would have been up first. His breakfast would have been waiting for him: the thick hot sweet tea mixed with fresh milk from his cows, the steaming porridge made of the ground maize from his shambas. His son would have already started the beautiful thin cattle and the sheep and the goats out of the kraal on their long walk toward water. Stephen grunted softly with annoyance. Elizabeth seldom got up before noon these days and her complaints would have been a blasphemy to her mother—old Wamwiu, so wrinkled and worn, her gums collapsed over the wreck of her teeth, dead now these twenty years. And Paul—one son, imagine only one son, one child. Paul with his idiot's beard, his single feather stuck in the headband like a red Indian. Paul!

Stephen set the dials for his breakfast. Fish cakes and eggs, toast and coffee. It didn't take long, a precise minute and a half. It wasn't worth the wait. The food was neither good nor bad. It simply kept a man going, like petrol in an engine.

He dressed with care: short-sleeved white shirt and tie, brown trousers creased for eternity, the soft gray boots that were the only concession made to outdoor work. He stepped outside and the door closed silently behind him.

Stephen's house stood on a high ridge, flanked by a thousand other houses that were exactly like it except for minor variations in color. He hated the houses and his hate was a constant source of surprise to him. As a boy, he had dreamed of houses like these. He had told himself that one day he would live in such a house, but he had not really believed it —not even after the promised *uhuru* had actually come and so many things had suddenly seemed possible. He remembered the old house, the sun-dried brick that crumbled when the rains came, the thatch on the roof, the good rich smell of smoke from the cooking fire. He had been told that the old house was not a good one and he had believed it —then.

He stood for a moment, drinking in the morning. To the north, not far away, he could see the outskirts of Nairobi. Already, a smudge was staining the air above the industrial complexes that ringed the city. He looked westward, across the plain that had once been Masailand. The great sky, that vast incredible Kenya sky, stretched away as it always had. The grass still grew—taller now, with better land management—and the flat-topped little acacia trees were still starkly black in the new sun. Unhappily, perhaps, a man could see far across that ancient savannah, and he could see clearly. Stephen could not ignore the glint of the electric fence that sealed off the game park and he could see the swollen metallic bubbles and gleaming towers of Safariland in the distance. Safariland was not open yet; the copters and the monorail would not begin to disgorge the tourists from Nairobi for another two hours. Filled or empty, though, it made no difference across the miles. Safariland was an alien thing, a growth that cut the earth but had no roots. Stephen knew it for what it was: garish, tasteless, a polished machine that sucked in money the way a hippo swallowed vegetation. And yet, he was strangely drawn to it. In a way, it was a part of his youth. He had wanted this, or something like this. It had not been forced upon him. He had welcomed it, grasped for it, fought for it. He had it now, and of course it was too late. The boy would have been enchanted, but the man was too old. The man had learned the hard way that the best dreams are not always those that come true. Still, a man can dream again, he must. . . .

Stephen tore his eyes away. He had more urgent problems. For one, the problem of the disappearing rhino horns. For another, the problem of the cattle that ate the forbidden grass . . .

He climbed into his car. It was only three years old, a Chevrolet. It was painted with black and white stripes that were supposed to look like zebra markings. There was neat, discreet lettering across each of the front doors: WARDEN, KENYA GAME COMMISSION. There was a good rifle, a .375 Magnum, clamped under the dashboard. On the back seat, resting

48

casually as though it had just been tossed in as an afterthought, was a wooden staff about six feet long with a fork in one end. It was always there now when Stephen worked.

He drove the car down from the hills and turned west, away from the city. The climbing sun was behind him. Ahead of him was the grassland and the wind.

He showed his identification at the gate, trying not to look at the huge signs. He had to look at them, of course; that was the kind of sign they were. One read: SEE WILD AFRICAN ANIMALS IN THEIR NATURAL HABITAT! That wasn't too bad, although many of the animals in the park were not really wild any longer and one could quibble about how natural the carefully managed habitat was. Another sign: SEE SAVAGE MASAI WARRIORS SPEAR A LION! The Masai weren't very savage these days, those that were left, and the spearing was a bloodless charade. Another: SEE SPEKE DISCOVER THE SOURCE OF THE NILE! That was staged in Safariland; the park was a long way from Lake Victoria. Another: SEE MAU MAU FREEDOM FIGHTERS! Well, they were at least in the right country, although the Mau Mau in Safariland were a far cry from the ragged, desperate men Stephen had known—when? Long ago, long ago. He had been a boy of seven when the Emergency had been declared. Another: SEE THE BASE ON THE MOON! It was a long way from the Mau Mau to the conquest of space, in more ways than one. But the broad theme of Safariland was exactly what the name suggested. A safari was just a journey, an expedition preferably into lands unknown. As a matter of fact, the space exploration exhibits at Safariland were among the best in the world. They were almost as good as those at Disneyland, which Stephen had visited. The Kenya government had been anxious to emphasize the future as well as the past in Safariland, and money had been spent.

Stephen drove into the park and there were no more signs. That was a blessing. At this time of the day, before the vehicles fanned out over the roads, a man could almost believe. . . .

He remembered this country as it had once been, not so very long ago. Stephen was a Kamba, and he had been born in 1945 in the hills near Machakos. (No tourist had ever heard of the Kamba; his people had not been colorful like the Masai or leaders in Mau Mau like the Kikuyu. A couple of anthropologists had written books about the Kamba, but no one had read them.) Stephen was now a man of fifty-five, but he had known this land well as a younger man. It had once been Masailand, which bordered on his own tribal territory of Ukambani. He had been here when there was no game park. He remembered the brown grasses, the clouds of red dust, the scummy green water in the shrinking pools. He remembered the Masai as they had been: the tall thin warriors with their cloaks the color of the red ocher they smeared on their faces, the long iron-bladed spears, the great herds of skinny zebu cattle, the brush fences around the brown breadloaf houses plastered with mud and manure, the flies everywhere. He remembered the fear that came with the Masai raids on the Kamba kraals, remembered his own father running for his bow and poisoned arrows....

There were no Masai visible now, although some would be on duty later, in costume, at Safariland. He *could* see some animals, even from the main road. (Stephen could remember when there had not been a single paved road of any consequence in all of Kenya outside the cities.) There were five giraffes in the bush to his left, their stalklike heads poked up above the screening acacias and watching him with typical giraffe curiosity. If he stopped the car and waited, they would walk right up and try to stick their heads in through the windows, their great long tongues uncoiling like snakes. There was an ostrich trotting with imperturbable dignity along the side of the road, looking for all the world like a long-distance runner in training for the Olympics. There were Tommys—Thomson's gazelles—everywhere, some of them stotting in their characteristic stiff-legged gait. It was odd, Stephen thought. As a boy, he had shared the attitudes of most Africans about wild animals. They were meat, pure and simple. He had saved his affection for his cows. Now, he had learned to admire them, even to envy them at times. He was not sentimental about them, like some of the British he had known, but he welcomed their presence on the land. His people needed them, yes; they brought in the tourist money. But it was more than that. They were not cows, but they were something. Of all the changes he had known in his life, this was one of the greatest. It was one of the few gifts of the white man that did not corrupt.

It took him nearly an hour to reach the field station. The sun was higher in the great sky, flooding the plains with golden light and welcome warmth. It was not hot and would not get hot even in the afternoon. Kenya was on the equator, but most of it was high plateau country and the air was cool and dry. For real heat you had to go to the coastal lowlands, to Mombasa on the shores of the Indian Ocean. But Stephen had no desire to go to *that* tourist trap with its swarming beaches. They called it the New Riviera, but, to Stephen, Mombasa would always be tainted. Mombasa had been the mainland starting point for the slavers from Zanzibar, and some of those Arab slave caravans had reached hungrily into Ukambani....

Ah no, he did not deceive himself. The good old days had been no

Eden. He had lost three sisters and a brother, all dead before they reached their fifth year. He remembered his father, so drunk on sugarcane beer in the afternoons that he could not speak. He remembered his mother, toiling endlessly in the fields, so bent over at the waist that she could hardly stand erect. He remembered the killing oaths, and the witches. He would not go back if he could. That dream was for the foolish young, who had never been there and so could not remember. And for the very old, perhaps, the elders lost in a new world and groping for the only alternative they knew.

He tried not to think about it as he checked the reports. He knew what he would find, out there on the sunlit savannah. He knew that they could not escape him.

His heart was heavy when he went out to the waiting copter. He did not relish this part of his job. It had to be done, yes, but it could not be done with joy. The past had been murdered enough.

The chopper climbed into the vault of the sky and swung toward the southwest. There was no Safariland here and only dirt trails cut through the thorny bush. Elephants, not gray as they were in zoos but rust-colored from the dust. Fat-bellied zebras, breaking into an oddly clumsy gallop as the shadow of the copter passed over them. Kongoni, those most ungainly of antelopes, unconcerned as always. One lazy lion, a male, flopped down asleep in the tall grass. Stephen knew him. They called him Lord Lugard, and Stephen was worried about his teeth.

"The damn fools," the pilot said. "Won't they ever learn?" He spoke in English. It still surprised the tourists, but English had been the major language in Kenya for years. The tribal languages were fading out, and Swahili was not what the doctor ordered for a nation trying hard to be modern.

"Wait a bit," Stephen said. "You'll get older and disappoint the old lady some night. Then you'll be out hunting rhino horn with the rest of them."

The pilot looked at him blankly. "I meant the cowboys."

Stephen did not reply. Cassius, the pilot, was a Luo and too clever by half. Stephen found him pretty hard to take. He was deliberately obtuse with Cassius, mostly to shut him up. It seldom worked.

"I mean, they haven't a chance when we can spot them from the air," Cassius said. "If they had half a brain between them they could figure that out."

"Africans ain't got no brains, don't you know that? We are like children."

Cassius lapsed into silence. He wasn't angry, just puzzled. Stephen was aware that he was something of an enigma to his colleagues, and he rather fancied the role.

The copter droned on, flying a search pattern. Stephen didn't bother to use his glasses. He could see well enough. He wouldn't miss a herd of cattle, not from the air or from the ground. He knew about where they had to be. Close enough to the fence to get them out at night, using a portable wooden walkway to get the animals over the electric fence. Close to the Tanzania border, away from the tourists and the game patrols.

Cassius was right. They were fools. But they were other things as well. He thought of his father, and of his grandfather. He thought of all the men of his clan, stretching backward into the mists of time, the men and their cattle, always the cattle. . . .

He saw the two peaks of Kilimanjaro thrusting up through the clouds, sharing the sky to his left. The snow and ice gleamed on the summits. According to legend, the Kamba had once lived on the slopes of Kilimanjaro. And now he was coming back—

"In a great silver bird," he muttered in self-mockery.

"How's that?"

"Nothing, man. An old joke."

The copter flew on. The sun climbed high in a sky that was a brilliant blue.

Quite suddenly, Stephen spotted them. They were nakedly exposed on the plains below. They could not hide any more than ants could hide on a greasy white plate.

"Take her down, Cassius."

Cassius stared at him. "We going in alone? Don't you think—"

"Take her down, Cassius."

The copter started down.

Stephen climbed out of the copter, his boots crushing the soft, fragrant grass. He carried no weapon. Cassius stayed behind, shouting into the radio. Stephen walked forward, hating what he had to do.

Almost, he thought, it was a timeless scene, a frieze from a ruined temple. There were the hump-backed cattle, beyond any man-made law, munching on the grass. And there were the herdsmen with their staffs, frozen like statues, only the eyes alive. Hostile eyes, fearful eyes, resigned eyes. Eyes that looked again on the destroyers of herds. . . .

But it was like all scenes now. There were distortions, bits and chunks of wrongness. A man had to edit to see what he wanted to see—or look beyond. There was the copter, for one thing, and that in a way was the least of it. The herdsmen—there were three of them—were very old, too old to be taking cattle to grass. That had been a job for boys, back when boys still did such things. The men were dressed in ragged, baggy suits— ripped by the thorns, stained by years of filth. One man even wore a tie although he had no shirt. And there were only sixteen cows in the herd. Three men for sixteen cows!

Stephen recognized one of the men as a Kamba. He could tell by the way his teeth had been filed, a custom that hadn't been practiced in fifty years.

Stephen spoke to him gently, the old language strange in his mouth. "*Nouvoo, mutumia?*" Is it peace, elder? A standard Kamba greeting once, but it had a literal meaning now.

The old man looked surprised, subtly pleased by the use of his language and his title. Hope flickered briefly in the cloudy eyes. He hesitated a moment, then nodded. "*Ii nesa.*" The ancient response. Yes, it is well, it is peace.

Stephen knew his job. Elders did not fight. "Old man," he said softly, "you cannot herd your cows here."

"Where can I herd them?" The elder's hands were trembling, more with age than fear.

"You cannot herd them anywhere. There is no land for cattle."

"There is land here. Much land."

"Not for cows. For wild animals."

The elder shook his head. This was madness. Stephen knew the memories in the old man's mind. When the British had come, it had been the same. The people had been moved to protect the animals. Then the white men had come to shoot the animals. It made no sense. "I must have cows," the old man said simply. "I have always had cows."

"That is all over. I am sorry." Stephen did not try to explain. There were no words to reach this man. Population growth rates, land short-ages, the necessity to increase agricultural yields—these things had no meaning for him. Irrigated farmland could support twenty times as many people as the same land spent on herding. Kenya could not support the luxury of cows.

The elder was beyond tears. He did not attempt to argue. He had suffered many blows in his long lifetime. He stood there, leaning on his staff, waiting for the next blow to fall.

Stephen waited with him, in silence. It took several hours; the sun started down the arc to the western horizon and the air was still. The flies were very bad. In time, the police trucks rolled up in showers of dust. The cattle were loaded. The three old men were arrested and put in with the cows. The trucks drove off.

That was that. Stephen looked for a moment at the distant Kilimanjaro. He could see only its dark base, rising so improbably out of the level plain. The peaks were hidden by clouds. He walked back to the copter and climbed in.

"Okay, Cassius. Another heroic mission accomplished. Chins up and all that."

"You're lucky you didn't get an arrow through you."

"You just don't understand savages, old boy. Just have to look them right in the eye and speak in a loud, clear voice."

"Ah, go to hell."

"Filthy superstition. I'm disappointed in you. Shall we have a go at the bloody rhino poachers?"

"What's with this crazy colonial talk? You could find yourself in a mess of trouble, Steve."

Stephen thought: We took their houses, their cars, their clothes, their schools, their courts, their money, their cities, their clubs, their guns, their books, and their whisky. Why not their patterns of speech? He said, "Some of my best friends are natives. I used to be one myself."

Cassius clamped his teeth together and turned to the controls. The chopper lifted with a great clatter into the blue sky. Down below, the good grass undulated in the wind from the whirling blades. Then all motion stopped and there was nothing.

They wasted a couple of long afternoon hours searching for signs of the rhino hunters. They found one dead rhino, its grotesque carcass bloating in the sun. The animal had been dead for days. The horns, both front and rear, had been neatly detached from the skull. The horns were missing, of course.

Stephen felt an anger that he had never been able to feel against the old men with their cattle. This rhino horn business had been going on for centuries. The passage of time does not necessarily make people less gullible. There were still millions of persons—in the Arab countries, in China—who believed that rhino horn was a cure for impotence. The horn, which was not a true horn at all, was ground up and served in a potion. It was incredible, but perhaps no more incredible than—say—astrology or statistics. Stephen didn't know how it worked out in the bedroom, but he did know the result in Africa. The rhino was virtually extinct.

It was no great trick to find the rhino carcasses, but catching the killers was something else again. It was not like trying to spot some old men with a herd of cattle. The poachers were well organized, and they could work at night. A rhino horn could be carried out of the country in a briefcase.

There was no point in aimless cruising, and the fuel was getting low. Cassius flew the copter back to the field station and landed. It was nearly five o'clock—quitting time.

It had been a depressing day and Stephen was in no mood to hurry home. He checked out, climbed into his Chevrolet, and drove the other way, toward Safariland. The highway was crowded with cars going back to Nairobi. Stephen studied the drivers as they flashed by. Black, brown, yellow, white—they all looked the same, faces tense, films exposed, wives bedraggled, kids sullen. There were times when Stephen felt very much alone.

Safariland was technically closed when he got there, with the maintenance crews engaged in picking up the day's debris. Stephen had no trouble in getting in; Safariland was situated in the game park, and Stephen was a senior warden. He preferred the place without the tourists and without the gimmicks. He had eyes. He could use them.

He ignored the buildings devoted to Africa's past. He didn't much care whether Stanley ever met Livingstone, and the source of the Nile was not a burning issue to him. He went straight to Spaceland and entered the great bubble of Moonbase.

He sat down in silence and looked at another world. He was the only one there. It was a good feeling.

The stars on the dome were very close, very bright. The animated lunar vehicles were still now with most of the power switched off for the night. The rockets were in their cradles with no fire in their tails. The helmeted human figures—so small, so lost in grandeur—did not move. The craters pocked the surface. Far away—it seemed—a lunar range thrust its ragged peaks into an unearthly sky.

The Mountains of the Moon. Once, they had called the Ruwenzoris that, those snow-capped mountains that separated East Africa from the Congo. Once, if it came to that, they had believed that the Ruwenzoris were the source of the Nile. . . .

Stephen felt a kind of peace growing within him. More than that, a kind of hope. (He remembered the false hope in the old herdsman's eyes. But a man had to have hope.) Here, of all places, there seemed to be an opportunity, a second chance—

It wasn't just the moon. The moon was nothing, a big hunk of barren rock. But the base on the moon stood for something, for everything. It was a sign for those who could read. It said: *It can be done.*

Stephen was not, by some standards, an educated man. He had finished high school, no more. But Stephen had read books and he had a brain. It was not a combination that led to happiness, but it had its uses. Stephen had been eighteen years old when Kenya became an independent nation. He had been in the Youth Wing. He had thought himself quite enlightened; he had dispensed with the past. Everything was going to be modern, up to date. He was going to have a car, a big house, a television set, a representative in the United Nations. . . .

Well, he had those things. When it was too late, he discovered what he had lost. Not just the old ways, although he saw the good in them now. It was not innocence that he had lost. No, the loss had been in the power of choice. By his eagerness to be "civilized" he had thrown away all of the alternatives. His people had given up what they had. In its place they had taken a bastard culture, and they had *wanted* to take it. Instead of the Kamba, the Masai, the Pokot, the Taita, the Samburu, they were all the same, ants in a western anthill. Not just the Africans. The whole world was stuck with the same culture—cities, industry, money, loneliness in the manswarm.

Stephen could not accept it. He did not believe that this was all that man could be. Other lifeways could have flowered from the old roots; even manure makes good fertilizer. There could have been warmth, kinship, purpose, fulfillment. For him, for all those on the earth today, it was too late. But clans do not die, they go on down through the generations. And one day, somewhere—

Space was vast. There were many worlds, not all of them barren like the moon. Mars was not the end. There would be other suns, other rivers, other grasslands. Surely, on just one world, at some time unimagined, man would find a life worth living. Perhaps even with thatch-roofed houses and cows and food plants that took root in good soil—who knew?

There was just one way to *get* to the stars. Stephen understood that. But then?

He took a last look around the silent Moonbase. He felt better. A million to one shot, a billion to one shot, was better than nothing. He went back to his Chevrolet and started the long drive home.

The lights were on when Stephen reached his house in the hills. Stephen felt a little guilty at being late but as always after a visit to Moonbase he was filled with his vision, he wanted to talk, to communicate—

He stepped inside. Elizabeth looked up coldly. "Where have *you* been?"

Paul was stretched out on the floor, staring at a Western on television. He had his feather on. Like so many of the young people, Paul didn't believe in anything. The Indian feather was the badge of his generation.

56

It was worn precisely because it made no sense. Paul didn't bother to greet his father.

Stephen felt a hot, sudden, irrational anger. His family seemed a waste and a betrayal. They had accepted it all, wallowed in it. They were blind, just as he had once been blind.

Stephen turned on his heel and walked back to his car. He took the wooden staff from the back seat. It was an elder's stick with the traditional fork at the top end; he was entitled to it at his age, even though the old age-grade system no longer had much significance. He went back into his house and crossed over to the TV set. He swung the staff once. Glass tinkled, a few sparks shot out, and the TV sputtered into silence.

Paul leaped to his feet, finally jolted into awareness. "Are you crazy? What did you do that for?"

Stephen gripped his staff. "You watch that damned thing too much, Paul. You should be studying. You should be reading."

"For Christ's sake!" Paul turned to his mother. "What's with him?"

Elizabeth fluttered her well-manicured hands. "Really, Stephen. I hardly know what to say."

"Don't say anything then. Paul is throwing his life away, can't you see that? It's *not* all over. There are things to do."

"Paul does very well in school. He's got a C average."

Stephen said a word—traditional indeed, it went all the way back to Anglo-Saxon. "Paul is going to learn the important things. He's going to be an engineer, a scientist. He's going to do it if I have to beat him with this stick. I'll call in the lineage elders—"

"Lineage elders!" Paul threw up his hands. "What'll they do—buy a goat to sacrifice? You know what you are, Pops? You're an Uncle Tom. A chief. A neocolonialist!"

Stephen advanced on him with his staff. Paul ran away and locked himself in his room.

Elizabeth looked at her husband, then lowered her eyes. She knew his moods. Stephen was a little mad sometimes. It was embarrassing, really. Why, he might even strike *her*.

"Fix me something to eat, Elizabeth. I'm going out."

Stephen went into their bedroom and changed his clothes. He knew he would be out all night. His anger was gone. The despair was back. He had handled Paul badly, as usual. He could not reach the boy, could not make contact with him. And yet he *had* to get through to him. He had to try. If fathers gave up on their sons, there was no hope, no chance. He remembered his own father. God knows, he had had reason to drink.

He ate his dinner. Elizabeth said nothing to him. He touched her when he was through. "I'll get the TV fixed tomorrow," he said. It was an apology of a sort.

"Will you be back tonight?"

"No. I'm going out to check the herd."

"You have no cows."

"I have a few—for a while."

She watched him go. Her face was hurt, puzzled. Stephen thought that the expression was better than the normal blankness.

He drove back into the park under the stars. The deep African night closed in around him, sheltering him. The blaze of the Nairobi lights was an intrusion, but he did not try to edit them out. You had to have the Nairobis to reach those stars.

He knew that the lions would be hunting this night. If he stopped the car he could hear their coughing roars, perhaps see their gleaming eyes. He did not stop, but it was not fear that prevented him. It was not lions that he feared. People were the problem, always, forever.

He drove to the silent field station and parked the Chevrolet. He walked to the holding pens. The cattle were there, the sixteen cows he had confiscated that day. They would be slaughtered after they had been inspected tomorrow. The meat would go to the hotels in Nairobi.

He opened the gate and went inside the pen. He closed the gate carefully behind him. He sat down on the earth. He had no plan. There was nothing he could do.

It was far different from the kraals he had known as a boy. The fence was steel, not thornbrush. There were no calves. There were no thatch-covered houses in the moonlight, no drums in the distance, no old men singing drunkenly along the trails.

But the smells were there, the warm rich milky smells of the cows. The cows were there, dark shadows under the moon. The textures were there, the feel of trodden earth and dung and hairy hides. There was a kind of continuity. A Kamba and his cows. . . .

Stephen smiled, alone there in the great night. Perhaps he was a little mad. Perhaps a man had to be a little mad in these times. He knew that he would never surrender. He would do his job as best he could, preserving something. He would keep after Paul, all the Pauls. Study, learn, work. Find the way. And then go, take the long way home—

It might never happen. For him, it would certainly never happen. But there were other men, other times. Clans do not die. When he too was a forgotten ancestor, the clan would live.

Stephen stayed there with the good smells all that night. He watched the red sun rise over the hills. He said good-by to the cows and got in his car.

He drove down the paved road to Safariland. He parked by the gates in his zebra-painted Chevrolet. He watched the tourists come in for a new day. They were all the same—black, brown, yellow, white. Dead people, groping for life.

For you too, Stephen thought. *For you. For you.*

FOR DISCUSSION: **Far From This Earth**

1. Authors frequently employ symbols in their stories. Here, the city of Nairobi may be said to be a symbol. What does it symbolize?
2. To involve a reader in a story, the author must create vivid, credible characters. Stephen, in this story, is such a character. Analyze how the author makes him seem to be a living person.
3. Like the characters of the bartender and the Spaceman in *The Last of the Romany*, Stephen and Cassius are two different kinds of men who hold different sets of values. This fact is evident during and after the encounter with the Kamba elders. What do Stephen's remarks to Cassius following the meeting indicate about Stephen himself? Does Cassius comprehend Stephen's feelings at this point?
4. What is the meaning of this statement by the author: "But Stephen had read books and he had a brain. It was not a combination that led to happiness but it had its uses."
5. No extraneous material may be included in a short story without weakening its structure. Each scene must serve its purpose which is to heighten the effect the author is seeking to achieve. What is the significance of the brief scene between Stephen and his son, Paul? Does it have any relationship to the encounter between Stephen and the Kamba elders?
6. Can you determine whether or not the author is sympathetic to Stephen? To Paul? To the Kamba elders?

Outer
Space

CHAPTER TWO

What might Columbus have felt as he set sail from Spain, the unknown his destination? What emotions might have been shared by such men as Admiral Byrd, Lewis and Clark, and other pioneering explorers as they journeyed through new lands and unfamiliar vistas?

Awe? Excitement?

What might Columbus have felt if he discovered that his ships had sprung unrepairable leaks in the middle of the Atlantic Ocean? What might Admiral Byrd have felt if he discovered one day that he could not find his way back from the Arctic?

Fear?

Awe. Excitement. Fear. These and other emotions must surely have been shared by all the men who explored the then unknown. They were probably also shared by the astronauts who manned the capsules that America and Russia have sent soaring into outer space.

Whatever their emotions and whatever the dangers, explorers will continue to travel to new frontiers. In this chapter, the reader will travel with some fictional explorers and learn what it is like to walk on other worlds and travel starward.

The authors of the stories will ask questions and pose problems which the reader will be asked to solve along with the protagonists of the stories. They will do this not by directly asking the questions or openly requesting solutions to the problems but by presenting the questions and problems in dramatic form so that the reader will be caught up in them and feel that he is experiencing the situations that embody the questions and the problems.

By so doing, the authors will have succeeded in their task of creating fiction that involves the reader. To do this, they must make the situations they describe vivid. They must add specific details to the events described so that they seem real. They must create characters who actually seem to live and breathe, wonder and worry. They must make the reader feel that he is living the story rather than merely reading it.

What we have been discussing are the techniques of fiction. They are the techniques by which writers throughout the ages have held the attention and interest of their readers. They are the very essence of story-telling.

In the stories included in this chapter, the authors have addressed themselves to various aspects of space travel and to conditions on worlds other than earth. Isaac Asimov's story, "Founding Father," for example, describes a planet on which the first men to arrive are doomed.

Tom Godwin, in "The Cold Equations," presents a problem. It is one with a terrible solution and Godwin makes his protagonist and the reader face that inevitable and awful solution.

Each story gives the reader an excellent example of the science-fiction author's art. Each contains drama, conflict, suspense, plot, characterization, and atmosphere. In addition to these story elements, Robert Sheckley supplies a dash of humor in his tale of a recalcitrant space ship crew member in "Holdout."

Each of these science-fiction stories contains the excitement and insight which encourage readers to turn to literature for a better understanding of themselves, of others, and of the world in which they live. The fact that the events depicted are beyond the experience of the reader at the present time does not prevent him from sharing the very real pain of the protagonist in "The Cold Equations." Nor does it prevent him from understanding the subtle point Sheckley makes about prejudice in "Holdout."

Science-fiction stories may be about worlds light years away from earth but they can and do, in the hands of the best practitioners of the art, teach us something about who we are and how we live despite the fact that the stories are not about our earth as it exists today.

INTRODUCTION: Maelstrom II

New frontiers have always beckoned to men. Men have found such new frontiers as the depths of the ocean or the surface of the moon irresistible. They have set out to explore them and to find ways to survive in their hostile environments. Facing life in these alien environments is a challenge men must meet if the new frontiers are to be tamed.

In this story, we meet a man in orbit around the moon who faces death in that alien environment. The story is an example of the fact that noted science-fiction writers, like other authors of stature, address themselves to the mysteries of human existence.

Maelstrom II
by Arthur C. Clarke

He was not the first man, Cliff Leyland told himself bitterly, to know the exact second and the precise manner of his death; times beyond number, condemned criminals had waited for their last dawn. Yet until the very end, they could have hoped for a reprieve; human judges can show mercy, but against the laws of nature there was no appeal.

And only six hours ago he had been whistling happily while he packed his ten kilos of personal baggage for the long fall home. He could still remember (even now, after all that had happened) how he had dreamed that Myra was already in his arms, that he was taking Brian and Sue on that promised cruise down the Nile. In a few minutes, as Earth rose above the horizon, he might see the Nile again; but memory alone could bring back the faces of his wife and children. And all because he had tried to save nine hundred fifty sterling dollars by riding home on the freight catapult instead of the rocket shuttle.

He had expected the first twelve seconds of the trip to be rough, as the electric launcher whipped the capsule along its ten-mile track and shot him off the Moon. Even with the protection of the water bath in which he had floated during countdown, he had not looked forward to the twenty G of takeoff. Yet when the acceleration had gripped the capsule, he had been hardly aware of the immense forces acting upon him. The only sound was a faint creaking from the metal walls; to anyone who had experienced the thunder of a rocket launch, the silence was uncanny. When the cabin speaker had announced, "T plus five seconds—speed two thousand miles an hour," he could scarcely believe it.

Two thousand miles an hour in five seconds from a standing start—with seven seconds still to go as the generators smashed their thunderbolts of power into the launcher. He was riding the lightning across the face of the Moon; and at T plus seven seconds, the lightning failed.

Even in the womblike shelter of the tank, Cliff could sense that something had gone wrong. The water around him, until now frozen almost rigid by its weight, seemed suddenly to become alive. Though the capsule was still hurtling along the track, all acceleration had ceased and it was merely coasting under its own momentum.

He had no time to feel fear, or to wonder what had happened, for the power failure lasted little more than a second. Then, with a jolt that shook the capsule from end to end and set off a series of ominous, tinkling crashes, the field came on again.

When the acceleration faded for the last time, all weight vanished with it. Cliff needed no instrument but his stomach to tell that the capsule had left the end of the track and was rising away from the surface of the Moon. He waited impatiently until the automatic pumps had drained the tank and the hot-air driers had done their work; then he drifted across the control panel and pulled himself down into the bucket seat.

"Launch Control," he called urgently, as he drew the restraining straps around his waist. "What the devil happened?"

A brisk but worried voice answered at once.

"We're still checking—call you back in thirty seconds. Glad you're okay," it added belatedly.

While he was waiting, Cliff switched to forward vision. There was nothing ahead except stars—which was as it should be. At least he had taken off with most of his planned speed and there was no danger that he would crash back to the Moon's surface immediately. But he would crash back sooner or later, for he could not possibly have reached escape velocity. He must be rising out into space along a great ellipse—and, in a few hours, he would be back at his starting point.

"Hello, Cliff," said Launch Control suddenly. "We've found what happened. The circuit breakers tripped when you went through section five of the track, so your take-off speed was seven hundred miles an hour low. That will bring you back in just over five hours—but don't worry; your course-correction jets can boost you into a stable orbit. We'll tell you when to fire them; then all you have to do is to sit tight until we can send someone to haul you down."

Slowly, Cliff allowed himself to relax. He had forgotten the capsule's vernier rockets; low-powered though they were, they could kick him into an orbit that would clear the Moon. Though he might fall back to within a few miles of the lunar surface, skimming over mountains and plains at a breath-taking speed, he would be perfectly safe.

Then he remembered those tinkling crashes from the control compartment, and his hopes dimmed again—for there were not many things that could break in a space vehicle without most unpleasant consequences.

He was facing those consequences, now that the final checks of the ignition circuits had been completed. Neither on manual nor on auto would the navigation rockets fire; the capsule's modest fuel reserves, which could have taken him to safety, were utterly useless. In five hours, he would complete his orbit—and return to his launching point.

I wonder if they'll name the new crater after me? thought Cliff. "Crater Leyland—diameter . . ." What diameter? Better not exaggerate—I don't suppose it will be more than a couple of hundred yards across. Hardly worth putting on the map.

Launch Control was still silent, but that was not surprising; there was little that one could say to a man already as good as dead. And yet, though he knew that nothing could alter his trajectory, even now he did not believe that he would soon be scattered over most of Farside. He was still soaring away from the Moon, snug and comfortable in his little cabin. The idea of death was utterly incongruous—as it is to all men until the final second.

And then, for a moment, Cliff forgot his own problem. The horizon ahead was no longer flat; something even more brilliant than the blazing lunar landscape was lifting against the stars. As the capsule curved round the edge of the Moon, it was creating the only kind of Earthrise that was possible—a man-made one. In a minute it was all over, such was his speed in orbit. By that time the Earth had leaped clear of the horizon and was climbing swiftly up the sky.

It was three-quarters full and almost too bright to look upon. Here was a cosmic mirror made not of dull rocks and dusty plains, but of snow and cloud and sea. Indeed, it was almost all sea, for the Pacific was turned toward him, and the blinding reflection of the Sun covered the Hawaiian Islands. The haze of the atmosphere—that soft blanket that should have cushioned his descent in a few hours' time—obliterated all geographical details; perhaps that darker patch emerging from night was New Guinea, but he could not be sure.

There was a bitter irony in the knowledge that he was heading straight toward that lovely, gleaming apparition. Another seven hundred miles an hour and he would have made it. Seven hundred miles an hour—that was all. He might as well ask for 7,000,000.

The sight of the rising Earth brought home to him, with irresistible force, the duty he feared but could postpone no longer. "Launch Control," he said, holding his voice steady with a great effort. "Please give me a circuit to Earth."

This was one of the strangest things he had ever done in his life—sitting here above the Moon, listening to the telephone ring in his own home a quarter of a million miles away. It must be near midnight down there in Africa and it would be some time before there would be any answer. Myra would stir sleepily—then, because she was a spaceman's wife, always alert for disaster, she would be instantly awake. But they had both hated to have a phone in the bedroom, and it would be at least fifteen seconds before she could switch on the lights, close the nursery door to avoid disturbing the baby, get down the stairs and—

Her voice came clear and sweet across the emptiness of space. He would recognize it anywhere in the Universe, and he detected at once the undertone of anxiety.

"Mrs. Leyland?" said the Earthside operator. "I have a call from your husband. Please remember the two-second time lag."

Cliff wondered how many people were listening to this call, either on the Moon, the Earth or the relay satellites. It was hard to talk for the last time to your loved ones, not knowing how many eavesdroppers there might be. But as soon as he began to speak, no one else existed but Myra and himself.

"Darling," he began. "This is Cliff. I'm afraid I won't be coming home as I promised. There's been a—a technical slip. I'm quite all right at the moment, but I'm in big trouble."

He swallowed, trying to overcome the dryness in his mouth, then went on quickly before she could interrupt. As briefly as he could, he explained the situation. For his own sake as well as hers, he did not abandon all hope.

"Everyone's doing their best," he said. "Maybe they can get a ship up to me in time—but in case they can't—well, I wanted to speak to you and the children."

She took it well, as he had known she would. He felt pride as well as love when her answer came back from the dark side of Earth.

"Don't worry, Cliff. I'm sure they'll get you out and we'll have our holiday after all, exactly the way we planned."

"I think so, too," he lied. "But just in case—would you wake the children? Don't tell them that anything's wrong."

It was an endless half minute before he heard their sleepy yet excited voices. Cliff would willingly have given these last few hours of his life to have seen their faces once again, but the capsule was not equipped with such luxuries as phonevision. Perhaps it was just as well, for he could not have hidden the truth had he looked into their eyes. They would know it soon enough, but not from him. He wanted to give them only happiness in these last moments together.

Yet it was hard to answer their questions, to tell them that he would soon be seeing them, to make promises that he could not keep. It needed all his self-control when Brian reminded him of the Moon dust he had forgotten once before—but had remembered this time.

"I've got it, Brian—it's in a jar right beside me—soon you'll be able to show it to your friends." (No: Soon it will be back on the world from which it came.) "And Susie—be a good girl and do everything that Mummy tells you. Your last school report wasn't too good, you know, especially those remarks about behavior ... Yes, Brian, I have those photographs, and the piece of rock from Aristarchus—"

It was hard to die at thirty-five; but it was hard, too, for a boy to lose his father at ten. How would Brian remember him in the years ahead? Perhaps as no more than a fading voice from space, for he had spent so little time on Earth. In these last few minutes, as he swung outward and then back to the Moon, there was little enough that he could do except project his love and his hope across the emptiness that he would never span again. The rest was up to Myra.

When the children had gone, happy but puzzled, there was work to do. Now was the time to keep one's head, to be businesslike and practical. Myra must face the future without him, but at least he could make the transition easier. Whatever happens to the individual, life goes on; and to modern man life involves mortgages and installments, insurance policies and joint bank accounts. Almost impersonally, as if they concerned someone else—which would soon be true enough—Cliff began to talk about these things. There was a time for the heart and a time for the brain. The heart would have its final say three hours from now, when he began his last approach to the surface of the Moon.

No one interrupted them; there must have been silent monitors maintaining the link between two worlds, but they might have been the only people alive. Sometimes, while he was speaking, Cliff's eyes would stray to the periscope and be dazzled by the glare of Earth—now more than halfway up the sky. It was impossible to believe that it was home for seven billion souls. Only three mattered to him now.

It should have been four, but with the best will in the world he could not put the baby on the same footing as the others. He had never seen his younger son; and now he never would.

At last, he could think of no more to say. For some things, a lifetime was not enough—but an hour could be too much. He felt physically and emotionally exhausted, and the strain on Myra must have been equally great. He wanted to be alone with his thoughts and with the stars, to compose his mind and to make his peace with the Universe.

"I'd like to sign off for an hour or so, darling," he said. There was no need for explanations; they understood each other too well. "I'll call you back in—in plenty of time. Goodbye for now."

He waited the two seconds for the answering goodbye from Earth; then he cut the circuit and stared blankly at the tiny control desk. Quite unexpectedly, without desire or volition, tears sprang into his eyes, and suddenly he was weeping like a child.

He wept for his loved ones and for himself. He wept for the future that might have been and the hopes that would soon be incandescent vapor, drifting between the stars. And he wept because there was nothing else to do.

After a while he felt much better. Indeed, he realized that he was extremely hungry; there was no point in dying on an empty stomach, and he began to rummage among the space rations in the closet-sized galley. While he was squeezing a tube of chicken-and-ham paste into his mouth, Launch Control called.

There was a new voice at the end of the line—a slow, steady and immensely competent voice that sounded as if it would brook no nonsense from inanimate machinery.

"This is Van Kessel, Chief of Maintenance, Space Vehicles Division. Listen carefully, Leyland—we think we've found a way out. It's a long shot—but it's the only chance you have."

Alternations of hope and despair are hard on the nervous system. Cliff felt a sudden dizziness; he might have fallen, had there been any direction in which to fall.

"Go ahead," he said faintly, when he had recovered. Then he listened to Van Kessel with an eagerness that slowly changed to incredulity.

"I don't believe it!" he said at last. "It just doesn't make sense!"

"You can't argue with the computers," answered Van Kessel. "They've checked the figures about twenty different ways. And it makes sense all right; you won't be moving so fast at apogee, and it doesn't need much of a kick then to change your orbit. I suppose you've never been in a deep-space rig before?"

"No, of course not."

"Pity—but never mind. If you follow instructions you can't go wrong. You'll find the suit in the locker at the end of the cabin. Break the seals and haul it out."

Cliff floated the full six feet from the control desk to the rear of the cabin, and pulled on the lever marked: EMERGENCY ONLY—TYPE 17 DEEP-

SPACE SUIT. The door opened and the shining silver fabric hung flaccid before him.

"Strip down to your underclothes and wriggle into it," said Van Kessel. "Don't bother about the biopack—you clamp that on later."

"I'm in," said Cliff presently. "What do I do now?"

"You wait twenty minutes—and then we'll give you the signal to open the air lock and jump."

The implications of that word "jump" suddenly penetrated. Cliff looked around the now familiar, comforting little cabin, and then thought of the lonely emptiness between the stars—the unreverberant abyss through which a man could fall until the end of time.

He had never been in free space; there was no reason why he should. He was just a farmer's boy with a master's degree in agronomy, seconded from the Sahara Reclamation Project and trying to grow crops on the Moon. Space was not for him; he belonged to the worlds of soil and rock, of Moon dust and vacuum-formed pumice.

"I can't do it," he whispered. "Isn't there any other way?"

"There's not," snapped Van Kessel. "We're doing our damnedest to save you, and this is no time to get neurotic. Dozens of men have been in far worse situations—badly injured, trapped in wreckage a million miles from help. But you're not even scratched, and already you're squealing! Pull yourself together—or we'll sign off and leave you to stew in your own juice."

Cliff turned slowly red, and it was several seconds before he answered.

"I'm all right," he said at last. "Let's go through those instructions again."

"That's better," said Van Kessel approvingly. "Twenty minutes from now, when you're at apogee, you'll go into the air lock. From that point, we'll lose communication: Your suit radio has only a ten-mile range. But we'll be tracking you on radar and we'll be able to speak to you when you pass over us again. Now, about the controls on your suit . . ."

The twenty minutes went quickly enough; at the end of that time, Cliff knew exactly what he had to do. He had even come to believe that it might work.

"Time to bail out," said Van Kessel. "The capsule's correctly orientated —the air lock points the way you want to go. But direction isn't critical— *speed* is what matters. Put everything you've got into that jump—and good luck!"

"Thanks," said Cliff inadequately. "Sorry that I—"

"Forget it," interrupted Van Kessel. "Now get moving!"

For the last time, Cliff looked round the tiny cabin, wondering if there was anything that he had forgotten. All his personal belongings would have to be abandoned, but they could be replaced easily enough. Then he remembered the little jar of Moon dust he had promised Brian; this time, he would not let the boy down. The minute mass of the sample—only a few ounces—would make no difference to his fate; he tied a piece of string round the neck of the jar and attached it to the harness of his suit.

The air lock was so small that there was literally no room to move; he stood sandwiched between inner and outer doors until the automatic pumping sequence was finished. Then the wall slowly opened away from him and he was facing the stars.

With his clumsy, gloved fingers, he hauled himself out of the air lock and stood upright on the steeply curving hull, bracing himself tightly against it with the safety line. The splendor of the scene held him almost paralyzed; he forgot all his fears of vertigo and insecurity as he gazed around him, no longer constrained by the narrow field of vision of the periscope.

The Moon was a gigantic crescent, the dividing line between night and day a jagged arc sweeping across a quarter of the sky. Down there the sun was setting, at the beginning of the long lunar night, but the summits of isolated peaks were still blazing with the last light of day, defying the darkness that had already encircled them.

That darkness was not complete. Though the Sun was gone from the land below, the almost full Earth flooded it with glory. Cliff could see, faint but clear in the glimmering Earthlight, the outlines of seas and highlands, the dim stars of mountain peaks, the dark circles of craters. He was flying above a ghostly, sleeping land—a land which was trying to drag him to his death. For now he was poised at the highest point of his orbit, exactly on the line between Moon and Earth. It was time to go.

He bent his legs, crouching against the hull. Then, with all his force, he launched himself toward the stars, letting the safety line run out behind him.

The capsule receded with surprising speed, and as it did so, he felt a most unexpected sensation. He had anticipated terror or vertigo—but not this unmistakable, haunting sense of familiarity. All this had happened before; not to him, of course, but to someone else. He could not pinpoint the memory, and there was no time to hunt for it now.

He flashed a quick glance at Earth, Moon and receding spacecraft, and made his decision without conscious thought. The line whipped away as he snapped the quick release; now he was alone, two thousand miles above the Moon, a quarter of a million miles from Earth. He could do nothing but wait; it would be two and a half hours before he would know if he could live—and if his own muscles had performed the task that the rockets had failed to do.

And then, as the stars slowly revolved around him, he suddenly knew the origin of that haunting memory. It had been many years since he had read Poe's short stories; but who could ever forget them?

He, too, was trapped in a maelstrom, being whirled down to his doom; he, too, hoped to escape by abandoning his vessel. Though the forces involved were totally different, the parallel was striking. Poe's fisherman had lashed himself to a barrel because stubby, cylindrical objects were being sucked down into the great whirlpool more slowly than his ship. It was a brilliant application of the laws of hydrodynamics; Cliff could only hope that his use of celestial mechanics would be equally inspired.

How fast had he jumped away from the capsule? At a good five miles an hour, surely. Trivial though that speed was by astronomical standards, it should be enough to inject him into a new orbit—one that, Van Kessel had promised him, would clear the Moon by several miles. That was not much of a margin, but it would be enough on this airless world, where there was no atmosphere to draw him down.

With a sudden spasm of guilt, Cliff realized that he had never made that second call to Myra. It was Van Kessel's fault; the engineer had kept him on the move, given him no time to brood over his own affairs. And Van Kessel was right: In a situation like this, a man could think only of himself. All his resources, mental and physical, must be concentrated on survival. This was no time or place for the distracting and weakening ties of love.

He was racing now toward the night side of the Moon, and the daylit crescent was shrinking even as he watched. The intolerable disk of the Sun, toward which he dared not look, was falling swiftly toward the curved horizon. The crescent moonscape dwindled to a burning line of light, a bow of fire set against the stars. Then the bow fragmented into a dozen shining beads, which one by one winked out as he shot into the shadow of the Moon.

With the going of the Sun, the Earthlight seemed more brilliant than ever, frosting his suit with silver as he rotated slowly along his orbit. It took him about ten seconds to make each revolution; there was nothing he could do to check his spin, and indeed he welcomed the constantly changing view. Now that his eyes were no longer distracted by occasional glimpses of the Sun, he could see the stars in thousands where there had been only hundreds before. The familiar constellations were drowned, and even the brightest of the planets were hard to find in that blaze of light.

The dark disk of the lunar nightland lay across the star field like an eclipsing shadow, and it was slowly growing as he fell toward it. At every instant some star, bright or faint, would pass behind its edge and wink out of existence. It was almost as if a hole were growing in space, eating up the heavens.

There was no other indication of his movement, or of the passage of time—except for his regular ten-second spin. When Cliff looked at his watch, he was astonished to see that he had left the capsule half an hour ago. He searched for it among the stars, without success. By now, it would be several miles behind—but presently it would draw ahead of him, as it moved on its lower orbit, and would be the first to reach the Moon.

Cliff was still puzzling over this paradox when the strain of the last few hours, combined with the euphoria of weightlessness, produced a result he would hardly have believed possible. Lulled by the gentle susurration of the air inlets, floating lighter than any feather as he turned beneath the stars, he fell into a dreamless sleep.

When he awoke at some prompting of his subconscious, the Earth was nearing the edge of the Moon. The sight almost brought on another wave of self-pity, and for a moment he had to fight for control of his emotions. This was the very last he might ever see of Earth, as his orbit took him back over Farside, into the land where the Earthlight never shone. The brilliant Antarctic ice caps, the equatorial cloud belts, the scintillation of the Sun upon the Pacific—all were sinking swiftly behind the lunar mountains. Then they were gone; he had neither Sun nor Earth to light him now, and the invisible land below was so black that it hurt his eyes.

Unbelievably, a cluster of stars had appeared *inside* the darkened disk, where no stars could possibly be. Cliff stared at them in astonishment for a few seconds, then realized he was passing above one of the Farside settlements. Down there beneath the pressure domes of their city, men were waiting out the lunar night—sleeping, working, loving, resting, quarreling . . . Did they know that he was speeding like an invisible meteor through their sky, racing above their heads at four thousand miles an hour? Almost certainly, for by now the whole Moon, and the whole Earth, must know of his predicament. Perhaps they were searching for him with radar and telescope, but they would have little time to find him. Within seconds, the unknown city had dropped out of sight, and he was once more alone above Farside.

It was impossible to judge his altitude above the blank emptiness speeding below, for there was no sense of scale or perspective. But he knew that he was still descending, and that at any moment one of the crater walls or mountain peaks that strained invisibly toward him might claw him from the sky.

For in the darkness somewhere ahead was the final obstacle—the hazard he feared most of all. Across the heart of Farside, spaning the equator from north to south in a wall more than a thousand miles long, lay the Soviet Range. He had been a boy when it was discovered, back in 1959, and could still remember his excitement when he had seen the first smudged photographs from Lunik III. He could never have dreamed that one day he would be flying toward those same mountains, waiting for them to decide his fate.

The first eruption of dawn took him completely by surprise. Light exploded ahead of him, leaping from peak to peak until the whole arc of the horizon was limned with flame. He was hurtling out of the lunar night, directly into the face of the Sun. At least he would not die in darkness, but the greatest danger was yet to come. For now he was almost back where he had started, nearing the lowest point of his orbit. He glanced at the suit chronometer, and saw that five full hours had now passed. Within minutes, he would have hit the Moon—or skimmed it and passed safely out into space.

As far as he could judge, he was less than twenty miles above the surface, and he was still descending, though very slowly now. Beneath him, the long shadows of the lunar dawn were daggers of darkness stabbing into the nightland. The steeply slanting sunlight exaggerated every rise in the ground, making even the smallest hills appear to be mountains. And now, unmistakably, the land ahead was rising, wrinkling into the foothills of the Soviet Range. More than 100 miles away, but approaching at a mile a second, a wave of rock was climbing from the face of the Moon. There was nothing he could do to avoid it; his path was fixed and unalterable. All that could be done had already been done, two and a half hours ago.

It was not enough. He was not going to rise above these mountains; they were rising above him.

Now he regretted his failure to make that second call to the woman who was still waiting, a quarter of a million miles away. Yet perhaps it was just as well, for there had been nothing more to say.

Other voices were calling in the space around him, as he came once more within range of Launch Control. They waxed and waned as he flashed through the radio shadow of the mountains; they were talking about him, but the fact scarcely registered on his emotions. He listened with an impersonal interest, as if to messages from some remote point of space or time, of no concern to him. Once he heard Van Kessel's voice say, quite distinctly: "Tell *Callisto*'s skipper we'll give him an intercept orbit, as soon as we know that Leyland's past perigee. Rendezvous time should be one hour, five minutes from now." I hate to disappoint you, thought Cliff, but that's one appointment I'll never keep.

For now the wall of rock was only fifty miles away, and each time he spun helplessly in space it came ten miles closer. There was no room for optimism now, as he sped more swiftly than a rifle bullet toward that implacable barrier. This was the end, and suddenly it became of great importance to know whether he would meet it face first, with open eyes, or with his back turned, like a coward.

No memories of his past life flashed through Cliff's mind as he counted the seconds that remained. The swiftly unrolling moonscape rotated beneath him, every detail sharp and clear in the harsh light of dawn. Now he was turned away from the onrushing mountains, looking back on the path he had traveled, the path that should have led to Earth. No more than three of his ten-second days were left to him.

And then the moonscape exploded into silent flame. A light as fierce as that of the Sun banished the long shadows, struck fire from the peaks and craters spread below. It lasted for only a fraction of a second, and had faded completely before he had turned toward its source.

Directly ahead of him, only twenty miles away, a vast cloud of dust was expanding toward the stars. It was as if a volcano had erupted in the Soviet Range—but that, of course, was impossible. Equally absurd was Cliff's second thought—that by some fantastic feat of organization and logistics the Farside Engineering Division had blasted away the obstacle in his path.

For it was gone. A huge, crescent-shaped bite had been taken out of the approaching skyline; rocks and debris were still rising from a crater that had not existed five seconds ago. Only the energy of an atomic bomb, exploded at precisely the right moment in his path, could have wrought such a miracle. And Cliff did not believe in miracles.

He had made another complete revolution and was almost upon the mountains when he remembered that all this while there had been a cosmic bulldozer moving invisibly ahead of him. The kinetic energy of the abandoned capsule—a thousand tons, traveling at over a mile a second —was quite sufficient to have blasted the gap through which he was now racing. The impact of the man-made meteor must have jolted the whole of Farside.

His luck held to the very end. There was a brief pitter-patter of dust particles against his suit, and he caught a blurred glimpse of glowing rocks and swiftly dispersing smoke clouds flashing beneath him. (How strange to see a cloud upon the Moon!) Then he was through the mountains, with nothing ahead but blessed, empty sky.

Somewhere up there, an hour in the future along his second orbit, *Callisto* would be moving to meet him. But there was no hurry now; he had escaped from the maelstrom. For better or for worse, he had been granted the gift of life.

There was the launching track, a few miles to the right of his path; it looked like a hairline scribed across the face of the Moon. In a few moments he would be within radio range; now, with thankfulness and joy, he could make that second call to Earth, to the woman who was still waiting in the African night.

FOR DISCUSSION: **Maelstrom II**

1. There are many elements involved in creating convincing fiction. Among them are suspense and conflict. The latter may be internal or external. Do you feel that these two ingredients are present in this story? If you do, can you give an example of both?
2. Does Cliff's taking the jar of Moon dust into space with him when he leaves the ship tell us anything about his view of his situation at that moment? Does it reveal anything about his character?
3. Convincing and specific details should be included in a story to make it seem real to the reader. How many such details can you find in this story?
4. Suppose it were impossible to blast a path through the Soviet Range. How would you conclude the story in light of such a problem?

INTRODUCTION: Founding Father

Throughout the world's fiction, regardless of the culture from which it springs, we encounter conflict. We discover stories of man against man, man against nature, and man against himself.

Science-fiction stories contain similar conflicts. In addition, they contain a scientific premise. Here is a story of man against nature, but not the nature we know. It is a story of victory within defeat. If that statement seems puzzling, the story will explain its meaning to the reader.

Founding Father
by Isaac Asimov

The original combination of catastrophes had taken place five years ago —five revolutions of this planet, HC-12549D by the charts, and nameless otherwise. Six-plus revolutions of Earth, but who was counting—any more?

If the men back home knew, they might say it was a heroic fight, an epic of the Galactic Corps; five men against a hostile world, holding their bitter own for five (or six-plus) years. And now they were dying, the battle lost after all. Three were in final coma, a fourth had his yellow-tinged eyeballs still open, and a fifth was yet on his feet.

But it was no question of heroism at all. It had been five men fighting off boredom and despair and maintaining their metallic bubble of livability only for the most unheroic reason that there was nothing else to do while life remained.

If any of them felt stimulated by the battle, he never mentioned it. After the first year, they stopped talking of rescue, and after the second, a moratorium descended on the word "Earth."

But one word remained always present. If unspoken it had to be found in their thoughts: "Ammonia."

It had come first while the landing was being scratched out against all odds on limping motors and in a battered space can.

You allow for bad breaks, of course; you expect a certain number—but one at a time. A stellar flare fries out the hyper-circuits—that can be repaired, given time. A meteorite disaligns the feeder-valves—they can be straightened, given time. A trajectory is miscalculated under tension and a momentarily unbearable acceleration tears out the jump-antennae and dulls the senses of every man on board—but antennae can be replaced and senses will recover, given time.

The chances are one in countless many that all three will happen at once; and still less that they will happen during a particularly tricky landing when the one necessary currency for the correction of all errors, time, is the one thing that is most lacking.

The *Cruiser John* hit that one chance in countless many, and it made a final landing, for it would never lift off a planetary surface again.

That it had landed essentially intact was itself a near-miracle. The five were given life for some years at least. Beyond that, only the blundering arrival of another ship could help, but no one expected that. They had had their lives' share of coincidences, they knew, and all had been bad.

That was that.

And the key word was "ammonia." With the surface spiralling upward, and death (mercifully quick) facing them at considerably better than even odds, Chou somehow had time to note the absorption spectrograph, which was registering raggedly.

"Ammonia," he cried out. The others heard but there was no time to pay attention. There was only the wrenching fight against a quick death for the sake of a slow one.

When they landed finally, on sandy ground with sparse, ragged, bluish vegetation; reedy grass; stunted treelike objects with blue bark and no leaves; no sign of animal life; and with an almost greenish cloudstreaked sky above—the word came back to haunt them.

"Ammonia?" said Peterson, heavily.

Chou said, "Four per cent."

"Impossible," said Peterson.

But it wasn't. The books didn't say impossible. What the Galactic Corps had discovered was that a planet of a certain mass and volume and at a certain temperature was an ocean planet and had one of two atmospheres: nitrogen/oxygen or nitrogen/carbon dioxide. In the former case, life was rampant; in the latter, it was primitive.

No one checked beyond mass, volume and temperature any longer. One took the atmosphere (one or the other of them) for granted. But the books didn't say it had to be so; just that it always was so. Other atmospheres were thermodynamically possible, but extremely unlikely, so they weren't found in actual practice.

Until now. The men of the *Cruiser John* had found one and were bathed for the rest of such life as they could eke out by a nitrogen/carbon dioxide/ammonia atmosphere.

The men converted their ship into an underground bubble of Earth-type surroundings. They could not lift off the surface, nor could they drive a communicating beam through hyperspace, but all else was salvageable. To make up for inefficiencies in the cycling system, they could even tap the planet's own water and air supply within limits; provided, of course, they subtracted the ammonia.

They organized exploring parties since their suits were in excellent condition and it passed the time. The planet was harmless; no animal life; sparse plant life everywhere. Blue, always blue; ammoniated chlorophyll; ammoniated protein.

They set up laboratories, analyzed the plant components, studied microscopic sections, compiled vast volumes of findings. They tried growing native plants in ammonia-free atmosphere and failed. They made themselves into geologists and studied the planet's crust; astronomers and studied the spectrum of the planet's sun.

Barrere would say sometimes, "Eventually, the Corps will reach this planet again and we'll leave a legacy of knowledge for them. It's a unique planet after all. There might not be another Earth-type with ammonia in all the Milky Way."

"Great," said Sandropoulos, bitterly. "What luck for us."

Sandropoulos worked out the thermodynamics of the situation. "A metastable system," he said. "The ammonia disappears steadily through geochemical oxidation that forms nitrogen; the plants utilize nitrogen and re-form ammonia, adapting themselves to the presence of ammonia. If the rate of plant formation of ammonia dropped two per cent, a declining spiral would set in. Plant life would wither, reducing the ammonia still further and so on."

"You mean if we killed enough plant life," said Vlassov, "we could wipe out the ammonia."

"If we had air-sleds and wide-angle blasters, and a year to work in, we might," said Sandropoulos, "but we haven't and there's a better way. If we could get our plants going, the formation of oxygen through photosynthesis would increase the rate of ammonia oxidation. Even a small localized rise would lower the ammonia in the region, stimulate Earth-plant growth further, and inhibit the native growth, drop the ammonia further and so on."

They became gardeners through all the growing season. That was, after all, routine for the Galactic Corps. Life on Earth-type planets was usually of the water/protein type, but variation was infinite and otherworld food was rarely nourishing and even more often it happened (not always, but often) that some types of Earth plants would overrun and drown out the native flora. With the native flora held down, other Earth plants could take root.

Dozens of planets had been converted into new Earths in this fashion. In the process, Earth plants developed hundreds of hardy varieties that flourished under extreme conditions—all the better with which to seed the next planet.

The ammonia would kill any Earth plant, but the seeds at the disposal of the *Cruiser John* were not true Earth plants but otherworld mutations of these plants. They fought hard but not well enough. Some varieties grew in a feeble, sickly manner and died.

At that they did better than did microscopic life. The planet's bacterioids were far more flourishing than was the planet's straggly blue plant life. The native microorganisms drowned out any attempt at competition from Earth samples. The attempt to seed the alien soil with Earth-type bacterial flora in order to aid the Earth plants failed.

Vlassov shook his head, "It wouldn't do anyway. If our bacteria survived, it would only be adapting to the presence of ammonia."

Sandropoulos said, "Bacteria won't help us. We need the plants; they carry the oxygen manufacturing systems."

"We could make some ourselves," said Peterson. "We could electrolyze water."

"How long will our equipment last? If we could only get our plants going it would be like electrolyzing water forever, little by little, but year after year, till the planet gave up."

Barrere said, "Let's treat the soil then. It's rotten with ammonium salts. We'll bake the salts out and replace the ammonia-free soil."

"And what about the atmosphere?" asked Chou.

"In ammonia-free soil, they may catch hold despite the atmosphere. They almost make it as it is."

They worked like longshoremen, but with no real end in view. None really thought it would work, and there was no future for themselves, personally, even if it did work. But working passed the days.

The next growing season, they had their ammonia-free soil, but Earth plants still grew only feebly. They even placed domes over several shoots and pumped ammonia-free air within. It helped slightly but not enough. They adjusted the chemical composition of the soil in every possible fashion. There was no reward.

The feeble shoots produced their tiny whiffs of oxygen, but not enough to topple the ammonia atmosphere off its base.

"One more push," said Sandropoulos, "one more. We're rocking it; we're rocking it; but we can't knock it over."

Their tools and equipment blunted and wore out with time and the future closed in steadily. Each month there was less room for maneuver.

When the end came at last, it was with almost gratifying suddenness. There was no name to place on the weakness and vertigo. No one actually suspected direct ammonia poisoning. Still, they were living off the algae growth of what had once been ship-hydroponics for years and the growths were themselves aberrant with possible ammonia contamination.

It could have been the workings of some native microorganism which might finally have learned to feed off them. It might even have been an Earthly microorganism, mutated under the conditions of a strange world.

So three died at last and did so, circumstances be praised, painlessly. They were glad to go, and leave the useless fight.

Chou said, in a voiceless whisper, "It's foolish to lose so badly."

Peterson, alone of the five to be on his feet (was he immune, whatever it was?) turned a grieving face toward his only living companion.

"Don't die," he said, "don't leave me alone."

Chou tried to smile. "I have no choice. But you can follow us, old friend. Why fight? The tools are gone and there is no way of winning now, if there ever was."

Even now, Peterson fought off final despair by concentrating on the fight against the atmosphere. But his mind was weary, his heart worn out, and when Chou died the next hour, he was left with four corpses to work with.

He stared at the bodies, counting over the memories, stretching them back (now that he was alone and dared wail) to Earth itself, which he had last seen on a visit eleven years before.

He would have to bury the bodies. He would break off the bluish branches of the native leafless trees and build crosses of them. He would hang the space helmet of each man on top and prop the oxygen cylinders below. Empty cylinders to symbolize the lost fight.

A foolish sentiment for men who could no longer care, and for future eyes that might never see.

But he was doing it for himself, to show respect for his friends, for he was not the kind of man to leave his friends untended in death while he himself could stand.

Besides—

Besides? He sat in weary thought for some moments.

While he was still alive, he would fight with such tools as were left. He would bury his friends.

He buried each in a spot of ammonia-free soil they had so laboriously built up; buried them without shroud and without clothing; leaving them naked in the hostile ground for the slow decomposition that would come with their own microorganisms before those, too, died with the inevitable invasion of the native bacterioids.

Peterson placed each cross, with its helmet and oxygen cylinders, propped each with rocks, then turned away, grim and sad-eyed, to return to the buried ship that he now inhabited alone.

He worked each day and eventually the symptoms came for him, too.

He strugged into his spacesuit and came to the surface for what he knew would be one last time.

He fell to his knees on the garden plots. The Earth plants were green. They had lived longer than ever before. They looked healthy, even vigorous.

They had patched the soil, babied the atmosphere, and now Peterson had used the last tool, the only one remaining at his disposal, and he had given them fertilizer as well—

Out of the slowly corrupting flesh of the Earthmen came the nutrients that supplied the final push. Out of the Earth plants came the oxygen that would beat back the ammonia and push the planet out of the un-accountable niche into which it had stuck.

If Earthmen ever came again (when? a million years hence?), they would find a nitrogen/oxygen atmosphere and a limited flora strangely reminiscent of Earth's.

The crosses would rot and decay, the metal rust and decompose. The bones might fossilize and remain to give a hint as to what happened. Their own records, sealed away, might be found.

But none of that mattered. If nothing at all was ever found, the planet itself, the whole planet, would be their monument.

And Peterson lay down to die in the midst of their victory.

FOR DISCUSSION: Founding Father

1. Science-fiction stories often begin with a known premise and then extrapolate from that premise. There is a point in this story where the author makes such an extrapolation. Can you identify it?
2. What does the behavior of the men in the story during their five years on the planet HC-12549D say about human nature in general?
3. Peterson has two reasons for burying his dead colleagues. What are they? Which is the more important reason, in your opinion?
4. Reread the last sentence in the story. What does it say about death in the circumstances described in the story?

INTRODUCTION: Holdout

"The crew of a spaceship must be friends."

This is the opening sentence in the story below and it immediately sets the stage for the situation to follow. The conflict in this story arises when one member of the ship's crew refuses to travel with the others because of his prejudice against a member of the crew.

Because of his refusal, he threatens to upset the world of the ship for, as the story's first sentence indicates, friendship is necessary if such a microcosmic world is to function smoothly and effectively.

The idea of racism aboard a space ship may be viewed in a larger context. The author's moral may well be applied to the planet Earth itself which is another kind of space ship.

Holdout
by Robert Sheckley

The crew of a space ship must be friends. They must live harmoniously in order to achieve the split-second interaction that becomes necessary from time to time. In space, one mistake is usually enough.

It is axiomatic that even the best ships have their accidents; the mediocre ones don't survive.

Knowing this, it can be understood how Captain Sven felt when, four hours before blastoff, he was told that radioman Forbes would not serve with the new replacement.

Forbes hadn't met the new replacement yet, and didn't want to. Hearing about him was enough. There was nothing personal in this, Forbes explained. His refusal was on purely racial grounds.

"Are you sure of this?" Captain Sven asked, when his chief engineer came to the bridge with the news.

"Absolutely certain, sir," said engineer Hao. He was a small, flat-faced, yellow-skinned man from Canton. "We tried to handle it ourselves. But Forbes wouldn't budge."

Captain Sven sat down heavily in his padded chair. He was deeply shocked. He had considered racial hatred a thing of the remote past. He was as astonished at a real-life example of it as he would have been to encounter a dodo, a moa, or a mosquito.

"Racialism in this day and age!" Sven said. "Really, it's too preposterous. It's like telling me they're burning heretics in the village square, or threatening warfare with cobalt bombs."

"There wasn't a hint of it earlier," said Hao. "It came as a complete surprise."

"You're the oldest man on the ship," Sven said. "Have you tried reasoning him out of this attitude?"

"I've talked to him for hours," Hao said. "I pointed out that for centuries we Chinese hated the Japanese, and vice versa. If we could overcome our antipathy for the sake of the Great Co-operation, why couldn't he?"

"Did it do any good?"

"Not a bit. He said it just wasn't the same thing."

Sven bit off the end of a cigar with a vicious gesture, lighted it, and puffed for a moment. "Well, I'm damned if I'll have anything like this on *my* ship. I'll get another radioman!"

"That won't be too easy, sir," Hao said. "Not here."

Sven frowned thoughtfully. They were on Discaya II, a small outpost planet in the Southern Star Reaches. Here they had unloaded a cargo of machine parts, and taken on the Company-assigned replacement who was the innocent source of all the trouble. Discaya had plenty of trained men, but they were all specialists in hydraulics, mining, and allied fields. The planet's single radio operator was happy where he was, had a wife and children on Discaya, owned a house in a pleasant suburb, and would never consider leaving.

"Ridiculous, absolutely ridiculous," Sven said. "I can't spare Forbes, and I'll not leave the new man behind. It wouldn't be fair. Besides, the Company would probably fire me. And rightly, rightly. A captain should be able to handle trouble aboard his own ship."

Hao nodded glumly.

"Where is this Forbes from?"

"A farm near an isolated village in the mountain country of the Southern United States. Georgia, sir. Perhaps you've heard of it?"

"I think so," said Sven, who had taken a course in Regional Characteristics at Uppsala, to better fit himself for the job of captain. "Georgia produces peanuts and hogs."

"And men," Hao added. "Strong, capable men. You'll find Georgians working on all frontiers, out of all proportions to their actual numbers. Their reputation is unexcelled."

"I know all this," Sven grumbled. "And Forbes is an excellent man. But this racialism—"

"Forbes can't be considered typical," Hao said. "He was raised in a small, isolated community, far from the mainstream of American life.

Similar communities all over the world develop and cling to strange folkways. I remember a village in Honan where—"

"I still find it hard to believe," Sven said, interrupting what promised to be a long dissertation on Chinese country life. "And there's simply no excuse for it. Every community everywhere has a heritage of some sort of racial feeling. But it's every individual's responsibility to rid himself of that when he enters the mainstream of Terran life. Others have. Why not Forbes? Why must he inflict his problems on us? Wasn't he taught anything about the Great Co-operation?"

Hao shrugged his shoulders. "Would you care to speak to him, Captain?"

"Yes. Wait, I'll speak to Angka first."

The chief engineer left the bridge. Sven remained deep in thought until he heard a knock at the door.

"Come in."

Angka entered. He was cargo foreman, a tall, spendidly proportioned man with skin the color of a ripe plum. He was a full-blooded Negro from Ghana, and a first-class guitar player.

"I assume," Sven said, "you know all about the trouble."

"It's unfortunate, sir," Angka said.

"Unfortunate? It's downright catastrophic! You know the risk involved in taking the ship up in this condition. I'm supposed to blast off in less than three hours. We can't sail without a radioman, and we need the replacement, too."

Angka stood impassively, waiting.

Sven flicked an inch of white ash from his cigar. "Now look, Angka, you must know why I called you here."

"I can guess, sir," Angka said, grinning.

"You're Forbes's best friend. Can't you do something with him?"

"I've tried, Captain, Lord knows I've tried. But you know Georgians."

"I'm afraid I don't."

"Good men, sir, but stubborn as mules. Once they've made up their minds, that's it. I've been talking to Forbes for two days about this. I got him drunk last night—strictly in line of duty, sir," Angka added hastily.

"It's all right. Go on."

"And I talked to him like I'd talk to my own son. Reminded him how good the crew got along. All the fun we'd had in all the ports. How good the Co-operation felt. Now look, Jimmy, I said to him, you keep on like this, you kill all that. You don't want that, do you, I asked him. He bawled like a baby, sir."

"But he wouldn't change his mind?"

"Said he *couldn't*. Told me I might as well quit trying. There was one and only one race in this galaxy he wouldn't serve with, and there was no sense talking about it. Said his pappy would spin in his grave if he were to do so."

"Is there any chance he'll change his mind?" Sven asked.

"I'll go on trying, but I don't think there's a chance."

He left. Captain Sven sat, his jaw cradled in one big hand. He glanced again at the ship's chronometer. Less than three hours before blastoff!

He lifted the receiver of the intercom and asked for a direct line to the spacefield tower. When he was in contact with the officer in charge he said, "I'd like to request permission to stay a few days longer."

"Wish I could grant it, Captain Sven," the officer said. "But we need the pit. We can only handle one interstellar ship at a time here. An ore boat from Calayo is due in five hours. They'll probably be short of fuel."

"They always are," Sven said.

"Tell you what we can do. If it's a serious mechanical difficulty, we could find a couple cranes, lower your ship to horizontal and drag it off the field. Might be quite a while before we could set it up again, though."

"Thanks, but never mind. I'll blast on schedule." He signed off. He couldn't allow his ship to become laid up like that. The Company would have his hide, not a doubt about it.

But there *was* a course of action he could take. An unpleasant one, but necessary. He got to his feet, discarded the dead cigar stump, and marched out of the bridge.

He came to the ship's infirmary. The doctor, in his white coat, was seated with his feet on a desk, reading a three-month-old German medical journal.

"Welcome, Cap. Care for a shot of strictly medicinal brandy?"

"I could use it," Sven said.

The young doctor poured out two healthy doses from a bottle marked *Swamp Fever Culture.*

"Why the label?" Sven asked.

"Discourages the men from sampling. They have to steal the cook's lemon extract." The doctor's name was Yitzhak Vilkin. He was an Israeli, a graduate of the new medical school at Beersheba.

"You know about the Forbes problem?" Sven asked.

"Everybody does."

"I wanted to ask you, in your capacity as medical officer aboard this ship: Have you ever observed any previous indications of racial hatred in Forbes?"

"Not one," Vilkin answered promptly.

"Are you sure?"

"Israelis are good at sensing that sort of thing. I assure you, it caught me completely by surprise. I've had some lengthy interviews with Forbes since, of course."

"Any conclusions?"

"He's honest, capable, straightforward, and slightly simple. He possesses some antiquated attitudes in the form of ancient traditions. The Mountain-Georgians, you know, have a considerable body of such custom. They've been much studied by anthropologists from Samoa and Fiji. Haven't you read *Coming of Age in Georgia*? Or *Folkways of Mountain-Georgia*?"

"I don't have time for such things," Sven said. "My time is pretty well occupied running this ship without me having to read up on the individual psychology of the entire crew."

"I suppose so, Cap," the doctor said. "Well, those books are in the ship's library, if you'd care to glance at them. I don't see how I can help you. Re-education takes time. I'm a medical officer anyhow, not a psychologist. The plain fact is this: There is one race that Forbes will not serve with, one race which causes him to enact all his ancient racial hostilities. Your new man, by some mischance, happens to be from that race."

"I'm leaving Forbes behind," Sven said abruptly. "The communications officer can learn how to handle the radio. Forbes can take the next ship back to Georgia."

"I wouldn't recommend that."

"Why not?"

"Forbes is very popular with the crew. They think he's damned unreasonable, but they wouldn't be happy sailing without him."

"*More* disharmony," Sven mused. "Dangerous, very dangerous. But damn it, I can't leave the new man behind. I won't. It isn't fair! Who runs this ship, me or Forbes?"

"A very interesting question," Vilkin observed, and ducked quickly as the irate captain hurled his glass at him.

Captain Sven went to the ship's library, where he glanced over *Coming of Age in Georgia* and *Folkways of Mountain-Georgia*. They didn't seem to help much. He thought for a moment, and glanced at his watch. Two hours to blastoff! He hurried to the Navigation Room.

Within the room was Ks'rat. A native of Venus, Ks'rat was perched on a stool inspecting the auxiliary navigating instruments. He was gripping a sextant in three hands, and was polishing the mirrors with his foot, his most dexterous member. When Sven walked in the Venusian turned orange-brown to show his respect for authority, then returned to his habitual green.

"How's everything?" Sven asked.

"Fine," said Ks'rat. "Except for the Forbes problem, of course." He was using a manual soundbox, since Venusians had no vocal chords. At first, these sound boxes had been harsh and metallic; but the Venusians had modified them until now, the typical Venusian "voice" was a soft, velvety murmur.

"Forbes is what I came to see you about," said Sven. "You're non-Terran. As a matter of fact, you're non-human. I thought perhaps you could throw a new light on the problem. Something I may have over-looked."

Ks'rat pondered, then turned gray, his "uncertain" color. "I'm afraid I can't help much, Captain Sven. We never had any racial problems on Venus. Although you might consider the *sclarda* situation a parallel—"

"Not really," Sven said. "That was more a religious problem."

"Then I have no further ideas. Have you tried reasoning with the man?"

"Everyone else has."

"You might have better luck, Captain. As an authority symbol, you might tend to supplant the father symbol within him. With that advantage, try to make him aware of the true basis for his emotional reaction."

"There *is* no basis for racial hatred."

"Perhaps not in terms of abstract logic. But in human terms, you might find an answer and a key. Try to discover what Forbes fears. Perhaps if you can put him in better reality-contact with his own motives, he'll come around."

"I'll bear all that in mind," said Sven, with a sarcasm that was lost on the Venusian.

The intercom sounded the captain's signal. It was the first mate. "Captain! Tower wants to know whether you're blasting on schedule."

"I am," Sven said. "Secure the ship." He put down the phone.

Ks'rat turned a bright red. It was the Venusian equivalent of a raised eyebrow.

"I'm damned if I do and damned if I don't," Sven said. "Thanks for your advice. I'm going to talk to Forbes now."

"By the way," Ks'rat said, "of what race is the man?"

"What man?"

"The new man that Forbes won't serve with."

"How the hell should I know?" shouted Sven, his temper suddenly snapping. "Do you think I sit on the bridge inspecting a man's racial background?"

"It might make a difference."

"Why should it? Perhaps it's a Mongolian that Forbes won't serve with, or a Pakistani, or a New Yorker or a Martian. What do I care what race his diseased, impoverished, little mind picks on?"

"Good luck, Captain Sven," Ks'rat said as Sven hurried out.

James Forbes saluted when he entered the bridge, though it was not customary aboard Sven's ship. The radioman stood at full attention. He was a tall, slender youth, tow-headed, light-skinned, freckled. Everything about him looked pliant, malleable, complaisant. Everything except his eyes, which were dark blue and very steady.

Sven didn't know how to begin. But Forbes spoke first.

"Sir," he said, "I want you to know I'm mighty well ashamed of myself. You've been a good Captain, sir, the very best, and this has been a happy ship. I feel like a worthless no-account for doing this."

"Then you'll reconsider?" asked Sven, with a faint glimmer of hope.

"I wish I could, I really do. I'd give my right arm for you, Cap'n, or anything else I possess."

"I don't want your right arm. I merely want you to serve with the new man."

"That's the one thing I can't do," Forbes said sadly.

"Why in hell can't you?" Sven roared, forgetting his determination to use psychology.

"You just don't understand us Georgia mountain boys," Forbes said. "That's how my pappy, bless his memory, raised me. That poor little old man would spin in his grave if I went against his dying wish."

Sven stifled a curse and said, "You know the situation that leaves me in, Forbes. Do you have any suggestions?"

"Only one thing to do, sir. Angka and me'll leave the ship. You'll be better off short-handed than with an unCo-operative crew, sir."

"Angka is leaving with you? Wait a minute! Who's *he* prejudiced against?"

"No one, sir. But him and me's been shipmates for close to five years now, ever since we met on the freighter *Stella*. Where one goes, the other goes."

A red light flickered on Sven's control board, indicating the ship's readiness for blastoff. Sven ignored it.

"I can't have both of you leaving the ship," Sven said. "Forbes, why won't you serve with the new man?"

"Racial reasons, sir," Forbes said tightly.

"Now listen closely. You have been serving under me, a Swede. Has that disturbed you?"

"Not at all, sir."

"The medical officer is an Israeli. The navigator is a Venusian. The engineer is Chinese. There are Russians, New Yorkers, Melanesians, Africans, and everything else in this crew. Men of all races, creeds, and colors. You have served with them."

"Of course I have. From earliest childhood us Mountain-Georgians expect to serve with all different races. It's our heritage. My pappy taught me that. But I will not serve with Blake."

"Who's Blake?"

"The new man, sir."

"Where's he from?" Sven asked wearily.

"Mountain-Georgia."

For a moment, Sven thought he hadn't heard right. He stared at Forbes, who stared nervously back.

"From the mountain country of Georgia?"

"Yes, sir. Not too far, I believe, from where I was born."

"This man Blake, is he white?"

"Of course, sir. White English-Scottish ancestry, same as me."

Sven had the sensation of discovering a new world, a world no civilized man had ever encountered. He was amazed to discover that weirder customs could be found on Earth than anywhere else in the galaxy.

He said to Forbes, "Tell me about the custom."

"I thought *everybody* knew about us Mountain-Georgians, sir. In the section I come from, we leave home at the age of sixteen and we don't come back. Our customs teach us to work with any race, live with any race . . . except our own."

"Oh," said Sven.

"This new man, Blake, is a white Mountain-Georgian. He should have looked over the roster and not signed for this ship. It's all his fault, really, and if he chooses to overlook the custom, I can't help that."

"But *why* won't you serve with your own kind?" Sven asked.

"No one knows, sir. It's been handed down from father to son for hundreds of years, ever since the Hydrogen War."

Sven stared at him closely, ideas beginning to form. "Forbes, have you ever had any . . . feeling about Negroes?"

"Yes, sir."

"Describe it."

"Well, sir, we Mountain-Georgians hold that the Negro is the white man's natural friend. I mean to say, whites can get along fine with Chinese and Martians and such, but there's something special about black and white—"

"Go on," Sven urged.

"Hard to explain it good, sir. It's just that—well, the qualities of the two seem to mesh, like good gears. There's a special understanding between black and white."

"Did you know," Sven said gently, "that once, long ago, your ancestors felt that the Negro was a lesser human being? That they created laws to keep him from interacting with whites? And that they kept on doing this long after the rest of the world had conquered its prejudices? That they kept on doing it, in fact, right up to the Hydrogen War?"

"That's a lie, sir!" Forbes shouted. "I'm sorry, I don't mean to call you a liar, sir, but it just isn't true. Us Georgians have always—"

"I can prove it to you in history books and anthropological studies. I have several in the ship's library, if you'd care to look!"

"Yankee books!"

"I'll show you Southern books, too. It's true, Forbes, and it's nothing to be ashamed of. Education is a long, slow process. You have a great deal to be proud of in your ancestry."

"*If* this is true," Forbes said, very hesitantly, "then what happened?"

"It's in the anthropology book. You know, don't you, that Georgia was hit during the war by a hydrogen bomb meant for Norfolk?"

"Yes, sir."

"Perhaps you didn't know that the bomb fell in the middle of the so-called Black Belt. Many whites were killed. But almost the entire Negro population of that section of Georgia was wiped out."

"I didn't know that."

"Now, you must take my word that there had been race riots before the Hydrogen War, and lynchings, and a lot of bad feeling between white and black. Suddenly the Negroes were gone—dead. This created a considerable feeling of guilt among the whites, particularly in isolated communities. Some of the more superstitious whites believed that they had been spiritually responsible for this wholesale obliteration. And it hit them hard, for they were religious men."

"What would that matter, if they hated the Negroes?"

"They didn't, that's the whole point! They feared intermarriage, economic competition, a change of hierarchy. But they didn't *hate* the Negroes. Quite the contrary. They always maintained, with considerable truth, that they liked the Negroes better than the 'liberal' Northerners did. It set up quite a conflict."

Forbes nodded, thinking hard.

"In an isolated community like yours, it gave rise to the custom of working away from home, with any race except their own. Guilt was at the bottom of it all."

Perspiration rolled down Forbes's freckled cheeks. "I can't believe it," he said.

"Forbes, have I ever lied to you?"

"No, sir."

"Will you believe me, then, when I swear to you that this is true?"

"I—I'll try, Captain Sven."

"Now you know the reason for the custom. Will you work with Blake?"

"I don't know if I can."

"Will you try?"

Forbes bit his lip and squirmed uncomfortably. "Captain, I'll try. I don't know if I can, but I'll try. And I'm doing it for you and the men, not on account of what you said."

"Just try," Sven said. "That's all I ask of you."

Forbes nodded and hurriedly left the bridge. Sven immediately signaled the tower that he was preparing for blastoff.

Down in the crew's quarters, Forbes was introduced to the new man, Blake. The replacement was tall, black-haired, and obviously ill at ease.

"Howdy," said Blake.

"Howdy," said Forbes. Each made a tentative gesture toward a handshake, but didn't follow it through.

"I'm from near Pompey," said Forbes.

"I'm from Almira."

"Practically next door," Forbes said, unhappily.

"Yeah, afraid so," Blake said.

They eyed each other in silence. After a long moment, Forbes groaned, "I can't do it, I just can't." He began to walk away.

"Suddenly he stopped, turned and blurted out, "You all white?"

"Can't say as how I am," Blake replied. "I'm one-eighth Cherokee on my mother's side."

"Cherokee, huh?"

"That's right."

"Well, man, why didn't you say so in the first place. Knew a Cherokee from Altahatchie once, name of Tom Little Sitting Bear. Don't suppose you're kin to him?"

"Don't believe so," Blake said. "Never knew no Cherokees, myself."

"Well, it don't make no never-mind. They should a told me in the first place you was a Cherokee. Come on, I'll show you your bunk."

When the incident was reported to Captain Sven, several hours after blastoff, he was completely perplexed. How, he asked himself, could one-eighth Cherokee blood make a man a Cherokee? Weren't the other seven-eights more indicative?

He decided he didn't understand American Southerners at all.

FOR DISCUSSION: Holdout

1. Despite his serious theme, the author includes a number of humorous comments that poke subtle fun at men and their occasionally unreasoning attitudes. What is the satirical point of the doctor's comment to the captain about Mountain-Georgians having been studied by anthropologists from Samoa and Fiji? Can you find other satirical remarks in the story that help to bring the issue of racism into focus?

2. Does Forbes actually want to serve with Blake? If you believe he does, support your argument with material from the story.

3. One of the turning points in this story, and the author's major argument, occurs when Ks'rat suggests that the captain should make an effort to determine what Forbes fears. The author does not labor the point but he is clearly suggesting something about the genesis of prejudice as later events in the story confirm. What is he pointing to as the real root of unreasoning bigotry?

4. Is the conflict in this story internal or external? Is the conflict of sufficient interest to maintain the reader's interest despite the lack of overt action?

INTRODUCTION: The Cold Equations

Literature of the world has often presented us with protagonists engaged in conflict who ultimately resolve their conflict satisfactorily. Rarer is the story of a protagonist who fails to satisfactorily resolve the conflict facing him as is the case in this story.

The Cold Equations
by Tom Godwin

He was not alone.

There was nothing to indicate the fact but the white hand of the tiny gauge on the board before him. The control room was empty but for himself; there was no sound other than the murmur of the drives—but the white hand had moved. It had been on zero when the little ship was launched from the *Stardust*; now, an hour later, it had crept up. There was something in the supplies closet across the room, it was saying, some kind of a body that radiated heat.

It could be but one kind of a body—a living, human body.

He leaned back in the pilot's chair and drew a deep, slow breath, considering what he would have to do. He was an EDS pilot, inured to the sight of death, long since accustomed to it and to viewing the dying of another man with an objective lack of emotion, and he had no choice in what he must do. There could be no alternative—but it required a few moments of conditioning for even an EDS pilot to prepare himself to walk across the room and coldly, deliberately, take the life of a man he had yet to meet.

He would, of course, do it. It was the law, stated very bluntly and definitely in grim Paragraph L, Section 8, of Interstellar Regulations: *Any stowaway discovered in an EDS shall be jettisoned immediately following discovery.*

It was the law, and there could be no appeal.

It was a law not of men's choosing but made imperative by the circumstances of the space frontier. Galactic expansion had followed the development of the hyperspace drive and as men scattered wide across the frontier there had come the problem of contact with the isolated first-colonies and exploration parties. The huge hyperspace cruisers were the product of the combined genius and effort of Earth and were long and expensive in the building. They were not available in such numbers that small colonies could possess them. The cruisers carried the colonists to their new worlds and made periodic visits, running on tight schedules, but they could not stop and turn aside to visit colonies scheduled to be visited at another time; such a delay would destroy their schedule and produce a confusion and uncertainty that would wreck the complex interdependence between old Earth and new worlds of the frontier.

Some method of delivering supplies or assistance when an emergency occurred on a world not scheduled for a visit had been needed and the Emergency Dispatch Ships had been the answer. Small and collapsible, they occupied little room in the hold of the cruiser; made of light metal and plastics, they were driven by a small rocket drive that consumed relatively little fuel. Each cruiser carried four EDS's and when a call for aid was received the nearest cruiser would drop into normal space long enough to launch an EDS with the needed supplies or personnel, then vanish again as it continued on its course.

The cruisers, powered by nuclear converters, did not use the liquid rocket fuel but nuclear converts were far too large and complex to permit their installation in the EDS's. The cruisers were forced by necessity to carry a limited amount of the bulky rocket fuel and the fuel was rationed with care; the cruiser's computers determining the exact amount of fuel each EDS would require for its mission. The computers considered the course coördinates, the mass of the EDS, the mass of pilot and cargo; they were very precise and accurate and omitted nothing from their calculations. They could not, however, foresee, and allow for, the added mass of a stowaway.

The *Stardust* had received the request from one of the exploration parties stationed on Woden; the six men of the party already being stricken with the fever carried by the green *kala* midges and their own supply of serum destroyed by the tornado that had torn through their camp. The *Stardust* had gone through the usual procedure; dropping into normal space to launch the EDS with the fever serum, then vanishing again in hyperspace. Now, an hour later, the gauge was saying there was something more than the small carton of serum in the supplies closet.

He let his eyes rest on the narrow white door of the closet. There, just inside, another man lived and breathed and was beginning to feel assured that discovery of his presence would now be too late for the pilot to alter the situation. It *was* too late—for the man behind the door it was far later than he thought and in a way he would find terrible to believe.

There could be no alternative. Additional fuel would be used during the hours of deceleration to compensate for the added mass of the stowaway; infinitesimal increments of fuel that would not be missed until the ship had almost reached its destination. Then, at some distance above the ground that might be as near as a thousand feet or as far as tens of thousands of feet, depending upon the mass of ship and cargo and the preceding period of deceleration, the unmissed increments of fuel would make their absence known; the EDS would expend its last drops of fuel with a sputter and go into whistling free fall. Ship and pilot and stowaway would merge together upon impact as a wreckage of metal and plastic, flesh and blood, driven deep into the soil. The stowaway had signed his own death warrant when he concealed himself on the ship; he could not be permitted to take seven others with him.

He looked again at the telltale white hand, then rose to his feet. What he must do would be unpleasant for both of them; the sooner it was over, the better. He stepped across the control room, to stand by the white door.

"Come out!" His command was harsh and abrupt above the murmur of the drive.

It seemed he could hear the whisper of a furtive movement inside the closet, then nothing. He visualized the stowaway cowering closer into one corner, suddenly worried by the possible consequences of his act and his self-assurance evaporating.

"I said *out!*"

He heard the stowaway move to obey and he waited with his eyes alert on the door and his hand near the blaster at his side.

The door opened and the stowaway stepped through it, smiling. "All right—I give up. Now what?"

It was a girl.

He stared without speaking, his hand dropping away from the blaster and acceptance of what he saw coming like a heavy and unexpected physical blow. The stowaway was not a man—she was a girl in her teens, standing before him in little white gypsy sandals with the top of her brown, curly head hardly higher than his shoulder, with a faint, sweet scent of perfume coming from her and her smiling face tilted up so her eyes could look unknowing and unafraid into his as she waited for his answer.

Now what? Had it been asked in the deep, defiant voice of a man he would have answered it with action, quick and efficient. He would have taken the stowaway's identification disk and ordered him into the air lock. Had the stowaway refused to obey, he would have used the blaster. It would not have taken long; within a minute the body would have been ejected into space—had the stowaway been a man.

He returned to the pilot's chair and motioned her to seat herself on the boxlike bulk of the drive-control units that set against the wall beside him. She obeyed, his silence making the smile fade into the meek and guilty expression of a pup that has been caught in mischief and knows it must be punished.

"You still haven't told me," she said. "I'm guilty, so what happens to me now? Do I pay a fine, or what?"

"What are you doing here?" he asked. "Why did you stow away on this EDS?"

"I wanted to see my brother. He's with the government survey crew on Woden and I haven't seen him for ten years, not since he left Earth to go into government survey work."

"What was your destination on the *Stardust?*"

"Mimir. I have a position waiting for me there. My brother has been sending money home all the time to us—my father and mother and I— and he paid for a special course in linguistics I was taking. I graduated sooner than expected and I was offered this job on Mimir. I knew it would be almost a year before Gerry's job was done on Woden so he could come on to Mimir and that's why I hid in the closet, there. There was plenty of room for me and I was willing to pay the fine. There were only the two of us kids—Gerry and I—and I haven't seen him for so long, and I didn't want to wait another year when I could see him now, even though I knew I would be breaking some kind of a regulation when I did it."

I knew I would be breaking some kind of a regulation—In a way, she could not be blamed for her ignorance of the law; she was of Earth and had not realized that the laws of the space frontier must, of necessity, be as hard and relentless as the environment that gave them birth. Yet, to protect such as her from the results of their own ignorance of the frontier, there had been a sign over the door that led to the section of the *Stardust* that housed EDS's; a sign that was plain for all to see and heed:

UNAUTHORIZED PERSONNEL
KEEP OUT!

"Does your brother know that you took passage on the *Stardust* for Mimir?"

"Oh, yes. I sent him a spacegram telling him about my graduation and about going to Mimir on the *Stardust* a month before I left Earth. I already knew Mimir was where he could be stationed in a little over a year. He gets a promotion then, and he'll be based on Mimir and not have to stay out a year at a time on field trips, like he does now."

There were two different survey groups on Woden, and he asked, "What is his name?"

"Cross—Gerry Cross. He's in Group Two—that was the way his address read. Do you know him?"

Group One had requested the serum; Group Two was eight thousand miles away, across the Western Sea.

"No, I've never met him," he said, then turned to the control board and cut the deceleration to a fraction of a gravity; knowing as he did so that it could not avert the ultimate end, yet doing the only thing he could do to prolong that ultimate end. The sensation was like that of the ship suddenly dropping and the girl's involuntary movement of surprise half lifted her from the seat.

"We're going faster now, aren't we?" she asked. "Why are we doing that?"

He told her the truth. "To save fuel for a little while."

"You mean, we don't have very much?"

He delayed the answer he must give her so soon to ask: "How did you manage to stow away?"

"I just sort of walked in when no one was looking my way," she said. "I was practicing my Gelanese on the native girl who does the cleaning in the Ship's Supply office when someone came in with an order for supplies for the survey crew on Woden. I slipped into the closet there after the ship was ready to go and just before you came in. It was an impulse of the moment to stow away, so I could get to see Gerry—and from the way you keep looking at me so grim, I'm not sure it was a very wise impulse.

"But I'll be a model criminal—or do I mean prisoner?" She smiled at him again. "I intended to pay for my keep on top of paying the fine. I can cook and I can patch clothes for everyone and I know how to do all kinds of useful things, even a little bit about nursing."

There was one more question to ask:

"Did you know what the supplies were that the survey crew ordered?"

"Why, no. Equipment they needed in their work, I supposed."

Why couldn't she have been a man with some ulterior motive? A fugitive from justice, hoping to lose himself on a raw new world; an opportunist, seeking transportation to the new colonies where he might find golden fleece for the taking; a crackpot, with a mission—

Perhaps once in his lifetime an EDS pilot would find such a stowaway on his ship; warped men, mean and selfish men, brutal and dangerous men—but never, before, a smiling, blue-eyed girl who was willing to pay her fine and work for her keep that she might see her brother.

He turned to the board and turned the switch that would signal the *Stardust*. The call would be futile but he could not, until he had exhausted that one vain hope, seize her and thrust her into the air lock as he would an animal—or a man. The delay, in the meantime, would not be dangerous with the EDS decelerating at fractional gravity.

A voice spoke from the communicator. "*Stardust*. Identify yourself and proceed."

"Barton, EDS 34G11. Emergency. Give me Commander Delhart."

There was a faint confusion of noises as the request went through the proper channels. The girl was watching him, no longer smiling.

"Are you going to order them to come back after me?" she asked.

The communicator clicked and there was the sound of a distant voice saying, "Commander, the EDS requests—"

"Are they coming back after me?" she asked again. "Won't I get to see my brother, after all?"

"Barton?" The blunt, gruff voice of Commander Delhart came from the communicator. "What's this about an emergency?"

"A stowaway," he answered.

"A stowaway?" There was a slight surprise to the question. "That's rather unusual—but why the 'emergency' call? You discovered him in time so there should be no appreciable danger and I presume you've informed Ship's Records so his nearest relatives can be notified."

"That's why I had to call you, first. The stowaway is still aboard and the circumstances are so different—"

"Different?" the commander interrupted, impatience in his voice. "How can they be different? You know you have a limited supply of fuel; you also know the law, as well as I do: 'Any stowaway discovered in an EDS shall be jettisoned immediately following discovery.'"

There was the sound of a sharply indrawn breath from the girl. "*What does he mean?*"

"The stowaway is a girl."

"*What?*"

"She wanted to see her brother. She's only a kid and she didn't know what she was really doing."

"I see." All the curtness was gone from the commander's voice. "So you called me in the hope I could do something?" Without waiting for an answer he went on. "I'm sorry—I can do nothing. This cruiser must maintain its schedule; the life of not one person but the lives of many depend on it. I know how you feel but I'm powerless to help you. You'll have to go through with it. I'll have you connected with Ship's Records."

The communicator faded to a faint rustle of sound and he turned back to the girl. She was leaning forward on the bench, almost rigid, her eyes fixed wide and frightened.

"What did he mean, to go through with it? To jettison me . . . to go through with it—what did he mean? Not the way it sounded . . . he couldn't have. What did he mean . . . what did he really mean?"

Her time was too short for the comfort of a lie to be more than a cruelly fleeting delusion.

"He meant it the way it sounded."

"*No!*" She recoiled from him as though he had struck her, one hand half upraised as though to fend him off and stark unwillingness to believe in her eyes.

"It will have to be."

"No! You're joking—you're insane! You can't mean it!"

"I'm sorry." He spoke slowly to her, gently. "I should have told you before—I should have, but I had to do what I could first; I had to call the *Stardust*. You heard what the commander said."

"But you can't—if you make me leave the ship, I'll *die*."

"I know."

She searched his face and the unwillingness to believe left her eyes, giving way slowly to a look of dazed terror.

"You—know?" She spoke the words far apart, numb and wonderingly.

"I know. It has to be like that."

"You mean it—you really mean it." She sagged back against the wall, small and limp like a little rag doll and all the protesting and disbelief gone.

"You're going to do it—you're going to make me die?"

"I'm sorry," he said again. "You'll never know how sorry I am. It has to be that way and no human in the universe can change it."

"You're going to make me die and I didn't do anything to die for—I didn't *do* anything—"

He sighed, deep and weary. "I know you didn't, child. I know you didn't—"

"EDS." The communicator rapped brisk and metallic. "This is Ship's Records. Give us all information on subject's identification disk."

He got out of his chair to stand over her. She clutched the edge of the seat, her upturned face white under the brown hair and the lipstick standing out like a blood-red cupid's bow.

"*Now?*"

"I want your identification disk," he said.

She released the edge of the seat and fumbled at the chain that suspended the plastic disk from her neck with fingers that were trembling and awkward. He reached down and unfastened the clasp for her, then returned with the disk to his chair.

"Here's your data, Records: Identification Number T837—"

"One moment," Records interrupted. "This is to be filed on the gray card, of course?"

"Yes."

"And the time of the execution?"

"I'll tell you later."

"Later? This is highly irregular; the time of the subject's death is required before—"

He kept the thickness out of his voice with an effort. "Then we'll do it in a highly irregular manner—you'll hear the disk read, first. The subject is a girl and she's listening to everything that's said. Are you capable of understanding that?"

There was a brief, almost shocked, silence, then Records said meekly: "Sorry. Go ahead."

He began to read the disk, reading it slowly to delay the inevitable for as long as possible, trying to help her by giving her what little time he could to recover from her first terror and let it resolve into the calm of acceptance and resignation.

"Number T8374 dash Y54. Name: Marilyn Lee Cross. Sex: Female. Born: July 7, 2160. *She was only eighteen.* Height: 5-3. Weight: 110. *Such a slight weight, yet enough to add fatally to the mass of the shell-thin bubble that was an EDS.* Hair: Brown. Eyes: Blue. Complexion: Light. Blood Type: O. *Irrelevant data.* Destination: Port City, Mimir. *Invalid data—*"

He finished and said, "I'll call you later," then turned once again to the girl. She was huddled back against the wall, watching him with a look of numb and wondering fascination.

"They're waiting for you to kill me, aren't they? They want me dead, don't they? You and everybody on the cruiser wants me dead, don't you?" Then the numbness broke and her voice was that of a frightened and bewildered child. "Everybody wants me dead and I didn't *do* anything. I didn't hurt anyone—I only wanted to see my brother."

"It's not the way you think—it isn't that way, at all," he said. "Nobody wants it this way; nobody would ever let it be this way if it was humanly possible to change it."

"Then why is it! I don't understand. Why is it?"

"This ship is carrying *kala* fever serum to Group One on Woden. Their own supply was destroyed by a tornado. Group Two—the crew your brother is in—is eight thousand miles away across the Western Sea and their helicopters can't cross it to help Group One. The fever is invariably fatal unless the serum can be had in time, and the six men in Group One will die unless this ship reaches them on schedule. These little ships are always given barely enough fuel to reach their destination and if you stay aboard your added weight will cause it to use up all its fuel before it reaches the ground. It will crash, then, and you and I will die and so will the six men waiting for the fever serum."

It was a full minute before she spoke, and as she considered his words the expression of numbness left her eyes.

"Is that it?" she asked at last. "Just that the ship doesn't have enough fuel?"

"Yes."

"I can go alone or I can take seven others with me—is that the way it is?"

"That's the way it is."

"And nobody wants me to have to die?"

"Nobody."

"Then maybe—Are you sure nothing can be done about it? Wouldn't people help me if they could?"

"Everyone would like to help you but there is nothing anyone can do. I did the only thing I could do when I called the *Stardust*."

"And it won't come back—but there might be other cruisers, mightn't there? Isn't there any hope at all that there might be someone, somewhere, who could do something to help me?"

She was leaning forward a little in her eagerness as she waited for his answer.

"No."

The word was like the drop of a cold stone and she again leaned back against the wall, the hope and eagerness leaving her face. "You're sure—you *know* you're sure?"

"I'm sure. There are no other cruisers within forty light-years; there is nothing and no one to change things."

She dropped her gaze to her lap and began twisting a pleat of her skirt between her fingers, saying no more as her mind began to adapt itself to the grim knowledge.

It was better so; with the going of all hope would go the fear; with the going of all hope would come resignation. She needed time and she could have so little of it. How much?

The EDS's were not equipped with hull-cooling units; their speed had to be reduced to a moderate level before entering the atmosphere. They were decelerating at .10 gravity; approaching their destination at a far higher speed than the computers had calculated on. The *Stardust* had been quite near Woden when she launched the EDS; their present velocity was putting them nearer by the second. There would be a critical point, soon to be reached, when he would have to resume deceleration. When he did so the girl's weight would be multiplied by the gravities of deceleration, would become, suddenly, a factor of paramount importance; the factor the computers had been ignorant of when they determined the amount of fuel the EDS should have. She would have to go when deceleration began; it could be no other way. When would that be—how long could he let her stay?

"How long can I stay?"

He winced involuntarily from the words that were so like an echo of his own thoughts. How long? He didn't know; he would have to ask the ship's computers. Each EDS was given a meager surplus of fuel to compensate for unfavorable conditions within the atmopshere and relatively little fuel was being consumed for the time being. The memory banks of the computers would still contain all data pertaining to the course set for the EDS; such data would not be erased until the EDS reached its destination. He had only to give the computers the new data; the girl's weight and the exact time at which he had reduced the deceleration to .10.

"Barton." Commander Delhart's voice came abruptly from the communciator, as he opened his mouth to call the *Stardust*. "A check with Records shows me you haven't completed your report. Did you reduce the deceleration?"

So the commander knew what he was trying to do.

"I'm decelerating at point ten," he answered. "I cut the deceleration at seventeen fifty and the weight is a hundred and ten. I would like to stay at point ten as long as the computers say I can. Will you give them the question?"

It was contrary to regulations for an EDS pilot to make any changes in the course or degree of deceleration the computers had set for him but the commander made no mention of the violation, neither did he ask the reason for it. It was not necessary for him to ask; he had not become commander of an interstellar cruiser without both intelligence and an understanding of human nature. He said only: "I'll have that given the computers."

The communicator fell silent and he and the girl waited, neither of them speaking. They would not have to wait long; the computers would give the answer within moments of the asking. The new factors would be fed into the steel maw of the first bank and the electrical impulses would go through the complex circuits. Here and there a relay might click, a tiny cog turn over, but it would be essentially the electrical impulses that found the answer; formless, mindless, invisible, determining with utter precision how long the pale girl beside him might live. Then five little segments of metal in the second bank would trip in rapid succession against an inked ribbon and a second steel maw would spit out the slip of paper that bore the answer.

The chronometer on the instrument board read 18:10 when the commander spoke again.

"You will resume deceleration at nineteen ten."

She looked toward the chronometer, then quickly away from it. "Is that when . . . when I go?" she asked. He nodded and she dropped her eyes to her lap again.

"I'll have the course corrections given you," the commander said. "Ordinarily I would never permit anything like this but I understand your position. There is nothing I can do, other than what I've just done, and you will not deviate from these new instructions. You will complete your report at nineteen ten. Now—here are the course corrections."

The voice of some unknown technician read them to him and he wrote them down on the pad clipped to the edge of the control board. There would, he saw, be periods of deceleration when he neared the atmosphere when the deceleration would be five gravities—and at five gravities, one hundred ten pounds would become five hundred fifty pounds.

The technician finished and he terminated the contact with a brief acknowledgment. Then, hesitating a moment, he reached out and shut off the communicator. It was 18:13 and he would have nothing to report until 19:10. In the meantime, it somehow seemed indecent to permit others to hear what she might say in her last hour.

He began to check the instrument readings, going over them with unnecessary slowness. She would have to accept the circumstances and there was nothing he could do to help her into acceptance; words of sympathy would only delay it.

It was 18:20 when she stirred from her motionlessness and spoke.

"So that's the way it has to be with me?"

He swung around to face her. "You understand now, don't you? No one would ever let it be like this if it could be changed."

"I understand," she said. Some of the color had returned to her face and the lipstick no longer stood out so vividly red. "There isn't enough fuel for me to stay; when I hid on this ship I got into something I didn't know anything about and now I have to pay for it."

She had violated a man-made law that said KEEP OUT but the penalty was not of men's making or desire and it was a penalty men could not revoke. A physical law had decreed: *h amount of fuel will power an EDS with a mass of m safely to its destination;* and a second physical law had decreed: *h amount of fuel will not power an EDS with a mass of m plus x safely to its destination.*

EDS's obeyed only physical laws and no amount of human sympathy for her could alter the second law.

"But I'm afraid. I don't want to die—not now. I want to live and nobody is doing anything to help me; everybody is letting me go ahead and acting just like nothing was going to happen to me. I'm going to die and nobody *cares.*"

"We all do," he said. "I do and the commander does and the clerk in Ship's Records; we all care and each of us did what little he could to help you. It wasn't enough—it was almost nothing—but it was all we could do."

"Not enough fuel—I can understand that," she said, as though she had not heard his own words. "But to have to die for it. *Me,* alone—"

How hard it must be for her to accept the fact. She had never known danger of death; had never known the environments where the lives of men could be as fragile and fleeting as sea foam tossed against a rocky shore. She belonged on gentle Earth, in that secure and peaceful society where she could be young and gay and laughing with the others of her kind; where life was precious and well-guarded and there was always the assurance that tomorrow would come. She belonged in that world of soft winds and warm suns, music and moonlight and gracious manners and not on the hard, bleak frontier.

"How did it happen to me, so terribly quickly? An hour ago I was on the *Stardust,* going to Mimir. Now the *Stardust* is going on without me and I'm going to die and I'll never see Gerry and Mama and Daddy again—I'll never see anything again."

He hesitated, wondering how he could explain it to her so she would really understand and not feel she had, somehow, been the victim of a reasonlessly cruel injustice. She did not know what the frontier was like; she thought in terms of safe-and-secure Earth. Pretty girls were not jettisoned on Earth; there was a law against it. On Earth her plight would have filled the newscasts and a fast black Patrol ship would have been racing to her rescue. Everyone, everywhere, would have known of Marilyn Lee Cross and no effort would have been spared to save her life. But this was not Earth and there were no Patrol ships; only the *Stardust,* leaving them behind at many times the speed of light. There was no one to help her, there would be no Marilyn Lee Cross smiling from the newscasts tomorrow. Marilyn Lee Cross would be but a poignant memory for an EDS pilot and a name on a gray card in Ship's Records.

"It's different here; it's not like back on Earth," he said. "It isn't that no one cares; it's that no one can do anything to help. The frontier is big and here along its rim the colonies and exploration parties are scattered so thin and far between. On Woden, for example, there are only sixteen men—sixteen men on an entire world. The exploration parties, the survey crews, the little first-colonies—they're all fighting alien environments, trying to make a way for those who will follow after. The environments fight back and those who go first usually make mistakes only once. There is no margin of safety along the rim of the frontier; there can't be until the way is made for the others who will come later, until the new worlds are tamed and settled. Until then men will have to pay the penalty for making mistakes with no one to help them because there is no one *to* help them."

"I was going to Mimir," she said. "I didn't know about the frontier; I was only going to Mimir and *it's* safe."

"Mimir is safe but you left the cruiser that was taking you there."

She was silent for a little while. "It was all so wonderful at first; there was plenty of room for me on this ship and I would be seeing Gerry so soon . . . I didn't know about the fuel, didn't know what would happen to me—"

Her words trailed away and he turned his attention to the viewscreen, not wanting to stare at her as she fought her way through the black horror of fear toward the calm gray of acceptance.

Woden was a ball, enshrouded in the blue haze of its atmosphere, swimming in space against the background of star-sprinkled dead blackness. The great mass of Manning's Continent sprawled like a gigantic hourglass in the Eastern Sea with the western half of the Eastern Continent still visible. There was a thin line of shadow along the right-hand edge of the globe and the Eastern Continent was disappearing into it as the planet turned on its axis. An hour before the entire continent had been in view, now a thousand miles of it had gone into the thin edge of shadow and around to the night that lay on the other side of the world. The dark blue spot that was Lotus Lake was approaching the shadow. It was somewhere near the southern edge of the lake that Group Two had their camp. It would be night there, soon, and quick behind the coming of night the rotation of Woden on its axis would put Group Two beyond the reach of the ship's radio.

He would have to tell her before it was too late for her to talk to her brother. In a way, it would be better for both of them should they not do so but it was not for him to decide. To each of them the last words would be something to hold and cherish, something that would cut like the blade of a knife yet would be infinitely precious to remember, she for her own brief moments to live and he for the rest of his life.

He held down the button that would flash the grid lines on the view-screen and used the known diameter of the planet to estimate the distance the southern tip of Lotus Lake had yet to go until it passed beyond radio range. It was approximately five hundred miles. Five hundred miles; thirty minutes—and the chronometer read 18:30. Allowing for error in estimating, it could not be later than 19:05 that the turning of Woden would cut off her brother's voice.

The first border of the Western Continent was already in sight along the left side of the world. Four thousand miles across it lay the shore of the Western Sea and the Camp of Group One. It had been in the Western Sea that the tornado had originated, to strike with such fury at the camp and destroy half their prefabricated buildings, including the one that housed the medical supplies. Two days before the tornado had not existed; it had been no more than great gentle masses of air out over the calm Western Sea. Group One had gone about their routine survey work, unaware of the meeting of the air masses out at sea, unaware of the force the union was spawning. It had struck their camp without warning; a thundering, roaring destruction that sought to annihilate all that lay before it. It had passed on, leaving the wreckage in its wake. It had destroyed the labor of months and had doomed six men to die and then, as though its task was accomplished, it once more began to resolve into gentle masses of air. But for all its deadliness, it had destroyed with neither malice nor intent. It had been a blind and mindless force, obeying the laws of nature, and it would have followed the same course with the same fury had men never existed.

Existence required Order and there was order; the laws of nature, irrevocable and immutable. Men could learn to use them but men could not change them. The circumference of a circle was always pi times the diameter and no science of Man would ever make it otherwise. The combination of chemical A with chemical B under condition C invariably produced reaction D. The law of gravitation was a rigid equation and it made no distinction between the fall of a leaf and the ponderous circling of a binary star system. The nuclear conversion process powered the cruisers that carried men to the stars; the same process in the form of a nova would destroy a world with equal efficiency. The laws *were*, and the universe moved in obedience to them. Along the frontier were arrayed all the forces of nature and sometimes they destroyed those who were fighting their way outward from Earth. The men of the frontier had long ago learned the bitter futility of cursing the forces that would destroy them for the forces were blind and deaf; the futility of looking to the heavens for mercy, for the stars of the galaxy swung in their long, long sweep of two hundred million years, as inexorably controlled as they by the laws that knew neither hatred nor compassion.

The men of the frontier knew—but how was a girl from Earth to fully understand? *H amount of fuel will not power an EDS with a mass of m plus x safely to its destination.* To himself and her brother and parents she was a sweet-faced girl in her teens; to the laws of nature she was *x*, the unwanted factor in a cold equation.

She stirred again on the seat. "Could I write a letter? I want to write to Mama and Daddy and I'd like to talk to Gerry. Could you let me talk to him over your radio there?"

"I'll try to get him," he said.

He switched on the normal-space transmitter and pressed the signal button. Someone answered the buzzer almost immediately.

"Hello. How's it going with you fellows now—is the EDS on its way?"

"This isn't Group One; this is the EDS," he said. "Is Gerry Cross there?"

"Gerry? He and two others went out in the helicopter this morning and aren't back yet. It's almost sundown, though, and he ought to be back right away—in less than an hour at the most."

"Can you connect me through to the radio in his 'copter?"

"Huh-uh. It's been out of commission for two months—some printed circuits went haywire and we can't get any more until the next cruiser stops by. Is it something important—bad news for him, or something?"

"Yes—it's very important. When he comes in get him to the transmitter as soon as you possibly can."

"I'll do that; I'll have one of the boys waiting at the field with a truck. Is there anything else I can do?"

"No, I guess that's all. Get him there as soon as you can and signal me."

He turned the volume to an inaudible minimum, an act that would not affect the functioning of the signal buzzer, and unclipped the pad of paper from the control board. He tore off the sheet containing his flight instructions and handed the pad to her, together with pencil.

"I'd better write to Gerry, too," she said as she took them. "He might not get back to camp in time."

She began to write, her fingers still clumsy and uncertain in the way they handled the pencil and the top of it trembling a little as she poised it between words. He turned back to the viewscreen, to stare at it without seeing it.

She was a lonely little child, trying to say her last good-by, and she would lay out her heart to them. She would tell them how much she loved them and she would tell them to not feel badly about it, that it was only something that must happen eventually to everyone and she was not afraid. The last would be a lie and it would be there to read between the sprawling, uneven lines; a valiant little lie that would make the hurt all the greater for them.

Her brother was of the frontier and he would understand. He would not hate the EDS pilot for doing nothing to prevent her going; he would know there had been nothing the pilot could do. He would understand, though the understanding would not soften the shock and pain when he learned his sister was gone. But the others, her father and mother—they would not understand. They were of Earth and they would think in the manner of those who had never lived where the safety margin of life was a thin, thin line—and sometimes not at all. What would they think of the faceless, unknown pilot who had sent her to her death?

They would hate him with cold and terrible intensity but it really didn't matter. He would never see them, never know them. He would have only the memories to remind him; only the nights to fear, when a blue-eyed girl in gypsy sandals would come in his dreams to die again—

He scowled at the viewscreen and tried to force his thoughts into less emotional channels. There was nothing he could do to help her. She had unknowingly subjected herself to the penalty of a law that recognized neither innocence nor youth nor beauty, that was incapable of sympathy or leniency. Regret was illogical—and yet, could knowing it to be illogical ever keep it away?

She stopped occasionally, as though trying to find the right words to tell them what she wanted them to know, then the pencil would resume its whispering to the paper. It was 18:37 when she folded the letter in a square and wrote a name on it. She began writing another, twice looking up at the chronometer as though she feared the black hand might reach its rendezvous before she had finished. It was 18:45 when she folded it as she had done the first letter and wrote a name and address on it.

She held the letters out to him. "Will you take care of these and see that they're enveloped and mailed?"

"Of course." He took them from her hand and placed them in a pocket of his gray uniform shirt.

"These can't be sent off until the next cruiser stops by and the *Star-*

dust will have long since told them about me, won't it?" she asked. He nodded and she went on, "That makes the letters not important in one way but in another way they're very important—to me, and to them."

"I know. I understand, and I'll take care of them."

She glanced at the chronometer, then back to him. "It seems to move faster all the time, doesn't it?"

He said nothing, unable to think of anything to say, and she asked, "Do you think Gerry will come back to camp in time?"

"I think so. They said he should be in right away."

She began to roll the pencil back and forth between her palms. "I hope he does. I feel sick and scared and I want to hear his voice again and maybe I won't feel so alone. I'm a coward and I can't help it."

"No," he said, "you're not a coward. You're afraid, but you're not a coward."

"Is there a difference?"

He nodded. "A lot of difference."

"I feel so alone. I never did feel like this before; like I was all by myself and there was nobody to care what happened to me. Always, before, there was Mama and Daddy there and my friends around me. I had lots of friends, and they had a going-away party for me the night before I left."

Friends and music and laughter for her to remember—and on the viewscreen Lotus Lake was going into the shadow.

"Is it the same with Gerry?" she asked. "I mean, if he should make a mistake, would have have to die for it, all alone and with no one to help him?"

"It's the same with all along the frontier; it will always be like that so long as there is a frontier."

"Gerry didn't tell us. He said the pay was good and he sent money home all the time because Daddy's little shop just brought in a bare living but he didn't tell us it was like this."

"He didn't tell you his work was dangerous?"

"Well—yes. He mentioned that, but we didn't understand. I always thought danger along the frontier was something that was a lot of fun; an exciting adventure, like in the three-D shows." A wan smile touched her face for a moment. "Only it's not, is it? It's not the same at all, because when it's real you can't go home after the show is over."

"No," he said. "No, you can't."

Her glance flicked from the chronometer to the door of the air lock then down to the pad and pencil she still held. She shifted her position slightly to lay them on the bench beside, moving one foot out a little. For the first time he saw that she was not wearing Vegan gypsy sandals but only cheap imitations; the expensive Vegan leather was some kind of grained plastic, the silver buckle was gilded iron, the jewels were colored glass. *Daddy's little shop just brought in a bare living*—She must have left college in her second year, to take the course in linguistics that would enable her to make her own way and help her brother provide for her parents, earning what she could by part-time work after classes were over. Her personal possessions on the *Stardust* would be taken back to her parents—they would neither be of much value nor occupy much storage space on the return voyage.

"Isn't it—" She stopped, and he looked at her questioningly. "Isn't it cold in here?" she asked, almost apologetically. "Doesn't it seem cold to you?"

"Why, yes," he said. He saw by the main temperature gauge that the room was at precisely normal temperature. "Yes, it's colder than it should be."

"I wish Gerry would get back before it's too late. Do you really think he will, and you didn't just say so to make me feel better?"

"I think he will—they said he would be in pretty soon." On the viewscreen Lotus Lake had gone into the shadow but for the thin blue line of its western edge and it was apparent he had overestimated the time she would have in which to talk to her brother. Reluctantly, he said to her, "His camp will be out of radio range in a few minutes; he's on that part of Woden that's in the shadow"—he indicated the viewscreen—"and the turning of Woden will put him beyond contact. There may not be much time left when he comes in—not much time to talk to him before he fades out. I wish I could do something about it—I would call him right now if I could."

"Not even as much time as I will have to stay?"

"I'm afraid not."

"Then—" She straightened and looked toward the air lock with pale resolution. "Then I'll go when Gerry passes beyond range. I won't wait any longer after that—I won't have anything to wait for."

Again there was nothing he could say.

"Maybe I shouldn't wait at all. Maybe I'm selfish—maybe it would be better for Gerry if you just told him about it afterward."

There was an unconscious pleading for denial in the way she spoke and he said, "He wouldn't want you to do that, to not wait for him."

"It's already coming dark where he is, isn't it? There will be all the long night before him, and Mama and Daddy don't know yet that I won't ever be coming back like I promised them I would. I've caused everyone I love to be hurt, haven't I? I didn't want to—I didn't intend to."

"It wasn't your fault," he said. "It wasn't your fault at all. They'll know that. They'll understand."

"At first I was so afraid to die that I was a coward and thought only of myself. Now, I see how selfish I was. The terrible thing about dying like this is not that I'll be gone but that I'll never see them again; never be able to tell them that I didn't take them for granted; never be able to tell them I knew of the sacrifices they made to make my life happier, that I knew all the things they did for me and that I loved them so much more than I ever told them. I've never told them any of those things. You don't tell them such things when you're young and your life is all before you—you're afraid of sounding sentimental and silly.

"But it's so different when you have to die—you wish you had told them while you could and you wish you could tell them you're sorry for all the little mean things you ever did or said to them. You wish you could tell them that you didn't really mean to ever hurt their feelings and for them to only remember that you always loved them far more than you ever let them know."

"You don't have to tell them that," he said. "They will know—they've always known it."

"Are you sure?" she asked. "How can you be sure? My people are strangers to you."

"Wherever you go, human nature and human hearts are the same."

"And they will know what I want them to know—that I love them?"

"They've always known it, in a way far better than you could ever put in words for them."

"I keep remembering the things they did for me, and it's the little things they did that seem to be the most important to me, now. Like Gerry—he sent me a bracelet of fire-rubies on my sixteenth birthday. It was beautiful—it must have cost him a month's pay. Yet, I remember him more for what he did the night my kitten got run over in the street. I was only six years old and he held me in his arms and wiped away my tears and told me not to cry, that Flossy was gone for just a little while, for just long enough to get herself a new fur coat and she would be on the foot of my bed the very next morning. I believed him and quit crying and went to sleep dreaming about my kitten coming back. When I woke up the next morning, there was Flossy on the foot of my bed in a brand-new white fur coat, just like he said she would be.

"It wasn't until a long time later that Mama told me Gerry had got the pet-shop owner out of bed at four in the morning and, when the man got mad about it, Gerry told him he was either going to go down and sell him the white kitten right then or he'd break his neck."

"It's always the little things you remember people by; all the little things they did because they wanted to do them for you. You've done the same for Gerry and your father and mother; all kinds of things that you've forgotten about but that they will never forget."

"I hope I have. I would like for them to remember me like that."

"They will."

"I wish—" She swallowed. "The way I'll die—I wish they wouldn't ever think of that. I've read how people look who die in space—their insides all ruptured and exploded and their lungs out between their teeth and then, a few seconds later, they're all dry and shapeless and horribly ugly. I don't want them to ever think of me as something dead and horrible, like that."

"You're their own, their child and their sister. They could never think of you other than the way you would want them to; the way you looked the last time they saw you."

"I'm still afraid," she said. "I can't help it, but I don't want Gerry to know it. If he gets back in time, I'm going to act like I'm not afraid at all and—"

The signal buzzer interrupted her, quick and imperative.

"Gerry!" She came to her feet. "It's Gerry, now!"

He spun the volume control knob and asked: "Gerry Cross?"

"Yes," her brother answered, an undertone of tenseness to his reply. "The bad news—what is it?"

She answered for him, standing close behind him and leaning down a little toward the communicator, her hand resting small and cold on his shoulder.

"Hello, Gerry." There was only a faint quaver to betray the careful casualness of her voice. "I wanted to see you—"

"Marilyn!" There was sudden and terrible apprehension in the way he spoke her name. "What are you doing on that EDS?"

"I wanted to see you," she said again. "I wanted to see you, so I hid on this ship—"

"You *hid* on it?"

"I'm a stowaway . . . I didn't know what it would mean—"

"*Marilyn!*" It was the cry of a man who calls hopeless and desperate to someone already and forever gone from him. "What have you done?"

"I . . . it's not—" Then her own composure broke and the cold little hand gripped his shoulder convulsively. "Don't, Gerry—I only wanted to see you; I didn't intend to hurt you. Please, Gerry, don't feel like that—"

Something warm and wet splashed on his wrist and he slid out of the chair, to help her into it and swing the microphone down to her own level.

"Don't feel like that—Don't let me go knowing you feel like that—"

The sob she had tried to hold back choked in her throat and her brother spoke to her. "Don't cry, Marilyn." His voice was suddenly deep and infinitely gentle, with all the pain held out of it. "Don't cry, Sis—you mustn't do that. It's all right, Honey—everything is all right."

"I—" Her lower lip quivered and she bit into it. "I didn't want you to feel that way—I just wanted us to say good-by because I have to go in a minute."

"Sure—sure. That's the way it will be, Sis. I didn't mean to sound the way I did." Then his voice changed to a tone of quick and urgent demand. "EDS—have you called the *Stardust*? Did you check with the computers?"

"I called the *Stardust* almost an hour ago. It can't turn back, there are no other cruisers within forty light-years, and there isn't enough fuel."

"Are you sure that the computers had the correct data—sure of everything?"

"Yes—do you think I could ever let it happen if I wasn't sure? I did everything I could do. If there was anything at all I could do now, I would do it."

"He tried to help me, Gerry." Her lower lip was no longer trembling and the short sleeves of her blouse were wet where she had dried her tears. "No one can help me and I'm not going to cry any more and everything will be all right with you and Daddy and Mama, won't it?"

"Sure—sure it will. We'll make out fine."

Her brother's words were beginning to come in more faintly and he turned the volume control to maximum. "He's going out of range," he said to her. "He'll be gone within another minute."

"You're fading out, Gerry," she said. "You're going out of range. I wanted to tell you—but I can't, now. We must say good-by so soon—but maybe I'll see you again. Maybe I'll come to you in your dreams with my hair in braids and crying because the kitten in my arms is dead; maybe I'll be the touch of a breeze that whispers to you as it goes by; maybe I'll be one of those gold-winged larks you told me about, singing my silly head off to you; maybe, at times, I'll be nothing you can see but you will know I'm there beside you. Think of me like that, Gerry; always like that and not—the other way."

Dimmed to a whisper by the turning of Woden, the answer came back: "Always like that, Marilyn—always like that and never any other way."

"Our time is up, Gerry—I have to go, now. Good—" Her voice broke in mid-word and her mouth tried to twist into crying. She pressed her hand hard against it and when she spoke again the words came clear and true:

"Good-by, Gerry."

Faint and ineffably poignant and tender, the last words came from the cold metal of the communicator:

"Good-by, little sister—"

She sat motionless in the hush that followed, as though listening to the shadow-echoes of the words as they died away, then she turned away from the communicator, toward the air lock, and he pulled the black lever beside him. The inner door of the air lock slid swiftly open, to reveal the bare little cell that was waiting for her, and she walked to it.

She walked with her head up and the brown curls brushing her shoulders, with the white sandals stepping as sure and steady as the fractional gravity would permit and the gilded buckles twinkling with little lights of blue and red and crystal. He let her walk alone and made no move to help her, knowing she would not want it that way. She stepped into the air lock and turned to face him, only the pulse in her throat to betray the wild beating of her heart.

"I'm ready," she said.

He pushed the lever up and the door slid its quick barrier between them, inclosing her in black and utter darkness for her last moments of life. It clicked as it locked in place and he jerked down the red lever. There was a slight waver to the ship as the air gushed from the lock, a vibration to the wall as though something had bumped the outer door in passing, then there was nothing and the ship was dropping true and steady again. He shoved the red lever back to close the door on the empty air lock and turned away, to walk to the pilot's chair with the slow steps of a man old and weary.

Back in the pilot's chair he pressed the signal button of the normal-space transmitter. There was no response; he had expected none. Her brother would have to wait through the night until the turning of Woden permitted contact through Group One.

It was not yet time to resume deceleration and he waited while the ship dropped endlessly downward with him and the drives purred softly. He saw that the white hand of the supplies closet temperature gauge was on zero. A cold equation had been balanced and he was alone on the ship. Something shapeless and ugly was hurrying ahead of him, going to Woden where its brother was waiting through the night, but the empty ship still lived for a little while with the presence of the girl who had not known about the forces that killed with neither hatred nor malice. It seemed, almost, that she still sat small and bewildered and frightened on the metal box beside him, her words echoing hauntingly clear in the void she had left behind her:

I didn't do anything to die for—I didn't do anything—

114

FOR DISCUSSION: The Cold Equations

1. What is the meaning of this story's title?
2. Barton is obviously a decisive man. Is it inconsistent with his character to hesitate to take the necessary action when he discovers that his stowaway is a girl?
3. What is the author telling us about frontiers? About the physical laws of the universe?
4. How does Marilyn's recounting of her brother's sympathy when her kitten was killed help to bring Gerry, a minor character in the story, to life? Can characterization be developed only through the actions and words of characters themselves or are there other ways to achieve this end?
5. Is Marilyn different just before her death from what she was when you first met her?

Human
and
Other Beings

CHAPTER THREE

Until Copernicus proved that the planets of our solar system revolved around the sun, people believed that the Earth was the center of the universe. This view had several important corollaries, the most significant of which was that man as a species and therefore as an individual was the most important creature in the universe. It was believed that the act of creation had placed man at the center of the universe and he was, therefore and obviously, the most significant being in it.

Science-fiction writers, like Copernicus, have often offered fresh and rather startling views of not only this universe but also universes of their imaginations. As as direct result, some authors have at times suggested, and suggested rather strongly, that man may not be quite as important in the vast scheme of things as he likes to think he is. These iconoclastic writers have dared to suggest on occasion that man, far from being the most important being in his or other universes, may actually be one of its lesser organisms. They have not been persecuted for their ideas as Copernicus was but they are frequently as intellectually revolutionary as was Copernicus.

One of the most exciting and instructive facets of science-fiction literature is its demonstrated capacity for taking generally accepted ideas and theories and disputing them vigorously in fictional terms. The result is a stimulating and mind-opening experience for the venturesome reader. What if there are aliens superior to man? If there are, what will happen when and if the two species meet? Are there malevolent machines? If there are, then what can be said of man, their creator?

When the reader has finished this chapter on human and non-human beings, he will hopefully think at least twice before calling every cow he encounters sacred.

One of the science-fiction story's greatest assets is its access to unlimited material. Everyone knows that man has not yet set foot on Mars. But that doesn't stop the science-fiction author from writing about the planet and what happens to men on it. Machines obviously are not human. However, Gene Wolfe, a skilled writer of contemporary science fiction, suggests in his story "Eyebem" that an android, which is technically a machine, wants very much to be human. Implicit in Wolfe's story are a number of interesting questions. Why would a machine want to be human? What is wrong with being an *almost* human machine?

The other stories in this chapter question a number of accepted assumptions about the forms life might possibly take on Earth and elsewhere. There is a story that places human beings in a distinctly inferior position to the inhabitants of another planet who use them very much as mankind uses its animals. There is a story that pokes fun at the almost unconscious prejudices human beings hold concerning their own value as a species.

Science-fiction writers are not necessarily accredited members of any establishment. If anything, they are quite often discovered to be intellectual renegades. They ask questions and then put their answers in the form of stories which provoke readers to think in new ways. They are not necessarily asking readers to believe their stories. Belief is beside the point. Learning to think, question, and criticize constructively is the point.

The writers of science fiction offer excitement and adventure in many of their stories, but most of their stories are meant to be thought about when the excitement fades and the adventure ends. A perfect example of this kind of story, the kind that deals with a subject much broader than the small canvas on which it is drawn, is Carol Carr's humorous treatment of a father's reaction when his daughter marries a Martian. The reader will probably laugh while reading it because the story is amusing. He will also probably give it serious attention as he considers its implications.

Copernicus fathered modern astronomy by careful observation of the skies which led him to the correct conclusion that the Earth turns on its axis which caused what most people of his time believed was the rising and setting of the stars. Science-fiction writers also father many important ideas which they clothe in fictional terms so that readers may discover new ways of looking at life and new ways of testing the values they may have held without subjecting them to critical analysis.

INTRODUCTION: The Father-thing

Horror in literature has a long and fascinating tradition. From tales of devils and soul-stealers in primitive cultures, it has moved onward to our own stories of horror in the classic tradition of such writers as Edgar Allan Poe and H. P. Lovecraft.

However, horror is not always created in such atmospheric settings as crumbling mansions or ruined and abandoned churches as is the case with most Gothic horror tales. Horror can exist in the midst of the everyday. Such a setting can chill the reader even more thoroughly because it confronts him with horror in the midst of the humdrum and ordinary.

Here is a story which introduces horror during a dinner of beef stew and frozen peas—an extraordinary horror that originates in an ordinary garage on an ordinary evening and one which affects a very ordinary family.

The Father-thing
by Philip K. Dick

"Dinner's ready," commanded Mrs. Walton. "Go get your father and tell him to wash his hands. The same applies to you, young man." She carried a steaming casserole to the neatly set table. "You'll find him out in the garage."

Charles hesitated. He was only eight years old, and the problem bothering him would have confounded Hillel. "I—" he began uncertainly.

"What's wrong?" June Walton caught the uneasy tone in her son's voice and her matronly bosom fluttered with sudden alarm. "Isn't Ted out in the garage? For heaven's sake, he was sharpening the hedge shears a minute ago. He didn't go over to the Andersons', did he? I told him dinner was practically on the table."

"He's in the garage," Charles said. "But he's—talking to himself."

"Talking to himself!" Mrs. Walton removed her bright plastic apron and hung it over the doorknob. "Ted? Why, he never talks to himself. Go tell him to come in here." She poured boiling black coffee in the little blue-and-white china cups and began ladling out creamed corn. "What's wrong with you? Go tell him!"

"I don't know which of them to tell," Charles blurted out desperately. "They both look alike."

June Walton's fingers lost their hold on the aluminum pan; for a moment the creamed corn slushed dangerously. "Young man—" she began angrily, but at that moment Ted Walton came striding into the kitchen, inhaling and sniffing and rubbing his hands together.

"Ah," he cried happily. "Lamb stew."

"Beef stew," June murmured. "Ted, what were you doing out there?"

Ted threw himself down at his place and unfolded his napkin. "I got the shears sharpened like a razor. Oiled and sharpened. Better not touch them—they'll cut your hand off." He was a good-looking man in his early thirties; thick blond hair, strong arms, competent hands, square face and flashing brown eyes. "Man, this stew looks good. Hard day at the office—Friday, you know. Stuff piles up and we have to get all the accounts out by five. Al McKinley claims the department could handle 20 per cent more stuff if we organized our lunch hours; staggered them so somebody was there all the time." He beckoned Charles over. "Sit down and let's go."

Mrs. Walton served the frozen peas. "Ted," she said, as she slowly took her seat, "is there anything on your mind?"

"On my mind?" He blinked. "No, nothing unusual. Just the regular stuff. Why?"

Uneasily, June Walton glanced over at her son. Charles was sitting bolt-upright at his place, face expressionless, white as chalk. He hadn't moved, hadn't unfolded his napkin or even touched his milk. A tension was in the air; she could feel it. Charles had pulled his chair away from his father's; he was huddled in a tense little bundle as far from his father as possible. His lips were moving, but she couldn't catch what he was saying.

"What is it?" she demanded, leaning toward him.

"*The other one,*" Charles was muttering under his breath. "The other one came in."

"What do you mean, dear?" June Walton asked out loud. "What other one?"

Ted jerked. A strange expression flitted across his face. It vanished at once; but in the brief instant Ted Walton's face lost all familiarity. Something alien and cold gleamed out, a twisting, wriggling mass. The eyes blurred and receded, as an archaic sheen filmed over them. The ordinary look of a tired, middle-aged husband was gone.

And then it was back—or nearly back. Ted grinned and began to wolf down his stew and frozen peas and creamed corn. He laughed, stirred his coffee, kidded and ate. But something terrible was wrong.

120

"The other one," Charles muttered, face white, hands beginning to tremble. Suddenly he leaped up and backed away from the table. "Get away!" he shouted. "Get out of here!"

"Hey," Ted rumbled ominously. "What's got into you?" He pointed sternly at the boy's chair. "You sit down there and eat your dinner, young man. Your mother didn't fix it for nothing."

Charles turned and ran out of the kitchen, upstairs to his room. June Walton gasped and fluttered in dismay. "What in the world—"

Ted went on eating. His face was grim; his eyes were hard and dark. "That kid," he grated, "is going to have to learn a few things. Maybe he and I need to have a little private conference together."

Charles crouched and listened.

The father-thing was coming up the stairs, nearer and nearer. "Charles!" it shouted angrily. "Are you up there?"

He didn't answer. Soundlessly, he moved back into his room and pulled the door shut. His heart was pounding heavily. The father-thing had reached the landing; in a moment it would come in his room.

He hurried to the window. He was terrified; it was already fumbling in the dark hall for the knob. He lifted the window and climbed out on the roof. With a grunt he dropped into the flower garden that ran by the front door, staggered and gasped, then leaped to his feet and ran from the light that streamed out the window, a patch of yellow in the evening darkness.

He found the garage; it loomed up ahead, a black square against the skyline. Breathing quickly, he fumbled in his pocket for his flashlight, then cautiously slid the door up and entered.

The garage was empty. The car was parked out front. To the left was his father's workbench. Hammers and saws on the wooden walls. In the back were the lawnmower, rake, shovel, hoe. A drum of kerosene. License plates nailed up everywhere. Floor was concrete and dirt; a great oil slick stained the center, tufts of weeds greasy and black in the flickering beam of the flashlight.

Just inside the door was a big trash barrel. On top of the barrel were stacks of soggy newspapers and magazines, moldy and damp. A thick stench of decay issued from them as Charles began to move them around. Spiders dropped to the cement and scampered off; he crushed them with his foot and went on looking.

The sight made him shriek. He dropped the flashlight and leaped wildly back. The garage was plunged into instant gloom. He forced himself to kneel down, and for an ageless moment, he groped in the darkness for the light, among the spiders and greasy weeds. Finally he had it again. He managed to turn the beam down into the barrel, down the well he had made by pushing back the piles of magazines.

The father-thing had stuffed it down in the very bottom of the barrel. Among the old leaves and torn-up cardboard, the rotting remains of magazines and curtains, rubbish from the attic his mother had lugged down here with the idea of burning someday. It still looked a little like his father, enough for him to recognize. He had found it—and the sight made him sick at his stomach. He hung onto the barrel and shut his eyes until finally he was able to look again. In the barrel were the remains of his father, his real father. Bits the father-thing had no use for. Bits it had discarded.

He got the rake and pushed it down to stir the remains. They were dry. They cracked and broke at the touch of the rake. They were like a discarded snake skin, flaky and crumbling, rustling at the touch. *An empty skin.* The insides were gone. The important part. This was all that remained, just the brittle, cracking skin, wadded down at the bottom of the trash barrel in a little heap. This was all the father-thing had left; it had eaten the rest. Taken the insides—and his father's place.

A sound.

He dropped the rake and hurried to the door. The father-thing was coming down the path, toward the garage. Its shoes crushed the gravel; it felt its way along uncertainly. "Charles!" it called angrily. "Are you in there? Wait'll I get my hands on you, young man!"

His mother's ample, nervous shape was outlined in the bright doorway of the house. "Ted, please don't hurt him. He's all upset about something."

"I'm not going to hurt him," the father-thing rasped; it halted to strike a match. "I'm just going to have a little talk with him. He needs to learn better manners. Leaving the table like that and running out at night, climbing down the roof—"

Charles slipped from the garage; the glare of the match caught his moving shape, and with a bellow the father-thing lunged forward.

"Come here!"

Charles ran. He knew the ground better than the father-thing; it knew a lot, had taken a lot when it got his father's insides, but nobody knew the way like *he* did. He reached the fence, climbed it, leaped into the Andersons' yard, raced past their clothesline, down the path around the side of their house, and out on Maple Street.

He listened, crouched down and not breathing. The father-thing hadn't come after him. It had gone back. Or it was coming around the sidewalk.

He took a deep, shuddering breath. He had to keep moving. Sooner or later it would find him. He glanced right and left, made sure it wasn't watching, and then started off at a rapid dog-trot.

"What do you want?" Tony Peretti demanded belligerently. Tony was fourteen. He was sitting at the table in the oak-panelled Peretti dining room, books and pencils scattered around him, half a ham-and-peanut-butter sandwich and a coke beside him. "You're Walton, aren't you?"

Tony Peretti had a job uncrating stoves and refrigerators after school at Johnson's Appliance Shop, downtown. He was big and blunt-faced. Black hair, olive skin, white teeth. A couple of times he had beaten up Charles; he had beaten up every kid in the neighborhood.

Charles twisted. "Say, Peretti. Do me a favor?"

"What do you want?" Peretti was annoyed. "You looking for a bruise?"

Gazing unhappily down, his fists clenched, Charles explained what had happened in short, mumbled words.

When he had finished, Peretti let out a low whistle. "No kidding."

"It's true." He nodded quickly. "I'll show you. Come on and I'll show you."

Peretti got slowly to his feet. "Yeah, show me. I want to see."

He got his b.b. gun from his room, and the two of them walked silently up the dark street, toward Charles' house. Neither of them said much. Peretti was deep in thought, serious and solemn-faced. Charles was still dazed; his mind was completely blank.

They turned down the Andersons' driveway, cut through the back yard, climbed the fence, and lowered themselves cautiously into Charles' back yard. There was no movement. The yard was silent. The front door of the house was closed.

They peered through the living room window. The shades were down, but a narrow crack of yellow streamed out. Sitting on the couch was Mrs. Walton, sewing a cotton T-shirt. There was a sad, troubled look on her large face. She worked listlessly, without interest. Opposite her was the father-thing. Leaning back in his father's easy chair, its shoes off, reading the evening newspaper. The TV was on, playing to itself in the corner. A can of beer rested on the arm of the easy chair. The father-thing sat exactly as his own father had sat; it had learned a lot.

"Looks just like him," Peretti whispered suspiciously. "You sure you're not bulling me?"

Charles led him to the garage and showed him the trash barrel. Peretti reached his long tanned arms down and carefully pulled up the dry, flaking remains. They spread out, unfolded, until the whole figure of his father was outlined. Peretti laid the remains on the floor and pieced broken parts back into place. The remains were colorless. Almost transparent. An amber yellow, thin as paper. Dry and utterly life-less.

"That's all," Charles said. Tears welled up in his eyes. "That's all that's left of him. The thing has the insides."

Peretti had turned pale. Shakily, he crammed the remains back in the trash barrel. "This is really something," he muttered. "You say you saw the two of them together?"

"Talking. They looked exactly alike. I ran inside." Charles wiped the tears away and sniveled; he couldn't hold it back any longer. "It ate him while I was inside. Then it came in the house. It pretended it was him. But it isn't. It killed him and ate his insides."

For a moment Peretti was silent. "I'll tell you something," he said suddenly. "I've heard about this sort of thing. It's a bad business. You have to use your head and not get scared. You're not scared, are you?"

"No," Charles managed to mutter.

"The first thing we have to do is figure out how to kill it." He rattled his b.b. gun. "I don't know if this'll work. It must be plenty tough to get hold of your father. He was a big man." Peretti considered. "Let's get out of here. It might come back. They say that's what a murderer does."

They left the garage. Peretti crouched down and peeked through the window again. Mrs. Walton had got to her feet. She was talking anxiously. Vague sounds filtered out. The father-thing threw down its newspaper. They were arguing.

"For God's sake!" the father-thing shouted. "Don't do anything stupid like that."

"Something's wrong," Mrs. Walton moaned. "Something terrible. Just let me call the hospital and see."

"Don't call anybody. He's all right. Probably up the street playing."

"He's never out this late. He never disobeys. He was terribly upset—afraid of you! I don't blame him." Her voice broke with misery. "What's wrong with you? You're so strange." She moved out of the room, into the hall. "I'm going to call some of the neighbors."

The father-thing glared after her until she had disappeared. Then a terrifying thing happened. Charles gasped; even Peretti grunted under his breath.

"Look," Charles muttered. "What—"

"Golly," Peretti said, black eyes wide.

As soon as Mrs. Walton was gone from the room, the father-thing sagged in its chair. It became limp. Its mouth fell open. Its eyes peered vacantly. Its head fell forward, like a discarded rag doll.

Peretti moved away from the window. "That's it," he whispered. "That's the whole thing."

"What is it?" Charles demanded. He was shocked and bewildered. "It looked like somebody turned off its power."

"Exactly." Peretti nodded slowly, grim and shaken. "It's controlled from outside."

Horror settled over Charles. "You mean, something outside our world?"

Peretti shook his head with disgust. "Outside the house! In the yard. You know how to find?"

"Not very well." Charles pulled his mind together. "But I know somebody who's good at finding." He forced his mind to summon the name. "Bobby Daniels."

"That little black kid? Is he good at finding?"

"The best."

"All right," Peretti said. "Let's go get him. We have to find the thing that's outside. That made *it* in there, and keeps it going. . . ."

"It's near the garage," Peretti said to the small, thin-faced Negro boy who crouched beside them in the darkness. "When it got him, he was in the garage. So look there."

"In the garage?" Daniels asked.

"*Around* the garage. Walton's already gone over the garage, inside. Look around outside. Nearby."

There was a small bed of flowers growing by the garage, and a great tangle of bamboo and discarded debris between the garage and the back of the house. The moon had come out; a cold, misty light filtered down over everything. "If we don't find it pretty soon," Daniels said, "I got to go back home. I can't stay up much later." He wasn't any older than Charles. Perhaps nine.

"All right," Peretti agreed. "Then get looking."

The three of them spread out and began to go over the ground with care. Daniels worked with incredible speed; his thin little body moved in a blur of motion as he crawled among the flowers, turned over rocks, peered under the house, separated stalks of plants, ran his expert hands over leaves and stems, in tangles of compost and weeds. No inch was missed.

Peretti halted after a short time. "I'll guard. It might be dangerous. The father-thing might come and try to stop us." He posted himself on the back step with his b.b. gun while Charles and Bobby Daniels searched. Charles worked slowly. He was tired, and his body was cold and numb. It seemed impossible, the father-thing and what had happened to his own father, his real father. But terror spurred him on; what if it happened to his mother, or to him? Or to everyone? Maybe the whole world.

"I found it!" Daniels called in a thin, high voice. "You all come around here quick!"

Peretti raised his gun and got up cautiously. Charles hurried over; he turned the flickering yellow beam of his flashlight where Daniels stood.

The Negro boy had raised a concrete stone. In the moist, rotting soil the light gleamed on a metallic body. A thin, jointed thing with endless crooked legs was digging frantically. Plated, like an ant; a red-brown bug that rapidly disappeared before their eyes. Its rows of legs scabbled and clutched. The ground gave rapidly under it. Its wicked-looking tail twisted furiously as it struggled down the tunnel it had made.

Peretti ran into the garage and grabbed up the rake. He pinned down the tail of the bug with it. "Quick! Shoot it with the b.b. gun!"

Daniels snatched the gun and took aim. The first shot tore the tail of the bug loose. It writhed and twisted frantically; its tail dragged uselessly and some of its legs broke off. It was a foot long, like a great millipede. It struggled desperately to escape down its hole.

"Shoot again," Peretti ordered.

Daniels fumbled with the gun. The bug slithered and hissed. Its head jerked back and forth; it twisted and bit at the rake holding it down. Its wicked specks of eyes gleamed with hatred. For a moment it struck futilely at the rake; then abruptly, without warning, it thrashed in a frantic convulsion that made them all draw away in fear.

Something buzzed through Charles' brain. A loud humming, metallic and harsh, a billion metal wires dancing and vibrating at once. He was tossed about violently by the force; the banging crash of metal made him deaf and confused. He stumbled to his feet and backed off; the others were doing the same, white-faced and shaken.

"If we can't kill it with the gun," Peretti gasped, "we can drown it. Or burn it. Or stick a pin through its brain." He fought to hold onto the rake, to keep the bug pinned down.

"I have a jar of formaldehyde," Daniels muttered. His fingers fumbled nervously with the b.b. gun. "How do this thing work? I can't seem to—"

Charles grabbed the gun from him. "I'll kill it." He squatted down, one eye to the sight, and gripped the trigger. The bug lashed and struggled. Its force-field hammered in his ears, but he hung onto the gun. His finger tightened . . .

"All right, Charles," the father-thing said. Powerful fingers gripped him, a paralyzing pressure around his wrists. The gun fell to the ground as he struggled futilely. The father-thing shoved against Peretti. The boy leaped away and the bug, free of the rake, slithered triumphantly down its tunnel.

"You have a spanking coming, Charles," the father-thing droned on. "What got into you? Your poor mother's out of her mind with worry."

It had been there, hiding in the shadows. Crouched in the darkness watching them. Its calm, emotionless voice, a dreadful parody of his father's, rumbled close to his ear as it pulled him relentlessly toward the garage. Its cold breath blew in his face, an icy-sweet odor, like decaying soil. Its strength was immense; there was nothing he could do.

"Don't fight me," it said calmly. "Come along, into the garage. This is for your own good. I know best, Charles."

"Did you find him?" his mother called anxiously, opening the back door.

"Yes, I found him."

"What are you going to do?"

"A little spanking." This father-thing pushed up the garage door. "In the garage." In the half-light a faint smile, humorless and utterly without emotion, touched its lips. "You go back in the living room, June. I'll take care of this. It's more in my line. You never did like punishing him."

The back door reluctantly closed. As the light cut off, Peretti bent down and groped for the b.b. gun. The father thing instantly froze.

"Go on home, boys," it rasped.

Peretti stood undecided, gripping the b.b. gun.

"Get going," the father-thing repeated. "Put down that toy and get out of here." It moved slowly toward Peretti, gripping Charles with one hand, reaching toward Peretti with the other. "No b.b. guns allowed in town, sonny. Your father know you have that? There's a city ordinance. I think you better give me that before—"

Peretti shot it in the eye.

The father-thing grunted and pawed at its ruined eye. Abruptly it slashed out at Peretti. Peretti moved down the driveway, trying to cock the gun. The father-thing lunged. Its powerful fingers snatched the gun from Peretti's hands. Silently, the father-thing mashed the gun against the wall of the house.

Charles broke away and ran numbly off. Where could he hide? It was between him and the house. Already, it was coming back toward him, a black shape creeping carefully, peering into the darkness, trying to make him out. Charles retreated. If there were only some place he could hide . . .

The bamboo.

He crept quickly into the bamboo. The stalks were huge and old. They closed after him with a faint rustle. The father-thing was fumbling in its pocket; it lit a match, then the whole pack flared up. "Charles," it said. "I know you're here, someplace. There's no use hiding. You're only making it more difficult."

His heart hammering, Charles crouched among the bamboo. Here, debris and filth rotted. Weeds, garbage, papers, boxes, old clothing, boards, tin cans, bottles. Spiders and salamanders squirmed around him. The bamboo swayed with the night wind. Insects and filth.

And something else.

A shape, a silent, unmoving shape that grew up from the mound of filth like some nocturnal mushroom. A white column, a pulpy mass that glistened moistly in the moonlight. Webs covered it, a moldy cocoon. It had vague arms and legs. An indistinct half-shaped head. As yet, the features hadn't formed. But he could tell what it was.

A mother-thing. Growing here in the filth and dampness, between the garage and the house. Behind the towering bamboo.

It was almost ready. Another few days and it would reach maturity. It was still a larva, white and soft and pulpy. But the sun would dry and warm it. Harden its shell. Turn it dark and strong. It would emerge from its cocoon, and one day when his mother came by the garage . . .

Behind the mother-thing were other pulpy white larvae, recently laid by the bug. Small. Just coming into existence. He could see where the father-thing had broken off; the place where it had grown. It had matured here. And in the garage, his father had met it.

Charles began to move numbly away, past the rotting boards, the filth and debris, the pulpy mushroom larvae. Weakly, he reached out to take hold of the fence—and scrambled back.

Another one. Another larva. He hadn't seen this one, at first. It wasn't white. It had already turned dark. The web, the pulpy softness, the moistness, were gone. It was ready. It stirred a little, moved its arm feebly.

The Charles-thing.

The bamboo separated, and the father-thing's hand clamped firmly around the boy's wrist. "You stay right here," it said. "This is exactly the place for you. Don't move." With its other hand it tore at the remains of the cocoon binding the Charles-thing. "I'll help it out—it's still a little weak."

The last shred of moist gray was stripped back, and the Charles-thing tottered out. It floundered uncertainly, as the father-thing cleared a path for it toward Charles.

"This way," the father-thing grunted. "I'll hold him for you. When you're fed you'll be stronger."

The Charles-thing's mouth opened and closed. It reached greedily toward Charles. The boy struggled wildly, but the father-thing's immense hand held him down.

"Stop that, young man," the father-thing commanded. "It'll be a lot easier for you if you—"

It screamed and convulsed. It let go of Charles and staggered back. Its body twitched violently. It crashed against the garage, limbs jerking. For a time it rolled and flopped in a dance of agony. It whimpered, moaned, tried to crawl away. Gradually it became quiet. The Charles-thing settled down in a silent heap. It lay stupidly among the bamboo and rotting debris, body slack, face empty and blank.

At last the father-thing ceased to stir. There was only the faint rustle of the bamboo in the night wind.

Charles got up awkwardly. He stepped down onto the cement driveway. Peretti and Daniels approached, wide-eyed and cautious. "Don't go near it," Daniels ordered sharply. "It ain't dead yet. Takes a little while."

"What did you do?" Charles muttered.

Daniels set down the drum of kerosene with a gasp of relief. "Found this in the garage. We Daniels always used kerosene on our mosquitoes, back in Virginia."

"Daniels poured kerosene down the bug's tunnel," Peretti explained, still awed. "It was his idea."

Daniels kicked cautiously at the contorted body of the father-thing. "It's dead, now. Died as soon as the bug died."

"I guess the others'll die, too," Peretti said. He pushed aside the bamboo to examine the larvae growing here and there among the debris. The Charles-thing didn't move at all, as Peretti jabbed the end of a stick into its chest. "This one's dead."

"We better make sure," Daniels said grimly. He picked up the heavy drum of kerosene and lugged it to the edge of the bamboo. "It dropped some matches in the driveway. You get them, Peretti."

They looked at each other.

"Sure," Peretti said softly.

"We better turn on the hose," Charles said. "To make sure it doesn't spread."

"Let's get going," Peretti said impatiently. He was already moving off. Charles quickly followed him and they began searching for the matches, in the moonlit darkness.

FOR DISCUSSION: The Father-thing

1. Why do you suppose the author did not have Charles tell his mother exactly what he saw occur in the garage? Why did he go instead to Peretti for help? Why did he not choose to tell a neighbor or the police?

2. How does the author aid the reader in willingly suspending disbelief in the fantastic events he portrays? Does the setting of the story help? Does the change of pronouns from "he" to "it" in reference to the father-thing help?

3. Daniels' solution to the problem of how to destroy the bug that has created the "things" is as ordinary as the setting of the story. Does this assist the reader in believing in the events of the story?

4. The author never explains how the father-thing has "eaten the insides" of Charles' father. Is such a detailed explanation necessary to achieve the story's effect on the reader? Is horror always the result of grisly or bloody events?

5. The author uses such words and phrases in his story as "filth," "pulpy mass," "webs covered it, a moldy cocoon." What effect do they have on the reader? Do they stimulate the principal emotion the author seeks to arouse in the reader?

INTRODUCTION: The Silk and the Song

Many stories, particularly mystery stories, are based on a riddle or a puzzle which the protagonist must solve. This story tells of the result of mankind's encounter with another race in outer space and what the results of that original encounter were many generations later. At the heart of this story is the riddle of the silk and the song which the young hero of the story solves, thereby escaping his fate.

The Silk and the Song
by Charles L. Fontenay

I

Alan first saw the Star Tower when he was twelve years old. His young master, Blik, rode him into the city of Falklyn that day.

Blik had to argue hard· before he got permission to ride Alan, his favorite boy. Blik's father, Wiln, wanted Blik to ride a man, because Wiln thought the long trip to the city might be too much for a boy as young as Alan.

Blik had his way, though. Blik was rather spoiled, and when he began to whistle, his father gave in.

"All right, the human is rather big for its age," surrendered Wiln. "You may ride it if you promise not to run it. I don't want you breaking the wind of any of my prize stock."

So Blik strapped the bridle-helmet with the handgrips on Alan's head and threw the saddle-chair on Alan's shoulders. Wiln saddled up Robb, a husky man he often rode on long trips, and they were off to the city at an easy trot.

The Star Tower was visible before they reached Falklyn. Alan could see its spire above the tops of the ttornot trees as soon as they emerged from the Blue Forest. Blik saw it at the same time. Holding onto the bridle-helmet with one four-fingered hand, Blik poked Alan and pointed.

"Look, Alan, the Star Tower!" cried Blik. "They say humans once lived in the Star Tower."

"Blik, when will you grow up and stop talking to the humans?" chided his father. "I'm going to punish you severely one of these days."

Alan did not answer Blik, for it was forbidden for humans to talk in the Hussir language except in reply to direct questions. But he kept his eager eyes on the Star Tower and watched it loom taller and taller ahead of them, striking into the sky far above the buildings of the city. He quickened his pace, so that he began to pull ahead of Robb, and Robb had to caution him.

Between the Blue Forest and Falklyn, they were still in wild country, where the land was eroded and there were no farms and fields. Little clumps of ttornot trees huddled here and there among the gullies and low hills, thickening back toward the Blue Forest behind them, thinning toward the northwest plain, beyond which lay the distant mountains.

They rounded a curve in the dusty road, and Blik whistled in excitement from Alan's shoulders. A figure stood on a little promontory overhanging the road ahead of them.

At first Alan thought it was a tall, slender Hussir, for a short jacket partly concealed its nakedness. Then he saw it was a young human girl. No Hussir ever boasted that mop of tawny hair, that tailless posterior curve.

"A Wild Human!" growled Wiln in astonishment. Alan shivered. It was rumored the Wild Humans killed Hussirs and ate other humans.

The girl was looking away toward Falklyn. Wiln unslung his short bow and loosed an arrow at her.

The bolt exploded the dust near her feet. With a toss of bright hair, she turned her head and saw them. Then she was gone like a deer.

When they came up to where she had stood, there was a brightness in the bushes beside the road. It was a pair of the colorful trousers such as Hussirs wore, only trimmer, tangled inextricably in a thorny bush. Evidently the girl had been caught as she climbed up from the road, and had had to crawl out of them.

"They're getting too bold," said Wiln angrily. "This close to civilization, in broad daylight!"

Alan was astonished when they entered Falklyn. The streets and buildings were of stone. There was little stone on the other side of the Blue Forest, and Wiln Castle was built of polished wooden blocks. The smooth stone of Falklyn's streets was hot under the double sun. It burned Alan's feet, so that he hobbled a little and shook Blik up. Blik clouted him on the side of the head for it.

There were so many strange new things to see in the city that they made Alan dizzy. Some of the buildings were as much as three stories high, and the windows of a few of the biggest were covered, not with wooden shutters, but with bright, transparent stuff that Wiln told Blik was called "glaz." Robb told Alan in the human language, which the Hussirs did not understand, that it was rumored humans themselves had invented this glaz and given it to their masters. Alan wondered how a human could invent anything, penned in open fields.

But it appeared that humans in the city lived closer to their masters. Several times Alan saw them coming out of houses, and a few that he saw were not entirely naked, but wore bright bits of cloth at various places on their bodies. Wiln expressed strong disapproval of this practice to Blik.

"Start putting clothing on these humans and they might get the idea they're Hussirs," he said. "If you ask me, that's why city people have more trouble controlling their humans than we do. Spoil the human and you make him savage, I say."

They had several places to go in Falklyn, and for a while Alan feared they would not see the Star Tower at close range. But Blik had never seen it before, and he begged and whistled until Wiln agreed to ride a few streets out of the way to look at it.

Alan forgot all the other wonders of Falklyn as the great monument towered bigger and bigger, dwarfing the buildings around it, dwarfing the whole city of Falklyn. There was a legend that humans had not only lived in the Star Tower once, but that they had built it and Falklyn had grown up around it when the humans abandoned it. Alan had heard this whispered, but he had been warned not to repeat it, for some Hussirs understood human language and repeating such tales was a good way to get whipped.

The Star Tower was in the center of a big circular park, and the houses around the park looked like dollhouses beneath it. It stretched up into the sky like a pointing finger, its strange dark walls reflecting the dual sunlight dully. Even the flying buttresses at its base curved up above the big trees in the park around it.

There was a railing round the park, and quite a few humans were chained or standing loose about it while their riders were looking at the Star Tower, for humans were not allowed inside the park. Blik was all for dismounting and looking at the inside of the tower, but Wiln would not hear of it.

"There'll be plenty of time for that when you're older and can understand some of the things you see," said Wiln.

They moved slowly around the street, outside the rail. In the park, the Hussirs moved in groups, some of them going up or coming down the long ramp that led into the Star Tower. The Hussirs were only about half the size of humans, with big heads and large pointed ears sticking straight out on each side, with thin legs and thick tails that helped to balance them. They wore loose jackets and baggy, colored trousers.

As they passed one group of humans standing outside the rail, Alan heard a familiar bit of verse, sung in an undertone:

> *"Twinkle, twinkle, golden star,*
> *I can reach you, though you're far.*
> *Shut my mouth and find my head,*
> *Find a worm—"*

Wiln swung Robb around quickly, and laid his keen whip viciously across the singer's shoulders. Slash, slash, and red welts sprang out on the man's back. With a muffled shriek, the man ducked his head and threw up his arms to protect his face.

"Where is your master, human?" demanded Wiln savagely, the whip trembling in his four-fingered hand.

"My master lives in Northwesttown, your greatness," whimpered the human. "I belong to the merchant Senk."

"Where is Northwesttown?"

"It is a section of Falklyn, sir."

"And you are here at the Star Tower without your master?"

"Yes, sir. I am on free time."

Wiln gave him another lash with the whip.

"You should know humans are not allowed to run loose near the Star Tower," Wiln snapped. "Now go back to your master and tell him to whip you."

The human ran off. Wiln and Blik turned their mounts homeward. When they were beyond the streets and houses of the town and the dust of the roads provided welcome relief to the burning feet of the humans, Blik asked:

"What did you think of the Star Tower, Alan?"

"Why has it no windows?" Alan asked, voicing the thought uppermost in his mind.

It was not, strictly speaking, an answer to Blik's question, and Alan risked punishment by speaking thus in Hussir. But Wiln had recovered his good humor, with the prospect of getting home in time for supper.

"The windows are in the very top, little human," said Wiln indulgently. "You couldn't see them, because they're inside."

Alan puzzled over this all the way to Wiln Castle. How could windows be inside and none outside? If windows were windows, didn't they always go through both sides of a wall?

When the two suns had set and Alan was bedded down with the other children in a corner of the meadow, the exciting events of the day repeated themselves in his mind like a series of colored pictures. He would have liked to question Robb, but the grown men and older boys were kept in a field well separated from the women and children.

A little distance away the women were singing their babies to sleep with the traditional songs of the humans. Their voices drifted to him on the faint breeze, with the perfume of the fragrant grasses.

> *"Rock-a-bye, baby, in mother's arm,*
> *Nothing's nearby to do baby harm.*
> *Sleep and sweet dreams, till both suns arise,*
> *Then will be time to open your eyes."*

That was a real baby song, the first he ever remembered. They sang others, and one was the song Wiln had interrupted at the Star Tower.

> *"Twinkle, twinkle, golden star,*
> *I can reach you, though you're far.*
> *Shut my mouth and find my head,*
> *Find a worm that's striped with red,*
> *Feed it to the turtle shell,*
> *Then go to sleep, for all is well."*

Half asleep, Alan listened. That song was one of the children's favorites. They called it "The Star Tower Song," though he had never been able to find out why.

It must be a riddle, he thought drowsily. *"Shut my mouth and find my head . . ."* Shouldn't it be the other way around—*"Find my head* (first) *and shut my mouth . . ."*? Why wasn't it? And those other lines. Alan knew worms, for he had seen many of the creepy, crawly creatures, long things in many bright colors. But what was a turtle?

The refrain of another song reached his ears, and it seemed to the sleepy boy that they were singing it to him.

> *"Alan saw a little zird,*
> *Its wings were all aglow.*
> *He followed it away one night.*
> *It filled his heart with woe."*

Only that wasn't the last line the children themselves sang. Optimistically, they always ended that song. *". . . To where he liked to go."*

Maybe he was asleep and dreamed it, or maybe he suddenly waked up with the distant music in his ears. Whichever it was, he was lying there, and a zird flew over the high fence and lit in the grass near him. Its luminous scales pulsed in the darkness, faintly lighting the faces of the children huddled asleep around him. It opened its beak and spoke to him in a raucous voice.

"Come with me to freedom, human," said the zird. "Come with me to freedom, human."

That was all it could say, and it repeated the invitation at least half a dozen times, until it grated on Alan's ears. But Alan knew that, despite the way the children sang the song, it brought only sorrow to a human to heed the call of a zird.

"Go away, zird," he said crossly, and the zird flew over the fence and faded into the darkness.

Sighing, Alan went back to sleep to dream of the Star Tower.

II

Blik died three years later. The young Hussir's death brought sorrow to Alan's heart, for Blik had been kind to him and their relationship was the close one of well-loved pet and master. The deprivation always would be associated to him with another emotional change in his life, for Blik's death came the day after Wiln caught Alan with the blond girl down by the stream and transferred him to the field with the older boys and men.

"Switch it, I hope the boy hasn't gotten her with child," grumbled Wiln to his oldest son, Snuk, as they drove Alan to the new meadow. "I hadn't planned to add that girl to the milking herd for another year yet."

"That comes of letting Blik make a pet out of the human," said Snuk, who was nearly grown now and was being trained in the art of managing Wiln Castle to succeed his father. "It should have been worked while Blik has been sick, instead of allowed to roam idly around among the women and children."

Through the welter of new emotions that confused him, Alan recognized the justice of that remark. It had been pure boredom with the play of the younger children that had turned his interest to more mature experimentation. At that, he realized that only the aloofness he had developed as a result of being Blik's pet had prevented his being taken to the other field at least two years earlier.

He looked back over his shoulder. The tearful girl stood forlornly, watching him go. She waved and called after him.

"Maybe we'll see each other again at mating time."

He waved back at her, drawing a sharp cut across the shoulders from Snuk's whip. They would not turn him in with the women at mating time for at least another three years, but the girl was almost of mating age. By the time she saw him again, she probably would have forgotten him.

His transfer into adulthood was an immediate ordeal. Wiln and Snuk remained just outside the fence and whistled delightedly at the hazing Alan was given by the men and older boys. The ritual would have been more difficult for him had it not been so long delayed, but he found a place in the scheme of things somewhat high for a newcomer because he was older than most of them and big for his age. Scratched and battered, he gained the necessary initial respect from his new associates by trouncing several boys his own size.

That night, lonely and unhappy, Alan heard the keening of the Hussirs rise from Wiln Castle. The night songs of the men, deeper and lustier than those of the women and children, faded and stopped as the sound of mourning drifted to them on the wind. Alan knew it meant that Blik's long illness was over, that his young master was dead.

He found a secluded corner of the field and cried himself to sleep under the stars. He had loved Blik.

After Blik's death, Alan thought he might be put with the laboring men, to pull the plows and work the crops. He knew he did not have the training for work in and around the castle itself, and he did not think he would be retained with the riding stock.

But Snuk had different ideas.

"I saw your good qualities as a riding human before Blik ever picked you out for a pet," Snuk told him, laying his pointed ears back viciously. Snuk used the human language, for it was Snuk's theory that one could control humans better when one could listen in on their conversations among themselves. "Blik spoiled all the temper out of you, but I'll change that. I may be able to salvage you yet."

It was only a week since Blik's death, and Alan was still sad. Dispiritedly, he cooperated when Snuk put the bridle-helmet and saddle-chair on him, and knelt for Snuk to climb on his back.

When Alan stood up, Snuk jammed spurs savagely into his sides.

Alan leaped three feet into the air with an agonized yell.

"Silence, human!" shouted Snuk, beating him over the head with the whip. "I shall teach you to obey. Spurs mean go, like so!"

And he dug the spurs into Alan's ribs again.

Alan twisted and turned momentarily, but his common sense saved him. Had he fallen to the ground and rolled, or tried to rub Snuk off against a ttornot tree, it would have meant death for him. There was no appeal from his new master's cruelty.

A third time Snuk applied the spurs and Alan spurted down the tree-lined lane away from the castle at a dead run. Snuk gave him his head and raked his sides brutally. It was only when he slowed to a walk, panting and perspiring, that Snuk pulled on the reins and turned him back toward the castle. Then the Hussir forced him to trot back.

Wiln was waiting at the corral when they returned.

"Aren't you treating it a little rough Snuk?" asked the older Hussir, looking the exhausted Alan up and down critically. Blood streamed from Alan's gashed sides.

"Just teaching it right at the outset who is master," replied Snuk casually. With an unnecessarily sharp rap on the head, he sent Alan to his knees and dismounted. "I think this one will make a valuable addition to my stable of riders, but I don't intend to pamper it like Blik."

Wiln flicked his ears.

"Well, you've proved you know how to handle humans by now, and you'll be master of them all in a few years," he said mildly. "Just take your father's advice, and don't break this one's wind."

The next few months were misery to Alan. He had the physical qualities Snuk liked in a mount, and Snuk rode him more frequently than any of his other saddle men.

Snuk liked to ride fast, and he ran Alan unmercifully. They would return at the end of a hot afternoon, Alan bathed in sweat and so tired his limbs trembled uncontrollably.

Besides, Snuk was an uncompromising master with more than a touch of cruelty in his make-up. He would whip Alan savagely for minor inattention, for failure to respond promptly to the reins, for speaking at all in his presence. Alan's back was soon covered with spur scars, and one eye often was half closed from a whip lash across the face.

In desperation, Alan sought the counsel of his old friend, Robb, whom he saw often now that he was in the men's field.

"There's nothing you can do," Robb said. "I just thank the Golden Star that Wiln rides me and I'll be too old for Snuk to ride when Wiln dies. But then Snuk will be master of us all, and I dread that day."

"Couldn't one of us kill Snuk against a tree?" asked Alan. He had thought of doing it himself.

"Never think such a thought," warned Robb quickly. "If that happened, all the riding men would be butchered for meat. The Wiln family has enough money to buy new riding stables in Falklyn if they wish, and no Hussir will put up with a rebellious human."

That night Alan nursed his freshest wounds beside the fence closest to the women's and children's field and gave himself up to nostalgia. He longed for the happy days of his childhood and Blik's kind mastery.

Across the intervening fields, faintly, he heard the soft voices of the women. He could not make out the words, but he remembered them from the tune:

> "Star light, star bright,
> Star that sheds a golden light,
> I wish I may, I wish I might,
> Reach you, star that shines at night."

From behind him came the voices of the men, nearer and louder:

> *"Human, see the little zird,*
> *Its wings are all aglow.*
> *Don't follow it away at night,*
> *For fear of grief and woe."*

The children had sung it differently. And there had been a dream . . .
"Come with me to freedom, human," said the zird.

Alan had seen many zirds at night—they appeared only at night—and had heard their call. It was the only thing they said, always in the human language: "Come with me to freedom, human."

As he had before, he wondered. A zird was only a scaly-winged little night creature. How could it speak human words? Where did zirds come from, and where did they go in the daytime? For the first time in his life, he asked the zird a question.

"What and where is freedom, zird?" Alan asked.

"Come with me to freedom, human," repeated the zird. It flapped its wings, rising a few inches above the fence, and settled back on its perch.

"Is that all you can say, zird?" asked Alan irritably. "How can I go with you when I can't fly?"

"Come with me to freedom, human," said the zird.

A great boldness surged in Alan's heart, spurred by the dreary prospect of having to endure Snuk's sadism again on the morrow. He looked at the fence.

Alan had never paid much attention to a fence before. Humans did not try to get out of the fenced enclosures, because the story parents told to children who tried it was that strayed humans were always recaptured and butchered for meat.

It was the strangest coincidence. It reminded him of that night long ago, the night after he had gone into Falklyn with Blik and first seen the Star Tower. Even as the words of the song died away in the night air, he saw the glow of the zird approaching. It lit on top of the fence and squawked down at him.

The links of the fence were close together, but he could get his fingers and toes through them. Tentatively, he tried it. A mounting excitement taking possession of him, he climbed.

It was ridiculously easy. He was in the next field. There were other fences, of course, but they could be climbed. He could go into the field with the women—his heart beat faster at the thought of the blonde girl— or he could even climb his way to the open road to Falklyn.

It was the road he chose, after all. The zird flew ahead of him across each field, lighting to wait for him to climb each fence. He crept along the fence past the crooning women with a muffled sigh, through the field of ripening akko grain, through the waist-high sento plants. At last he climbed the last fence of all.

He was off the Wiln estate. The dust of the road to Falklyn was beneath his feet.

What now? If he went into Falklyn, he would be captured and returned to Wiln Castle. If he went the other way the same thing would happen. Stray humans were spotted easily. Should he turn back now? It would be easy to climb his way back to the men's field—and there would be innumerable nights ahead of him when the women's field would be easily accessible to him.

But there was Snuk to consider.

For the first time since he had climbed out of the men's field, the zird spoke.

"Come with me to freedom, human," it said.

It flew down the road, away from Falklyn, and lit in the dust, as though waiting. After a moment's hesitation, Alan followed.

The lights of Wiln Castle loomed up to his left, up the lane of ttornot trees. They fell behind and disappeared over a hill. The zird flew, matching its pace to his slow trot.

Alan's resolution began to weaken.

Then a figure loomed up beside him in the gloom, a human hand was laid on his arm and a female voice said:

"I thought we'd never get another from Wiln Castle. Step it up a little, fellow. We've a long way to travel before dawn."

III

They traveled at a fast trot all that night, the zird leading the way like a giant firefly. By the time dawn grayed the eastern sky, they were in the mountains west of Falklyn, and climbing.

When Alan was first able to make out details of his nocturnal guide, he thought for a minute she was a huge Hussir. She wore the Hussir loose jacket, open at the front, and the baggy trousers. But there was no tail, and there were no pointed ears. She was a girl, his own age.

She was the first human Alan had ever seen fully clothed. Alan thought she looked rather ridiculous and, at the same time, he was slightly shocked, as by sacrilege.

They entered a high valley through a narrow pass, and slowed to a walk. For the first time since they left the vicinity of Wiln Castle, they were able to talk in other than short, disconnected phrases.

"Who are you, and where are you taking me?" asked Alan. In the cold light of dawn he was beginning to doubt his impetuousness in fleeing the castle.

"My name is Mara," said the girl. "You've heard of the Wild Humans? I'm one of them, and we live in these mountains."

The hair prickled on the back of Alan's neck. He stopped in his tracks, and half turned to flee. Mara caught his arm.

"Why do all the slaves believe those fairy tales about cannibalism?" she asked scornfully. The word *cannibalism* was unfamiliar to Alan. "We aren't going to eat you, boy, we're going to make you free. What's your name?"

"Alan," he answered in a shaky voice, allowing himself to be led onward. "What is this freedom the zird was talking about?"

"You'll find out," she promised. "But the zird doesn't know. Zirds are just flying animals. We train them to say that one sentence and lead slaves to us."

"Why don't you just come in the fields yourselves?" he asked curiously, his fear dissipating. "You could climb the fences easily."

"That's been tried. The silly slaves just raise a clamor when they recognize a stranger. The Hussirs have caught several of us that way."

The two suns rose, first the blue one, the white one only a few minutes late. The mountains around them awoke with light.

In the dawn, he had thought Mara was dark, but her hair was tawny gold in the pearly morning. Her eyes were deep brown, like the fruit of the ttornot tree.

They stopped by a spring that gushed from between huge rocks, and Mara took the opportunity to appraise his slender, well-knit frame.

"You'll do," she said. "I wish all of them we get were as healthy."

In three weeks, Alan could not have been distinguished from the other Wild Humans—outwardly. He was getting used to wearing clothing and, somewhat awkwardly, carried the bow and arrows with which he was armed. He and Mara were ranging several miles from the caves in which the Wild Humans lived.

They were hunting animals for food, and Alan licked his lips in anticipation. He liked cooked meat. The Hussirs fed their human herds bean meal and scraps from the kitchens. The only meat he had ever eaten was raw meat from small animals he had been swift enough to catch in the fields.

They came up on a ridge and Mara, ahead of him, stopped. He came up beside her.

Not far below them, a Hussir moved, afoot, carrying a short, heavy bow and a quiver of arrows. The Hussir looked from side to side, as if hunting, but did not catch sight of them.

A quiver of fear ran through Alan. In that instant, he was a disobedient member of the herd, and death awaited him for his escape from the fields.

There was a sharp twang beside him, and the Hussir stumbled and fell, transfixed through the chest with an arrow. Mara calmly lowered her bow, and smiled at the fright in his eyes.

"There's one that won't find Haafin," she said. "Haafin" was what the Wild Humans called their community.

"The—there are Hussirs in the mountains?" he quavered.

"A few. Hunters. If we get them before they run across the valley, we're all right. Some have seen us and gotten away, though. Haafin has been moved a dozen times in the last century, and we've always lost a lot of people fighting our way out. Those little devils attack in force."

"But what's the good of all this, then?" he asked hopelessly. "There aren't more than four or five hundred humans in Haafin. What good is hiding, and running somewhere else when the Hussirs find you, when sooner or later there'll come a time when they'll wipe you out?"

Mara sat down on a rock.

"You learn fast," she remarked. "You'll probably be surprised to learn that this community has managed to hang on in these mountains for more than a thousand years, but you've still put your finger right on the problem that has faced us for generations."

She hesitated and traced a pattern thoughtfully in the dust with a moccasined foot.

"It's a little early for you to be told, but you might as well start keeping your ears open," she said. "When you've been here a year, you'll be accepted as a member of the community. The way that's done is for you to have an interview with The Refugee, the leader of our people, and he always asks newcomers for their ideas on the solution of that very problem."

"But what will I listen for?" asked Alan anxiously.

"There are two different major ideas on how to solve the problem, and I'll let you hear them from the people who believe in them," she said. "Just remember what the problem is: to save ourselves from death and the hundreds of thousands of other humans in the world from slavery, we have to find a way to force the Hussirs to accept humans as equals, not as animals."

Many things about Alan's new life in Haafin were not too different from the existence he had known. He had to do his share of work in the little fields that clung to the edges of the small river in the middle of the valley. He had to help hunt animals for meat, he had to help make tools such as the Hussirs used. He had to fight with his fists, on occasion, to protect his rights.

But this thing the Wild Humans called "freedom" was a strange element that touched everything they were and did. The word meant basically, Alan found, that the Wild Humans did not belong to the Hussirs, but were their own masters. When orders were given, they usually had to be obeyed, but they came from humans, not Hussirs.

There were other differences. There were no formal family relationships, for there were no social traditions behind people who for generations had been nothing more than domestic animals. But the pressure and deprivations of rigidly enforced mating seasons were missing, and some of the older couples were mated permanently.

"Freedom," Alan decided, meant a dignity which made a human the equal of a Hussir.

The anniversary of that night when Alan followed the zird came, and Mara led him early in the morning to the extreme end of the valley. She left him at the mouth of a small cave, from which presently emerged the man of whom Alan had heard much but whom he saw now for the first time.

The Refugee's hair and beard were gray, and his face was lined with years.

"You are Alan, who came to us from Wiln Castle," said the old man.

"That is true, your greatness," replied Alan respectfully.

"Don't call me 'your greatness.' That's slave talk. I am Roand, The Refugee."

"Yes, sir."

"When you leave me today, you will be a member of the community of Haafin, only free human community in the world," said Roand. "You will have a member's rights. No man may take a woman from you without her consent. No one may take from you the food you hunt or grow without your consent. If you are first in an empty cave, no one may move into it with you unless you give permission. That is freedom.

"But, as you were no doubt told long ago, you must offer your best idea on how to make all humans free."

"Sir—" began Alan.

"Before you express yourself," interrupted Roand, "I'm going to give you some help. Come into the cave."

Alan followed him inside. By the light of a torch, Roand showed him a series of diagrams drawn on one wall with soft stone, as one would draw things in the dust with a stick.

"These are maps, Alan," said Roand, and he explained to the boy what a map was. At last Alan nodded in comprehension.

"You know by now that there are two ways of thinking about what to do to set all humans free, but you do not entirely understand either of them," said Roand. "These maps show you the first one, which was conceived a hundred and fifty years ago but which our people have not been able to agree to try.

"This map shows how, by a surprise attack, we could take Falklyn, the central city of all this Hussir region, although the Hussirs in Falklyn number almost ten thousand. Holding Falklyn, we could free the nearly forty thousand humans in the city and we would have enough strength then to take the surrounding area and strike at the cities around it, gradually, as these other maps show."

Alan nodded.

"But I like the other way better," Alan said. "There must be a reason why they won't let humans enter the Star Tower."

Roand's toothless smile did not mar the innate dignity of his face.

"You are a mystic, as I am, young Alan," he said. "But the tradition says that for a human to enter the Star Tower is not enough. Let me tell you of the tradition.

"The tradition says that the Star Tower was once the home of all humans. There were only a dozen or so humans then, but they had powers that were great and strange. But when they came out of the Star Tower, the Hussirs were able to enslave them through mere force of numbers.

"Three of those first humans escaped to these mountains and became the first Wild Humans. From them has come the tradition that has passed to their descendants and to the humans who have been rescued from Hussir slavery.

"The tradition says that a human who enters the Star Tower can free all the humans in the world—if he takes with him the Silk and the Song."

Roand reached into a crevice.

"This is the Silk," he said, drawing forth a peach-colored scarf on which something had been painted. Alan recognized it as writing, such as the Hussirs used and were rumored to have been taught by humans. Roand read it to him, reverently.

" 'REG. B-XII. CULTURE V. SOS.' "

"What does it mean?" asked Alan.

"No one knows," said Roand. "It is a great mystery. It may be a magical incantation."

He put the Silk back into the crevice.

"This is the only other writing we have handed down by our forebears," said Roand, and pulled out a fragment of very thin, brittle, yellowish material. To Alan it looked something like thin cloth that had

144

hardened with age, yet it had a different texture. Roand handled it very carefully.

"This was torn and the rest of it lost centuries ago," said Roand, and he read. "'October 3, 2 . . . ours to be the last . . . three lost expeditions . . . too far to keep trying . . . how we can get . . .'"

Alan could make no more sense of this than he could of the words of the Silk.

"What is the Song?" asked Alan.

"Every human knows it from childhood," said Roand. "It is the best known of all human songs."

"'Twinkle, twinkle, golden star,'" quoted Alan at once, "'I can reach you, though you're far. . . .'"

"That's right, but there is a second verse that only the Wild Humans know. You must learn it. It goes like this:

> "Twinkle, twinkle, little bug,
> Long and round, of shiny hue.
> In a room marked by a cross,
> Sting my arm when I've found you.
> Lay me down, in bed so deep,
> And then there's naught to do but sleep."

"It doesn't make sense," said Alan. "No more than the first verse— though Mara showed me what a turtle looks like."

"They aren't supposed to make sense until you sing them in the Star Tower," said Roand, "and then only if you have the Silk with you."

Alan cogitated a while. Roand was silent, waiting.

"Some of the people want one human to try to reach the Star Tower and think that will make all humans miraculously free," said Alan at last. "The others think that is but a child's tale and we must conquer the Hussirs with bows and spears. It seems to me, sir, that one or the other must be tried. I'm sorry that I don't know enough to suggest another course."

Roand's face fell.

"So you will join one side or the other and argue about it for the rest of your life," he said sadly. "And nothing will ever be done, because the people can't agree."

"I don't see why that has to be, sir."

Roand looked at him with sudden hope.

"What do you mean?"

"Can't you or someone else order them to take one course or another?"

Roand shook his head.

"Here there are rules, but no man tells another what to do," he said. "We are free here."

"Sir, when I was a small child, we played a game called Two Herds," said Alan slowly. "The sides would be divided evenly, each with a tree for a haven. When two of opposite sides met in the field, the one last from his haven captured the other and took him back to join his side."

"I've played that game, many years ago," said Roand. "I don't see your point, boy."

"Well, sir, to win, one side had to capture all the people on the other side. But, with so many captures back and forth, sometimes night fell and the game was not ended. So we always played that, then, the side with the most children when the game ended was the winning side.

"Why couldn't it be done that way?"

Comprehension dawned slowly in Roand's face. There was something there, too, of the awe-inspiring revelation that he was present at the birth of a major advance in the science of human government.

"Let them count those for each proposal, eh, and agree to abide by the proposal having the majority support?"

"Yes, sir."

Roand grinned his toothless grin.

"You have indeed brought us a new idea, my boy, but you and I will have to surrender our own viewpoint by it, I'm afraid. I keep close count. There are a few more people in Haafin who think we should attack the Hussirs with weapons than believe in the old tradition."

IV

When the armed mob of Wild Humans approached Falklyn in the dusk, Alan wore the Silk around his neck. Roand, one of the oldsters who stayed behind at Haafin, had given it to him.

"When Falklyn is taken, my boy, take the Silk with you into the Star Tower and sing the Song," were Roand's parting words. "There may be something to the old traditions after all."

After much argument among those Wild Humans who had given it thought for years, a military plan had emerged blessed with all the simplicity of a non-military race. They would just march into the city, killing all Hussirs they saw, and stay there, still killing all Hussirs they saw. Their own strength would increase gradually as they freed the city's enslaved humans. No one could put a definite finger on anything wrong with the idea.

Falklyn was built like a wheel. Around the park in which stood the Star Tower, the streets ran in concentric circles. Like spokes of the wheel, other streets struck from the park out to the edge of the city.

Without any sort of formation, the humans entered one of these spoke streets and moved inward, a few adventurous souls breaking away from the main body at each cross street. It was suppertime in Falklyn, and few Hussirs were abroad. The humans were jubilant as those who escaped their arrows fled, whistling in fright.

They were about a third of the way to the center of Falklyn when the bells began ringing, first near at hand and then all over the city. Hussirs popped out of doors and onto balconies, and arrows began to sail in among the humans to match their own. The motley army began to break up as its soldiers sought cover. Its progress was slowed, and there was some hand-to-hand fighting.

Alan found himself with Mara, crouching in a doorway. Ahead of them and behind them, Wild Humans scurried from house to house, still moving forward. An occasional Hussir hopped hastily across the street, sometimes making it, sometimes falling from a human arrow.

"This doesn't look so good," said Alan. "Nobody seemed to think of the Hussirs being prepared for an attack, but those bells must have been an alarm system."

"We're still moving ahead," replied Mara confidently.

Alan shook his head.

"That may just mean we'll have more trouble getting out of the city," he said. "The Hussirs outnumber us twenty to one, and they're killing more of us than we're killing of them."

The door beside them opened and a Hussir leaped all the way out before seeing them. Alan dispatched him with a blow from his spear. Mara at his heels, he ran forward to the next doorway. Shouts of humans and whistles and cries of Hussirs echoed back and forth down the street.

The fighting humans were perhaps halfway to the Star Tower when from ahead of them came the sound of shouting and chanting. From the dimness it seemed that a solid river of white was pouring toward them, filling the street from wall to wall.

A Wild Human across the street from Alan and Mara shouted in triumph.

"They're humans! The slaves are coming to help us!"

A ragged shout went up from the embattled Wild Humans. But as it died down, they were able to distinguish the words of the chanting and the shouting from that naked mass of humanity.

"Kill the Wild Humans! Kill the Wild Humans! Kill the Wild Humans!"

Remembering his own childhood fear of Wild Humans, Alan suddenly understood. With a confidence fully justified, the Hussirs had turned the humans' own people against them.

The invaders looked at each other in alarm, and drew closer together beneath the protection of overhanging balconies. Hussir arrows whistled near them unheeded.

They could not kill their enslaved brothers, and there was no chance of breaking through that oncoming avalanche of humanity. First by ones and twos, and then in groups, they turned to retreat from the city.

But the way was blocked. Up the street from the direction in which they had come moved orderly ranks of armed Hussirs. Some of the Wild Humans, among them Alan and Mara, ran for the nearest cross streets. Along them, too, approached companies of Hussirs.

The Wild Humans were trapped in the middle of Falklyn.

Terrified, the men and women of Haafin converged and swirled in a helpless knot in the center of the street. Hussir arrows from nearby windows picked them off one by one. The advancing Hussirs in the street were almost within bow-shot, and the yelling, unarmed slave humans were even closer.

"Your clothes!" shouted Alan, on an inspiration. "Throw away your clothes and weapons! Try to get back to the mountains!"

In almost a single swift shrug he divested himself of the open jacket and baggy trousers and threw his bow, arrows and spear from him. Only the Silk still fluttered from his neck.

As Mara stood openmouthed beside him, he jerked at her jacket impatiently. Suddenly getting his idea, she stripped quickly. The other Wild Humans began to follow suit.

The arrows of the Hussir squads were beginning to fall among them. Grabbing Mara's hand, Alan plunged headlong toward the avalanche of slave humans.

Slowed as he was by Mara, a dozen other Wild Humans raced ahead of him to break into the wall of humanity. Angry hands clutched at them as they tried to lose themselves among the slaves, and Alan and Mara, clinging to each other, were engulfed in a sudden swirl of shouting confusion.

There were naked, sweating bodies moving on all sides of them. They were buffeted back and forth like chips in the surf. Desperately, they gripped hands and stayed close together.

They were crowded to one side of the street, against the wall. The human tide scraped them along the rough stone and battered them roughly into a doorway. The door yielded to the tremendous pressure and flew inward. Somehow, only the two of them lost their balance and sprawled on the carpeted floor inside.

A Hussir appeared from an inside door, a barbed spear upraised.

"Mercy, your greatness!" cried Alan in the Hussir tongue, groveling.

The Hussir lowered the spear.

"Who is your master, human?" he demanded.

A distant memory thrust itself into Alan's mind, haltingly.

"My master lives in Northwesttown, your greatness."

The spear moved in the Hussir's hand.

"This is Northwesttown, human," he said ominously.

"Yes, your greatness," whimpered Alan, and prayed for no more coincidences. "I belong to the merchant, Senk."

The spear point dropped to the floor again.

"I felt sure you were a town human," said the Hussir, his eyes on the scarf around Alan's neck. "I know Senk well. And you, woman, who is your master?"

Alan did not wait to find out whether Mara spoke Hussir.

"She also belongs to my lord Senk, your greatness." Another recollection came to his aid, and he added, "It's mating season, your greatness."

The Hussir gave the peculiar whistle that served for a laugh among his race. He beckoned to them to rise.

"Go out the back door and return to your pen," he said kindly. "You're lucky you weren't separated from each other in that herd."

Gratefully, Alan and Mara slipped out the back door and made their way up a dark alley to a street. He led her to the left.

"We'll have to find a cross street to get out of Falklyn," he said. "This is one of the circular streets."

"I hope most of the others escape," she said fervently. "There's no one left in Haafin but the old people and the small children."

"We'll have to be careful," he said. "They may have guards at the edge of the city. We outtalked that Hussir, but you'd better go ahead of me till we get to the outskirts. It'll look less suspicious if we're not together."

At the cross street, they turned right. Mara moved ahead about thirty feet, and he followed. He watched her slim white figure swaying under the flickering gas lights of Falklyn and suddenly he laughed quietly. The memory of the blonde girl at Wiln Castle had returned to him, and it occurred to him, too, that he had never missed her.

The streets were nearly empty. Once or twice a human crossed ahead of them at a trot, and several times Hussirs passed them. For a while Alan heard shouting and whistling not far away, then these sounds faded.

They had not been walking long when Mara stopped. Alan came up beside her.

"We must have reached the outskirts," she said, waving her hand at the open space ahead of them.

They walked quickly.

But there was something wrong. The cross street just ahead curved too much, and there was the glimmer of lights some distance beyond it.

"We took the wrong turn when we left the alley," said Alan miserably. "Look—straight ahead!"

Dimly against the stars loomed the dark bulk of the Star Tower.

V

The great metal building stretched up into the night sky, losing itself in the blackness. The park around it was unlighted, but they could see the glow of the lamps at the Star Tower's entrance, where the Hussir guards remained on duty.

"We'll have to turn back," said Alan dully.

She stood close to him and looked up at him with large eyes.

"All the way back through the city?" There was a tremor in her voice.

"I'm afraid so." He put his arm around her shoulders and they turned away from the Star Tower. He fumbled at his scarf as they walked slowly back down the street.

His scarf! He stopped, halting her with a jerk. The Silk!

He grasped her shoulders with both hands and looked down into her face.

"Mara," he said soberly, "we aren't going back to the mountains. We aren't going back out of the city. We're going into the Star Tower!"

They retraced their steps to the end of the spoke street. They raced across the last and smallest of the circular streets, vaulted the rail, slipped like wraiths into the shadow of the park.

They moved from bush to bush and from tree to tree with the quiet facility of creatures born to nights in the open air. Little knots of guards were scattered all over the park. Probably the guard had been strengthened because of the Wild Human invasion of Falklyn. But the guards all had small, shaded lights, and Hussirs could not see well in the dark. The two humans were able to avoid them easily.

They came up behind the Star Tower and circled it cautiously. At its base, the entrance ramp was twice Alan's height. There were two guards, talking in low tones under the lamps that hung on each side of the dark, open door to the tower.

"If we could only have brought a bow!" exclaimed Alan in a whisper. "I could handle one of them without a weapon, but not two."

"Couldn't both of us?" she whispered back.

"No! They're little, but they're strong. Much stronger than a woman."

Against the glow of the light, something projected a few inches over the edge of the ramp above them.

"Maybe it's a spear," whispered Alan. "I'll lift you up."

In a moment she was down again, the object in her hands.

"Just an arrow," she muttered in disgust. "What good is it without a bow?"

"It may be enough," he said. "You stay here, and when I get to the foot of the ramp, make a noise to distract them. Then run for it—"

He crept on his stomach to the point where the ramp angled to the ground. He looked back. Mara was a lightness against the blackness of the corner.

Mara began banging against the side of the ramp with her fists and chanting in a low tone. Grabbing their bows, both Hussir guards moved quickly to the edge. Alan stood up and ran as fast as he could up the ramp, the arrow in his hand.

Their bows were drawn to shoot down where Mara was, when they felt the vibration of the ramp. They turned quickly.

Their arrows, hurriedly loosed, missed him. He plunged his own arrow through the throat of one and grappled with the other. In a savage burst of strength, he hurled the Hussir over the side to the ground below.

Mara cried out. A patrol of three Hussirs had been too close. She nearly reached the foot of the ramp, when one of them plunged from the darkness and locked his arms around her hips from behind. The other two were hopping up the ramp toward Alan, spears in hand.

Alan snatched up the bow and quiver of the Hussir he had slain. His first arrow took one of the approaching Hussirs, halfway down the ramp. The Hussir that had seized Mara hurled her away from him to the ground and raised his spear for the kill.

Alan's arrow only grazed the creature, but it dropped the spear, and Mara fled up the ramp.

The third Hussir lurched at Alan behind its spear. Alan dodged. The blade missed him, but the haft burned his side, almost knocking him from the ramp. The Hussir recovered like lightning, poised the spear again. It was too close for Alan to use the bow, and he had no time to pick up a spear.

Mara leaped on the Hussir's back, locking her legs around its body and grappling its spear arm with both her hands. Before it could shake her off, Alan wrested the spear from the Hussir's hand and dispatched it.

The other guards were coming up from all directions. Arrows rang against the sides of the Star Tower as the two humans ducked inside.

There was a light inside the Star Tower, a softer light than the gas lamps but more effective. They were inside a small chamber, from which another door led to the interior of the tower.

The door, swung back against the wall on its hinges, was two feet thick and its diameter was greater than the height of a man. Both of them together were unable to move it.

Arrows were coming through the door. Alan had left the guards' weapons outside. In a moment the Hussirs would gain courage to rush the ramp.

Alan looked around in desperation for a weapon. The metal walls were bare except for some handrails and a panel from which projected three metal sticks. Alan wrenched at one, trying to pull it loose for a club. It pulled down and there was a hissing sound in the room, but it would not come loose. He tried a second, and again it swung down but stayed fast to the wall.

Mara shrieked behind him, and he whirled.

The big door was closing, by itself, slowly, and outside the ramp was raising itself from the ground and sliding into the wall of the Star Tower below them. The few Hussirs who had ventured onto the end of the ramp were falling from it to the ground, like ants.

The door closed with a clang of finality. The hissing in the room went on for a moment, then stopped. It was as still as death in the Star Tower.

The went through the inner door, timidly, holding hands. They were in a curved corridor. The other side of the corridor was a blank wall. They followed the corridor all the way around the Star Tower, back to the door, without finding an entrance through the inner wall.

But there was a ladder that went upward. They climbed it, Alan first, then Mara. They were in another corridor, and another ladder went upward.

Up and up they climbed, past level after level, the blank inner wall gave way to spacious rooms, in which was strange furniture. Some were compartmented, and on the compartment doors for three levels, red crosses were painted.

Both of them were bathed with perspiration when they reached the room with the windows. And here there were no more ladders.

"Mara, we're at the top of the Star Tower!" exclaimed Alan.

The room was domed, and from head level all the dome was windows. But, though the windows faced upward, those around the lower periphery showed the lighted city of Falklyn spread below them. There was even one of them that showed a section of the park, and the park was right under them, but they knew it was the park because they could see the Hussirs scurrying about in the light of the two gas lamps that still burned beside the closed door of the Star Tower.

All the windows in the upper part of the dome opened on the stars.

The lower part of the walls was covered with strange wheels and metal sticks and diagrams and little shining circles of colored lights.

"We're in the top of the Star Tower!" shouted Alan in a triumphant frenzy. "I have the Silk and I shall sing the Song!"

152

VI

Alan raised his voice and the words reverberated back at them from the walls of the domed chamber.

> *"Twinkle, twinkle, golden star,*
> *I can reach you, though you're far.*
> *Shut my mouth and find my head,*
> *Find a worm that's striped with red,*
> *Feed it to the turtle shell,*
> *Then go to sleep, for all is well."*

Nothing happened.

Alan sang the second verse, and still nothing happened.

"Do you suppose that if we went back out now the Hussirs would let all humans go free?" asked Mara doubtfully.

"That's silly," he said, staring at the window where an increasing number of Hussirs was crowding into the park. "It's a riddle. We have to do what it says."

"But how can we? What does it mean?"

"It has something to do with the Star Tower," he said thoughtfully. "Maybe the *'golden star'* means the Star Tower, though I always thought it meant the Golden Star in the southern sky. Anway, we've reached the Star Tower, and it's silly to think about reaching a real star.

"Let's take the next line. *'Shut my mouth, and find my head.'* How can you shut anyone's mouth before you find their head?"

"We had to shut the door to the Star Tower before we could climb to the top," she ventured.

"That's it!" he exclaimed. "Now, let's *'find a worm that's striped with red'!*"

They looked all over the big room, in and under the strange, crooked beds that would tilt forward to make chairs, behind the big, queer-looking objects that stood all over the floor. The bottom part of the walls had drawers and they pulled these out, one by one.

At last Mara dropped a little disc of metal and it popped in half on the floor. A flat spool fell out, and white tape unrolled from it in a tangle.

"Worm!" shouted Alan. "Find one striped with red!"

They popped open disc after metal disc—and there it was: a tape crossed diagonally with red stripes. There was lettering on the metal discs and Mara spelled out the letters on this one.

"EMERGENCY. TERRA. AUTOMATIC BLASTDOWN."

Neither of them could figure out what that meant. So they looked for the *"turtle shell,"* and of course that would be the transparent dome-shaped object that sat on a pedestal between two of the chair-beds.

It was an awkward job trying to feed the striped worm to the turtle shell, for the only opening in the turtle shell was under it and to one side. But with Alan lying in one cushioned chair-bed and Mara lying in the other, and the two of them working together, they got the end of the worm into the turtle shell's mouth.

Immediately the turtle shell began eating the striped worm with a clicking chatter that lasted only a moment before it was drowned in a great rumbling roar from far down in the bowels of the Star Tower.

Then the windows that looked down on the park blossomed into flame that was almost too bright for human eyes to bear, and the lights of Falklyn began to fall away in the other windows around the rim of the dome. There was a great pressure that pushed them mightily down into the cushions on which they lay, and forced their senses from them.

Many months later, they would remember the second verse of the song. They would go into one of the chambers marked with a cross, they would sting themselves with the bugs that were hypodermic needles and sink down in the sleep of suspended animation.

But now they lay, naked and unconscious, in the control room of the accelerating starship. In the breeze from the air conditioners, the silken message to Earth fluttered pink against Alan's throat.

FOR DISCUSSION: The Silk and the Song

1. Although this story is obviously science fiction, the author uses some of the techniques of the mystery-story writer. The writer of mysteries must present clues to his readers without destroying his story's mystery or suspense in the process. He must engage the reader in a search for the answer to the mystery confronting his main characters. Do you think the author succeeds in doing this in the story you have just read?

2. The author gives Alan certain characteristics which make it possible for him to later solve the riddle of the silk and the song. What are these characteristics and in what scenes are they displayed?

3. What does Alan's grief over the death of Blik say about Alan himself? What does it indicate about the conditioning Alan has experienced all his life?

4. In telling the story of the enslavement of humans by an alien race, do you think the author may also be commenting on the behavior of men in the world today? Explain.

5. Identify two elements in the story which allow the Hussirs to maintain the status quo in their society.

INTRODUCTION: Eyebem

Writers throughout the centuries have addressed themselves to the human condition. They have asked themselves what it means to be a man and they have presented their answers in their stories.

Science-fiction writers have also concerned themselves with this important subject. In addition, some have concerned themselves with what it means to be a machine that possesses many human abilities and characteristics.

In our contemporary world where computers can talk to their programmers, such a concern is not misplaced. It can lead to sensitive portraits of men-like machines as in this story.

Eyebem
by Gene Wolfe

I am lying, I say again, in the dark; in the dark in the hut Mark has built of frozen earth and pounded snow. My pack transformer ratio .06 and I am dying. My identity, I say again, is 887332 and my friends call me Eyebem.

Inside me, I know, my words are going around and around in slow circles as they have all my life; I never thought it would matter—when you are young you think you will live forever. I remember very clearly old Ceedeesy describing this interior looped tape all of us contain. (I think setting my pack transformer ratio so low has called all these memories forth, though why it should I can't comprehend; memory chips burning bright as the spark dies.) A tape going around and around, Ceedeesy said, recording the last half hour of our talk, and then when end meets beginning writing over it so that only the last half hour remains. It was an idea, he told us, more than a hundred years old, having been originally used to record the last transmissions of those picturesque air-burning rockets called jets.

Ceedeesy was my group's principal instructor at the creche and I looked up to him. Now I want to talk about him, and though since it doesn't pertain to the cause of my death you won't like it, what can you do about it? I will be beyond the reach of your vindictive reprogramming, voltage gone, mind and memory zeroed.

To tell the truth I have said a great many things you would not like during the past eighteen or twenty hours as I lay here talking to myself in the dark. Yes, talking, even though the voltage in my speaker is so low that Mark, lying a few feet away, cannot hear me. He cannot hear me, but I know he is awake, lying there eating and thinking. I cannot see his eyes, but how they burn in the dark!

Ceedeesy, as I said, was old. So old that he could no longer be repaired sufficiently for active service, which was why we youngsters received the benefit of the deep wisdom he had won during his decades in the wild parts of the world. I recall his saying, "How many times, Eyebem, I've seen the trumpeter swans black against the morning sun!" then the little pause as he searched—the pause that told of hysteresis gathering on his aging mind like cobwebs. "A hundred and twenty-three times, Eyebem. That's an average of 3.8622 times a year, but the hundred and twenty-fourth time will never come for me."

No. Nor will the first for me.

Ceedeesy's skin had yellowed. They said at the creche that it was an older type of vinyl and that they had since improved the color stability so that our own will be virtually unaffected by the ultraviolet in sunlight, but I suspect that when my creche-mates are as old as Ceedeesy, their skin too will be yellowed at the back of the neck and the back of the hands, where the harsh noon light will have seen it too often.

It was because his skin was yellowed—or so I used to think—that Ceedeesy never left the compound. I was too young then to know that humans could always identify one of us in a second or two in spite of new skin and different face patterns with each creche-cycle. Once I persuaded him to go with me to a little store my creche-mates and I had found scarcely more than a block from the compound gate. It was run by a plump woman who, in order to get our custom, pretended to be too simple to recognize us. I think, too, that having us there attracted tourists for her. At least several times when I was there people—humans, I mean —entered the store and stared, only buying something when the plump woman pressed it into their hands. As young as I was I understood that she was exerting some form of psychological pressure on them.

Since our faces within the creche-cycle were all the same, this woman pretended to think we were all the same human person, a young man who was her best customer, coming ten or twenty times a day into her little shop. Pretending, as I said, to think we were all the same person, she called us all Mark; one of my creche-mates had told her to, no doubt; it's the name stupid youngsters always give when they want to pass, useful because it's a human name as well as being one of ours. How ironic that seems now.

We would wander about the store one at a time looking at the trusses and contraceptives we had no use for, and pretending to drink a carbonated liquid until the woman, with what I realize now was the most elephantine tact, contrived to turn her back so that we could pour it into a conveniently placed spittoon.

On the one occasion that Ceedeesy accompanied me we sat on high, swiveling stools sloshing the sweet drinks in our cups and occasionally putting the straws to our mouths. Ceedeesy, I am certain, was only doing it to please me. He must have known I was the only one being deceived, but at the time I believe he felt I was weak in marine biology, and he was ready to take any opportunity to tutor me before the junior examination. The store faced west, and as we talked I watched a spot of sunlight creep along the floor to his feet, then up his faded denim trousers, then past the moose-hide belt he had made himself and over his patched hunting shirt until his face and throat, and the hand that held his cup, were all brightly illuminated. I looked at them then, cracked with minute cracks and discolored, and it was as though Ceedeesy were an old piece of furniture covered with stiff, peeling plastic; it was terrible. I thought then that the woman *must* know (being too innocent to realize that she had known when the first of us walked in), but she was puttering in the back of the store—waiting, no doubt, for the display at her soda fountain to attract tourists.

To keep myself from staring at Ceedeesy I began watching the crowds on the street outside. In the space of a few minutes a thousand human beings must have passed the store. It made me interrupt Ceedeesy's lecture to ask, "When it's so beautiful out there—as the training tapes show and you and the other old ones say—why don't some of them"—I waved a hand at the window—"go out and look at it? Why send us?"

Ceedeesy laughed. "When I was a youngster, the explanation given was always blackflies."

"Blackflies?"

"A stinging insect. That explanation's just a put-off, of course. There are repellents to take care of them."

"Then—"

"A few of them do go out," Ceedeesy said. He went on to tell me about a man he had once rescued in the gorge of the Colorado. The man had been a fanatic Ecumenical Neo-Catholic, and had wanted to shoot the river on an air mattress because St. Kennedy the Less was reputed to have done something of the kind. "He was so naïve," Ceedeesy said, "that he called me Ranger the whole time he was with me. Or perhaps he was just afraid of me, out there away from the cities, and thought that was safest. I doubt if there are ten human rangers left in the world now."

A pot-bellied man leading two children came into the store then, pointing at Ceedeesy and me and whispering; we left.

I think that was the only time Ceedeesy went out of the compound. Last month (it seems so much longer) when we graduated he saw us off as we climbed into the trucks that would take us to the launch area. I was on the last truck, and I can still picture him waving as we went through the compound gate. At the time I was eager to leave.

The launch area was a new world to all of us, a huge building filled with bustling humans and machines, with the ships rising outside on columns of fire. I wasn't thinking about it then, but I suppose it's having these ships, as well as being able to synthesize food, that have caused human beings to concentrate more and more in the cities. In the old days they had to go out to get from one to another, or at least fly low enough that treetops and lakes became familiar. Now—well, my own experience was typical, I suppose. We were issued tickets, and after several hours (we sat around and compared tickets—the North for me) my ship was called. An enclosed traveling walk put me into it. That was the last I saw of my creche-mates.

After a few minutes more a human girl with inquisitive fingers came and strapped me to my couch, giving herself a lesson on how our anatomy differs from theirs. Another wait, a recorded announcement, and the ship was rising under me, slowly at first, then faster and faster until the acceleration drove me down against the upholstery so hard I could sense there wasn't enough strength in my servos to move my arms.

And then nothing. The acceleration faded and I was disoriented, feeling sure that something had gone wrong. After a short time the disoriented feeling changed to one of descending in an elevator. The couch was beneath me again and we were going down. Slowly. There was no sensation of speed.

This time instead of the enclosed walk there was an aluminum ramp; the building was older and the concrete pad small enough for its edges to be visible, but there was no more feeling of having traveled or having been out of the city than I would have gotten from going to the top of the central shop complex in our compound.

For me there was, however, at least one valid difference in emotional quality. I was alone, and as I carried my one small bag into the old and rather grimy port building, I came to realize what that meant. There were several machines moving smoothly over the terrazzo floor, but to these machines I was a man. There were a number of humans waiting for their ships to leave or greeting arriving relatives, but to them I was a machine in spite of my pointed, broad-brimmed field hat and high-laced boots, and they stared.

158

My orders had stated that I would be met here by someone from my assigned station, but for over an hour I was by myself in the middle of that crowd. In retrospect I think the experience was good for me, and perhaps it was planned that way. I had been anticipating the loneliness of duty in some remote part of the wilderness outside of the cities, and I had been trained for that. But this was different. It taught me that I was vulnerable after all, and I think it made me accept Mark, when he came, more than I would have otherwise.

I still remember how glad I was when I saw a hat like mine over the heads of that surging mass of people. I took off my own and waved it over my head to let him know where I was, and grasped his hand eagerly when he extended it. Half shouting to make myself heard, I said, "Identity 887332. Call me Eyebem."

He said, "Call me Mark."

I still don't know whether "Mark" is really Mark's name or merely one he has assumed to put us at our ease. I could ask him now, turning up my speaker until he heard me over the whistling wind, but he is thinking. All our own names, of course, derive from the dawn age of cybernetics: Ceedeesy's from the old Control Data Corporation computers, and "Mark" from the famous series which included the Mark VII and Mark VIII. At any rate I had been expecting one of us, and the name postponed for half a minute at least my discovery that Mark was human. To be truthful, I don't believe I was really sure of it until we were alone in the cab of the copter. Then, sitting next to him as he started the engine, I could study the skin of his neck. After that it seemed best to say something so he wouldn't realize I was staring, so I asked where we were going.

"Main station," he said. "About thirty miles up the Kobuk River." I could tell that he wasn't accustomed to talking a great deal, but he was perfectly friendly. I asked if it were far, and he said two hundred and fifty miles farther north. We had lifted off by then and I was too busy looking at the country to want to ask more questions. It was rocky, with conifers on the higher ground and alders following the watercourses. In places they had already shed their leaves, and I knew this must be one of the last good days we would have before the short Arctic summer ended and winter closed in.

At the main station I was reassured to find that Mark was the only human. The station boss was one of us, very imposing in a huge old grey cabinet with sensors scattered all over the station, but he made me welcome in a hearty, pleasant voice that made me feel right at home. There was another fellow too, from the creche-cycle two years ahead of mine as it turned out, who had come in from a tour to report and rest up.

With my own anxiety gone I began to feel sorry for Mark. He had to prepare food when the rest of us were sitting around recharging our power packs, and a lot of the little jokes and things that were said pretty well left him out—not intentionally but just by the nature of things. Since I had the least seniority I had to cut wood for the fireplace and do the odd jobs the station boss couldn't be bothered with around the low-yield pile that kept our generator running, but I didn't mind and I felt sure Mark would have traded places with me gladly if he could.

Then the pleasant time at the station was over and Mark and I left for our tour. By then I had learned that Mark, who was nearly thirty, would be retiring the next year, and I was to work with him until then, learning the territory and getting the specialized knowledge that can only be acquired in the field. We could have flown since the first big storm of the winter hadn't come yet, but Mark was afraid that if we did we wouldn't be able to get the copter back out when it turned nasty, so we took a snow jeep instead.

The first night that we camped I knew that I had reached the life in which I could fulfill myself, the thing I had been made and trained for. Without his asking I carried water up from the creek for Mark so that he could wash and make coffee. After he had gone to bed I sat up half the night staring at the polestar—so bright and so high here—and listening to the sounds the wind made in the little spruce trees around us.

The next day Mark showed me the tracks of a bear overlapping my own beside the creek. "He came before the frost got to the mud," Mark said, "so it must have been pretty early in the evening. Did you see him?"

I shook my head. "He's not dangerous, is he?"

"I wouldn't want to blunder into him in the dark, and he might go after the grub I've got locked in the jeep."

I hadn't thought of that. The bear couldn't eat amperes out of my power pack, but if it got to Mark's food—not here where we could easily get back to the station, but when we were farther out—Mark might starve. That knowledge hung like a dark cloud at the back of my mind while we broke camp and loaded the snow jeep. I hadn't realized I was allowing the worry to show on my face, but when we were under way Mark asked, "What's the matter, Eyebem?"

I told him what was troubling me and he laughed. "I'm an old hand. Funny, but while you were worrying about me I was fretting about you and the boss and the rest of you; wondering if you'll be all right when I leave."

"About us?" Frankly, I was shocked.

"Uh-huh." He swung the snow jeep around a fallen tree. "I know there are a lot of these completely automated stations operating successfully, but I still worry."

Completely automated? I suppose in a sense Mark was right, but I hadn't thought of it that way. I said as gently as I could, "We're designed for it, Mark. This is our home out here. If anyone's out of place it's you, and I'm sure the station boss and all of us will feel a lot less concern when you go to one of the cities."

Mark didn't say anything to that, but I could see he didn't really agree. To change the subject I said, "The bears will be going into hibernation soon, I suppose. Then we won't have to worry about them."

"Most of them are in already." Mark sounded like a bear himself. "The one we had around camp was probably an old male; some of them don't go until the last bit of food's gone, and they'll stick their heads out any time during the winter when there's a little stretch of better than average weather."

I know all that, of course. I had asked the question to give him something to talk about that wouldn't hurt his pride. It worked, too. Bears around camp are always a problem, and he told bear stories for the rest of that day as we picked our way north.

The storm came on our fifth day out, but we were expecting it and had made ourselves as secure as possible, pitching our tent in a sheltered spot and weighing down the edges with rocks until it looked almost like a stone house. The storm kept us there for three days, but when it was over we could put the skis on the snow jeep and skim along where we had had to pick our way before. We looked in on the sea otter rookeries north of the abandoned city of Kivalina, then followed the coast north toward Point Hope. We were still about two days' travel south of it when the second storm came.

That one held us five days, and when it was over Mark decided we'd better cut our tour short and head back toward the station. We dug the snow jeep out of the drifts and got ready to leave, but when Mark engaged the transmission the engine died and would not restart.

I know very little about turbines—I've only so much program capacity after all—but Mark seemed to be quite familiar with them, so while I built a snow wall to give him some shelter from the wind, he tore the engine down.

A drive shaft bearing race had shattered. It was broken so badly it wouldn't even keep the shaft in place, much less allow it to turn. It had jammed the turbine, and the overtorque breaker was what had actually shut down the engine; the trouble with the bearing had probably been due to cold-shortness, the weakness that will make an ax head fly into a thousand pieces sometimes when it's been left outside all night in subzero cold and you slam it into a frozen knot. All our equipment is supposed to be tested against it, but apparently this slipped through, or more likely, as Mark says, some mechanic doing an overhaul made an unauthorized substitution.

For as long as the battery lasted we tried to raise the station boss on the radio, but the cold reduced its efficiency so badly that we were forced to disconnect it from time to time so that we could carry it into the tent to warm up. For a while we considered tearing the entire radio out of the jeep so that we could take it inside, but we were afraid we'd damage something in the process (neither of us were too clear on how closely its wiring was integrated with the jeep's), and by the time we had about made up our minds to do it, the battery failed completely.

After that we had to reassess our position pretty thoroughly and we did, sitting by our little stove in the tent that night. Mark had food for at least ten days more, twenty with rationing, but it was too heavy to carry with us together with our other gear, and the loss of the snow jeep's engine meant no more power-pack recharges for me. We decided the smart thing to do was to stay with the jeep and our equipment, making what we had last as long as possible. We could burn the jeep's fuel in our stove, and if we kept the snow off it, just having it near us would make us a lot more visible to a search party than we would be otherwise. When we failed to return from our tour on schedule the station boss would send someone after us, and if we conserved what we had we thought he ought to find us in pretty good shape.

At first everything went quite well. I cut my pack transformer ratio: first to .5, then as the days went by to .3 without seeming to lose too much. I wasn't strong, of course, but as I told Mark it kept my monitor on, kept me going, and I didn't feel too bad. If you're not familiar with us, you who are hearing this tape, you may wonder why I didn't simply turn myself off altogether and instruct Mark to reactivate me when rescue came. The reason is that my memory is dependent on subminiature semiconductor chips which make up bistable circuits. When there is no electromotive force on them, the semiconductors "forget" their position, and that would mean wiping out every memory I possess—the total erasure of my personality as well as the loss of all my training.

Two days ago Mark built that hut of earth and snow for us with the tent as a liner, but I was too weak to help him much. The truth is that for the past week I have been simply lying here conserving as much energy as I can. Yesterday Mark went out and was able to shoot a seal on the beach, and when he dragged it inside I know he thought I was dead. He knelt beside me and passed his hand in front of my eyes, then slipped it inside my parka to feel the place in my chest above the heaters that prevent my hydraulic pump's freezing. There was so little current that he felt nothing, and I could see him shake his head as he drew his hand out.

I should not have done it, but for some reason that made me angry, and I turned up the power to my speaker until I could make myself heard and said, "I'm alive, Mark. Don't junk me yet."

He said, "I wouldn't junk you, Eyebem."

Then it all burst out of me, all the horror and frustration of these past days. I shouldn't have talked to Mark that way, he has never done me any harm and in fact has done whatever he could to help me, but I lost control of myself. Perhaps the long period at reduced voltage had something to do with it. Perhaps I am going mad, but I told him over and over how unjust it was: "We are the advance of the future, not you men. All your stupid human history has been just your own replacement by us, and there's nothing, not one thing, that you can do that we can't do better. Why don't you help me?" I suppose I was raving.

He only took my hand and said, "I'll think of something, Eyebem; turn down your power before you exhaust yourself."

And now another storm has come up, which means that whoever has been sent out to look for me, if anyone has, is pinned down just as we are; sitting in his tent while my power drains ampere by ampere, electron by electron on the way to nothing while Mark lies across from me in the dark eating his filthy seal blubber. Has the half-hour loop completed its cycle yet? Have I already erased the last beginning I made? I have no way of knowing.

I am lying, I say again, in the dark. . . .

FOR DISCUSSION: Eyebem

1. An author of a story must grip the reader's interest from the outset if he wants him to continue reading. By what device—by posing what question in the reader's mind concerning Eyebem in the opening paragraph—does the author of this story make you want to continue reading? What is it you want to find out?

2. What does the scene in the store run by the plump woman tell you about the attitudes of Eyebem and Ceedeesy toward themselves and toward human beings?

3. Why do you suppose the author chose to have Mark wear a hat exactly like the one worn by Eyebem?

4. There are indications in the story of the fact that Eyebem thinks of himself as somewhat superior to humans. Is it a firmly established

attitude? Does it in any way account for Eyebem's outburst at the conclusion of the story?

5. The theme of this story is the relative value of human beings versus androids. What conclusion does the story reach concerning this question?

6. Near the end of the story, Mark says, "I wouldn't junk you, Eyebem." What does his remark tell us about him and about his understanding of Eyebem's attitudes?

INTRODUCTION: Puppet Show

Although this story is dated in terms of its reference to the famous ventriloquist of an earlier day, Edgar Bergen, and to his two equally famous puppets, Charlie McCarthy and Mortimer Snerd, it is not dated in the ideas it includes or the philosophy it presents.

It is an example of a story which has no definitely stated resolution. This is but one of the elements that lend the story its appeal. Another is its author's skillful use of misdirection.

Puppet Show
by Fredric Brown

Horror came to Cherrybell at a little after noon on a blistering hot day in August.

Perhaps that is redundant; any August day in Cherrybell, Arizona, is blistering hot. It is on Highway 89, about 40 miles south of Tucson and about 30 miles north of the Mexican border. It consists of two filling stations, one on each side of the road to catch travelers going in both directions, a general store, a beer-and-wine-license-only tavern, a tourist-trap-type trading post for tourists who can't wait until they reach the border to start buying serapes and huaraches, a deserted hamburger stand, and a few 'dobe houses inhabited by Mexican Americans who work in Nogales, the border town to the south, and who, for God knows what reason, prefer to live in Cherrybell and commute, some of them in Model T Fords. The sign on the Highway says, CHERRYBELL, POP. 42, but the sign exaggerates; Pop died last year—Pop Anders, who ran the now deserted hamburger stand—and the correct figure should be 41.

Horror came to Cherrybell mounted on a burro led by an ancient, dirty and gray-bearded desert rat of a prospector who later gave the name of Dade Grant. Horror's name was Garvane. He was approximately nine feet tall but so thin, almost a stickman, that he could not have weighed over a hundred pounds. Old Dade's burro carried him easily, despite the fact that his feet dragged in the sand on either side. Being dragged through the sand for, as it later turned out, well over five miles hadn't caused the slightest wear on the shoes—more like buskins, they were—which constituted all that he wore except for a pair of what could

165

have been swimming trunks, in robin's-egg blue. But it wasn't his dimensions that made him horrible to look upon; it was his skin. It looked red, raw. It looked as though he had been skinned alive, and the skin replaced raw side out. His skull, his face, were equally narrow or elongated; otherwise in every visible way he appeared human—or at least humanoid. Unless you count such little things as the fact that his hair was a robin's-egg blue to match his trunks, as were his eyes and his boots. Blood red and light blue.

Casey, owner of the tavern, was the first one to see them coming across the plain, from the direction of the mountain range to the east. He'd stepped out of the back door of his tavern for a breath of fresh, if hot, air. They were about 100 yards away at that time, and already he could see the utter alienness of the figure on the led burro. Just alienness at that distance, the horror came only at close range. Casey's jaw dropped and stayed down until the strange trio was about 50 yards away, then he started slowly toward them. There are people who run at the sight of the unknown, others who advance to meet it. Casey advanced, slowly, to meet it.

Still in the wide open, 20 yards from the back of the little tavern, he met them. Dade Grant stopped and dropped the rope by which he was leading the burro. The burro stood still and dropped its head. The stickman stood up simply by planting his feet solidly and standing, astride the burro. He stepped one leg across it and stood a moment, leaning his weight against his hands on the burro's back, and then sat down in the sand. "High gravity planet," he said. "Can't stand long."

"Kin I get water fer my burro?" the prospector asked Casey. "Must be purty thirsty by now. Hadda leave water bags, some other things, so it could carry—" He jerked a thumb toward the red-and-blue horror.

Casey was just realizing that it was a horror. At a distance the color combination seemed only mildly hideous, but close up—the skin was rough and seemed to have veins on the outside and looked moist (although it wasn't) and *damn* if it didn't look just like he had his skin peeled off and put back on inside out. Or just peeled off, period. Casey had never seen anything like it and hoped he wouldn't ever see anything like it again.

Casey felt something behind him and looked over his shoulder. Others had seen now and were coming, but the nearest of them, a pair of boys, were 10 yards behind him. "*Muchachos*," he called out, "*Agua por el burro. Un pozal. Pronto.*"

He looked back and said, "What—? Who—?"

"Name's Dade Grant," said the prospector, putting out a hand, which

Casey took absently. When he let go of it, it jerked back over the desert rat's shoulder, thumb indicating the thing that sat on the sand. "His name's Garvane, he tells me. He's an extra something or other, and he's some kind of minister."

Casey nodded at the stick-man and was glad to get a nod in return instead of an extended hand. "I'm Manuel Casey," he said. "What does he mean, an extra something?"

The stick-man's voice was unexpectedly deep and vibrant. "I am an extraterrestrial. And a minister plenipotentiary."

Surprisingly, Casey was a moderately well-educated man and knew both of those phrases; he was probably the only person in Cherrybell who would have known the second one. Less surprisingly, considering the speaker's appearance, he believed both of them.

"What can I do for you, Sir?" he asked. "But first, why not come in out of the sun?"

"No, thank you. It's a bit cooler here than they told me it would be, but I'm quite comfortable. This is equivalent to a cool spring evening on my planet. And as to what you can do for me, you can notify your authorities of my presence. I believe they will be interested."

Well, Casey thought, by blind luck he's hit the best man for his purpose within at least 20 miles. Manuel Casey was half Irish, half Mexican. He had a half-brother who was half Irish and half assorted-American, and the half-brother was a bird colonel at Davis-Monthan Air Force Base in Tucson.

He said, "Just a minute, Mr. Garvane, I'll telephone. You, Mr. Grant, would you want to come inside?"

"Naw, I don't mind sun. Out in it all day ever' day. An' Garvane here, he ast me if I'd stick with him till he was finished with what he's gotta do here. Said he'd gimme somethin' purty vallable if I did. Somethin'— a 'lectronic—"

"An electronic battery-operated portable ore indicater," Garvane said. "A simple little device, indicates presence of a concentration of ore up to two miles, indicates kind, grade, quantity and depth."

Casey gulped, excused himself, and pushed through the gathering crowd into his tavern. He had Colonel Casey on the phone in one minute, but it took him another four minutes to convince the colonel that he was neither drunk nor joking.

Twenty-five minutes after that there was a noise in the sky, a noise that swelled and then died as a four-man helicopter set down and shut off its rotors a dozen yards from an extraterrestrial, two men and a burro. Casey alone had had the courage to rejoin the trio from the desert; there were other spectators, but they still held well back.

Colonel Casey, a major, a captain and a lieutenant who was the helicopter's pilot all came out and ran over. The stick-man stood up, all nine feet of him; from the effort it cost him to stand you could tell that he was used to a much lighter gravity than Earth's. He bowed, repeated his name and the identification of himself as an extraterrestrial and a minister plenipotentiary. Then he apologized for sitting down again, explained why it was necessary, and sat down.

The colonel introduced himself and the three who had come with him. "And now, Sir, what can we do for you?"

The stick-man made a grimace that was probably intended as a smile. His teeth were the same light blue as his hair and eyes.

"You have a cliché, 'Take me to your leader.' I do not ask that. In fact, I must remain here. Nor do I ask that any of your leaders be brought here to me. That would be impolite. I am perfectly willing for you to represent them, to talk to you and let you question me. But I do ask one thing.

"You have tape recorders. I ask that before I talk or answer questions you have one brought. I want to be sure that the message your leaders eventually receive is full and accurate."

"Fine," the colonel said. He turned to the pilot. "Lieutenant, get on the radio in the whirlybird and tell them to get us a tape recorder faster than possible. It can be dropped by para—No, that'd take longer, rigging it for a drop. Have them send it by another helicopter." The lieutenant turned to go. "Hey," the colonel said. "Also 50 yards of extension cord. We'll have to plug it in inside Manny's tavern."

The lieutenant sprinted for the helicopter.

The others sat and sweated a moment and then Manuel Casey stood up. "That's a half-an-hour wait," he said, "and if we're going to sit here in the sun, who's for a bottle of cold beer? You, Mr. Garvane?"

"It is a cold beverage, is it not? I am a bit chilly. If you have something hot—?"

"Coffee, coming up. Can I bring you a blanket?"

"No, thank you. It will not be necessary."

Casey left and shortly returned with a tray with half-a-dozen bottles of cold beer and a cup of steaming coffee. The lieutenant was back by then. Casey put the tray down and served the stick-man first, who sipped the coffee and said, "It is delicious."

Colonel Casey cleared his throat. "Serve our prospector friend next, Manny. As for us—well, drinking is forbidden on duty, but it was 112 in the shade in Tucson, and this is hotter and also is *not* in the shade. Gentlemen, consider yourselves on official leave for as long as it takes you to drink one bottle of beer, or until the tape recorder arrives, whichever comes first."

The beer was finished first, but by the time the last of it had vanished, the second helicopter was within sight and sound. Casey asked the stick-man if he wanted more coffee. The offer was politely declined. Casey looked at Dade Grant and winked and the desert rat winked back, so Casey went in for two more bottles, one apiece for the civilian terrestrials. Coming back he met the lieutenant arriving with the extension cord and returned as far as the doorway to show him where to plug it in.

When he came back, he saw that the second helicopter had brought its full complement of four, besides the tape recorder. There were, besides the pilot who had flown it, a technical sergeant who was skilled in its operation and who was now making adjustments on it, and a lieutenant-colonel and a warrant officer who had come along for the ride or because they had been made curious by the request for a tape recorder to be rushed to Cherrybell, Arizona, by air. They were standing gaping at the stick-man and whispered conversations were going on.

The colonel said "Attention" quietly, but it brought complete silence. "Please sit down, gentlemen. In a rough circle. Sergeant, if you rig your mike in the center of the circle, will it pick up clearly what any one of us may say?"

"Yes, Sir. I'm almost ready."

Ten men and one extraterrestrial humanoid sat in a rough circle, with the microphone hanging from a small tripod in the approximate center. The humans were sweating profusely; the humanoid shivered slightly. Just outside the circle, the burro stood dejectedly, its head low. Edging closer, but still about five yards away, spread out now in a semicircle, was the entire population of Cherrybell who had been at home at the time; the stores and the filling stations were deserted.

The technical sergeant pushed a button and the tape recorder's reel started to turn. "Testing . . . testing," he said. He held down the rewind button for a second and then pushed the playback button. "Testing . . . testing," said the recorder's speaker. Loud and clear. The sergeant pushed the rewind button, then the erase one to clear the tape. Then the stop button.

"When I push the next button, Sir," he said to the colonel, "we'll be recording."

The colonel looked at the tall extraterrestrial, who nodded, and then the colonel nodded at the sergeant. The sergeant pushed the recording button.

"My name is Garvane," said the stick-man, slowly and clearly. "I am from a planet of a star which is not listed in your star catalogs, although the globular cluster in which it is one of 90,000 stars is known to you. It is, from here, in the direction of the center of the galaxy at a distance of over 4,000 light-years.

"However, I am not here as a representative of my planet or my people, but as minister plenipotentiary of the Galactic Union, a federation of the enlightened civilizations of the galaxy, for the good of all. It is my assignment to visit you and decide, here and now, whether or not you are to be welcomed to join our federation.

"You may now ask questions freely. However, I reserve the right to postpone answering some of them until my decision has been made. If the decision is favorable, I will then answer all questions, including the ones I have postponed answering meanwhile. Is that satisfactory?"

"Yes," said the colonel. "How did you come here? A spaceship?"

"Correct. It is overhead right now, in orbit 22,000 miles out, so it revolves with the earth and stays over this one spot. I am under observation from it which is one reason I prefer to remain here in the open. I am to signal it when I want it to come down to pick me up."

"How do you know our language so fluently? Are you telepathic?"

"No. I am not. And nowhere in the galaxy is any race telepathic except among its own members. I was taught your language for this purpose. We have had observers among you for many centuries—by we, I mean the Galactic Union, of course. Quite obviously, I could not pass as an Earthman, but there are other races who can. Incidentally, they are not spies, or agents; they have in no way tried to affect you; they are observers and that is all."

"What benefits do we get from joining your union, if we are asked and if we accept?" the colonel asked.

"First, a quick course in the fundamental social sciences which will end your tendency to fight among yourselves and end or at least control your aggressions. After we are satisfied that you have accomplished that and it is safe for you to do so, you will be given space travel, and many other things, as rapidly as you are able to assimilate them."

"And if we are not asked, or refuse?"

"Nothing. You will be left alone; even our observers will be withdrawn. You will work out your own fate—either you will render your planet uninhabited and uninhabitable within the next century, or you will master social science yourselves and again be candidates for membership and again be offered membership. We will check from time to time and if and when it appears certain that you are not going to destroy yourselves, you will again be approached."

"Why the hurry, now that you're here? Why can't you stay long enough for our leaders, as you call them, to talk to you in person?"

"Postponed. The reason is not important but it is complicated, and I simply do not wish to waste time explaining."

"Assuming your decision is favorable, how will we get in touch with you to let you know our decision? You know enough about us, obviously, to know that I can't make it."

"We will know your decision through our observers. One condition of acceptance is full and uncensored publication in your newspapers of this interview, verbatim from the tape we are now using to record it. Also of all deliberations and decisions of your government."

"And other governments? We can't decide unilaterally for the world."

"Your government has been chosen for a start. If you accept, we shall furnish the techniques that will cause the others to fall in line quickly— and those techniques do not involve force or the threat of force."

"They must be some techniques," said the colonel wryly, "if they'll make one certain country I don't have to name fall into line without even a threat."

"Sometimes the offer of reward is more significant than the use of a threat. Do you think the country you do not wish to name would like your country colonizing planets of far stars before they even reach the moon? But this is a minor point, relatively. You may trust the techniques."

"It sounds almost too good to be true. But you said that you are to decide, here and now, whether or not we are to be invited to join. May I ask on what factors you will base your decision?"

"One is that I am—was, since I already have—to check your degree of xenophobia. In the loose sense in which you use it, that means fear of strangers. We have a word that has no counterpart in your vocabulary: it means fear of and revulsion toward aliens. I—or at least a member of my race—was chosen to make the first overt contact with you. Because I am what you would call roughly humanoid—as you are what I would call roughly humanoid—I am probably more horrible, more repulsive, to you than many completely different species would be. Because to you I am a caricature of a human being, I am more horrible to you than a being who bears no remote resemblance to you.

"You may think you do feel horror at me, and revulsion, but believe me, you have passed that test. There are races in the galaxy who can never be members of the federation, no matter how they advance otherwise, because they are violently and incurably xenophobic; they could never face or talk to an alien of any species. They would either run screaming from him or try to kill him instantly. From watching you and these people"—he waved a long arm at the civilian population of Cherrybell not far outside the circle of the conference—"I know you feel revulsion at the sight of me, but believe me, it is relatively slight and certainly curable. You have passed that test satisfactorily."

"And are there other tests?"

"One other. But I think it is time that I—" Instead of finishing the sentence, the stick-man lay back flat on the sand and closed his eyes.

The colonel started to his feet. "What in hell?" he said. He walked quickly around the mike's tripod and bent over the recumbent extraterrestrial, putting an ear to the bloody-appearing chest.

As he raised his head, Dade Grant, the grizzled prospector, chuckled. "No heartbeat, Colonel, because no heart. But I may leave him as a souvenir for you and you'll find much more interesting things inside him than heart and guts. Yes, he is a puppet who I have been operating, as your Edgar Bergen operates his—what's his name?—oh yes, Charlie McCarthy. Now that he has served his purpose, he is deactivated. You can go back to your place, Colonel."

Colonel Casey moved back slowly. "Why?" he asked.

Dade Grant was peeling off his beard and wig. He rubbed a cloth across his face to remove makeup and was revealed as a handsome young man. He said, "What he told you, or what you were told through him, was true as far as it went. He is only a simulacrum, yes, but he is an exact duplicate of a member of one of the intelligent races of the galaxy, the one toward whom you would be disposed—if you were violently and incurably xenophobic—to be most horrified by, according to our psychologists. But we did not bring a real member of his species to make first contact because they have a phobia of their own, agoraphobia—fear of space. They are highly civilized and members in good standing of the federation, but they never leave their own planet.

"Our observers assure us you don't have that phobia. But they were unable to judge in advance the degree of your xenophobia, and the only way to test it was to bring along something in lieu of someone to test it against, and presumably to let him make the intial contact."

The colonel sighed audibly. "I can't say this doesn't relieve me in one way. We could get along with humanoids, yes, and we will when we have to. But I'll admit it's a relief to learn that the master race of the galaxy is, after all, human instead of only humanoid. What is the second test?"

"You are undergoing it now. Call me—" He snapped his fingers. "What's the name of Bergen's second-string puppet, after Charlie McCarthy?"

The colonel hesitated, but the tech sergeant supplied the answer. "Mortimer Snerd."

"Right. So call me Mortimer Snerd, and now I think it is time that I—" He lay back flat on the sand and closed his eyes just as the stick-man had done a few minutes before.

The burro raised its head and put it into the circle over the shoulder of the tech sergeant.

"That takes care of the puppets, Colonel," it said. "And now, what's this bit about it being important that the master race be human or at least humanoid? What is a master race?"

FOR DISCUSSION: Puppet Show

1. There are basically only a limited number of themes in literature. The same is true for science-fiction literature. This story deals with a visitor to Earth who comes from another planet. Does the author successfully supply a fresh look at the basic theme?
2. Would you say that the alien visitor is superior to the race of man in any way? If your answer is affirmative, can you support your conclusion with quotes from the story?
3. The alien assures his listeners that he can provide techniques that do not involve force or the threat of force to persuade other nations to join the Galactic Union. What does this promise imply about the current state of the alien's own culture and its development?
4. The second test the alien mentions is not specifically described in the story but it is hinted at in the burro's final question. What is the second test?
5. The author does not tell us whether mankind passes the alien's test the first time. In your opinion, does he pass or does he fail? What is the reason for your answer?

INTRODUCTION: Look, You Think You've Got Troubles

In the introduction to the previous story, it was pointed out that there are a limited number of themes in both general literature and in science fiction. Here is a science-fiction story which deals with one of the themes basic to all literature—love. However, it also deals with other matters of importance, among which are prejudice and family relationships.

Look, You Think You've Got Troubles
by Carol Carr

To tell you the truth, in the old days we would have sat shivah for the whole week. My so-called daughter gets married, my own flesh and blood, and not only he doesn't look Jewish, he's not even human.

"Papa," she says to me, two seconds after I refuse to speak to her again in my entire life, "if you know him you'll love him, I promise." So what can I answer—the truth, like I always tell her: "If I know him I'll vomit, that's how he affects me. I can help it? He makes me want to throw up on him."

With silk gloves you have to handle the girl, just like her mother. I tell her what I feel, from the heart, and right away her face collapses into a hundred cracks and water from the Atlantic Ocean makes a soggy mess out of her paper sheath. And that's how I remember her after six months —standing in front of me, sopping wet from the tears and making me feel like a monster—me—when all the time it's her you-should-excuse-the-expression husband who's the monster.

After she's gone to live with him (New Horizon Village, Crag City, Mars), I try to tell myself it's not me who has to—how can I put it?—deal with him intimately; if she can stand it, why should I complain? It's not like I need somebody to carry on the business; my business is to enjoy myself in my retirement. But who can enjoy? Sadie doesn't leave me alone for a minute. She calls me a criminal, a worthless no-good with gallstones for a heart.

"Hector, where's your brains?" she says, having finally given up on my

174

emotions. I can't answer her. I just lost my daughter, I should worry about my brains too? I'm silent as the grave. I can't eat a thing. I'm empty—drained. It's as though I'm waiting for something to happen but I don't know what. I sit in a chair that folds me up like a bee in a flower and rocks me to sleep with electronic rhythms when I feel like sleeping, but who can sleep? I look at my wife and I see Lady Macbeth. Once I caught her whistling as she pushed the button for her bath. I fixed her with a look like an icicle tipped with arsenic.

"What are you so happy about? Thinking of your grandchildren with the twelve toes?"

She doesn't flinch. An iron woman.

When I close my eyes, which is rarely, I see our daughter when she was fourteen years old, with skin just beginning to go pimply and no expression yet on her face. I see her walking up to Sadie and asking her what she should do with her life now she's filling out, and my darling Sadie, my life's mate, telling her why not marry a freak; you got to be a beauty to find a man here, but on Mars you shouldn't know from so many fish. "I knew I could count on you, Mama," she says, and goes ahead and marries a plant with legs.

Things go on like this—impossible—for months. I lose twenty pounds, my nerves, three teeth and I'm on the verge of losing Sadie, when one day the mailchute goes ding-dong and it's a letter from my late daughter. I take it by the tips of two fingers and bring it in to where my wife is punching ingredients for the gravy I won't eat tonight.

"It's a communication from one of your relatives."

"Oh-oh-oh." My wife makes a grab for it, meanwhile punching CREAM-TOMATO-SAUCE-BEEF DRIPPINGS. No wonder I have no appetite.

"I'll give it to you on one condition only," I tell her, holding it out of her trembling reach. "Take it into the bedroom and read it to yourself. Don't even move your lips for once; I don't want to know. If she's, God forbid, dead, I'll send him a sympathy card."

Sadie has a variety of expressions but the one thing they have in common is they all wish me misfortune in my present and future life.

While she's reading the letter I find suddenly I have nothing to do. The magazines I read already. Breakfast I ate (like a bird). I'm all dressed to go out if I felt like, but there's nothing outside I don't have inside. Frankly, I don't feel like myself—I'm nervous. I say a lot of things I don't really intend and now maybe this letter comes to tell me I've got to pay for my meanness. Maybe she got sick up there; God knows what they eat, the kind of water they drink, the creatures they run around with. Not wanting to think about it too much, I go over to my chair and turn it on to brisk massage. It doesn't take long till I'm dreaming (fitfully).

I'm someplace surrounded by sand, sitting in a baby's crib and bouncing a diapered kangaroo on my knee. It gurgles up at me and calls me grandpa and I don't know what I should do. I don't want to hurt its feelings, but if I'm a grandpa to a kangaroo, I want no part of it; I only want it should go away. I pull out a dime from my pocket and put it into its pouch. The pouch is full of tiny insects which bite my fingers. I wake up in a sweat.

"Sadie! Are you reading, or rearranging the sentences? Bring it in here and I'll see what she wants. If it's a divorce, I know a lawyer."

Sadie comes into the room with her I-told-you-so waddle and gives me a small wet kiss on the cheek—a gold star for acting like a mensch. So I start to read it, in a loud monotone so she shouldn't get the impression I give a damn:

"Dear Daddy, I'm sorry for not writing sooner. I suppose I wanted to give you a chance to simmer down first." (Ingrate! Does the sun simmer down?) "I know it would have been inconvenient for you to come to the wedding, but Mor and I hoped you would maybe send us a letter just to let us know you're okay and still love me, in spite of everything."

Right at this point I feel a hot sigh followed by a short but wrenching moan.

"Sadie, get away from my neck. I'm warning you . . ."

Her eyes are going flick-a-fleck over my shoulder, from the piece of paper I'm holding to my face, back to the page, flick-a-fleck, flick-a-fleck.

"All right, already," she shoo-shoos me. "I read it, I know what's in it. Now it's your turn to see what kind of a lousy father you turned out to be." And she waddles back into the bedroom, shutting the door extra careful, like she's handling a piece of snow-white velvet.

When I'm certain she's gone, I sit myself down on the slab of woven dental floss my wife calls a couch and press a button on the arm that reads SEMI-CL.: FELDMAN TO FRIML. The music starts to slither out from the speaker under my left armpit. The right speaker is dead and buried and the long narrow one at the base years ago got drowned from the dog, who to this day hasn't learned to control himself when he hears "Desert Song."

This time I'm lucky; it's a piece by Feldman that comes on. I continue to read, calmed by the music.

"I might as well get to the point, Papa, because for all I know you're so mad you tore up this letter without even reading it. The point is that Mor and I are going to have a baby. Please, please don't throw this into the disintegrator. It's due in July, which gives you over three months to plan the trip up here. We have a lovely house, with a guest room that you and Mama can stay in for as long as you want."

I have to stop here to interject a couple of questions, since my daughter never had a head for logic and it's my strong point.

176

First of all, if she were in front of me in person right now I would ask right off what means "Mor and I are going to have a baby." Which? Or both? The second thing is, when she refers to it as "it" is she being literal or just uncertain? And just one more thing and then I'm through for good: Just how lovely can a guest room be that has all the air piped in and you can't even see the sky or take a walk on the grass because there is no grass, only simulated this and substituted that?

All the above notwithstanding, I continue to read:

"By the way, Papa, there's something I'm not sure you understand. Mor, you may or may not know, is as human as you and me, in all the important ways—and frankly a bit more intelligent."

I put down the letter for a minute just to give the goosebumps a chance to fly out of my stomach ulcers before I go on with her love and best and kisses and hopes for seeing us soon, Lorinda.

I don't know how she manages it, but the second I'm finished, Sadie is out of the bedroom and breathing hard.

"Well, do I start packing or do I start packing? And when I start packing, do I pack for us or do I pack for me?"

"Never. I should die three thousand deaths, each one with a worse prognosis."

It's a shame a company like Interplanetary Aviation can't afford, with the fares they charge, to give you a comfortable seat. Don't ask how I ever got there in the first place. Ask my wife—she's the one with the mouth. First of all, they only allow you three pounds of luggage, which if you're only bringing clothes is plenty, but we had a few gifts with us. We were only planning to stay a few days and to sublet the house was Sadie's idea, not mine.

The whole trip was supposed to take a month, each way. This is one reason Sadie thought it was impractical to stay for the weekend and then go home, which was the condition on which I'd agreed to go.

But now that we're on our way, I decide I might as well relax. I close my eyes and try to think of what the first meeting will be like.

"How." I put up my right hand in a gesture of friendship and trust. I reach into my pocket and offer him beads.

But even in my mind he looks at me blank, his naked pink antennas waving in the breeze like a worm's underwear. Then I realize there isn't any breeze where we're going. So they stop waving and wilt.

I look around in my mind. We're alone, the two of us, in the middle of a vast plain, me in my business suit and him in his green skin. The scene looks familiar, like something I had experienced, or read about . . .

"We'll meet at Philippi," I think, and stab him with my sword.

Only then am I able to catch a few winks.

The month goes by. When I begin to think I'll never remember how to use a fork, the loudspeaker is turned on and I hear this very smooth, modulated voice, the tranquilized tones of a psychiatrist sucking glycerine, telling us it's just about over, and we should expect a slight jolt upon landing.

That slight jolt starts my life going by so fast I'm missing all the good parts. But finally the ship is still and all you can hear are the wheezes and sighs of the engines—the sounds remind me of Sadie when she's winding down from a good argument. I look around. Everybody is very white. Sadie's five fingers are around my upper arm like a tourniquet.

"We're here," I tell her. "Do I get a hacksaw or can you manage it yourself?"

"Oh, my goodness." She loosens her grip. She really looks a mess—completely pale, not blinking, not even nagging.

I take her by the arm and steer her into customs. All the time I feel that she's a big piece of unwilling luggage I'm smuggling in. There's no cooperation at all in her feet and her eyes are going every which way.

"Sadie, shape up!"

"If you had a little more curiosity about the world you'd be a better person," she says, tolerantly.

While we're waiting to be processed by a creature in a suit like ours who surprises me by talking English, I sneak a quick look around.

It's funny. If I didn't know where we are I'd think we're in the back yard. The ground stretches out pure green, and it's only from the leaflet they give you in the ship to keep your mind off the panic that I know it's 100% Acrispan we're looking at, not grass. The air we're getting smells good, too, like fresh-cut flowers, but not too sweet.

By the time I've had a good look and a breathe, what's-its-name is handing us back our passports with a button that says to keep Mars beautiful don't litter.

I won't tell you about the troubles we had getting to the house, or the misunderstanding about the tip, because to be honest I wasn't paying attention. But we do manage to make it to the right door, and considering that the visit was a surprise, I didn't really expect they would meet us at the airport. My daughter must have been peeking, though, because she's in front of us even before we have a chance to knock.

"Mother!" she says, looking very round in the stomach. She hugs and kisses Sadie, who starts bawling. Five minutes later, when they're out of the clinch, Lorinda turns to me, a little nervous.

You can say a lot of things about me, but basically I'm a warm person, and we're about to be guests in this house, even if she is a stranger to me. I shake her hand.

"Is he home, or is he out in the back yard, growing new leaves?"

Her face (or what I can see of it through the climate adapter) crumbles a little at the chin line, but she straightens it out and puts her hand on my shoulder.

"Mor had to go out, Daddy—something important came up—but he should be back in an hour or so. Come on, let's go inside."

Actually there's nothing too crazy about the house, or even interesting. It has walls, a floor and a roof, I'm glad to see, even a few relaxer chairs, and after the trip we just had, I sit down and relax. I notice my daughter is having a little trouble looking me straight in the face, which is only as it should be, and it isn't long before she and Sadie are discussing pregnancy, gravitational exercise, labor, hospitals, formulas and sleep-taught toilet training. When I'm starting to feel that I'm getting over-educated, I decide to go into the kitchen and make myself a bite to eat. I could have asked them for a little something but I don't want to interfere with their first conversation. Sadie has all engines going and is interrupting four times a sentence, which is exactly the kind of game they always had back home—my daughter's goal is to say one complete thought out loud. If Sadie doesn't spring back with a non sequitur, Lorinda wins that round. A full-fledged knockout with Sadie still champion is when my daughter can't get a sentence in for a week. Sometimes I can understand why she went to Mars.

Anyway, while they're at the height of their simultaneous monologues, I go quietly off to the kitchen to see what I can dig up. (Ripe parts of Mor wrapped in plastic? Does he really regenerate, I wonder. Does Lorinda fully understand how he works, or one day will she make an asparagus omelet out of one of his appendages, only to learn that's the part that doesn't grow back? "Oh, I'm so *sorry*," she says. "Can you ever forgive me?")

The refrigerator, though obsolete on Earth, is well stocked—fruits of a sort, steaks, it seems, small chicken-type things that might be stunted pigeons. There's a bowl of a brownish, creamy mess—I can't even bring myself to smell it. Who's hungry, anyway, I think. The rumbling in my stomach is the symptom of a father's love turning sour.

I wander into the bedroom. There's a large portrait of Mor hanging on the wall—or maybe his ancestor. Is it true that instead of hearts, Martians have a large avocado pit? There's a rumor on Earth that when Martians get old they start to turn brown at the edges, like lettuce.

There's an object on the floor and I bend down and pick it up. A piece of material—at home I would have thought it was a man's handkerchief. Maybe it is a handkerchief. Maybe they have colds like us. They catch a germ, the sap rises to combat the infection and they have to blow their stamens. I open up a drawer to put the piece of material in (I like to be neat), but when I close it, something gets stuck. Another thing I can't recognize. It's small, round and either concave or convex, depending on how you look at it. It's made of something black and shiny. A cloth bowl? What would a vegetable be doing with a cloth bowl? Some questions are too deep for me, but what I don't know I eventually find out—and not by asking, either.

I go back to the living room.

"Did you find anything to eat?" Lorinda asks. "Or would you like me to fix—"

"Don't even get up," Sadie says quickly. "I can find my way around any kitchen, I don't care whose."

"I'm not hungry. It was a terrible trip. I thought I'd never wake up from it in one piece. By the way, I heard a good riddle on the ship. What's round and black, either concave or convex, depending on how you look at it, and made out of a shiny material?"

Lorinda blushed. "A skullcap? But that's not funny."

"So who needs funny? Riddles have to be a laugh a minute all of a sudden? You think Oedipus giggled all the way home from seeing the Sphinx?"

"Look, Daddy, I think there's something I should tell you."

"I think there are all sorts of things you should tell me."

"No. I mean about Mor."

"Who do you think *I* mean, the grocery boy? You elope with a cucumber from outer space and you want I should be satisfied because he's human in all the important ways? What's important—that he sneezes and hiccups? If you tell me he snores, I should be ecstatic? Maybe he sneezes when he's happy and hiccups when he's making love and snores because it helps him think better. Does that make him human?"

"Daddy, *please.*"

"Okay, not another word." Actually I'm starting to feel quite guilty. What if she has a miscarriage right on the spot? A man like me doesn't blithely torture a pregnant woman, even if she does happen to be his daughter. "What's so important it can't wait till later?"

"Nothing, I guess. Would you like some chopped liver? I just made some fresh."

"What?"

"Chopped liver—you know, chopped liver."

Oh yes, the ugly mess in the refrigerator. "You made it, that stuff in the bowl?"

"Sure. Daddy, there's something I really have to tell you."

She never does get to tell me, though, because her husband walks in, bold as brass.

180

I won't even begin to tell you what he looks like. Let me just say he's a good dream cooked up by Mary Shelley. I won't go into it, but if it gives you a small idea, I'll say that his head is shaped like an acorn on top of a stalk of broccoli. Enormous blue eyes, green skin and no hair at all except for a small blue round area on top of his head. His ears are adorable. Remember Dumbo the Elephant? Only a little smaller—I never exaggerate, even for effect. And he looks boneless, like a filet.

My wife, God bless her, I don't have to worry about; she's a gem in a crisis. One look at her son-in-law and she faints dead away. If I didn't know her better, if I wasn't absolutely certain that her simple mind contained no guile, I would have sworn she did it on purpose, to give everybody something to fuss about. Before we know what's happening, we're all in a tight, frantic conversation about what's the best way to bring her around. But while my daughter and her husband are in the bathroom looking for some deadly chemical, Sadie opens both eyes at once and stares up at me from the floor.

"What did I miss?"

"You didn't miss anything—you were only unconscious for fifteen seconds. It was a cat nap, not a coma."

"Say hello, Hector. Say hello to him or so help me I'll close my eyes for good."

"I'm very glad to meet you, Mr. Trumbnick," he says. I'm grateful that he's sparing me the humiliation of making the first gesture, but I pretend I don't see the stalk he's holding out.

"S'mutual," I say.

"I beg your pardon?"

"S'mutual. How are you? You look better than your pictures." He does, too. Even though his skin is green, it looks like the real thing up close. But his top lip sort of vibrates when he talks, and I can hardly bear to look at him except sideways.

"I hear you had some business this afternoon. My daughter never did tell me what your line is, uh, Morton."

"Daddy, his name is Mor. Why don't you call him Mor?"

"Because I prefer Morton. When we know each other better I'll call him something less formal. Don't rush me, Lorinda; I'm still getting adjusted to the chopped liver."

My son-in-law chuckles and his top lip really goes crazy. "Oh, were you surprised? Imported meats aren't a rarity here, you know. Just the other day one of my clients was telling me about an all-Earth meal he had at home."

"Your client?" Sadie asks. "You wouldn't happen to be a lawyer?" (My wife amazes me with her instant familiarity. She could live with a tyrannosaur in perfect harmony. First she faints, and while she's out cold everything in her head that was strange becomes ordinary and she wakes up a new woman.)

"No, Mrs. Trumbnick. I'm a—"

"—rabbi, of course," she finishes. "I knew it. The minute Hector found that skullcap I knew it. Him and his riddles. A skullcap is a skullcap and nobody not Jewish would dare wear one—not even a Martian." She bites her lip but recovers like a pro. "I'll bet you were out on a Bar Mitzvah—right?"

"No, as a matter of fact—"

"—a Bris. I knew it."

She's rubbing her hands together and beaming at him. "A Bris, how *nice*. But why didn't you tell us, Lorinda? Why would you keep such a thing a secret?"

Lorinda comes over to me and kisses me on the cheek, and I wish she wouldn't because I'm feeling myself go soft and I don't want to show it.

"Mor isn't *just* a rabbi, Daddy. He converted because of me and then found there was a demand among the colonists. But he's never given up his own beliefs, and part of his job is to minister to the Kopchopees who camp outside the village. That's where he was earlier, conducting a Kopchopee menopausal rite."

"A what!"

"Look, to each his own," says my wife with the open mind. But me, I want facts, and this is getting more bizarre by the minute.

"Kopchopee. He's a Kopchopee priest to his own race and a rabbi to ours, and that's how he makes his living? You don't feel there's a contradiction between the two, Morton?"

"That's right. They both pray to a strong silent god, in different ways of course. The way my race worships, for instance—"

"Listen, it takes all kinds," says Sadie.

"And the baby, whatever it turns out to be—will it be a Choptapi or a Jew?"

"Jew, shmoo," Sadie says with a wave of dismissal. "All of a sudden it's Hector the Pious—such a megilla out of a molehill." She turns away from me and addresses herself to the others, like I've just become invisible. "He hasn't seen the inside of a synagogue since we got married—what a rain that night—and now he can't take his shoes off in a house until he knows its race, color and creed." With a face full of fury, she brings me back into her sight. "Nudnick, what's got into you?"

I stand up straight to preserve my dignity. "If you'll excuse me, my things are getting wrinkled in the suitcase."

Sitting on my bed (with my shoes on), I must admit I'm feeling a little different. Not that Sadie made me change my mind. Far from it; for many years now her voice is the white sound that lets me think my own thoughts. But what I'm realizing more and more is that in a situation like this a girl needs her father, and what kind of a man is it who can't sacrifice his personal feelings for his only daughter? When she was going out with Herbie the Hemopheliac and came home crying it had to end because she was afraid to touch him, he might bleed, didn't I say pack your things, we're going to Grossinger's Venus for three weeks? When my twin brother Max went into kitchen sinks, who was it that helped him out at only four per cent? Always, I stood ready to help my family. And if Lorinda ever needed me, it's now when she's pregnant by some religious maniac. Okay—he makes me retch, so I'll talk to him with a tissue over my mouth. After all, in a world that's getting smaller all the time, it's people like me who have to be bigger to make up for it, no?

I go back to the living room and extend my hand to my son-in-law the cauliflower. (Feh.)

FOR DISCUSSION: Look, You Think You've Got Troubles

1. Do you think Hector means everything he says? Does he tend to overdramatize incidents and emotions? Is he completely honest with himself?
2. Is Hector's ultimate willingness to accept his son-in-law strictly the result of Mor's conversion to Judaism? Or has Hector all along been seeking a way to reconcile himself with his daughter and Mor's conversion merely provides him with a rationale for doing so?
3. Prejudice, the theme of this story, is usually treated in a serious fashion in literature. Does the presence of humor in this author's treatment of the theme in any way negate the seriousness of the subject?
4. Do you think the author had a particular reason for using a Jewish family in her story? Does the fact that the family is Jewish in any way reinforce the moral of the story?

Somewhere/
Somewhen

CHAPTER FOUR

Science fiction deals not only with travel in outer space but also travel in time. As a result, its authors have been able to examine periods in the world's past history through the eyes of characters who have traveled backward in time. Mark Twain was one of the authors who used the idea of time travel to create a contemporary man's view of a particular period in history in his story *A Connecticut Yankee in King Arthur's Court.*

There are many stories concerning time travel. Not all of them deal with travel backward in time. Some authors have transported their characters into the future. Others have brought persons living in the future back to our own time. The results of such travels are as varied as the stories themselves.

The concept of time travel poses a number of interesting questions which have intrigued science-fiction writers. Consider, for example, one basic question involved in the concept of time travel. What would happen if an individual traveled backward in time and murdered a man? Would the descendants of the murdered man still exist after the murder which shattered an established segment of the structure of the past? By altering the structure of time, no matter how minutely, does one not automatically alter the nature of the future?

The intriguing nature of such questions is in part what leads authors to write time travel stories and students to read them. The questions also give birth to some surprising insights and points of view concerning man and his behavior presented in terms of this science-fiction theme.

Imagine, for example, what it would be like to travel back to some chosen moment in history. Such a traveler could be an eyewitness to the crucifixion of Christ or to the devastation resulting from the bombing of Hiroshima. He could attend an opening night performance of one of Shakespeare's plays at England's historic Globe Theater.

Science-fiction writers have dealt with this particular idea many times.

They have also gone several steps farther and postulated such events as a man stranded in time and criminals condemned to a prison in the past.

Like other themes in science fiction, time travel offers fascinating fare for the adventurous mind. The theme also offers an opportunity for the reader to examine seriously some of the accepted physical laws now known in the universe. It very definitely allows writers to create some highly unusual variations on this one basic theme.

The idea behind the stories in this chapter—the concept of traveling in time—gives imaginative and creative writers an opportunity to explore beyond known boundaries and to ask questions that do not always occur to people. Their questioning leads them directly to fascinating speculations concerning what men might do and what might happen to them if time travel were to become a reality.

All authors are men of ideas and ideas are boundless. Nowhere are these facts more evident than in the literature included in this book. Science fiction recognizes few intellectual or ideological boundaries. Those that it does recognize are those inevitably imposed by the limits of each writer's mind, imagination, and ability.

To illustrate the literary creativity involved in the idea of time travel, let us pose a question. In the last story in this chapter, "The Good Provider" by Marion Gross, the author constructs a situation in which a time machine is built. But the vehicle is flawed. It will only take a person back twenty years and always to the corner of Main and Center Streets for only twenty minutes. Its inventor is disappointed because twenty years ago, in the story, is in the midst of the Depression and he has seen more than enough of that time and its problems. However, the inventor's wife sees what her husband considers a flaw as a splendid opportunity. The question: what is the opportunity that she sees which has escaped her husband?

We ask the question here to give the student an opportunity to put himself in the place of the author of this particular story. While reading it, he might try constructing his own answer to the question before it is revealed by the author. By so doing, he will come to understand something of the process of plotting and develop a sense of how such stories are created.

INTRODUCTION: Young Girl at an Open Half-door

One of the major variations on the theme of time travel is the visitor from the future who returns to our own time. Here is such a story which employs an original setting and situation and which underscores the poignancy of finding the right girl at the wrong time.

Young Girl at an Open Half-door
by Fred Saberhagen

That first night there was a police vehicle, what I think they call a K-9 unit, in the little employees' lot behind the Institute. I parked my car beside it and got out. The summer moon was dull above the city's air, but floodlights glared at a small door set in the granite flank of the great building. I carried my toolbox there, pushed a button, and stood waiting.

Within half a minute, a uniformed guard appeared inside the reinforced glass of the door. Before he had finished unlocking, two uniformed policemen were standing beside him, and beside them a powerful leashed dog whose ears were aimed my way.

The door opened. "Electronic Watch," I said, holding out my identification. The dog inspected me, while the three uniformed men peered at my symbols and were satisfied.

With a few words and nods the police admitted me to fellowship. In the next moment they were saying goodbye to the guard. "It's clean here, Dan, we're gonna shove off."

The guard agreed they might as well. He gave them a jovial farewell and locked them out, and then turned back to me, still smiling, an old and heavy man, now adopting a fatherly attitude. He squinted with the effort of remembering what he had read on my identification card. "Your name Joe?"

"Joe Ricci."

"Well, Joe, our system's acting up." He pointed. "The control room's up this way."

"I know, I helped install it." I walked beside the guard named Dan through silent passages and silent marble galleries, all carved by night lights into one-third brilliance and two-thirds shadow. We passed through new glass doors that were opened for us by photocells. Maintenance men in green uniforms were cleaning the glass; the white men among them were calling back and forth in Polish.

Dan whistled cheerfully as we went up the wide four-branched central stair, passing under a great skylight holding out the night. From the top landing of the stair, a plain door, little noticed in the daytime, opens through classical marble into a science-fiction room of fluorescent lights and electronic consoles. In that room are three large wall panels, marked Security, Fire, and Interior Climate. As we entered, another guard was alone in the room, seated before the huge security panel.

"Gallery two-fifteen showed again," the seated guard said in a faintly triumphant voice, turning to us and pointing to one of the indicator lights on the panel. The little panel lights were laid out within an outline of the building's floor plan. "You'd swear it was someone in there."

I set down my kit and stood looking at the panel, mentally reviewing the general layout of the security circuitry. Electronic Watch has not for a long time used anything as primitive as photocells, which are relegated to such prosaic jobs as opening doors. After closing hours in the Institute, when the security system is switched on, invisible electric fields permeate the space of every room where there is anything of value. A cat cannot prowl the building without leaving a track of disturbances across the Security panel.

At the moment all its indicators were dim and quiet. I opened my kit, took out a multimeter and a set of probes, and began a preliminary check of the panel itself.

"You'd swear someone's in two-fifteen when it happens," said the guard named Dan. Standing close and watching me, he gave a little laugh. "And then a man starts over to investigate, and before he can get there it stops."

Of course there was nothing nice and obvious wrong with the panel. I had not expected there would be; neat, simple troubles are too much to expect from the complexities of modern electronic gear. I tapped the indicator marked 215 but its glow remained dim and steady. "You get the signal from just the one gallery?" I asked.

"Yeah," said the guard in the chair. "Flashing a couple times, real quick, on and off. Then it stays on steady for a while, like someone's just standing in the middle of the room over there. Then like he said, it goes off while a man's trying to get over there. We called the officers and then we called you."

I put the things back in my kit and closed it up and lifted it. "I'll walk over there and look around."

"You know where two-fifteen is?" Dan had just unwrapped a sandwich. "I can walk over with you."

"That's all right, I can find it." I delayed on my way out of the room, smiling back at the two guards. "I've been here in the daytime, looking at the pictures."

"Oh. You bring your girl here, hey?" The guards laughed, a little relieved that I had broken my air of grim intentness. I know I often strike people that way.

Walking alone through the half-lit halls, I found it pleasant to think of myself as a man who came there in two such different capacities. Electronics and art were both in my grasp. I had a good start at knowing everything of importance. Renaissance Man, I thought, of the New Renaissance of the Space Age.

Finding the gallery I wanted was no problem, for all of them are numbered plainly, more or less in sequence. Through rising numbers, I traversed the Thirteenth Century, the Fourteenth, the Fifteenth. A multitude of Christs and virgins, saints and noblemen watched my passage from their walls of glare and shadow.

From several rooms away I saw the girl, through a real doorway framing the painted one she stands in. My steps slowed as I entered gallery two-fifteen. About twenty other paintings hang there, but for me it was empty of any presence but hers.

That night I had not thought of her until I saw her, which struck me then as odd, because on my occasional daytime visits I had always stopped before her door. I had no girl of the kind to take to an art gallery, whatever the guards might surmise.

The painter's light is full only on her face, and on her left hand, which rests on the closed bottom panel of a divided door. She is leaning very slightly out through the half-open doorway, her head of auburn curls turned just an inch to her left but her eyes looking the other way. She watches and listens, that much is certain. To me it had always seemed that she is expecting someone. Her full, vital body is chaste in a plain dark dress. Consider her attitude, her face, and wonder that so much is made of the smile of Mona Lisa.

The card on the wall beside the painting reads:

REMBRANDT VAN RIJN
DUTCH 1606-1669
YOUNG GIRL AT AN OPEN HALF-DOOR   dated 1645

She might have been seventeen when Rembrandt saw her, and seventeen she has remained, while the faces passing her doorway have grown up and grown old and disappeared, wave after wave of them.

She waits.

I broke out of my reverie, at last, with an effort. My eye was caught by the next painting, Saftleven's *Witches' Sabbath*, which once in the daylight had struck me as amusing. When I had freed my eyes from that I looked into the adjoining galleries, trying to put down the sudden feeling of being watched. I squinted up at the skylight ceiling of gallery two-fifteen, through which a single glaring spotlight shone.

Holding firmly to thoughts of electronics, I peered in corners and under benches, where a forgotten transistor radio might lurk to interfere, conceivably, with the electric field of the alarm. There was none.

From my kit I took a small field-strength meter, and like a priest swinging a censer I moved it gently through the air around me. The needle swayed, as it should have, with the invisible presence of the field.

There was a light gasp, as of surprise. A sighing momentary movement in the air, something nearby come and gone in a moment, and in that moment the meter needle jumped over violently, pegging so that with a technician's reflex my hand flew to switch it to a less sensitive scale.

I waited there alone for ten more minutes, but nothing further happened.

"It's working now; I could follow you everywhere you moved," said the guard in the chair, turning with assurance to speak to me just as I re-entered the science-fiction room. Dan and his sandwich were gone.

"Something's causing interference," I said, in my voice the false authority of the expert at a loss. "So. You never have any trouble with any other gallery, hey?"

"No, least I've never seen any—well, look at that now. Make a liar out of me." The guard chuckled without humor. "Something showing in two-twenty-seven now. That's Modern Art."

Half an hour later I was creeping on a catwalk through a clean crawl space above gallery two-twenty-seven, tracing a perfectly healthy microwave system. The reflected glare of night lights below filtered up into the crawl space, through a million holes in acoustical ceiling panels.

A small, bright auburn movement, almost directly below me, caught my eye. I crouched lower on the catwalk, putting my eyes close to the holes in one thin panel, bringing into my view almost the whole of the enormous room under the false ceiling.

The auburn was in a girl's hair. It came near matching the hair of the girl in the painting, but that could only have been coincidence, if such a thing exists. The girl below me was alive in the same sense I am, solid and fleshly and three-dimensional. She wore a kind of stretch suit, of a green shade that set off her hair, and she held a shiny object raised like a camera in her hands.

From my position almost directly above her, I could not see her face, only the curved grace of her body as she took a step forward, holding the shiny thing high. Then she began another step, and halfway through it she was gone, vanished in an instant from the center of an open floor.

Some time passed before I eased up from the strain of my bent position. All the world was silent and ordinary, so that alarm and astonishent would have seemed out of place. I inched back through the crawl space to my borrowed ladder, climbed down, walked along a corridor and turned a corner into the vast shadow-and-glare of gallery two-two-seven.

Standing in the brightly lit spot where I had seen the girl, I realized she had been raising her camera at a sculpture—a huge, flowing mass of bronze blobs and curved holes, on the topmost blob a face that looked like something scratched there by a child. I went up to it and thumped my knuckles on the nearest bulge of bronze, and the great thing sounded hollowly. Looking at the card on its marble base I had begun to read— RECLINING FIGURE, 1957—when a sound behind me made me spin round.

Dan asked benignly: "Was that you raising a ruckus in here about five minutes ago? Looked like a whole mob of people was running around."

I nodded, feeling the beginning of a strange contentment.

Next day I awoke at the usual time, to afternoon sunlight pushing at the closed yellow shades of my furnished apartment, to the endless street noises coming in. I had slept well and felt alert at once, and I began thinking about the girl.

Even if I had not seen her vanish, it would have been obvious that her comings and goings at the Institute were accomplished by no ordinary prowlers' or burglars' methods. Nor was she there on any ordinary purpose; if she had stolen or vandalized, I would most certainly have been awakened early.

I ate an ordinary breakfast, not noticing much or being noticed, sitting at the counter in the restaurant on the ground floor of the converted hotel where I rented my apartment. The waitress wore green, although her hair was black. Once I had tried half-heartedly to talk to her, to know her, to make out, but she had kept on working and loafing, talking to me and everyone else alike.

When the sun was near going down, I started for work as usual. I bought the usual newspaper to take along, but did not read it when I saw the headline PEACE TALKS FAILING. That evening I felt the way I supposed a lover should feel, going to his beloved.

Dan and two other guards greeted me with smiles of the kind that people wear when things that are clearly not their fault are going wrong for their employer. They told me that the pseudo-prowler had once more visited gallery two-fifteen, had vanished as usual from the panel just as a guard approached that room, and then had several times appeared on the indicators for gallery two-twenty-seven. I went to two-twenty-seven, making a show of carrying in tools and equipment, and settled myself on a bench in a dim corner, to wait.

The contentment I had known for twenty-four hours became impatience, and with slowly passing time the tension of impatience made me uncontrollably restless. I felt sure that she could somehow watch me waiting; she must know I was waiting for her; she must be able to see that I meant her no harm. Beyond meeting her, I had no plan at all.

Not even a guard came to disturb me. Around me, in paint and bronze and stone and welded steel, crowded the tortured visions of the Twentieth Century. I got up at last in desperation and found that not everything was torture. There on the wall were Monet's water lilies; at first nothing but vague flat shapes of paint, then the surface of a pond and a deep curve of reflected sky. I grew dizzy staring into that water, a dizziness of relief that made me laugh. When I looked away at last, the walls and ceiling were shimmering as if the glare of the night lights was reflected from Monet's pond.

I understood then that something was awry, something was being done to me, but I could not care. Giggling at the world, I stood there breathing air that seemed to sparkle in my lungs. The auburn-haired girl came to my side and took my arm and guided me to the bench where my unused equipment lay.

Her voice had the beauty I had expected, though with a strange strong accent. "Oh, I am sorry to make you weak and sick. But you insist to stay here and span much time, the time in which I must do my work."

For the moment I could say nothing. She made me sit on the bench, and bent over me with concern, turning her head with something of the same questioning look as the girl in the Rembrandt painting. Again she said, "Oh, I am sorry."

"S'all right." My tongue was heavy, and I still wanted to laugh.

She smiled and hurried away, flowed away. Again she was dressed in a green stretch suit, setting off the color of her hair. This time she vanished from my sight in normal fashion, going around one of the gallery's low partitions. Coming from behind that partition were flashes of light.

I got unsteadily to my feet and went after her. Rounding the corner, I saw three devices set up on tripods, the tripods spaced evenly around the *Reclining Figure*. From the three devices, which I could not begin to identify, little lances of light flicked like stings or brushes at the sculpture. And whirling around it like dancers, on silent rubbery feet, moved another pair of machine-shapes, busy with some purpose that was totally beyond me.

The girl reached to support me as I swayed. Her hands were strong, her eyes were darkly blue, and she was tall in slender curves. Smiling, she said, "It is all right, I do no harm."

"I don't care about that," I said. "I want only—not to tangle things with you."

"What?" She smiled, as if at someone raving. She had drugged me, with subtle gasses in the air that sparkled in my lungs. I knew that but I did not care.

"I always hold back," I said, "and tangle things with people. Not this time. I want to love you without any of that. This is a simple miracle, and I just want it to go on. Now tell me your name."

She was so silent and solemn for a moment, watching me, that I feared that I had angered her. But then she shook her head and smiled again. "My name is Day-ell. Now don't fall down!" and she took her supporting arm away.

For the moment I was content without her touching me. I leaned against the partition and looked at her busy machines. "Will you steal our *Reclining Figure*?" I asked, giggling again as I wondered who would want it.

"Steal?" she was thoughtful. "The two greatest works of this house I must save. I will replace them with copies so well made that no one will ever know, before—" She broke off. After a moment she added, "Only you will know." And then she turned away to give closer attention to her silent and ragingly busy machines. When she made an adjustment on a tiny thing she held in her hand, there were suddenly two *Reclining Figures* visible, one of them smaller and transparent but growing larger, moving toward us from some dark and distant space that was temporarily within the gallery.

I was thinking over and over what Day-ell had said. Addled and joyful, I plotted what seemed to me a clever compliment, and announced, "I know what the two greatest works in this house are."

"Oh?" The word in her voice was a soft bell. But she was still busy.

"One is Rembrandt's girl."

"You are right!" Day-ell, pleased, turned to me. "Last night I took that one to safety. Where I take them, the originals, they will be safe forever."

"But the best—is you." I pushed away from the partition. "I make you my girl. My love. Forever, if it can be. But how long doesn't matter."

Her face changed and her eyes went wide, as if she truly understood how marvelous were such words, from anyone, from grim Joe Ricci in particular. She took a step toward me.

"If you could mean that," she whispered, "then I would stay with you, in spite of everything."

My arms went round her and I could feel forever passing. "Stay, of course I mean it, stay with me."

"Come, Day-ell, come," intoned a voice, soft, but still having metal in its timbre. Looking over her shoulder, I saw the machine-shapes waiting, balancing motionless now on their silent feet. There was again only one *Reclining Figure*.

My thoughts were clearing and I said to her, "You're leaving copies, you said, and no one will know the difference, before. Before what? What's going to happen?"

When my girl did not answer, I held her at arms' length. She was shaking her head slowly, and tears had come into her eyes. She said, "It does not matter what happens, since I have found here a man of life who will love me. In my world there is no one like that. If you will hold me, I can stay."

My hands holding her began to shake. I said, "I won't keep you here, to die in some disaster. I'll go with you instead."

"Come, Day-ell, come." It was a terrible steel whisper.

And she stepped back, compelled by the machine-voice now that I had let her go. She said to me, "You must not come. My world is safe for paint, safe for bronze, not safe for men who love. Why do you think that we must steal—?"

She was gone, the machines and lights gone with her.

The *Reclining Figure* stands massive and immobile as ever, bronze blobs and curved holes, with a face like something scratched on by a child. Thump it with a knuckle, and it sounds hollowly. Maybe three hundred years' perspective is needed to see it as one of the two greatest in this house. Maybe eyes are needed, accustomed to more dimensions than ours; eyes of those who sent Day-ell diving down through time to save choice fragments from the murky wreckage of the New Renaissance, plunged in the mud of the ignorant and boastful Twentieth Century.

Not that her world is better. *Safe for paint, safe for bronze, not safe for men who love.* I could not live there now.

The painting looks unchanged. A girl of seventeen still waits, frozen warmly in Rembrandt's light, three hundred years and more on the verge of smiling, secure that long from age and death and disappointment. But will a war incinerate her next week, or an earthquake swallow her next month? Or will our city convulse and die in mass rioting madness, a

194

witches' Sabbath come true? What warning can I give? When they found me alone and weeping in the empty gallery that night, they talked about a nervous breakdown. The indicators on the Security panel are always quiet now, and I have let myself be argued out of the little of my story that I told.

No world is safe for those who love.

FOR DISCUSSION: Young Girl at an Open Half-door

1. Why does the author emphasize the Rembrandt painting which gives the story its title? Is it only because he has chosen an art museum as the setting for his story?
2. Is there any significance to the mention of the newspaper headline in terms of the story itself? Does its inclusion hint at the possible reason for Day-ell's visits to the museum?
3. Joe Ricci does not think much of the artistic value of the sculpture called *Reclining Figure*. But Day-ell steals it as well as the Rembrandt. Does this difference in their opinions tell us something about art criticism? About time itself?
4. Authors build their stories unit by unit. Extraneous elements that serve no purpose in the story are omitted. This technique is evident here in the inclusion of a reference to the painting *Witches' Sabbath*. Can you link the painting with the point of the story?

INTRODUCTION: The Man Who Came Early

The man who came early in this story is a twentieth century soldier who is thrust backward in time to Iceland in the late tenth century. The conflict of cultures is one of the forces at work in the story and it, together with human passions, brings about the story's climax.

One of the major accomplishments of the author is his detailed, accurate, and convincing re-creation of the customs, language, attitudes, and beliefs of an earlier age. Of importance, too, is the light the story casts on the similarities of human behavior in both the world of the tenth century and that of the twentieth.

The Man Who Came Early
by Poul Anderson

Yes, when a man grows old he has heard so much that is strange there's little more can surprise him. They say the king in Miklagard has a beast of gold before his high seat, which stands up and roars. I have it from Eilif Eiriksson, who served in the guard down there, and he is a steady fellow when not drunk. He has also seen the Greek fire used, it burns on water.

So, priest, I am not unwilling to believe what you say about the White Christ. I have been in England and France myself, and seen how the folk prosper. He must be a very powerful god, to ward so many realms ... and did you say that everyone who is baptized will be given a white robe? I would like to have one. They mildew, of course, in this cursed wet Iceland weather, but a small sacrifice to the houseelves should—No sacrifices? Come now! I'll give up horseflesh if I must, my teeth not being what they were, but every sensible man knows how much trouble the elves make if they're not fed.

... Well, let's have another cup and talk about it. How do you like the beer? It's my own brew, you know. The cups I got in England, many years back. I was a young man then ... times goes, time goes. Afterward I came back and inherited this, my father's steading, and have not left it since. Well enough to go in viking as a youth, but grown older you see where the real wealth lies: here, in the land and the cattle.

Stoke up the fires, Hjalti. It's growing cold. Sometimes I think the winters are colder than when I was a boy. Thorbrand of the Salmondale

196

says so, but he believes the gods are angry because so many are turning from them. You'll have trouble winning Thorbrand over, priest. A stubborn man. Myself I am open-minded, and willing to listen at least.

... Now then. There is one point on which I must correct you. The end of the world is not coming in two years. This I know.

And if you ask me how I know, that's a very long tale, and in some ways a terrible one. Glad I am to be old, and safely in the earth before that great tomorrow comes. It will be an eldritch time before the frost giants march... oh, very well, before the angel blows his battle horn. One reason I hearken to your preaching is that I know the White Christ will conquer Thor. I know Iceland is going to be Christian erelong, and it seems best to range myself on the winning side.

No, I've had no visions. This is a happening of five years ago, which my own household and neighbors can swear to. They mostly did not believe what the stranger told; I do, more or less, if only because I don't think a liar could wreak so much harm. I loved my daughter, priest, and after it was over I made a good marriage for her. She did not naysay it, but now she sits out on the ness-farm with her husband and never a word to me; and I hear he is ill pleased with her silence and moodiness, and spends his nights with an Irish concubine. For this I cannot blame him, but it grieves me.

Well, I've drunk enough to tell the whole truth now, and whether you believe it or not makes no odds to me. Here ... you girls! ... fill these cups again, for I'll have a dry throat before I finish the telling.

It begins, then, on a day in early summer, five years ago. At that time, my wife Ragnhild and I had only two unwed children still living with us: our youngest son Helgi, of seventeen winters, and our daughter Thorgunna, of eighteen. The girl, being fair, had already had suitors. But she refused them, and I am not a man who would compel his daughter. As for Helgi, he was ever a lively one, good with his hands but a breakneck youth. He is now serving in the guard of King Olaf of Norway. Besides these, of course, we had about ten housefolk—two Irish thralls, two girls to help with the women's work, and half a dozen hired carles. This is not a small steading.

You have not seen how my land lies. About two miles to the west is the bay; the thorps at Reykjavik are about five miles south. The land rises toward the Long Jökull, so that my acres are hilly; but it's good hayland, and there is often driftwood on the beach. I've built a shed down there for it, as well as a boathouse.

There had been a storm the night before, so Helgi and I were going down to look for drift. You, coming from Norway, do not know how precious wood is to us Icelanders, who have only a few scrubby trees and must bring all our timber from abroad. Back there men have often been burned in their houses by their foes, but we count that the worst of deeds, though it's not unknown.

I was on good terms with my neighbors, so we took only hand weapons. I my ax, Helgi a sword, and the two carles we had with us bore spears. It was a day washed clean by the night's fury, and the sun fell bright on long wet grass. I saw my garth lying rich around its courtyard, sleek cows and sheep, smoke rising from the roof hole of the hall, and knew I'd not done so ill in my lifetime. My son Helgi's hair fluttered in the low west wind as we left the steading behind a ridge and neared the water. Strange how well I remember all which happened that day; somehow it was a sharper day than most.

When we came down to the strand, the sea was beating heavy, white and gray out to the world's edge. A few gulls flew screaming above us, frightened off a cod washed up onto the shore. I saw there was a litter of no few sticks, even a baulk of timber . . . from some ship carrying it that broke up during the night, I suppose. That was a useful find, though, as a careful man, I would later sacrifice to be sure the owner's ghost wouldn't plague me.

We had fallen to and were dragging the baulk toward the shed when Helgi cried out. I ran for my ax as I looked the way he pointed. We had no feuds then, but there are always outlaws.

This one seemed harmless, though. Indeed, as he stumbled nearer across the black sand I thought him quite unarmed and wondered what had happened. He was a big man and strangely clad—he wore coat and breeches and shoes like anyone else, but they were of peculiar cut and he bound his trousers with leggings rather than thongs. Nor had I ever seen a helmet like his: it was almost square, and came down to cover his neck, but it had no nose guard; it was held in place by a leather strap. And this you may not believe, but it was *not metal yet had been cast in one piece!*

He broke into a staggering run as he neared, and flapped his arms and croaked something. The tongue was none I had ever heard, and I have heard many; it was like dogs barking. I saw that he was clean-shaven and his black hair cropped short, and thought he might be French. Otherwise he was a young man, and good-looking, with blue eyes and regular features. From his skin I judged that he spent much time indoors, yet he had a fine manly build.

"Could he have been shipwrecked?" asked Helgi.

"His clothes are dry and unstained," I said; "nor has he been wandering long, for there's no stubble on his chin. Yet I've heard of no strangers guesting hereabouts."

We lowered our weapons, and he came up to us and stood gasping. I saw that his coat and the shirt behind were fastened with bonelike buttons rather than laces, and were of heavy weave. About his neck he had fastened a strip of cloth tucked into his coat. These garments were all in brownish hues. His shoes were of a sort new to me, very well cobbled. Here and there on his coat were bits of brass, and he had three broken stripes on each sleeve; also a black band with white letters, the same letters being on his helmet. Those were not runes, but Roman letters—thus: MP. He wore a broad belt, with a small clublike thing of metal in a sheath at the hip and also a real club.

"I think he must be a warlock," muttered my carle Sigurd. "Why else all those tokens?"

"They may only be ornament, or to ward against witchcraft," I soothed him. Then, to the stranger. "I hight Ospak Ulfsson of Hillstead. What is your errand?"

He stood with his chest heaving and a wildness in his eyes. He must have run a long way. Then he moaned and sat down and covered his face.

"If he's sick, best we get him to the house," said Helgi. His eyes gleamed—we see so few new faces here.

"No . . . no . . ." The stranger looked up. "Let me rest a moment—"

He spoke the Norse tongue readily enough, though with a thick accent not easy to follow and with many foreign words I did not understand.

The other carle, Grim, hefted his spear. "Have vikings landed?" he asked.

"When did vikings ever come to Iceland?" I snorted. "It's the other way around."

The newcomer shook his head, as if it had been struck. He got shakily to his feet. "What happened?" he said. "What happened to the city?"

"What city?" I asked reasonably.

"Reykjavik!" he groaned. "Where is it?"

"Five miles south, the way you came—unless you mean the bay itself," I said.

"No! There was only a beach, and a few wretched huts, and—"

"Best not let Hjalmar Broadnose hear you call his thorp that," I counseled.

"But there was a city!" he cried. Wildness lay in his eyes. "I was crossing the street, it was a storm, and there was a crash and then I stood on the beach and the city was gone!"

"He's mad," said Sigurd, backing away. "Be careful . . . if he starts to foam at the mouth, it means he's going berserk."

"Who are you?" babbled the stranger. "What are you doing in those clothes? Why the spears?"

"Somehow," said Helgi, "he does not sound crazed—only frightened and bewildered. Something evil has happened to him."

"I'm not staying near a man under a curse!" yelped Sigurd, and started to run away.

"Come back!" I bawled. "Stand where you are or I'll cleave your louse-bitten head!"

That stopped him, for he had no kin who would avenge him; but he would not come closer. Meanwhile the stranger had calmed down to the point where he could at least talk evenly.

"Was it the *aitchbomb?*" he asked. "Has the war started?"

He used that word often, *aitchbomb,* so I know it now, though unsure of what it means. It seems to be a kind of Greek fire. As for the war, I knew not which war he meant, and told him so.

"There was a great thunderstorm last night," I added. "And you say you were out in one too. Perhaps Thor's hammer knocked you from your place to here."

"But where is here?" he replied. His voice was more dulled than otherwise, now that the first terror had lifted.

"I told you. This is Hillstead, which is on Iceland."

"But that's where I was!" he mumbled. "Reykjavik . . . what happened? Did the *aitchbomb* destroy everything while I was unconscious?"

"Nothing has been destroyed," I said.

"Perhaps he means the fire at Olafsvik last month," said Helgi.

"No, no no!" He buried his face in his hands. After a while he looked up and said, "See here. I am Sergeant Gerald Roberts of the United States Army base on Iceland. I was in Reykjavik and got struck by lightning or something. Suddenly I was standing on the beach, and got frightened and ran. That's all. Now, can you tell me how to get back to the base?"

Those were more or less his words, priest. Of course, we did not grasp half of it, and made him repeat it several times and explain the words. Even then we did not understand, except that he was from some country called the United States of America, which he said lies beyond Greenland to the west, and that he and some others were on Iceland to help our folk against their enemies. Now this I did not consider a lie— more a mistake or imagining. Grim would have cut him down for thinking us stupid enough to swallow that tale, but I could see that he meant it.

200

Trying to explain it to us cooled him off. "Look here," he said, in too reasonable a tone for a feverish man, "perhaps we can get at the truth from your side. Has there been no war you know of? Nothing which— well, look here. My country's men first came to Iceland to guard it against the Germans ... now it is the Russians, but then it was the Germans. When was that?"

Helgi shook his head. "That never happened that I know of," he said. "Who are these Russians?" He found out later that Gardariki was meant. "Unless," he said, "the old warlocks—"

"He means the Irish monks," I explained. "There were a few living here when the Norsemen came, but they were driven out. That was, hm, somewhat over a hundred years ago. Did your folk ever help the monks?"

"I never heard of them!" he said. His breath sobbed in his throat. "You ... didn't you Icelanders come from Norway?"

"Yes, about a hundred years ago," I answered patiently. "After King Herald Fairhair took all the Norse lands and—"

"A hundred years ago!" he whispered. I saw whiteness creep up under his skin. "What year is this?"

We gaped at him. "Well, it's the second year after the great salmon catch," I tried.

"What year after Christ, I mean?" It was a hoarse prayer.

"Oh, so you are a Christian? Hm, let me think ... I talked with a bishop in England once, we were holding him for ransom, and he said ... let me see ... I think he said this Christ man lived a thousand years ago, or maybe a little less."

"A thousand—" He shook his head; and then something went out of him, he stood with glassy eyes—yes, I have seen glass, I told you I am a traveled man—he stood thus, and when we led him toward the garth he went like a small child.

You can see for yourself, priest, that my wife Ragnhild is still good to look upon even in eld, and Thorgunna took after her. She was—is tall and slim, with a dragon's hoard of golden hair. She being a maiden then, it flowed loose over her shoulders. She had great blue eyes and a small heart-shaped face and very red lips. Withal she was a merry one, and kind-hearted, so that all men loved her. Sverri Snorrason went in viking when she refused and was slain, but no one had the wit to see that she was unlucky.

We led this Gerald Samsson—when I asked, he said his father was named Sam—we led him home, leaving Sigurd and Grim to finish gathering the driftwood. There are some who would not have a Christian in their house, for fear of witchcraft, but I am a broad-minded man and

Helgi, of course, was wild for anything new. Our guest stumbled like a blind man over the fields, but seemed to wake up as we entered the yard. His eyes went around the buildings that enclosed it, from the stables and sheds to the smokehouse, the brewery, the kitchen, the bathhouse, the god-shrine, and thence to the hall. And Thorgunna was standing in the doorway.

Their gazes locked for a moment, and I saw her color but thought little of it then. Our shoes rang on the flagging as we crossed the yard and kicked the dogs aside. My two thralls paused in cleaning out the stables to gawk, until I got them back to work with the remark that a man good for naught else was always a pleasing sacrifice. That's one useful practice you Christians lack; I've never made a human offering myself, but you know not how helpful is the fact that I could do so.

We entered the hall and I told the folk Gerald's name and how we had found him. Ragnhild set her maids hopping, to stoke up the fire in the middle trench and fetch beer, while I led Gerald to the high seat and sat down by him. Thorgunna brought us the filled horns.

Gerald tasted the brew and made a face. I felt somewhat offended, for my beer is reckoned good, and asked him if there was aught wrong. He laughed with a harsh note and said no, but he was used to beer that foamed and was not sour.

"And where might they make such?" I wondered testily.

"Everywhere. Iceland, too—no . . ." He stared emptily before him. "Let's say . . . in Vinland."

"Where is Vinland?" I asked.

"The country to the west whence I came. I thought you knew . . . wait a bit." He shook his head. "Maybe I can find out—have you heard of a man named Leif Eiriksson?"

"No," I said. Since then it has struck me that this was one proof of his tale, for Leif Eiriksson is now a well-known chief; and I also take more seriously those tales of land seen by Bjarni Herjulfsson.

"His father, maybe—Eirik the Red?" asked Gerald.

"Oh yes," I said. "If you mean the Norseman who came hither because of a manslaughter, and left Iceland in turn for the same reason, and has now settled with other folk in Greenland."

"Then this is . . . a little before Leif's voyage," he muttered. "The late tenth century."

"See here," demanded Helgi, "we've been patient with you, but this is no time for riddles. We save those for feasts and drinking bouts. Can you not say plainly whence you come and how you got here?"

Gerald covered his face, shaking.

"Let the man alone, Helgi," said Thorgunna. "Can you not see he's troubled?"

He raised his head and gave her the look of a hurt dog that someone has patted. It was dim in the hall, enough light coming in by the loft windows so no candles were lit, but not enough to see well by. Nevertheless, I marked a reddening in both their faces.

Gerald drew a long breath and fumbled about; his clothes were made with pockets. He brought out a small parchment box and from it took a little white stick that he put in his mouth. Then he took out another box, and a wooden stick from it which burst into flame when scratched. With the fire he kindled the stick in his mouth, and sucked in the smoke.

We all stared. "Is that a Christian rite?" asked Helgi.

"No . . . not just so." A wry, disappointed smile twisted his lips. "I'd have thought you'd be more surprised, even terrified."

"It's something new," I admitted, "but we're a sober folk on Iceland. Those fire sticks could be useful. Did you come to trade in them?"

"Hardly." He sighed. The smoke he breathed in seemed to steady him, which was odd, because the smoke in the hall had made him cough and water at the eyes. "The truth is . . . something you will not believe. I can scarce believe it myself."

We waited. Thorgunna stood leaning forward, her lips parted.

"That lightning bolt—" Gerald nodded wearily. "I was out in the storm, and somehow the lightning must have struck me in just the right way, a way that happens only once in many thousands of times. It threw me back into the past."

Those were his words, priest. I did not understand, and told him so.

"It's hard to see," he agreed. "God give that I'm only dreaming. But if this is a dream, I must endure till I wake up . . . well, look. I was born one thousand, nine hundred and thirty-two years after Christ, in a land to the west which you have not yet found. In the twenty-third year of my life, I was in Iceland as part of my country's army. The lightning struck me, and now . . . now it is less than one thousand years after Christ, and yet I am here—almost a thousand years before I was born, I am here!"

We sat very still. I signed myself with the Hammer and took a long pull from my horn. One of the maids whimpered, and Ragnhild whispered so fiercely I could hear. "Be still. The poor fellow's out of his head. There's no harm in him."

I agreed with her, though less sure of the last part of it. The gods can speak through a madman, and the gods are not always to be trusted. Or he could turn berserker, or he could be under a heavy curse that would also touch us.

He sat staring before him, and I caught a few fleas and cracked them while I thought about it. Gerald noticed and asked with some horror if we had many fleas here.

"Why, of course," said Thorgunna. "Have you none?"

"No." He smiled crookedly. "Not yet."

"Ah," she sighed, "you *must* be sick."

She was a level-headed girl. I saw her thought, and so did Ragnhild and Helgi. Clearly, a man so sick that he had no fleas could be expected to rave. There was still some worry about whether we might catch the illness, but I deemed it unlikely; his trouble was all in the head, perhaps from a blow he had taken. In any case, the matter was come down to earth now, something we could deal with.

As a godi, a chief who holds sacrifices, it behooved me not to turn a stranger out. Moreover, if he could fetch in many of those little fire-kindling sticks, a profitable trade might be built up. So I said Gerald should go to bed. He protested, but we manhandled him into the shut-bed and there he lay tired and was soon asleep. Thorgunna said she would take care of him.

The next day I decided to sacrifice a horse, both because of the timber we had found and to take away any curse there might be on Gerald. Furthermore, the beast I had picked was old and useless, and we were short of fresh meat. Gerald had spent the day lounging moodily around the garth, but when I came into supper I found him and my daughter laughing.

"You seem to be on the road to health," I said.

"Oh yes. It ... could be worse for me." He sat down at my side as the carles set up the trestle table and the maids brought in the food. "I was ever much taken with the age of the vikings, and I have some skills."

"Well," I said, "if you've no home, we can keep you here for a while."

"I can work," he said eagerly. "I'll be worth my pay."

Now I knew he was from a far land, because what chief would work on any land but his own, and for hire at that? Yet he had the easy manner of the highborn, and had clearly eaten well all his life. I overlooked that he had made no gifts; after all, he was shipwrecked.

"Maybe you can get passage back to your United States," said Helgi. "We could hire a ship. I'm fain to see that realm."

"No," said Gerald bleakly. "There is no such place. Not yet."

"So you still hold to that idea you came from tomorrow?" grunted Sigurd. "Crazy notion. Pass the pork."

"I do," said Gerald. There was a calm on him now. "And I can prove it."

"I don't see how you speak our tongue, if you come from so far away," I said. I could not call a man a liar to his face, unless we were swapping brags in a friendly way, but . . .

"They speak otherwise in my land and time," he replied, "but it happens that in Iceland the tongue changed little since the old days, and I learned it when I came there."

"If you are a Christian," I said, "you must bear with us while we sacrifice tonight."

"I've naught against that," he said. "I fear I never was a very good Christian. I'd like to watch. How is it done?"

I told him how I would smite the horse with a hammer before the god, and cut his throat, and sprinkle the blood about with willow twigs; thereafter we would butcher the carcass and feast. He said hastily:

"There's my chance to prove what I am. I have a weapon that will kill the horse with . . . with a flash of lightning."

"What is it?" I wondered. We all crowded around while he took the metal club out of his sheath and showed it to us. I had my doubts; it looked well enough for hitting a man, perhaps, but had no edge, though a wonderously skillful smith had forged it. "Well, we can try," I said.

He showed us what else he had in his pockets. There were some coins of remarkable roundness and sharpness, a small key, a stick with lead in it for writing, a flat purse holding many bits of marked paper; when he told us solemnly that some of this paper was money, even Thorgunna had to laugh. Best of all was a knife whose blade folded into the handle. When he saw me admiring that, he gave it to me, which was well done for a shipwrecked man. I said I would give him clothes and a good ax, as well as lodging for as long as needful.

No, I don't have the knife now. You shall hear why. It's a pity, for it was a good knife, though rather small.

"What were you ere the war arrow went out in your land?" asked Helgi. "A merchant?"

"No," said Gerald. "I was an . . . *engineer* . . . that is, I was learning how to be one. That's a man who builds things, bridges and roads and tools . . . more than just an artisan. So I think my knowledge could be of great value here." I saw a fever in his eyes. "Yes, give me time and I'll be a king!"

"We have no king in Iceland," I grunted. "Our forefathers came hither to get away from kings. Now we meet at the Things to try suits and pass new laws, but each man must get his own redress as best he can."

"But suppose the man in the wrong won't yield?" he asked.

"Then there can be a fine feud," said Helgi, and went on to relate with sparkling eyes some of the killings there had lately been. Gerald looked unhappy and fingered his *gun*. That is what he called his fire-spitting club.

"Your clothing is rich," said Thorgunna softly. "Your folk must own broad acres at home."

"No," he said, "our . . . our king gives every man in the army clothes like these. As for my family, we owned no land, we rented our home in a building where many other families also dwelt."

I am not purse-proud, but it seemed to me he had not been honest, a landless man sharing my high seat like a chief. Thorgunna covered my huffiness by saying, "You will gain a farm later."

After dark we went out to the shrine. The carles had built a fire before it, and as I opened the door the wooden Odin appeared to leap forth. Gerald muttered to my daughter that it was a clumsy bit of carving, and since my father had made it I was still more angry with him. Some folks have no understanding of the fine arts.

Nevertheless, I let him help me lead the horse forth to the altar stone. I took the blood-bowl in my hands and said he could now slay the beast if he would. He drew his gun, put the end behind the horse's ear, and squeezed. There was a crack, and the beast quivered and dropped with a hole blown through its skull, wasting the brains—a clumsy weapon. I caught a whiff of smell, sharp and bitter like that around a volcano. We all jumped, one of the women screamed, and Gerald looked proud. I gathered my wits and finished the rest of the sacrifice as usual. Gerald did not like having blood sprinkled over him, but then, of course, he was a Christian. Nor would he take more than a little of the soup and flesh.

Afterward Helgi questioned him about the *gun*, and he said it could kill a man at bowshot distance but there was no witchcraft in it, only use of some tricks we did not know as yet. Having heard of the Greek fire, I believed him. A *gun* could be useful in a fight, as indeed I was to learn, but it did not seem very practical—iron costing what it does, and months of forging needed for each one.

I worried more about the man himself.

And the next morning I found him telling Thorgunna a great deal of foolishness about his home, buildings tall as mountains and wagons that flew or went without horses. He said there were eight or nine thousand thousands of folk in his city, a burgh called New Jorvik or the like. I enjoy a good brag as well as the next man, but this was too much and I told him gruffly to come along and help me get in some strayed cattle.

After a day scrambling around the hills I knew well enough that Gerald could scarce tell a cow's prow from her stern. We almost had the strays

206

once, but he ran stupidly across their path and turned them so the work was all to do again. I asked him with strained courtesy if he could milk, shear, wield scythe or flail, and he said no, he had never lived on a farm.

"That's a pity," I remarked, "for everyone on Iceland does, unless he be outlawed."

He flushed at my tone. "I can do enough else," he answered. "Give me some tools and I'll show you metalwork well done."

That brightened me, for truth to tell, none of our household was a very gifted smith. "That's an honorable trade," I said, "and you can be of great help. I have a broken sword and several bent spearheads to be mended, and it were no bad idea to shoe all the horses." His admission that he did not know how to put on a shoe was not very dampening to me then.

We had returned home as we talked, and Thorgunna came angrily forward. "That's no way to treat a guest, father!" she said. "Making him work like a carle, indeed!"

Gerald smiled. "I'll be glad to work," he said. "I need a ... a stake ... something to start me afresh. Also, I want to repay a little of your kindness."

That made me mild toward him, and I said it was not his fault they had different customs in the United States. On the morrow he could begin work in the smithy, and I would pay him, yet he would be treated as an equal, since craftsmen are valued. This earned him black looks from the housefolk.

That evening he entertained us well with stories of his home; true or not, they made good listening. However, he had no real polish, being unable to compose even two lines of verse. They must be a raw and backward lot in the United States. He said his task in the army had been to keep order among the troops. Helgi said this was unheard-of, and he must be a brave man who would offend so many men, but Gerald said folk obeyed him out of fear of the king. When he added that the term of a levy in the United States was two years, and that men could be called to war even in harvest time, I said he was well out of a country with so ruthless and powerful a king.

"No," he answered wistfully, "we are a free folk, who say what we please."

"But it seems you may not do as you please," said Helgi.

"Well," he said, "we may not murder a man just because he offends us."

"Not even if he has slain your own kin?" asked Helgi.

"No. It is for the ... the king to take vengeance on behalf of us all."

I chuckled. "Your yarns are good," I said, "but there you've hit a snag. How could the king even keep track of all the murders, let alone avenge them? Why, the man wouldn't even have time to beget an heir!"

He could say no more for all the laughter that followed.

The next day Gerald went to the smithy, with a thrall to pump the bellows for him. I was gone that day and night, down to Reykjavik to dicker with Hjalmar Broadnose about some sheep. I invited him back for an overnight stay, and we rode into the garth with his son Ketill, a red-haired sulky youth of twenty winters who had been refused by Thorgunna.

I found Gerald sitting gloomily on a bench in the hall. He wore the clothes I had given him, his own having been spoiled by ash and sparks— what had he awaited, the fool? He was talking in a low voice with my daughter.

"Well," I said as I entered, "how went it?"

My man Grim snickered. "He has ruined two spearheads, but we put out the fire he started ere the whole smithy burned."

"How's this?" I cried. "I thought you said you were a smith."

Gerald stood up, defiantly. "I worked with other tools, and better ones, at home," he replied. "You do it differently here."

It seemed he had built up the fire too hot; his hammer had struck everywhere but the place it should; he had wrecked the temper of the steel through not knowing when to quench it. Smithcraft takes years to learn, of course, but he should have admitted he was not even an apprentice.

"Well," I snapped, "what can you do, then, to earn your bread?" It irked me to be made a fool of before Hjalmar and Ketill, whom I had told about the stranger.

"Odin alone knows," said Grim. "I took him with me to ride after your goats, and never have I seen a worse horseman. I asked him if he could even spin or weave, and he said no."

"That was no question to ask a man!" flared Thorgunna. "He should have slain you for it!"

"He should indeed," laughed Grim. "But let me carry on the tale. I thought we would also repair your bridge over the foss. Well, he can just barely handle a saw, but he nearly took his own foot off with the adz."

"We don't use those tools, I tell you!" Gerald doubled his fists and looked close to tears.

I motioned my guests to sit down. "I don't suppose you can butcher a hog or smoke it either," I said.

"No." I could scare hear him.

"Well, then, man . . . what *can* you do?"

"I—" He could get no words out.

"You were a warrior," said Thorgunna.

"Yes—that I was!" he said, his face kindling.

"Small use in Iceland when you have no other skills," I grumbled, "but perhaps, if you can get passage to the eastlands, some king will take you in his guard." Myself I doubted it, for a guardsman needs manners that will do credit to his master; but I had not the heart to say so.

Ketill Hjalmarsson had plainly not liked the way Thorgunna stood close to Gerald and spoke for him. Now he sneered and said: "I might even doubt your skill in fighting."

"That I have been trained for," said Gerald grimly.

"Will you wrestle with me then?" asked Ketill.

"Gladly!" spat Gerald.

Priest, what is a man to think? As I grow older, I find life to be less and less the good-and-evil, black-and-white thing you say it is; we are all of us some hue of gray. This useless fellow, this spiritless lout who could even be asked if he did women's work and not lift ax, went out in the yard with Ketill Hjalmarsson and threw him three times running. There was some trick he had of grabbing the clothes as Ketill charged . . . I called a stop when the youth was nearing murderous rage, praised them both, and filled the beer-horns. But Ketill brooded sullenly on the bench all evening.

Gerald said something about making a *gun* like his own. It would have to be bigger, a *cannon* he called it, and could sink ships and scatter armies. He would need the help of smiths, and also various stuffs. Charcoal was easy, and sulfur could be found in the volcano country, I suppose, but what is this saltpeter?

Also, being suspicious by now, I questioned him closely as to how he would make such a thing. Did he know just how to mix the powder? No, he admitted. What size would the *gun* have to be? When he told me—at least as long as a man—I laughed and asked him how a piece that size could be cast or bored, even if we could scrape together that much iron. This he did not know either.

"You haven't the tools to make the tools to make the tools," he said. I don't know what he meant by that. "God help me, I can't run through a thousand years of history all by myself."

He took out the last of his little smoke sticks and lit it. Helgi had tried a puff earlier and gotten sick, though he remained a friend of Gerald's. Now my son proposed to take a boat in the morning and go up to Ice Fjord, where I had some money outstanding I wanted to collect. Hjalmar and Ketill said they would come along for the trip, and Thorgunna pleaded so hard that I let her come along too.

"An ill thing," muttered Sigurd. "All men know the landtrolls like not a woman aboard a ship. It's unlucky."

"How did your father ever bring women to this island?" I grinned.

Now I wish I had listened to him. He was not a clever man, but he often knew whereof he spoke.

At this time I owned a half share in a ship that went to Norway, bartering wadmal for timber. It was a profitable business until she ran afoul of vikings during the disorders while Olaf Tryggvason was overthrowing Jarl Haakon there. Some men will do anything to make a living—thieves, cutthroats, they ought to be hanged, the worthless robbers pouncing on honest merchantmen. Had they any courage or honesty they would go to Ireland, which is full of plunder.

Well, anyhow, the ship was abroad, but we had three boats and took one of these. Besides myself, Thorgunna, and Helgi, Hjalmar and Ketill went along, with Grim and Gerald. I saw how the stranger winced at the cold water as we launched her, and afterward took off his shoes and stockings to let his feet dry. He had been surprised to learn we had a bathhouse—did he think us savages?—but still, he was dainty as a woman and soon moved upwind of our feet.

There was a favoring breeze, so we raised mast and sail. Gerald tried to help, but of course did not know one line from another and got them tangled. Grim snarled at him and Ketill laughed nastily. But erelong we were under way, and he came and sat by me where I had the steering oar.

He had plainly lain long awake thinking, and now he ventured timidly: "In my land they have . . . will have a rig and rudder which are better than this. With them, you can criss-cross against the wind."

"Ah, so now our skilled sailor must give us redes!" sneered Ketill.

"Be still," said Thorgunna sharply. "Let Gerald speak."

He gave her a sly look of thanks, and I was not unwilling to listen. "This is something which could easily be made," he said. "I've used such boats myself, and know them well. First, then, the sail should not be square and hung from a yardarm, but three-cornered, with the third corner lashed to a yard swiveling from the mast. Then, your steering oar is in the wrong place—there should be a rudder in the middle of the stern, guided by a bar." He was eager now, tracing the plan with his fingernail on Thorgunna's cloak. "With these two things, and a deep keel—going down to about the height of a man for a boat this size—a ship can move across the path of the wind . . . so. And another sail can be hung between the mast and the prow."

Well, priest, I must say the idea had its merits, and were it not for fear of bad luck—for everything of his was unlucky—I might even now play with it. But there are clear drawbacks, which I pointed out to him in a reasonable way.

"First and worst," I said, "this rudder and deep keel would make it all but impossible to beach the ship or sail up a shallow river. Perhaps they have many harbors where you hail from, but here a craft must take what landings she can find, and must be speedily launched if there should be an attack. Second, this mast of yours would be hard to unstep when the wind dropped and oars came out. Third, the sail is the wrong shape to stretch as an awning when one must sleep at sea."

"The ship could lie out, and you could go to land in a small boat," he said. "Also, you could build cabins aboard for shelter."

"The cabins would get in the way of the oars," I said, "unless the ship were hopelessly broad-beamed or unless the oarsmen sat below a deck like the galley slaves of Miklagard; and free men would not endure rowing in such foulness."

"Must you have oars?" he asked like a very child.

Laughter barked along the hull. Even the gulls hovering to starboard, where the shore rose darkly, mewed their scorn. "Do they also have tame winds in the place whence you came?" snorted Hjalmar. "What happens if you're becalmed—for days, maybe, with provisions running out—"

"You could build a ship big enough to carry many weeks' provisions," said Gerald.

"If you have the wealth of a king, you could," said Helgi. "And such a king's ship, lying helpless on a flat sea, would be swarmed by every viking from here to Jomsborg. As for leaving the ship out on the water while you make camp, what would you have for shelter, or for defense if you should be trapped there?"

Gerald slumped. Thorgunna said to him gently: "Some folks have no heart to try anything new. I think it's a grand idea."

He smiled at her, a weary smile, and plucked up the will to say something about a means for finding north even in cloudy weather—he said there were stones which always pointed north when hung by a string. I told him kindly that I would be most interested if he could find me some of this stone; or if he knew where it was to be had, I could ask a trader to fetch me a piece. But this he did not know, and fell silent. Ketill opened his mouth, but got such an edged look from Thorgunna that he shut it again; his looks declared plainly enough what a liar he thought Gerald to be.

The wind turned contrary after a while, so we lowered the mast and took to the oars. Gerald was strong and willing, though clumsy; however, his hands were so soft that erelong they bled. I offered to let him rest, but he kept doggedly at the work.

Watching him sway back and forth, under the dreary creak of the tholes, the shaft red and wet where he gripped it, I thought much about him. He had done everything wrong which a man could do—thus I imagined then, not knowing the future—and I did not like the way Thorgunna's eyes strayed to him and rested there. He was no man for my daughter, landless and penniless and helpless. Yet I could not keep from liking him. Whether his tale was true or only a madness, I felt he was honest about it; and surely there was something strange about the way he had come. I noticed the cuts on his chin from my razor; he had said he was not used to our kind of shaving and would grow a beard. He had tried hard. I wondered how well I would have done, landing alone in this witch country of his dreams, with a gap of forever between me and my home.

Perhaps that same misery was what had turned Thorgunna's heart. Women are a kittle breed, priest, and you who leave them alone belike understand them as well as I who have slept with half a hundred in six different lands. I do not think they even understand themselves. Birth and life and death, those are the great mysteries, which none will ever fathom, and a woman is closer to them than a man.

—The ill wind stiffened, the sea grew iron gray and choppy under low, leaden clouds, and our headway was poor. At sunset we could row no more, but must pull in to a small unpeopled bay and make camp as well as could be on the strand.

We had brought firewood along, and tinder. Gerald, though staggering with weariness, made himself useful, his little sticks kindling the blaze more easily than flint and steel. Thorgunna set herself to cook our supper. We were not warded by the boat from a lean, whining wind; her cloak fluttered like wings and her hair blew wild above the streaming flames. It was the time of light nights, the sky a dim dusky blue, the sea a wrinkled metal sheet and the land like something risen out of dream-mists. We men huddled in our cloaks, holding numbed hands to the fire and saying little.

I felt some cheer was needed, and ordered a cask of my best and strongest ale broached. An evil Norn made me do that, but no man escapes his weird. Our bellies seemed all the emptier now when our noses drank in the sputter of a spitted joint, and the ale went swiftly to our heads. I remember declaiming the death song of Ragnar Hairybreeks for no other reason than that I felt like declaiming it.

Thorgunna came to stand over Gerald where he slumped. I saw how her fingers brushed his hair, ever so lightly, and Ketill Hjalmarsson did too. "Have they no verses in your land?" she asked.

"Not like yours," he said, looking up. Neither of them looked away again. "We sing rather than chant. I wish I had my *guitar* here—that's a kind of harp."

"Ah, an Irish bard!" said Hjalmar Broadnose.

I remember strangely well how Gerald smiled, and what he said in his own tongue, though I know not the meaning: "*Only on me mither's side, begorra.*" I suppose it was magic.

"Well, sing for us," asked Thorgunna.

"Let me think," he said. "I shall have to put it in Norse words for you." After a little while, staring up at her through the windy night, he began a song. It had a tune I liked, thus:

> *From this valley they tell me you're leaving,*
> *I shall miss your bright eyes and sweet smile.*
> *You will carry the sunshine with you,*
> *That has brightened my life all the while . . .*

I don't remember the rest, except that it was not quite decent.

When he had finished, Hjalmar and Grim went over to see if the meat was done. I saw a glimmering of tears in my daughter's eyes. "That was a lovely thing," she said.

Ketill sat upright. The flames splashed his face with wild, running hues. There was a rawness in his tone: "Yes, we've found what this fellow can do: sit about and make pretty songs for the girls. Keep him for that, Ospak."

Thorgunna whitened, and Helgi clapped hand to sword. I saw how Gerald's face darkened, and his voice was thick: "That was no way to talk. Take it back."

Ketill stood up. "No," he said, "I'll ask no pardon of an idler living off honest yeomen."

He was raging, but he had sense enough to shift the insult from my family to Gerald alone. Otherwise he and his father would have had the four of us to deal with. As it was, Gerald stood up too, fists knotted at his sides, and said, "Will you step away from here and settle this?"

"Gladly!" Ketill turned and walked a few yards down the beach, taking his shield from the boat. Gerald followed. Thorgunna stood with stricken face, then picked up his ax and ran after him.

"Are you going weaponless?" she shrieked.

Gerald stopped, looking dazed. "I don't want that," he mumbled. "Fists—"

Ketill puffed himself up and drew sword. "No doubt you're used to fighting like thralls in your land," he said. "So if you'll crave my pardon, I'll let this matter rest."

Gerald stood with drooped shoulders. He stared at Thorgunna as if he were blind, as if asking her what to do. She handed him the ax.

"So you want me to kill him?" he whispered.

"Yes," she answered.

Then I knew she loved him, for otherwise why should she have cared if he disgraced himself?

Helgi brought him his helmet. He put it on, took the ax, and went forward.

"Ill is this," said Hjalmar to me. "Do you stand by the stranger, Ospak?"

"No," I said. "He's no kin or oath-brother of mine. This is not my quarrel."

"That's good," said Hjalmar. "I'd not like to fight with you, my friend. You were ever a good neighbor."

We went forth together and staked out the ground. Thorgunna told me to lend Gerald my sword, so he could use a shield too, but the man looked oddly at me and said he would rather have the ax. They squared away before each other, he and Ketill, and began fighting.

This was no holmgang, with rules and a fixed order of blows and first blood meaning victory. There was death between those two. Ketill rushed in with the sword whistling in his hand. Gerald sprang back, wielding the ax awkwardly. It bounced off Ketill's shield. The youth grinned and cut at Gerald's legs. I saw blood well forth and stain the ripped breeches.

It was murder from the beginning. Gerald had never used an ax before. Once he even struck with the flat of it. He would have been hewed down at once had Ketill's sword not been blunted on his helmet and had he not been quick on his feet. As it was, he was soon lurching with a dozen wounds.

"Stop the fight!" Thorgunna cried aloud and ran forth. Helgi caught her arms and forced her back, where she struggled and kicked till Grim must help. I saw grief on my son's face but a malicious grin on the carle's.

Gerald turned to look. Ketill's blade came down and slashed his left hand. He dropped the ax. Ketill snarled and readied to finish him. Gerald drew his *gun*. It made a flash and a barking noise. Ketill fell, twitched for a moment, and was quiet. His lower jaw was blown off and the back of his head gone.

214

There came a long stillness, where only the wind and the sea had voice.

Then Hjalmar trod forth, his face working but a cold steadiness over him. He knelt and closed his son's eyes, as token that the right of vengeance was his. Rising, he said. "That was an evil deed. For that you shall be outlawed."

"It wasn't magic," said Gerald in a numb tone. "It was like a . . . a bow. I had no choice. I didn't want to fight with more than my fists."

I trod between them and said the Thing must decide this matter, but that I hoped Hjalmar would take weregild for Ketill.

"But I killed him to save my own life!" protested Gerald.

"Nevertheless, weregild must be paid, if Ketill's kin will take it," I explained. "Because of the weapon, I think it will be doubled, but that is for the Thing to judge."

Hjalmar had many other sons, and it was not as if Gerald belonged to a family at odds with his own, so I felt he would agree. However, he laughed coldly and asked where a man lacking wealth would find the silver.

Thorgunna stepped up with a wintry calm and said we would pay it. I opened my mouth, but when I saw her eyes I nodded. "Yes, we will," I said, "in order to keep the peace."

"Then you make this quarrel your own?" asked Hjalmar.

"No," I answered. "This man is no blood of my own. But if I choose to make him a gift of money to use as he wishes, what of it?"

Hjalmar smiled. There was sorrow crinkled around his eyes, but he looked on me with old comradeship.

"Erelong this man may be your son-in-law," he said. "I know the signs, Ospak. Then indeed he will be of your folk. Even helping him now in his need will range you on his side."

"And so?" asked Helgi, most softly.

"And so, while I value your friendship, I have sons who will take the death of their brother ill. They'll want revenge on Gerald Samsson, if only for the sake of their good names, and thus our two houses will be sundered and one manslaying will lead to another. It has happened often enough erenow." Hjalmar sighed. "I myself wish peace with you, Ospak, but if you take this killer's side it must be otherwise."

I thought for a moment, thought of Helgi lying with his skull cloven, of my other sons on their garths drawn to battle because of a man they had never seen, I thought of having to wear byrnies every time we went down for driftwood and never knowing when we went to bed whether we would wake to find the house ringed in by spearmen.

"Yes," I said, "you are right, Hjalmar. I withdraw my offer. Let this be a matter between you and him alone."

We gripped hands on it.

Thorgunna gave a small cry and fled into Gerald's arms. He held her close. "What does this mean?" he asked slowly.

"I cannot keep you any longer," I said, "but belike some crofter will give you a roof. Hjalmar is a law-abiding man and will not harm you until the Thing has outlawed you. That will not be before midsummer. Perhaps you can get passage out of Iceland ere then."

"A useless one like me?" he replied bitterly.

Thorgunna whirled free and blazed that I was a coward and a perjurer and all else evil. I let her have it out, then laid my hands on her shoulders.

"It is for the house," I said. "The house and the blood, which are holy. Men die and women weep, but while the kindered live our names are remembered. Can you ask a score of men to die for your own hankerings?"

Long did she stand, and to this day I know not what her answer would have been. It was Gerald who spoke.

"No," he said. "I suppose you have right, Ospak ... the right of your time, which is not mine." He took my hand, and Helgi's. His lips brushed Thorgunna's cheek. Then he turned and walked out into the darkness.

I heard, later, that he went to earth with Thorvald Hallsson, the crofter of Humpback Fell, and did not tell his host what had happened. He must have hoped to go unnoticed until he could arrange passage to the eastlands somehow. But of course word spread. I remember his brag that in the United States men had means to talk from one end of the land to another. So he must have looked down on us, sitting on our lonely garths, and not know how fast word could get around. Thorvald's son, Hrolf, went to Brand Sealskin-boots to talk about some matter, and of course mentioned the stranger, and soon all the western island had the tale.

Now if Gerald had known he must give notice of a manslaying at the first garth he found, he would have been safe at least till the Thing met, for Hjalmar and his sons are sober men who would not kill a man still under the protection of the law. But as it was, his keeping the matter secret made him a murderer and therefore at once an outlaw. Hjalmar and his kin rode up to Humpback Fell and haled him forth. He shot his way past them with the *gun* and fled into the hills. They followed him, having several hurts and one more death to avenge. I wonder if Gerald thought the strangeness of his weapon would unnerve us. He may not have known that every man dies when his time comes, neither sooner nor later, so that fear of death is useless.

At the end, when they had him trapped, his weapon gave out on him. Then he took up a dead man's sword and defended himself so valiantly that Ulf Hjalmarsson has limped ever since. It was well done, as even his foes admitted; they are an eldritch race in the United States, but they do not lack manhood.

When he was slain, his body was brought back. For fear of the ghost, he having perhaps been a warlock, it was burned, and all he had owned was laid in the fire with him. That was where I lost the knife he had given me. The barrow stands out on the moor, north of here, and folk shun it, though the ghost has not walked. Now, with so much else happening, he is slowly being forgotten.

And that is the tale, priest, as I saw it and heard it. Most men think Gerald Samsson was crazy, but I myself believed he did come from out of time, and that his doom was that no man may ripen a field before harvest season. Yet I look into the future, a thousand years hence, when they fly through the air and ride in horseless wagons and smash whole cities with one blow. I think of this Iceland then, and of the young United States men there to help defend us in a year when the end of the world hovers close. Perhaps some of them, walking about on the heaths, will see that barrow and wonder what ancient warrior lies buried there, and they may even wish they had lived long ago in his time when men were free.

FOR DISCUSSION: **The Man Who Came Early**

1. This story is told after its events have occurred by a participant in those events. Nevertheless, the story possesses a sense of immediacy. How does the author achieve this effect even though the events being described took place five years ago?
2. Foreshadowing later events in a story is a literary technique. An example of foreshadowing is Gerald's fight with Ketill in which he throws Ketill "three times running." This incident foreshadows Gerald's eventual death. Can you explain the meaning of foreshadowing as a literary technique?
3. One character in the story provides an opportunity for the flaring of emotion that contributes to Gerald's death. Who is that character and what is the emotion involved?
4. This is clearly an adventure story. It offers the reader excitement and thrills. It also gives him facts concerning another age with which

he may not have been familiar. How many areas of Icelandic daily life in the tenth century are touched upon? What have you learned about such things as Icelandic law and religion in the tenth century from reading this story?

5. Does the fact that the author chose a soldier to return in time carry any significance in terms of the events of the story?

INTRODUCTION: Soldier

Like "The Man Who Came Early," this story is about a soldier plucked out of his own time. The previous story took a soldier from "today" and returned him to "yesterday." This story takes a soldier from "tomorrow" and returns him to "today."

Both stories have similarities. Both are different from one another. Both succeed in entertaining the reader while presenting points of view concerning interpersonal strife which, when sufficiently magnified, becomes war between nations.

Soldier
by Harlan Ellison

Qarlo hunkered down further into the firmhole, gathering his cloak about him. Even the triple-lining of the cape could not prevent the seeping cold of the battlefield from reaching him; and even through one of those linings—lead impregnated—he could feel the faint tickle of dropout, all about him, eating at his tissues. He began to shiver again. The Push was going on to the South, and he had to wait, had to listen for the telepathic command of his superior officer.

He fingered an edge of the firmhole, noting he had not steadied it up too well with the firmer. He drew the small molecule-hardening instrument from his pouch, and examined it. The calibrator had slipped a notch, which explained why the dirt of the firmhole had not become as hard as he had desired.

Off to the left the hiss of an eighty-thread beam split the night air, and he shoved the firmer back quickly. The spider-web tracery of the beam lanced across the sky, poked tentatively at an armor center, throwing blood-red shadows across Qarlo's crag-like features.

The armor center backtracked the thread beam, retaliated with a blinding flash of its own batteries. One burst. Two. Three. The eighty-thread reared once more, feebly, then subsided. A moment later the concussion of its power chambers exploding shook the earth around Qarlo, causing bits of unfirmed dirt and small pebbles to tumble in on him. Another moment, and the shrapnel came through.

Qarlo lay flat on the ground, soundlessly hoping for a bit more life

amidst all this death. He knew his chances of coming back were infinitesimal. What was it? Three out of every thousand came back? He
had no illusions. He was a common footman, and he knew he would die
out here, in the midst of the Great War VII.

As though the detonation of the eighty-thread had been a signal, the
weapons of Qarlo's company opened up, full-on. The webbings criss-
crossed the blackness overhead with delicate patterns—appearing, disappearing, changing with every second, ranging through the spectrum,
washing the bands of colors outside the spectrum Qarlo could catalog.
Qarlo slid into a tiny ball in the slush-filled bottom of the firmhole,
waiting.

He was a good soldier. He knew his place. When those metal and
energy beasts out there were snarling at each other, there was nothing a
lone foot soldier could do—but die. He waited, knowing his time would
come much too soon. No matter how violent, how involved, how push-
button-ridden wars became, it always simmered down to the man on
foot. It had to, for men fought men still.

His mind dwelled limply in a state between reflection and alertness. A
state all men of war came to know when there was nothing but the thunder of the big guns abroad in the night.

The stars had gone into hiding.

Abruptly, the thread beams cut out, the traceries winked off, silence
once again descended. Qarlo snapped to instant attentiveness. This was
the moment. His mind was now keyed to one sound, one only. Inside
his head the command would form, and he would act; not entirely of his
own volition. The strategists and psychmen had worked together on this
thing: the tone of command was keyed into each soldier's brain. Printed
in, probed in, sunken in. It was there, and when the Regimenter sent his
telepathic orders, Qarlo would leap like a puppet, and advance on direction.

Thus, when it came, it was as though he had anticipated it; as though
he knew a second before the mental rasping and the *Advance!* erupted
within his skull, that the moment had arrived.

A second sooner than he should have been, he was up, out of the firmhole, hugging his Brandelmeier to his chest, the weight of the plastic
bandoliers and his pouch reassuring across his stomach, back, and hips.
Even before the mental word actually came.

Because of this extra moment's jump on the command, it happened,
and it happened just that way. No other chance coincidences could have
done it, but done just that way.

When the first blasts of the enemy's zeroed-in batteries met the combined rays of Qarlo's own guns, also pin-pointed, they met at a point that

should by all rights have been empty. But Qarlo had jumped too soon, and when they met, the soldier was at the focal point.

Three hundred distinct beams latticed down, joined in a coruscating rainbow, threw negatively charged particles five hundred feet in the air, shorted out . . . and warped the soldier off the battlefield.

Nathan Schwachter had his heart attack right there on the subway platform.

The soldier materialized in front of him, from nowhere, filthy and ferocious-looking, a strange weapon cradled to his body . . . just as the old man was about to put a penny in the candy machine.

Qarlo's long cape was still, the dematerialization and subsequent re-appearance having left him untouched. He stared in confusion at the sallow face before him, and started violently at the face's piercing shriek.

Qarlo watched with growing bewilderment and terror as the sallow face contorted and sank to the littered floor of the platform. The old man clutched his chest, twitched and gasped several times. His legs jerked spasmodically, and his mouth opened wildly again and again. He died with mouth open, eyes staring at the ceiling.

Qarlo looked at the body disinterestedly for a moment; death . . . what did one death matter . . . every day during the War, ten thousand died . . . more horribly than this . . . this was as nothing to him.

The sudden universe-filling scream of an incoming express train broke his attention. The black tunnel that his war-filled world had become, was filled with the rusty wail of an unseen monster, bearing down on him out of the darkness.

The fighting man in him made his body arch, sent it into a crouch. He poised on the balls of his feet, his rifle levering horizontal instantly, pointed at the sound.

From the crowds packed on the platform, a voice rose over the thunder of the incoming train:

"*Him!* It was *him!* He shot that old man . . . he's crazy!" Heads turned; eyes stared; a little man with a dirty vest, his bald head reflecting the glow of the overhead lights, was pointing a shaking finger at Qarlo.

It was as if two currents had been set up simultaneously. The crowd both drew away and advanced on him. Then the train barreled around the curve, drove past, blasting sound into the very fibers of the soldier's body. Qarlo's mouth opened wide in a soundless scream, and more from reflex than intent, the Brandelmeier erupted in his hands.

A triple-thread of cold blue beams sizzled from the small bellmouth of the weapon, streaked across the tunnel, and blasted full into the front of the train.

The front of the train melted down quickly, and the vehicle ground to a stop. The metal had been melted like a coarse grade of plastic on a burner. Where it had fused into a soggy lump, the metal was bright and smeary—more like the gleam of oxidized silver than anything else.

Qarlo regretted having fired the moment he felt the Brandelmeier buck. He was not where he should be—*where* he was, that was still another, more pressing problem—and he knew he was in danger. Every movement had to be watched as carefully as possible . . . and perhaps he had gotten off to a bad start already. But that noise . . .

He had suffered the screams of the battlefield, but the reverberations of the train, thundering back and forth in that enclosed space, was a nightmare of indescribable horror.

As he stared dumbly at his handiwork, from behind him, the crowd made a concerted rush.

Three burly, charcoal-suited executives—each carrying an attaché case which he dropped as he made the lunge, looking like unhealthy carbon-copies of each other—grabbed Qarlo above the elbows, around the waist, about the neck.

The soldier roared something unintelligible and flung them from him. One slid across the platform on the seat of his pants, bringing up short, his stomach and face smashing into a tiled wall. The second spun away, arms flailing, into the crowd. The third tried to hang onto Qarlo's neck. The soldier lifted him bodily, arched him over his head—breaking the man's insecure grip—and pitched him against a stanchion. The executive hit the girder, slid down, and lay quite still, his back oddly twisted.

The crowd emitted scream after scream, drew away once more. Terror rippled back through its ranks. Several women, near the front, suddenly became aware of the blood pouring from the face of one of the executives, and keeled onto the dirty platform unnoticed. The screams continued, seeming echoes of the now-dead express train's squealing.

But as an entity, the crowd backed the soldier down the platform. For a moment Qarlo forgot he still held the Brandelmeier. He lifted the gun to a threatening position, and the entity that was the crowd pulsed back.

Nightmare! It was all some sort of vague, formless nightmare to Qarlo. This was not the war, where anyone he saw, he blasted. This was something else, some other situation, in which he was lost, disoriented. What was happening?

Qarlo moved toward the wall, his back prickly with fear sweat. He had expected to die in the war, but something as simple and direct and expected as that had not happened. He was *here*, not *there*—wherever *here* was, and wherever *there* had gone—and these people were unarmed, obviously civilians. Which would not have kept him from murdering them . . . but what was happening? Where was the battlefield?

His progress toward the wall was halted momentarily as he backed cautiously around a stanchion. He knew there were people behind him, as well as the white-faced knots before him, and he was beginning to suspect there was no way out. Such confusion boiled up in his thoughts, so close to hysteria was he—plain soldier of the fields—that his mind forcibly rejected the impossibility of being somehow transported from the War into this new—and in many ways more terrifying—situation. He concentrated on one thing only, as a good soldier should. *Out!*

He slid along the wall, the crowd flowing before him, opening at his approach, closing in behind. He whirled once, driving them back further with the black hole of the Brandelmeier's bell mouth. Again he hesitated (not kowing why) to fire upon them.

He sensed they were enemies. But still they were unarmed. And yet, that had never stopped him before. The village in TetraOmsk Territory, beyond the Volga somewhere. They had been unarmed there, too, but the square had been filled with civilians he had not hesitated to burn. Why was he hesitating now?

The Brandelmeier continued in its silence.

Qarlo detected a commotion behind the crowd, above the crowd's inherent commotion. And a movement. Something was happening there. He backed tightly against the wall as a blue-suited, brass-buttoned man broke through the crowd.

The man took one look, caught the unwinking black eye of the Brandelmeier, and threw his arms back, indicating to the crowd to clear away. He began screaming at the top of his lungs, veins standing out in his temples, "Geddoudahere! The guy's a cuckaboo! Somebody'll get kilt! Beat it, run!"

The crowd needed no further impetus. It broke in the center and streamed toward the stairs.

Qarlo swung around, looking for another way out, but both accessible stairways were clogged by fighting commuters, shoving each other mercilessly to get out. He was effectively trapped.

The cop fumbled at his holster. Qarlo caught a glimpse of the movement from the corner of his eye. Instinctively he knew the movement for what it was; a weapon was about to be brought into use. He swung about, leveling the Brandelmeier. The cop jumped behind a stanchion just as the soldier pressed the firing stud.

A triple-thread of bright blue energy leaped from the weapon's bell mouth. The beam went over the heads of the crowd, neatly melting away a five-foot segment of wall supporting one of the stairways. The stairs creaked, and the sound of tortured metal adjusting to poor support and an overcrowding of people, rang through the tunnel. The cop looked fearfully above himself, saw the beams curving, then settle under the weight, and turned a wide-eyed stare back at the soldier.

The cop fired twice from behind the stanchion, the booming of the explosions catapulting back and forth in the enclosed space.

The second bullet took the soldier above the wrist in his left arm. The Brandelmeier slipped uselessly from his good hand, as blood stained the garment he wore. He stared at his shattered lower arm in amazement. Doubled amazement.

What manner of weapon was this the blue-coated man had used? No beam, that. Nothing like anything he had ever seen before. No beam to fry him in his tracks. It was some sort of power that hurled a projectile ... that had ripped his body. He stared stupidly as blood continued to flow out of his arm.

The cop, less anxious now to attack this man with the weird costume and unbelievable rifle, edged cautiously from behind his cover, skirting the edge of the platform, trying to get near enough to Qarlo to put another bullet into him, should he offer further resistance. But the soldier continued to stand, spraddle-legged, staring at his wound, confused at where he was, what had happened to him, the screams of the trains as they bulleted past, and the barbarian tactics of his blue-coated adversary.

The cop moved slowly, steadily, expecting the soldier to break and run at any moment. The wounded man stood rooted, however. The cop bunched his muscles and leaped the few feet intervening.

Savagely, he brought the barrel of his pistol down on the side of Qarlo's neck, near the ear. The soldier turned slowly, anchored in his tracks, and stared unbelievingly at the policeman for an instant.

Then his eyes glazed, and he collapsed to the platform.

As a grey, swelling mist bobbed up around his mind, one final thought impinged incongruously: *he struck me ... physical contact? I don't believe it!*

What have I gotten into?

Light filtered through vaguely. Shadows slithered and wavered, sullenly formed into solids.

"Hey, Mac. Got a light?"

Shadows blocked Qarlo's vision, but he knew he was lying on his back, staring up. He turned his head, and a wall oozed into focus, almost at his nose tip. He turned his head the other way. Another wall, about three feet away, blending in his sight into a shapeless grey blotch. He abruptly realized the back of his head hurt. He moved slowly, swiveling his head, but the soreness remained. Then he realized he was lying on some hard metal surface, and he tried to sit up. The pains throbbed higher, making him feel nauseated, and for an instant his vision receded again.

Then it steadied, and he sat up slowly. He swung his legs over the sharp edge of what appeared to be a shallow, sloping, metal trough. It was a mattressless bunk, curved in its bottom, from hundreds of men who had lain there before him.

He was in a cell.

"Hey! I said you got a match there?"

Qarlo turned from the empty rear wall of the cell and looked through the bars. A bulb-nosed face was thrust up close to the metal barrier. The man was short, in filthy rags whose odor reached Qarlo with tremendous offensiveness. The man's eyes were bloodshot, and his nose was criss-crossed with blue and red veins. Acute alcoholism, reeking from every pore; *acne rosacea* that had turned his nose into a hideous, cracked and pocked blob.

Qarlo knew he was in detention, and from the very look, the very smell of this other, he knew he was not in a military prison. The man was staring in at him, oddly.

"Match, Charlie? You got a match?" he puffed his fat, wet lips at Qarlo, forcing the bit of cigarette stub forward with his mouth. Qarlo stared back; he could not understand the man's words. They were so slowly spoken, so sharp and yet unintelligible. But he knew what to answer.

"Marnames Qarlo Clobregnny, pyrt, sizfifwunohtootoonyn," the soldier muttered by rote, surly tones running together.

"Whaddaya mad at *me* for, buddy? I didn't putcha in here," argued the match-seeker. "All I wanted was a light for this here butt." He held up two inches of smoked stub. "How come they gotcha inna cell, and not runnin' around loose inna bull pen like us?" he cocked a thumb over his shoulder, and for the first time Qarlo realized others were in this jail.

"Ah, ta hell wit ya," the drunk muttered. He cursed again, softly under his breath, turning away. He walked across the bull pen and sat down with the four other men—all vaguely similar in facial content—who lounged around a rough-hewn table-bench combination. The table and benches, all one piece, like a picnic table, were bolted to the floor.

"A screwloose," the drunk said to the others, nodding his balding head at the soldier in his long cape and metallic skin tight suit. He picked up the crumpled remnants of an ancient magazine and leafed through it as though he knew every line of type, every girlie illustration, by heart.

Qarlo looked over the cell. It was about ten feet high by eight across, a sink with one thumb-push spigot running cold water, a commode without seat or paper, and metal trough, roughly the dimensions of an average-sized man, fastened to one wall. One enclosed bulb burned feebly in the ceiling. Three walls of solid steel. Ceiling and floor of the same, riveted together at the seams. The fourth wall was the barred door.

The firmer might be able to wilt that steel, he realized, and instinctively reached for his pouch. It was the first moment he had had a chance to think of it, and even as he reached, knew the satisfying weight of it was gone. His bandoliers also. His Brandelmeier, of course. His boots, too, and there seemed to have been some attempt to get his cape off, but it was all part of the skintight suit of metallic-mesh cloth.

The loss of the pouch was too much. Everything that had happened, had happened so quickly, so blurrily meshed, and the soldier was abruptly overcome by confusion and a deep feeling of hopelessness. He sat down on the bunk, the ledge of metal biting into his thighs. His head still ached from a combination of the blow dealt him by the cop, and the metal bunk where he had lain. He ran a shaking hand over his head, feeling the fractional inch of his brown hair, cut battle-style. Then he noticed that his left hand had been bandaged quite expertly. There was hardly any throbbing from his wound.

That brought back to sharp awareness all that had transpired, and the war leaped into his thoughts. The telepathic command, the rising from the firmhole, the rifle at the ready . . .

. . . then a sizzling shussssss, and the universe had exploded around him in a billion tiny flickering novas of color and color and color. Then suddenly, just as suddenly as he had been standing on the battlefield of Great War VII, advancing on the enemy forces of Ruskie-Chink, he was *not* there.

He was here.

He was in some dark, hard tunnel, with a great beast roaring out of the blackness onto him, and a man in a blue coat had shot him, and clubbed him. Actually *touched* him! Without radiation gloves! How had the man known Qarlo was not booby-trapped with radiates? He could have died in an instant.

Where was he? What war was this he was engaged in? Were these Ruskie-Chink or his own Tri-Continenters? He did not know, and there was no sign of an explanation.

Then he thought of something more important. If he had been captured, then they must want to question him. There was a way to combat *that*, too. He felt around in the hollow tooth toward the back of his mouth. His tongue touched each tooth till it hit the right lower bicuspid. It was empty. The poison glob was gone, he realized in dismay. *It must have dropped out when the blue-coat clubbed me,* he thought.

He realized he was at *their* mercy; who *they* might be was another thing to worry about. And with the glob gone, he had no way to stop their extracting information. It was bad. Very bad, according to the warning conditioning he had received. They could use Probers, or dyoxlscopalite, or hypno-scourge, or any one of a hundred different methods, any one of which would reveal to them the strength of numbers in his company, the battery placements, the gun ranges, the identity and thought wave band of every officer . . . in fact, a good deal. More than he thought he knew.

He had become a very important prisoner of war. He *had* to hold out, he realized!

Why?

The thought popped up, and was gone. All it left in its wake was the intense feeling: I despise war, all war and *the* war! Then, even that was gone, and he was alone with the situation once more, to try and decide what had happened to him . . . what secret weapon had been used to capture him . . . and if these unintelligible barbarians with the projectile weapons *could*, indeed, extract his knowledge from him.

I swear they won't get anything out of me but my name, rank, and serial number, he thought desperately.

He mumbled those particulars aloud, as reassurance: "Marnames Qarlo Clobregnny, pryt, sixfifwunohtootoonyn."

The drunks looked up from their table and their shakes, at the sound of his voice. The man with the rosedrop nose rubbed a dirty hand across fleshy chin folds, repeated his philosophy of the strange man in the locked cell.

"Screwloose!"

He might have remained in jail indefinitely, considered a madman or a mad rifleman. But the desk sergeant who had booked him, after the soldier had received medical attention, grew curious about the strangely shaped weapon.

As he put the things into security, he tested the Brandelmeier—hardly realizing what knob or stud controlled its power, never realizing what it could do—and melted away one wall of the safe room. Three-inch plate steel, and it melted bluely, fused solidly.

He called the Captain, and the Captain called the F.B.I., and the F.B.I. called Internal Security, and Internal Security said, "Preposterous!" and checked back. When the Brandelmeier had been thoroughly tested

—as much as *could* be tested, since the rifle had no seams, no apparent power source, and fantastic range—they were willing to believe. They had the soldier removed from his cell, transported along with the pouch and a philologist named Soames, to the I.S. general headquarters in Washington, D.C. The Brandelmeier came by jet courier, and the soldier was flown in by helicopter, under sedation. The philologist named Soames, whose hair was long and rusty, whose face was that of a starving artist, whose temperament was that of a saint, came in by specially chartered plane from Columbia University. The pouch was sent by sealed Brink's truck to the airport, where it was delivered under heaviest guard to a mail plane. They all arrived in Washington within ten minutes of one another, and without seeing anything of the surrounding countryside, were whisked away to the subsurface levels of the I.S. Buildings.

When Qarlo came back to consciousness, he found himself again in a cell, this time quite unlike the first. No bars, but just as solid to hold him in, with padded walls. Qarlo paced around the cell a few times, seeking breaks in the walls, and found what was obviously a door, in one corner. But he could not work his fingers between the pads, to try and open it.

He sat down on the padded floor, and rubbed the bristled top of his head in wonder. Was he *never* to find out what had happened to himself? And *when* was he going to shake this strange feeling that he was being watched?

Overhead, through a pane of one-way glass that looked like a ventilator grille, the soldier was being watched.

Lyle Sims and his secretary knelt before the window in the floor, along with the philologist named Soames. Where Soames was shaggy, ill-kempt, hungry-looking and placid... Lyle Sims was lean, collegiate-seeming, brusque and brisk. He had been special advisor to an unnamed branch office of Internal Security for five years, dealing with every strange or offbeat problem too outré for regulation inquiry. Those years had hardened him in an odd way; he was quick to recognize authenticity, even quicker to recognize fakery.

As he watched, his trained instincts took over completely, and he knew in a moment of spying, that the man in the cell below was out of the ordinary. Not so in any fashion that could be labeled—"drunkard," "foreigner," "psychotic"—but so markedly different, so *other* he was taken aback.

"Six feet three inches," he recited to the girl kneeling beside him. She made the notation on her pad, and he went on calling out characteristics of the soldier below. "Brown hair, clipped so short you can see the scalp. Brown... no, black eyes. Scars. Above the left eye, running down to

228

center of left cheek; bridge of nose; three parallel scars on the right side of chin; tiny one over right eyebrow; last one I can see, runs from back of left ear, into hairline.

"He seems to be wearing an all-over, skintight suit something like, oh, I suppose it's like a pair of what do you call those pajamas kids wear ... the kind with the back door, the kind that enclose the feet?"

The girl inserted softly, "You mean snuggies?"

The man nodded, slightly embarrassed for no good reason, continued, "Mmm. Yes, that's right. Like those. The suit encloses his feet, seems to be joined to the cape, and comes up to his neck. Seems to be some sort of metallic cloth.

"Something else ... may mean nothing at all, or on the other hand ..." he pursed his lips for a moment, then described his observation carefully. "His head seems to be oddly shaped. The forehead is larger than most, seems to be pressing forward in front, as though he had been smacked hard and it was swelling. That seems to be everything."

Sims settled back on his haunches, fished in his side pocket, and came up with a small pipe, which he cold-puffed in thought for a second. He rose slowly, still staring down through the floor window. He murmured something to himself, and when Soames asked what he had said, the special advisor repeated, "I think we've got something almost too hot to handle."

Soames clucked knowingly, and gestured toward the window. "Have you been able to make out anything he's said yet?"

Sims shook his head. "No. That's why you're here. It seems he's saying the same thing, over and over, but it's completely unintelligible. Doesn't seem to be any recognizable language, or any dialect we've been able to pin down."

"I'd like to take a try at him," Soames said, smiling gently. It was the man's nature that challenge brought satisfaction; solutions brought unrest, eagerness for a new, more rugged problem.

Sims nodded agreement, but there was a tense, strained film over his eyes, in the set of his mouth. "Take it easy with him, Soames. I have a strong hunch this is something completely new, something we haven't even begun to understand."

Soames smiled again, this time indulgently. "Come, come, Mr. Sims. After all ... he *is* only an alien of some sort ... all we have to do is find out what country he's from."

"Have you heard him talk yet?"

Soames shook his head.

"Then don't be too quick to think he's just a foreigner. The word *alien* may be more correct than you think—only not in the *way* you think."

A confused look spread across Soames's face. He gave a slight shrug, as though he could not fathom what Lyle Sims meant . . . and was not particularly interested. He patted Sims reassuringly, which brought an expression of annoyance to the advisor's face, and he clamped down on the pipestem harder.

They walked downstairs together; the secretary left them to type her notes, and Sims let the philologist into the padded room, cautioning him to deal gently with the man. "Don't forget," Sims warned, "we're not sure *where* he comes from, and sudden movements may make him jumpy. There's a guard overhead, and there'll be a man with me behind this door, but you never know."

Soames looked startled. "You sound as though he's an aborigine or something. With a suit like that, he *must* be very intelligent. You suspect something, don't you?"

Sims made a neutral motion with his hands. "What I suspect is too nebulous to worry about now. Just take it easy . . . and above all, figure out what he's saying, where he's from."

Sims had decided long before, that it would be wisest to keep the power of the Brandelmeier to himself. But he was fairly certain it was not the work of a foreign power. The trial run on the test range had left him gasping, confused.

He opened the door, and Soames passed through, uneasily.

Sims caught a glimpse of the expression on the stranger's face as the philologist entered. It was even more uneasy than Soames's had been.

It looked to be a long wait.

Soames was white as paste. His face was drawn, and the complacent attitude he had shown since his arrival in Washington was shattered. He sat across from Sims, and asked him in a quavering voice for a cigarette. Sims fished around in his desk, came up with a crumpled pack and idly slid them across to Soames. The philologist took one, put it in his mouth, and then, as though it had been totally forgotten in the space of a second, he removed it, held it while he spoke.

His tones were amazed. "Do you know what you've got up there in that cell?"

Sims said nothing, knowing what was to come would not startle him too much; he had expected something fantastic.

"That man . . . do you know where he . . . that soldier—and by God, Sims, that's what he *is*—comes from, from—now you're going to think I'm insane to believe it, but somehow I'm convinced—he comes from the future!"

230

Sims tightened his lips. Despite himself, he *was* shocked. He knew it was true. It *had* to be true, it was the only explanation that fit all the facts.

"What can you tell me?" he asked the philologist.

"Well, at first I tried solving the communications problem by asking him simple questions . . . pointing to myself and saying 'Soames,' pointing to him and looking quizzical, but all he'd keep saying was a string of gibberish. I tried for hours to equate his tones and phrases with all the dialects and subdialects of every language I'd every known, but it was no use. He slurred too much. And then I finally figured it out. He had to write it out—which I couldn't understand, of course, but it gave me a clue—and then I kept having him repeat it. Do you know what he's speaking?"

Sims shook his head.

The linguist spoke softly. "He's speaking English. It's that simple. Just English.

"But an English that has been corrupted and run together, and so slurred, it's incomprehensible. It must be the future trend of the language. Sort of an extrapolation of gutter English, just contracted to a fantastic extreme. At any rate, I got it out of him."

Sims leaned forward, held his dead pipe tightly. "What?"

Soames read it off a sheet of paper:

"My name is Qarlo Clobregnny. Private. Six-five-one-oh-two-two-nine."

Sims murmured in astonishment. "My God . . . name, rank and—"

Soames finished for him, "—and serial number. Yes, that's all he'd give me for over three hours. Then I asked him a few innocuous questions, like where did he come from, and what was his impression of where he was now."

The philologist waved a hand vaguely. "By that time, I had an idea what I was dealing with, though not where he had come from. But when he began telling me about the War, the War he was fighting when he showed up here, I knew immediately he was either from some other world—which is fantastic—or, or . . . well, I just didn't know!"

Sims nodded his head in understanding. "From *when* do you think he comes?"

Soames shrugged. "Can't tell. He says the year he is in—doesn't seem to realize he's in the past—is K79. He doesn't know when the other style of dating went out. As far as he knows, it's been 'K' for a long time, though he's heard stories about things that happened during a time they dated 'GV'. Meaningless, but I'd wager it's more thousands of years than we can imagine."

Sims ran a hand nervously through his hair. This problem was, indeed, larger than he'd thought.

"Look, Professor Soames, I want you to stay with him, and teach him current English. See if you can work some more information out of him, and let him know we mean him no hard times.

"Though Lord knows," the special advisor added with a tremor, "*he* can give us a harder time than we can give him. What knowledge he must have!"

Soames nodded in agreement, "Is it all right if I catch a few hours sleep? I was with him almost ten hours straight, and I'm sure *he* needs it as badly as I do."

Sims nodded also, in agreement, and the philologist went off to a sleeping room. But when Sims looked down through the window, twenty minutes later, the soldier was still awake, still looking about nervously. It seemed he did *not* need sleep.

Sims was terribly worried, and the coded telegram he had received from the President, in answer to his own, was not at all reassuring. The problem was in his hands, and it was an increasingly worrisome problem.

Perhaps a deadly problem.

He went to another sleeping room, to follow Soames's example. It looked like sleep was going to be scarce.

Problem:

A man from the future. An ordinary man, without any special talents, without any great store of intelligence. The equivalent of "the man in the street." A man who owns a fantastic little machine that turns sand into solid matter, harder than steel—but who hasn't the vaguest notion of how it works, or how to analyze it. A man whose knowledge of past history is as vague and formless as any modern man's. A soldier. With no other talent than fighting. What is to be done with such a man?

Solution:

Unknown.

Lyle Sims pushed the coffee cup away. If he ever had to look at another cup of the disgusting stuff, he was sure he would vomit. Three sleepless days and nights, running on nothing but Dexedrine and hot black coffee, had put his nerves more on edge than usual. He snapped at the clerks and secretaries, he paced endlessly, and he had ruined the stems of five pipes. He felt muggy and his stomach was queasy. Yet there was no solution.

It was impossible to say, "All right, we've got a man from the future. So what? Turn him loose and let him make a life for himself in our time, since he can't return to his own."

It was impossible to do that for several reasons: (1) what if he *couldn't* adjust? He was then a potential menace, of *incalculable* potential. (2) What if an enemy power—and God knows there were enough powers around anxious to get a secret weapon as valuable as Qarlo—grabbed him, and *did* somehow manage to work out the concepts behind the rifle, the firmer, the mono-atomic anti-gravity device in the pouch? What then? (3) A man used to war, knowing only war, would eventually *seek* or foment war.

There were dozens of others, they were only beginning to realize. No, something had to be done with him.

Imprison him?

For what? The man had done no real harm. He had not intentionally caused the death of the man on the subway platform. He had been frightened by the train. He had been attacked by the executives—one of whom had a broken neck, but was alive. No, he was just "a stranger and afraid, in a world I never made," as Housman had put it so terrifyingly clearly.

Kill him?

For the same reasons, unjust and brutal . . . not to mention wasteful.

Find a place for him in society?

Doing what?

Sims raged in his mind, mulled it over and tried every angle. It was an insoluble problem. A simple dogface, with no other life than that of a professional soldier, what good was he?

All Qarlo knew was war.

The question abruptly answered itself: If he knows no other life than that of a soldier . . . why, make him a soldier. (But . . . who was to say that with his knowledge of futuristic tactics and weapons, he might not turn into another Hitler, or Genghis Khan?) No, making him a soldier would only heighten the problem. There could be no peace of mind were he in a position where he might organize.

As a tactician **then**?

It might work at that.

Sims slumped behind his desk, pressed down the key of his intercom, spoke to the secretary, "Get me General Mainwaring, General Polk and the Secretary of Defense."

He clicked the key back. It just might work at that. If Qarlo could be persuaded to detail fighting plans, now that he realized where he was, and that the men who held him were not his enemies and allies of Ruskie-Chink (and what a field of speculation *that* pair of words opened!).

It just might work . . .

. . . but Sims doubted it.

Mainwaring stayed on to report when Polk and the Secretary of Defense went back to their regular duties. He was a big man, with softness written across his face and body, and a pompous white moustache. He shook his head sadly, as though the Rosetta Stone had been stolen from him just before an all-important experiment.

"Sorry, Sims, but the man is useless to us. Brilliant grasp of military tactics, so long as it involves what he calls 'eighty-thread beams' and telepathic contacts.

"Do you know those wars up there are fought as much mentally as they are physically? Never heard of a tank or a mortar, but the stories he tells of brain-burning and spore-death would make you sick. It isn't pretty the way they fight.

"I thank God I'm not going to be around to see it; I *thought* our wars were filthy and unpleasant. They've got us licked all down the line for brutality and mass death. And the strange thing is, this Qarlo fellow *despises* it! For a while there—felt foolish as hell—but for a while there, when he was explaining it, I almost wanted to chuck my career, go out and start beating the drum for disarmament."

The General summed up, and it was apparent Qarlo was useless as a tactician. He had been brought up with one way of waging war, and it would take a lifetime for him to adjust enough to be of any tactical use.

But it didn't really matter, for Sims was certain the General had given him the answer to the problem, inadvertently.

He would have to clear it with Security, and the President, of course. And it would take a great deal of publicity to make the people realize this man actually *was* the real thing, an inhabitant of the future. But if it worked out, Qarlo Clobregnny, the soldier and nothing *but* the soldier, could be the most valuable man Time had ever spawned.

He set to work on it, wondering foolishly if he wasn't too much the idealist.

Ten soldiers crouched in the frozen mud. Their firmers had been jammed, had turned the sand and dirt of their holes only to icelike conditions. The cold was seeping up through their suits, and the jammed firmers were emitting hard radiation. One of the men screamed as the radiation took hold in his gut, and he felt the organs watering away. He leaped up, vomiting blood and phlegm—and was caught across the face by a robot-tracked triple beam. The front of his face disappeared, and the nearly decapitated corpse flopped back into the firmhole, atop a comrade.

That soldier shoved the body aside carelessly, thinking of his four children, lost to him forever in a Ruskie-Chink raid on Garmatopolis, sent to the bogs to work. His mind conjured up the sight of the three girls and the little boy with such long, long eyelashes—each dragging through the stinking bog, a mineral bag tied to their neck, collecting fuel rocks for the enemy. He began to cry softly. The sound and mental image of crying was picked up by a Ruskie-Chink telepath somewhere across the lines, and even before the man could catch himself, blank his mind, the telepath was on him.

The soldier raised up from the firmhole bottom, clutching with crooked hands at his head. He began to tear at his features wildly, screaming high and piercing, as the enemy telepath burned away his brain. In a moment his eyes were empty, staring shells, and the man flopped down beside his comrade, who had begun to deteriorate.

A thirty-eight-thread whined its beam overhead, and the eight remaining men saw a munitions wheel go up with a deafening roar. Hot shrapnel zoomed across the field, and a thin, brittle, knife-edged bit of plasteel arced over the edge of the firmhole, and buried itself in one soldier's head. The piece went in crookedly, through his left earlobe, and came out skewering his tongue, half-extended from his open mouth. From the side it looked as though he were wearing some sort of earring. He died in spasms, and it took an awfully long while. Finally, the twitching and gulping got so bad, one of his comrades used the butt of a Brandelmeier across the dying man's nose. It splintered the nose, sent bone chips into the brain, killing the man instantly.

Then the attack call came!

In each of their heads, the telepathic cry came to advance, and they were up out of the firmhole, all seven of them, reciting their daily prayer, and knowing it would do no good. They advanced across the slushy ground, and overhead they could hear the buzz of leech bombs, coming down on the enemy's thread emplacements.

All around them in the deep-set night the varicolored explosions popped and sugged, expanding in all directions like fireworks, then dimming the scene against the blackness.

One of the soldiers caught a beam across the belly, and he was thrown sidewise for ten feet, to land in a soggy heap, his stomach split open, the organs glowing and pulsing wetly from the charge of the threader. A head popped out of a firmhole before them, and three of the remaining six fired simultaneously. The enemy was a booby—rigged to backtrack their kill urge, rigged to a telepathic hookup—and even as the body exploded under their combined firepower, each of the men caught fire. Flames leaped from their mouths, from their pores, from the instantly charred spaces where their eyes had been. A pyrotic-telepath had been at work.

The remaining three split and cut away, realizing they might be thinking, might be giving themselves away. That was the horror of being just a dogface, not a special telepath behind the lines. Out here there was nothing but death.

A doggie-mine slithered across the ground, entwined itself in the legs of one soldier, and blew the legs out from under him. He lay there clutching the shredded stumps, feeling the blood soaking into the mud, and then unconsciousness seeped into his brain. He died shortly thereafter.

Of the two left, one leaped a barbwall, and blasted out a thirty-eight-thread emplacement of twelve men, at the cost of the top of his head. He was left alive, and curiously, as though the war had stopped, he felt the top of himself, and his fingers pressed lightly against convoluted, slick matter for a second before he dropped to the ground.

His braincase was open, glowed strangely in the night, but no one saw it.

The last soldier dove under a beam that zzzzzzzed through the night, and landed on his elbows. He rolled with the tumble, felt the edge of a leech-bomb crater, and dove in head-first. The beam split up his passage, and he escaped charring by an inch. He lay in the hole, feeling the cold of the battlefield seeping around him, and drew his cloak closer.

The soldier was Qarlo . . .

He finished talking, and sat down on the platform . . .

The audience was silent . . .

Sims shrugged into his coat, fished around in the pocket for the cold pipe. The dottle had fallen out of the bowl, and he felt the dark grains at the bottom of the pocket. The audience was filing out slowly, hardly anyone speaking, but each staring at others around him. As though they were suddenly realizing what had happened to them, as though they were looking for a solution.

Sims passed such a solution. The petitions were there, tacked up alongside the big sign—duplicate of the ones up all over the city. He caught the heavy black type on them as he passed through the auditorium's vestibule:

SIGN THIS PETITION! PREVENT WHAT YOU HAVE HEARD TONIGHT!

People were flocking around the petitions, but Sims knew it was only a token gesture at this point: the legislation had gone through that morning. No more war . . . under any conditions. And intelligence reported the long playing records, the piped broadcasts, the p.a. trucks, had all done their jobs. Similar legislation was going through all over the world.

It looked as though Qarlo had done it, single-handed.

Sims stopped to refill his pipe, and stared up at the big black-lined poster near the door.

HEAR QARLO, THE SOLDIER FROM THE FUTURE! SEE THE MAN FROM TOMORROW, AND HEAR HIS STORIES OF THE WONDERFUL WORLD OF THE FUTURE! FREE! NO OBLIGATIONS! HURRY!

The advertising had been effective, and it was a fine campaign.

Qarlo had been more valuable just telling about his wars, about how men died in that day in the future, than he could ever have been as a strategist.

It took a real soldier, who hated war, to talk of it, to show people that it was ugly, and unglamorous. And there was a certain sense of foul defeat, of hopelessness, in knowing the future was the way Qarlo described it. It made you want to stop the flow of Time, say, "No. The future will *not* be like this! We will abolish war!"

Certainly enough steps in the right direction had been taken. The legislation was there, and those who had held back, who had tried to keep animosity alive, were being disposed of every day.

Qarlo had done his work well.

There was just one thing bothering special advisor Lyle Sims. The soldier had come back in time, so he was here. That much they knew for certain.

But a nagging worry ate at Sim's mind, made him say prayers he had thought himself incapable of inventing. Made him fight to get Qarlo heard by everyone . . .

Could the future be changed?

Or was it inevitable?

Would the world Qarlo left inevitably appear?

Would all their work be for nothing?

It couldn't be! It dare not be!

He walked back inside, got in line to sign the petitions again, though it was his fiftieth time.

FOR DISCUSSION: Soldier

1. Anderson had his soldier struck by lightning to cause his backtracking in time. Ellison uses "three hundred distinct beams" to "warp" the soldier of his story off the battlefield and into our own time. Which method do you prefer? Why?

2. In Anderson's story, you saw that human jealousy was much the

same in the tenth century as it is today. In this story, Ellison tells us that a soldier's method of identification when captured is the same in the future as it is today. What purpose does the inclusion of such similarities among different eras serve in science-fiction stories?

3. The author allows us to see Sims' attempts to solve the problem of what to do with Qarlo. But when Sims does find what he feels to be a satisfactory solution to the problem, the author does not let us know that solution immediately. Why not?

4. The scene depicting war in the future is horrifying because it is brutally graphic. Why do you think the author wrote it in this manner? Does the scene highlight the theme of the story? Explain.

INTRODUCTION: The Good Provider

The short-short story of usually no more than 1,000 to 1,200 words is a challenge to an author's literary skills. He must create living characters, a believable situation, usually a surprise ending, and do it all in an extremely limited number of words.

In the short-short story, it is far more necessary than in the novel, for example, to eliminate all non-essential material—all material that does not directly contribute to the point of the story. "The Good Provider" is an excellent example of the skillful storyteller's handling of this difficult form.

The Good Provider
by Marion Gross

Minnie Leggety turned up the walk of her Elm Street bungalow and saw that she faced another crisis. When Omar sat brooding like that, not smoking, not "studying," but just scrunched down inside of himself, she knew enough after forty years to realize that she was facing a crisis. As though it weren't enough just trying to get along on Omar's pension these days, without having to baby him through another one of his periods of discouragement! She forced a gaiety into her voice that she actually didn't feel.

"Why, hello there, Pa, what are you doing out here? Did you have to come up for air?" Minnie eased herself down beside Omar on the stoop and put the paper bag she had been carrying on the sidewalk. Such a little bag, but it had taken most of their week's food budget! Protein, plenty of lean, rare steaks and chops, that's what that nice man on the radio said old folks needed, but as long as he couldn't tell you how to buy it with steak at $1.23 a pound, he might just as well save his breath to cool his porridge. And so might she, for all the attention Omar was paying her. He was staring straight ahead as though he didn't even see her. This looked like one of his real bad spells. She took his gnarled hand and patted it.

"What's the matter, Pa? Struck a snag with your gadget?" The "gadget" filled three full walls of the basement and most of the floor space besides, but it was still a "gadget" to Minnie—another one of his ideas that didn't quite work.

239

Omar had been working on gadgets ever since they were married. When they were younger, she hotly sprang to his defense against her sisters-in-law: "Well, it's better than liquor, and it's cheaper than pinochle; at least I know where he is nights." Now that they were older, and Omar was retired from his job, his tinkering took on a new significance. It was what kept him from going to pieces like a lot of men who were retired and didn't have enough activity to fill their time and their minds.

"What's the matter, Pa?" she asked again.

The old man seemed to notice her for the first time. Sadly he shook his head. "Minnie, I'm a failure. The thing's no good; it ain't practical. After all I promised you, Minnie, and the way you stuck by me and all, it's just not going to work."

Minnie never had thought it would. It just didn't seem possible that a body could go gallivanting back and forth the way Pa had said they would if the gadget worked. She continued to pat the hand she held and told him soothingly, "I'm not sure but it's for the best, Pa. I'd sure have gotten airsick, or timesick, or whatever it was. What're you going to work on now that you're giving up the time machine?" she asked anxiously.

"You don't understand, Min," the old man said. "I'm through. I've failed. I've failed at everything I've ever tried to make. They always *almost* work, and yet there's always something I can't get just right. I never knew enough, Min, never had enough schooling, and now it's too late to get any. I'm just giving up altogether. I'm through!"

This *was* serious. Pa with nothing to tinker at down in the basement, Pa constantly underfoot, Pa with nothing to keep him from just slipping away like old Mr. Mason had, was something she didn't like to think about. "Maybe it isn't as bad as all that," she told him. "All those nice parts you put into your gadget, maybe you could make us a television or something with them. Land, a television, that would be a nice thing to have."

"Oh, I couldn't do that, Min. I wouldn't know how to make a television; besides, I told you, it almost works. It's just that it ain't practical. It ain't the way I pictured it. Come down, I'll show you." He dragged her into the house and down into the basement.

The time machine left so little free floor space, what with the furnace and coal bin and washtubs, that Minnie had to stand on the stairway while Pa explained it to her. It needed explanation. It had more colored lights than a pinball machine, more plugs than the Hillsdale telephone exchange, and more levers than one of those newfangled voting booths.

"Now see," he said, pointing to various parts of the machine, "I rigged this thing up so we could move forward or back in time and space both.

I thought we could go off and visit foreign spots, and see great things happening, and have ourselves an interesting old age."

"Well, I don't rightly know if I'd have enjoyed that, Pa," Minnie interrupted. "I doubt I'd know how to get along with all them foreigners, and their strange talk and strange ways and all."

Omar shook his head in annoyance. "The Holy Land. You'd have wanted to see the Holy Land, wouldn't you? You could have sat with the crowd at Galilee and listened to the Lord's words right from His lips. You'd have enjoyed that, wouldn't you?"

"Omar, when you talk like that you make the whole thing sound sacrilegious and against the Lord's ways. Besides, I suppose the Lord would have spoke in Hebrew, and I don't know one word of that and you don't either. I don't know but what I'm glad you couldn't get the thing to work," she said righteously.

"But Min, it does work!" Omar was indignant.

"But you said—"

"I never said it don't work. I said it ain't practical. It don't work good enough, and I don't know enough to make it work better."

Working on the gadget was one thing, but believing that it worked was another. Minnie began to be alarmed. Maybe folks had been right—maybe Omar had gone off his head at last. She looked at him anxiously. He seemed all right and, now that he was worked up at her, the depression seemed to have left him.

"What do you mean it works, but not good enough?" she asked him.

"Well, see here," Omar told her, pointing to an elaborate control board. "It was like I was telling you before you interrupted with your not getting along with foreigners, and your sacrilegion and all. I set this thing up to move a body in time and space any which way. There's a globe of the world worked in here, and I thought that by turning the globe and setting these time controls to whatever year you had in mind you could go wherever you had a mind to. Well, it don't work like that. I've been trying it out for a whole week and no matter how I set the globe, no matter how I set the time controls, it always comes out the same. It lands me over at Main and Center, right in front of Purdey's meat market."

"What's wrong with that?" Minnie asked. "That might be real convenient."

"You don't understand," Omar told her. "It isn't *now* when I get there, it's twenty years ago! That's the trouble, it don't take me none of the places I want to go, just Main and Center. And it don't take me none of the times I want to go, just twenty years ago, and I saw enough of the depression so I don't want to spend my old age watching people sell apples. Then on top of that, this here timer don't work." He pointed to another dial. "It's supposed to set to how long you want to stay, where-ever you want to go, but it don't work at all. Twenty minutes, and then woosh, you're right back here in the basement. Nothing works like I want it to."

Minnie had grown thoughtful as Omar recounted the faults of the machine. Wasn't it a caution the way even a smart man like Pa, a man smart enough to make a time machine, didn't have a practical ounce to his whole hundred and forty-eight pounds? She sat down heavily on the cellar steps and, emptying the contents of her purse on her broad lap, began examining the bills.

"What you looking for, Min?" Omar asked.

Minnie looked at him pityingly. Wasn't it a caution . . .

Purdey the butcher was leaning unhappily against his chopping block. The shop was clean and shining, the floor was strewn with fresh sawdust, and Purdey himself, unmindful of the expense, had for the sake of his morale donned a fresh apron. But for all that, Purdey wished that he was hanging on one of his chromium-plated meat hooks.

The sky was blue and smogless, something it never was when the shops were operating and employing the valley's five thousand breadwinners. Such potential customers as were abroad had a shabby, threadbare look to them. Over in front of the Bijou old Mr. Ryan was selling apples.

While he watched, a stout, determined-looking woman appeared at the corner of Main and Center. She glanced quickly around, brushing old Mr. Ryan and his apples with her glance, and then came briskly toward Purdey's shop. Purdey straightened up.

"Afternoon, Ma'am, what can I do for you?" He beamed as though the light bill weren't three months overdue.

"I'll have a nice porterhouse," the lady said hesitantly. "How much is porterhouse?"

"Forty-five a pound, best in the house." Purdey held up a beauty, expecting her to change her mind.

"I'll take it," the lady said. "And six lamb chops. I want a rib roast for Sunday, but I can come back for that. No use carrying too much," she explained. "Could you please hurry with that? I haven't very much time."

"New in town?" Purdey asked as he turned to ring up the sale on the cash register.

"Yes, you might say so," the woman said. By the time Purdey turned back to ask her name, she was gone. But Purdey knew she'd be back. She wanted a rib roast for Sunday. "It just goes to show you," Purdey said to himself, surveying the satisfactory tab sticking up from the register, "there still is some money around. Two dollars, and she never even batted an eyelash. It goes to show you!"

FOR DISCUSSION: The Good Provider

1. The first and second paragraphs of this story define the problem Minnie is concerned with when the story begins. At the same time, these paragraphs foreshadow her solution to the problem when confronted by the time machine Omar deems a failure. How do they foreshadow the solution?
2. Omar says his machine isn't "practical." Is the use of this word important in terms of the story? If the word "worthwhile" were substituted for "practical," would the new word have the same significance in the story's terms?
3. Why does Minnie suggest that Omar might convert the time machine to a television set? Is it only because she would enjoy having a television set?

Special
Talents

CHAPTER FIVE

Society pays honor to those of its members who manifest particular abilities and talents. Musicians, dancers, painters, poets, actors—such people are generally respected and renowned because of the special talents they possess.

But talent, of course, is not limited to artists. There are other men and women of special talent who also receive society's tribute—people who are particularly skilled in sports and innovative scientists, to name only two categories.

There are other kinds of talented people as well. There are the mountain climbers, adventurers like Thor Heyerdahl and John Glenn, and statesmen.

All these people possess special talents that make them stand out among their fellowmen. They are admired and envied. The admiration and envy society accords them testifies to our evaluation of their talents. We honor them at public ceremonies and we often seek to emulate them in some way.

The theme of special talents in science fiction reflects our interest in remarkable people. But here, as in other science-fiction themes, the subject matter is never mundane or ordinary. The talents written about in science-fiction stories can range from telepathy and telekinesis to skills resulting from genetic mutation. We enjoy these stories for much the same reason that we pay attention to the performances of our celebrated actors and applaud the feats accomplished by our astronauts.

Science-fiction authors examine special talents within a scientific framework. The science involved may be mathematical physics. The talent may be telepathy. In the case of the last story in this chapter, the talent is one resulting from a symbiotic relationship between a human being and an alien life form.

Just as literature in general reflects life, so does science fiction reflect it but in its own way and on its own terms. Science-fiction authors deal with talents not yet documented, talents that mystify us at the moment but may be proven to exist someday.

We tend to think of talent as something highly desirable. But one of the stories in this chapter, Richard Matheson's "Witch War", describes the talents of seven pretty little girls as gifts few would desire to possess.

In this chapter, science-fiction authors once again examine some of the possibilities inherent in a given theme as they present their five different views of talented individuals. But the individuals portrayed in these stories are not the kinds of talented people we were talking about earlier in this introduction. The people in these stories are talented in strange and sometimes bizarre ways. But their talents might be said to be secondary to the people themselves. The reader will notice that the stories are not only about special talents. They are also about the people who possess these talents. The emphasis throughout remains on the people involved as it does in all good literature from Homer's *Odyssey* and Chaucer's *Canterbury Tales* to such contemporary classics as *The Catcher in the Rye* by J. D. Salinger or *1984* by George Orwell.

Readers turn to literature to learn something about other people and in learning about these fictional people they frequently learn something about themselves. In these stories, the reader will learn about people who are remarkably talented and what happens to them as a result. What is important, however, may not be so much what he learns from these stories as it is the fact that they provide him with an opportunity to learn while he is enjoying fine examples of the science-fiction author's talent.

Chapter Five: *Special Talents*

INTRODUCTION: A Message from Charity

The theme of time travel in science fiction deals with ways to reach past or future societies. In this story, the basic theme falls within the category of special talents. It is a story of an unusual talent shared by a boy and girl who make contact with one another although they are living in ages hundreds of years apart.

It can be said to be a "boy meets girl" story. But by dealing with this traditional situation in science-fiction terms, it presents the reader with a fascinating and original version of a familiar story situation.

A Message from Charity
by William M. Lee

That summer of the year 1700 was the hottest in the memory of the very oldest inhabitants. Because the year ushered in a new century, some held that the events were related and that for a whole hundred years Bay Colony would be as torrid and steamy as the Indies themselves.

There was a good deal of illness in Annes Towne, and a score had died before the weather broke at last in late September. For the great part they were oldsters who succumbed, but some of the young were sick too, and Charity Payne as sick as any.

Charity had turned eleven in the spring and had still the figure and many of the ways of thinking of a child, but she was tall and strong and tanned by the New England sun, for she spent many hours helping her father in the fields and trying to keep some sort of order in the dooryard and garden.

During the weeks when she lay bedridden and, for a time, burning up with the fever, Thomas Carter and his good wife Beulah came as neighbors should to lend a hand, for Charity's mother had died abirthing and Obie Payne could not cope all alone.

Charity lay on a pallet covered by a straw-filled mattress which her father, frantic to be doing something for her and finding little enough to do beyond the saying of short, fervent prayers, refilled with fresh straw as often as Beulah would allow. A few miles down Harmon Brook was a famous beaver pond where in winter the Annes Towne people cut ice to be stored under layers of bark and chips. It had been used heavily early in the summer, and there was not very much ice left, but those families

247

with sickness in the home might draw upon it for the patient's comfort. So Charity had bits of ice folded into a woolen cloth to lay on her forehead when the fever was bad.

William Trowbridge, who had apprenticed in medicine down in Philadelphia, attended the girl, and pronounced her illness a sort of summer cholera which was claiming victims all up and down the brook. Trowbridge was only moderately esteemed in Annes Towne, being better, it was said, at delivering lambs and foals than at treating human maladies. He was a gruff and notional man, and he was prone to state his views on a subject and then walk away instead of waiting to argue and perhaps be refuted. Not easy to get along with.

For Charity he prescribed a diet of beef tea with barley and another tea, very unpleasant to the taste, made from pounded willow bark. What was more, all her drinking water was to be boiled. Since there was no other advice to be had, they followed it and in due course Charity got well.

She ran a great fever for five days, and it was midway in this period when the strange dreams began. Not dreams really, for she was awake though often out of her senses, knowing her father now and then, other times seeing him as a gaunt and frightening stranger. When she was better, still weak but wholly rational, she tried to tell her visitors about these dreams.

"Some person was talking and talking," she recalled. "A man or perchance a lad. He talked not to me, but I could hear or understand all that he said. 'Twas strange talk indeed, a porridge of the King's English and other words of no sense at all. And with the talk I did see some fearful sights."

"La, now, don't even think of it," said Dame Beulah.

"But I would fen both think and talk of it, for I am no longer afeared. Such things I saw in bits and flashes, as 'twere seen by a strike of lightning."

"Talk and ye be so minded, then. There's naught impious in y'r conceits. Tell me again about the carriages which travelled along with nary horse."

Annes Towne survived the Revolution and the War of 1812, and for a time seemed likely to become a larger, if not an important community. But when its farms became less productive and the last virgin timber disappeared from the area, Annes Towne began to disappear too, dwindling from two score of homes to a handful, then to none; and the last foundation had crumbled to rubble and been scattered a hundred years before it could have been nominated a historic site.

In time dirt tracks became stone roads, which gave way to black

248

meanderings of macadam, and these in their turn were displaced by never ending bands of concrete. The cross-roads site of Annes Towne was presently cleared of brambles, sumac and red cedar, and overnight it was a shopping center. Now, for mile on spreading mile the New England hills were dotted with ranch houses, salt boxes and split-level colonial homes.

During four decades Harmon Brook had been fouled and poisoned by a textile bleach and dye works. Rising labor costs had at last driven the small company to extinction. With that event and increasingly rigorous legislation, the stream had come back to the extent that it could now be bordered by some of these prosperous homes and by the golf course of the Anniston Country Club.

With aquatic plants and bull frogs and a few fish inhabiting its waters, it was not obvious to implicate the Harmon for the small outbreak of typhoid which occurred in the hot, dry summer of 1965. No one was dependent on it for drinking water. To the discomfort of a local milk distributor, who was entirely blameless, indictment of the stream was delayed and obscured by the fact that the organisms involved were not a typical strain of *Salmonella typhosa*. Indeed, they ultimately found a place in the American Type Culture Collection, under a new number.

Young Peter Wood, whose home was one of those pleasantly situated along the stream, was the most seriously ill of all the cases, partly because he was the first, mostly because his symptoms went unremarked for a time. Peter was sixteen and not highly communicative to either parents or friends. The Wood Seniors both taught, at Harvard and Wellesley respectively. They were intelligent and well-intentioned parents, but sometimes a little off-hand, and like many of their friends, they raised their son to be a miniature adult in as many ways as possible. His sports, tennis and golf, were adult sports. His reading tastes were catholic, ranging from Camus to Al Capp to science fiction. He had been carefully held back in his progress through the lower grades so that he would not enter college more than a year or so ahead of his age. He had an adequate number of friends and sufficient areas of congeniality with them. He had gotten a driver's license shortly after his sixteenth birthday and drove seriously and well enough to be allowed nearly unrestricted use of the second car.

So Peter Wood was not the sort of boy to complain to his family about headache, mild nausea and other symptoms. Instead, after they had persisted for forty-eight hours, he telephoned for an appointment on his own initiative and visited their family doctor. Suddenly, in the waiting room, he became much worse, and was given a cot in an examining room until Dr. Maxwell was free to drive him home. The doctor did not seriously suspect typhoid, though it was among several possibilities which he counted as less likely.

Peter's temperature rose from 104° to over 105° that night. No nurse was to be had until morning, and his parents alternated in attendance in his bedroom. There was no cause for alarm, since the patient was full of wide-spectrum antibiotic. But he slept only fitfully with intervals of waking delirium. He slapped at the sheet, tossed around on the bed and muttered or spoke now and then. Some of the talk was understandable.

"There's a forest," he said.

"What?" asked his father.

"There's a forest the other side of the stream."

"Oh."

"Can you see it?"

"No, I'm sitting inside here with you. Take it easy, son."

"Some deer are coming down to drink, along the edge of Weller's pasture."

"Is that so?"

"Last year a mountain lion killed two of them, right where they drank. Is it raining?"

"No, it isn't. It would be fine if we could have some."

"It's raining. I can hear it on the roof." A pause. "It drips down the chimney."

Peter turned his head to look at his father, momentarily clear-eyed.

"How long since there's been a forest across the stream?"

Dr. Wood reflected on the usual difficulty of answering explicit questions and on his own ignorance of history.

"A long time. I expect this valley has been farm land since colonial days."

"Funny," Peter said. "I shut my eyes and I can see a forest. Really big trees. On our side of the stream there's a kind of a garden and an apple tree and a path goes down to the water."

"It sounds pleasant."

"Yeah."

"Why don't you try going to sleep?"

"OK."

The antibiotic accomplished much less than it should have done in Peter's case, and he stayed very sick for several days. Even after diagnosis, there appeared no good reason to move him from home. A trained nurse was on duty after that first night, and tranquilizers and sedatives reduced her job to no more than keeping a watch. There were only a few sleepy communications from her young patient. It was on the fourth night, the last one when he had any significant fever, that he asked:

250

"Were you ever a girl?"

"Well, thanks a lot. I'm not as old as all that."

"I mean, were you ever inside a girl?"

"I think you'd better go back to sleep, young man."

"I mean—I guess I don't know what I mean."

He uttered no oddities thereafter, at least when there was anyone within hearing. During the days of his recovery and convalescence, abed and later stretched out on a chaise lounge on the terrace looking down toward Harmon Brook, he took to whispering. He moved his lips hardly at all, but vocalized each word, or if he fell short of this, at least put each thought into carefully chosen words and sentences.

The idea that he might be in mental communication with another person was not, to him, very startling. Steeped in the lore of science fiction whose heroes were, as like as not, adept at telepathy, the event seemed almost an expected outcome of his wishes. Many nights he had lain awake sending out (he hoped) a mental probe, trying and trying to find the trick, for surely there must be one, of making a contact.

Now that such a contact was established he sought, just as vainly, for some means to prove it. How do you know you're not dreaming, he asked himself. How do you know you're not still delirious?

The difficulty was that his communication with Charity Payne could be by mental route only. Had there been any possibility for Peter to reach the girl by mail, by telephone, by travel and a personal visit, their rapport on a mental level might have been confirmed, and their messages cross-checked.

During their respective periods of illness, Peter and Charity achieved a communion of a sort which consisted at first of brief glimpses, each of the other's environment. They were not—then—seeing through one another's eyes, so much as tapping one another's visual recollections. While Peter stared at a smoothly plastered ceiling, Charity looked at rough hewn beams. He, when his aching head permitted, could turn on one side and watch a television program. She, by the same movement, could see a small smoky fire in a monstrous stone fireplace, where water was heated and her beef and barley broth kept steaming.

Instead of these current images, current for each of them in their different times, they saw stored-up pictures, not perfect, for neither of them was remembering perfectly; rather like pictures viewed through a badly ground lens, with only the objects of principal interest in clear detail.

Charity saw her fearful sights with no basis for comprehension—a section of dual highway animated by hurtling cars and trucks and not a person, recognizable as a person, in sight; a tennis court, and what on earth could it be, a jet plane crossing the sky; a vast and many-storied building which glinted with glass and the silvery tracings of untarnished steel.

At the start she was terrified nearly out of her wits. It's all very well to dream, and a nightmare is only a bad dream after you waken, but a nightmare is assembled from familiar props. You could reasonably be chased by a dragon (like the one in the picture that St. George had to fight) or be lost in a cave (like the one on Parish Hill, only bigger and darker). To dream of things which have no meaning at all is worse.

She was spared prolongation of her terror by Peter's comprehension of their situation and his intuitive realization of what the experience, assuming a two-way channel, might be doing to her. The vignettes of her life which he was seeing were in no way disturbing. Everything he saw through her mind was within his framework of reference. Horses and cattle, fields and forest, rutted lanes and narrow wooden bridges, were things he knew, even if he did not live among them. He recognized Harmon Brook because, directly below their home, there was an immense granite boulder parting the flow, shaped like a great bear-like animal with its head down, drinking. It was strange that the stream, in all those years, had neither silted up nor eroded away to hide or change the seeming of the rock, but so it was. He saw it through Charity's eyes and knew the place in spite of the forest on the far hill.

When he first saw this partly familiar, partly strange scene, he heard from somewhere within his mind the frightened cry of a little girl. His thinking at that time was fever distorted and incoherent. It was two days later after a period of several hours of normal temperature, when he conceived the idea—with sudden virtual certainty—these pastoral scenes he had been dreaming were truly something seen with other eyes. There were subtle perceptual differences between those pictures and his own seeing.

To his mother, writing at a table near the windows, he said, "I think I'm feeling better. How about a glass of orange juice?"

She considered. "The doctor should be here in an hour or so. In the meantime you can make do with a little more ice water. I'll get it. Drink it slowly, remember."

Two hundred and sixty-five years away, Charity Payne thought suddenly, "How about a glass of orange juice?" She had been drowsing, but her eyes popped wide open. "Mercy," she said aloud. Dame Beulah bent over the pallet.

"What is it, child?"

"How about a glass of orange juice?" Charity repeated.

"La, 'tis gibberish." A cool hand was laid on her forehead. "Would ye like a bit of ice to bite on?"

Orange juice, whatever that might be, was forgotten.

Over the next several days Peter Wood tried time and again to address the stranger directly, and repeatedly failed. Some of what he said to others reached her in fragments and further confused her state of mind. What she had to say, on the other hand, was coming through to him with increasing frequency. Often it was only a word or a phrase with a quaint twist like a historical novel, and he would lie puzzling over it, trying to place the person on the other end of their erratic line of communication. His recognition of Bear Rock, which he had seen once again through her eyes, was disturbing. His science-fiction conditioning led him naturally to speculate about the parallel worlds concept, but that seemed not to fit the facts as he saw them.

Peter reached the stage of convalescence when he could spend all day on the terrace and look down, when he wished, at the actual rock. There, for the hundredth time he formed the syllables, "Hello, who are you?" and for the first time received a response. It was a silence, but a silence reverberating with shock, totally different in quality from the blankness which had met him before.

"My name is Peter Wood."

There was a long pause before the answer came, softly and timidly.

"My name is Charity Payne. Where are you? What is happening to me?"

The following days of enforced physical idleness were filled with exploration and discovery. Peter found out almost at once that, while they were probably no more than a few feet apart in their respective worlds, a gulf of more than a quarter of a thousand years stretched between them. Such a contact through time was a greater departure from known physical laws, certainly, than the mere fact of telepathic communication. Peter revelled in his growing ability.

In another way the situation was heart breaking. No matter how well they came to know one another, he realized, they could never meet, and after no more than a few hours of acquaintance he found that he was regarding this naïve child of another time with esteem and a sort of affection.

They arrived shortly at a set of rules whiᴄh seemed to govern and limit their communications. Each came to be able to hear the other speak, whether aloud or subvocally. Each learned to perceive through the other's senses, up to a point. Visual perception became better and better especially for direct seeing while, as they grew more skillful, the remembered scene became less clear. Tastes and odors could be transmitted, if not accurately, at least with the expected response. Tactile sensations could not be perceived in the slightest degree.

There was little that Peter Wood could learn from Charity. He came to recognize her immediate associates and liked them, particularly her gaunt, weather-beaten father.   He formed a picture of Puritanism which, as an ethic, he had to respect, while the supporting dogma evoked nothing but impatience.   At first he exposed her to the somewhat scholarly agnosticism which prevailed in his own home, but soon found that it distressed her deeply and he left off. There was so much he could report from the vantage of 1965, so many things he could show her which did not conflict with her tenets and faith.

He discovered that Charity's ability to read was remarkable, though what she had read was naturally limited—the Bible from cover to cover, *Pilgrim's Progress*, several essays and two of Shakespeare's plays.   Encouraged by a schoolmaster who must have been an able and dedicated man, she had read and reread everything permitted to her.   Her quite respectable vocabulary was gleaned from these sources and may have equalled Peter's own in size.   In addition she possessed an uncanny word sense which helped her greatly in understanding Peter's jargon.

She learned the taste of bananas and frankfurters, chocolate ice cream and coke, and displayed such an addiction to these delicacies that Peter rapidly put on some of the pounds he had lost.   One day she asked him what he looked like.

"Well, I told you I am sixteen, and I'm sort of thin."

"Does thee possess a mirror?" she asked.

"Yes, of course."

At her urging and with some embarrassment he went and stood before a mirrored door in his mother's bedroom.

"Marry," she said after a dubious pause, "I doubt not thee is comely. But folk have changed."

"Now let me look at you," he demanded.

"Nay, we have no mirror."

"Then go and look in the brook.   There's a quiet spot below the rock where the water is dark."

He was delighted with her appearance, having remembered Hogarth's unkind representations of a not much later period and being prepared for disappointment.   She was in fact very much prettier by Peter's standards than by those of her own time, which favored plumpness and smaller mouths.   He told her she was a beauty, and her tentative fondness for him turned instantly to adulation.

Previously, Peter had had fleeting glimpses of her slim, smoothly muscled body, as she had bathed or dressed.   Now, having seen each other face to face, they were overcome by embarrassment and both of them, when not fully clothed, stared resolutely into the corners of the room.

For a time Charity believed that Peter was a dreadful liar.   The sight

254

and sound of planes in the sky were not enough to convince her of the fact of flying, so he persuaded his father to take him along on a business flight to Washington. After she had recovered from the marvels of airplane travel, he took her on a walking tour of the Capitol. Now she would believe anything, even that the American Revolution had been a success. They joined his father for lunch at an elegant French restaurant and she experienced, vicariously, the pleasures of half of a half-bottle of white wine and a chocolate eclair. Charity was by way of getting spoiled.

Fully recovered and with school only a week away, Peter decided to brush up his tennis. When reading or doing nothing in particular, he was always dimly aware of Charity and her immediate surroundings, and by sharpening his attention he could bring her clearly to the forefront of his mind. Tennis displaced her completely and for an hour or two each day he was unaware of her doings.

Had he been a few years older and a little more knowledgeable and realistic about the world, he might have guessed the peril into which he was leading her. Fictional villainy abounded, of course, and many items in the news didn't bear thinking about, but by his own firsthand experience, people were well-intentioned and kindly, and for the most part they reacted to events with reasonable intelligence. It was what he expected instinctively.

A first hint of possible consequences reached him as he walked home from one of his tennis sessions.

"Ursula Miller said an ill thing to me today."

"Oh?" His answer was abstracted since, in all truth, he was beginning to run out of interest in the village gossip which was all the news she had to offer.

"Yesterday she said it was an untruth about the thirteen states. Today she avowed that I was devil-ridden. And Ursula has been my best friend."

"I warned you that people wouldn't believe you and you might get yourself laughed at," he said. Then suddenly he caught up in his thinking. "Good Lord—Salem."

"Please, Peter, thee must stop taking thy Maker's name."

"I'll try to remember. Listen, Charity, how many people have you been talking to about our—about what's been happening?"

"As I have said. At first to Father and Aunt Beulah. They did believe I was still addled from the fever."

"And to Ursula."

"Aye, but she vowed to keep it secret."

"Do you believe she will, now that she's started name calling?"

A lengthy pause.

"I fear she may have told the lad who keeps her company."

"I should have warned you. Damn it, I should have laid it on the line."

"Peter!"

"Sorry. Charity, not another word to anybody. Tell Ursula you've been fooling—telling stories to amuse her."

"'Twould not be right."

"So what. Charity, don't be scared, but listen. People might get to thinking you're a witch."

"Oh, they couldn't."

"Why not?"

"Because I am not one. Witches are—oh, no, Peter."

He could sense her growing alarm.

"Go tell Ursula it was a pack of lies. Do it now."

"I must milk the cow."

"Do it now."

"Nay, the cow must be milked."

"Then milk her faster than she's ever been milked before."

On the Sabbath, three little boys threw stones at Charity as she and her father left the church. Obadiah Payne caught one of them and caned him, and then would have had to fight the lad's father save that the pastor intervened.

It was on the Wednesday that calamity befell. Two tight-lipped men approached Obadiah in the fields.

"Squire wants to see thy daughter Charity."

"Squire?"

"Aye. Squire Hacker. He would talk with her at once."

"Squire can talk to me if so be he would have her reprimanded. What has she been up to?"

"Witchcraft, that's what," said the second man, sounding as if he were savoring the dread news. "Croft's old ewe delivered a monstrous lamb. Pointy pinched-up face and an extra eye." He crossed himself.

"Great God!"

"'Twill do ye no good to blaspheme, Obadiah. She's to come with us now."

"I'll not have it. Charity's no witch, as ye well know, and I'll not have her converse with Squire. Ye mind the Squire's lecherous ways."

"That's not here nor there. Witchcraft is afoot again and all are saying 'tis your Charity at bottom of it."

"She shall not go."

First one, then the other displayed the stout truncheons they had held concealed behind their backs.

"'Twas of our own good will we told thee first. Come now and instruct thy daughter to go with us featly. Else take a clout on the head and sleep tonight in the gaol house."

They left Obie Payne gripping a broken wrist and staring in numbed bewilderment from his door stoop, and escorted Charity, not touching her, walking at a cautious distance to either side, to Squire Hacker's big house on the hill. In the village proper, little groups of people watched from doorways and, though some had always been her good friends, none had the courage now to speak a word of comfort.

Peter went with her each reluctant step of the way, counting himself responsible for her plight and helpless to do the least thing about it. He sat alone in the living room of his home, eyes closed to sharpen his reading of her surroundings. She offered no response to his whispered reassurances and perhaps did not hear them.

At the door her guards halted and stood aside, leaving her face to face with the grim-visaged squire. He moved backward step by step, and she followed him, as if hypnotised, into the shadowed room.

The squire lowered himself into a high-backed chair. "Look at me."

Unwillingly she raised her head and stared into his face.

Squire Hacker was a man of medium height, very broad in the shoulder and heavily muscled. His face was disfigured by deep pock marks and the scar of a knife cut across the jaw, souvenirs of his earlier years in the Carib Islands. From the Islands he had also brought some wealth which he had since increased manyfold by the buying of land, share cropping and money lending.

"Charity Payne," he said sternly, "take off thy frock."

"No. No, please."

"I command it. Take off thy garments for I must search thee for witch marks."

He leaned forward, seized her arm and pulled her to him. "If thee would avoid public trial and condemnation, thee will do as I say." His hands began to explore her body.

Even by the standards of the time, Charity regularly spent extraordinary hours at hard physical labor and she possessed a strength which would have done credit to many young men. Squire Hacker should have been more cautious.

"Nay," she shouted and drawing back her arm, hit him in the nose with all the force she could muster. He released her with a roar of rage, then, while he was mopping away blood and tears with the sleeve of his ruffled shirt and shouting imprecations, she turned and shot out the door. The guards, converging, nearly grabbed her as she passed but, once away, they stood no chance of catching her and for a wonder none of the villagers took up the chase.

She was well on the way home and covering the empty road at a fast trot before Peter was able to gain her attention.

"Charity," he said, "Charity, you mustn't go home. If that s. o. b. of a squire has any influence with the court, you just fixed yourself."

She was beginning to think again and could even translate Peter's strange language.

"Influence!" she said. "Marry, he is the court. He is the judge."

"Ouch!"

"I wot well I must not be found at home. I am trying to think where to hide. I might have had trial by water. Now they will burn me for a surety. I do remember what folk said about the last witch trials."

"Could you make your way to Boston and then maybe to New York— New Amsterdam?"

"Leave my home forever! Nay. And I would not dare the trip."

"Then take to the woods. Where can you go?"

"Take to—? Oh. To the cave, mayhap."

"Don't too many people know about it?"

"Aye. But there is another across the brook and beyond Tom Carter's freehold. I do believe none know of it but me. 'Tis very small. We must ford the brook just yonder, then walk that fallen tree. There is a trail which at sundown will be tromped by a herd of deer."

"You're thinking about dogs?"

"Aye, on the morrow. There is no good pack in Annes Towne."

"You live in a savage age, Charity."

"Aye," she said wryly. " 'Tis fortunate we have not invented the bomb."

"Damn it," Peter said, "I wish we'd never met. I wish I hadn't taken you on that plane trip. I wish I'd warned you to keep quiet about it."

"Ye could not guess I would be so foolish."

"What can you do out here without food?"

"I'd liefer starve than be in the stocks, but there is food to be had in the forest, some sorts of roots and toadstools and autumn berries. I shall hide myself for three days, I think, then seek out my father by night and do as he tells me."

When she was safely hidden in the cave, which was small indeed but well concealed by a thicket of young sassafras, she said:

"Now we can think. First, I would have an answer from thy superior wisdom. Can one be truly a witch and have no knowledge of it?"

"Don't be foolish. There's no such thing as a witch."

"Ah well, 'tis a matter for debate by scholars. I do feel in my heart that I am not a witch, if there be such creatures. That book, Peter, of which ye told me, which recounts the history of these colonies."

"Yes?"

"Will ye look in it and learn if I come to trial and what befell me?"

"There'd be nothing about it. It's just a small book. But—"

To his parents' puzzlement, Peter spent the following morning at the Boston Public Library. In the afternoon he shifted his operations to the Historical Society. He found at last a listing of the names of women known to have been tried for witchcraft between the years 1692 and 1697. Thereafter he could locate only an occasional individual name. There was no record of any Charity Payne in 1700 or later.

He started again when the reading room opened next day, interrupting the task only momentarily for brief exchanges with Charity. His lack of success was cheering to her, for she overestimated the completeness of the records.

At close to noon he was scanning the pages of a photostated doctoral thesis when his eye caught a familiar name.

"Jonas Hacker," it read. "Born Liverpool, England, date uncertain, perhaps 1659, was the principal figure in a curious action of law which has not become a recognized legal precedent in English courts.

"Squire Hacker, a resident of Annes Towne (cf. Anniston), was tried and convicted of willful murder and larceny. The trial was posthumous, several months after his decease from natural causes in 1704. The sentence pronounced was death by hanging which, since it could not be imposed, was commuted to forfeiture of his considerable estate. His land and other possessions reverted to the Crown and were henceforward administered by the Governor of Bay Colony.

"While the motivation and procedure of the court may have been open to question, evidence of Hacker's guilt was clear-cut. The details are these . . ."

"Hey, Charity," Peter rumbled in his throat.

"Aye?"

"Look at this page. Let me flatten it out."

"Read it please, Peter. Is it bad news?"

"No. Good, I think." He read the paragraphs on Jonas Hacker.

"Oh, Peter, can it be true?"

"It has to be. Can you remember any details?"

"Marry, I remember well when they disappeared, the ship's captain and a common sailor. They were said to have a great sack of gold for some matter of business with Squire. But it could not be, for they never reached his house."

"That's what Hacker said, but the evidence showed that they got there —got there and never got away. Now here's what you must do. Late tonight, go home."

"I would fen do so, for I am terrible athirst."

"No, wait. What's your parson's name?"

"John Hix."

"Can you reach his house tonight without being seen?"

"Aye. It backs on a glen."

"Go there. He can protect you better than your father can until your trial."

"Must I be tried?"

"Of course. We want to clear your name. Now let's do some planning."

The town hall could seat no more than a score of people, and the day was fair; so it was decided that the trial should be held on the common, in discomforting proximity to the stocks.

Visitors came from as far as twenty miles away, afoot or in carts, and nearly filled the common itself. Squire Hacker's own armchair was the only seat provided. Others stood or sat on the patchy grass.

The squire came out of the inn presently, fortified with rum, and took his place. He wore a brocaded coat and a wide-rimmed hat and would have been more impressive if it had not been for his still swollen nose, now permanently askew.

A way was made through the crowd then, and Charity, flanked on one side by John Hix, on the other by his tall son, walked to the place where she was to stand. Voices were suddenly stilled. Squire Hacker did not condescend to look directly at the prisoner, but fixed a cold stare on the minister; a warning that his protection of the girl would not be forgiven. He cleared his throat.

"Charity Payne, is thee willing to swear upon the Book?"

"Aye."

"No mind. We may forego the swearing. All can see that ye are fearful."

"Nay," John Hix interrupted. "She shall have the opportunity to swear to her word. 'Twould not be legal otherwise." He extended a Bible to Charity, who placed her fingers on it and said, "I do swear to speak naught but the truth."

Squire Hacker glowered and lost no time coming to the attack. "Charity Payne, do ye deny being a witch?"

"I do."

"Ye do be one?"

"Nay, I do deny it."

"Speak what ye mean. What have ye to say of the monstrous lamb born of Master Croft's ewe?"

"I know naught of it."

"Was't the work of Satan?"

"I know not."

"Was't then the work of God?"

"I know not."

"Thee holds then that He might create such a monster?"

"I know naught about it."

"In thy own behalf will thee deny saying that this colony and its neighbors will in due course make war against our King?"

"Nay, I do not deny that."

There was a stir in the crowd and some angry muttering.

"Did ye tell Mistress Ursula Miller that ye had flown a great journey through the air?"

"Nay."

"Mistress Ursula will confound thee in that lie."

"I did tell Ursula that someday folk would travel in that wise. I did tell her that I had seen such travel through eyes other than my own."

Squire Hacker leaned forward. He could not have hoped for a more damning statement. John Hix' head bowed in prayer.

"Continue."

"Aye. I am blessed with a sort of second sight."

"Blessed or cursed?"

"God permits it. It cannot be accursed."

"Continue. What evil things do ye see by this second sight?"

"Most oftentimes I see the world as it will one day be. Thee said evil. Such sights are no more and no less evil than we see around us."

Hacker pondered. There was an uncomfortable wrongness about this child's testimony. She should have been gibbering with fear, when in fact she seemed self-possessed. He wondered if by some strange chance she really had assistance from the devil's minions.

"Charity Payne, thee has confessed to owning second sight. Does thee use this devilish power to spy on thy neighbors?"

It was a telling point. Some among the spectators exchanged discomfited glances.

"Nay, 'tis not devilish, and I cannot see into the doings of my neighbors —except—"

"Speak up, girl. Except what?"

"Once I did perceive by my seeing a most foul murder."

"Murder!" The squire's voice was harsh. A few in the crowd made the sign of the cross.

"Aye. To tell true, two murders. Men whose corpses do now lie buried unshriven in a dark cellar close onto this spot. 'Tween them lies a satchel of golden guineas."

It took a minute for the squire to find his voice.

"A cellar?" he croaked.

"Aye, a root cellar, belike the place one would keep winter apples." She lifted her head and stared straight into the squire's eyes, challenging him to inquire further.

The silence was ponderous as he strove to straighten out his thoughts. To this moment he was safe, for her words described every cellar in and about the village. But she knew. Beyond any question, she knew. Her gaze, seeming to penetrate the darkest corners of his mind, told him that, even more clearly than her words.

Squire Hacker believed in witches and considered them evil and deserving of being destroyed. He had seen and shuddered at the horrible travesty of a lamb in farmer Croft's stable yard, but he had seen like deformities in the Caribbee and did not hold the event an evidence of witchcraft. Not for a minute had he thought Charity a witch, for she showed none of the signs. Her wild talk and the growing rumors had simply seemed to provide the opportunity for some dalliance with a pretty young girl and possibly, in exchange for an acquittal, a lien upon her father's land.

Now he was unsure. She must indeed have second sight to have penetrated his secret, for it had been stormy that night five years ago, and none had seen the missing sailors near to his house. Of that he was confident. Further, shockingly, she knew how and where they lay buried. Another question and answer could not be risked.

He moved his head slowly and looked right and left at the silent throng.

"Charity Payne," he said, picking his words with greatest care, "has put her hand on the Book and sworn to tell true, an act, I opine, she could scarce perform, were she a witch. Does any person differ with me?"

John Hix looked up in startled hopefulness.

"Very well. The lambing at Master Croft's did have the taint of witchcraft, but Master Trowbridge has stated his belief that some noxious plant is growing in Croft's pasture, and 'tis at the least possible. Besides, the ewe is old and she has thrown runty lambs before.

"To quote Master Trowbridge again, he holds that the cholera which has afflicted us so sorely comes from naught but the drinking of bad water. He advises boiling it. I prefer adding a little rum."

He got the laughter he sought. There was a lessening of tension.

"As to second sight." Again he swept the crowd with his gaze. "Charity had laid claim to it, and I called it a devilish gift to test her, but second sight is not witchcraft, as ye well know. My own grandmother had it, and a better woman ne'er lived. I hold it to be a gift of God. Would any challenge me?

"Very well. I would warn Charity to be cautious in what she sees and tells, for second sight can lead to grievous disputations. I do not hold with her story of two murdered men although I think that in her own sight she is telling true. If any have aught of knowledge of so dire a crime, I adjure him to step forth and speak."

He waited. "Nobody? Then, by the authority conferred on me by his Excellency the Governor, I declare that Charity Payne is innocent of the charges brought. She may be released."

This was not at all the eventuality which a few of Squire Hacker's cronies had foretold. The crowd had clearly expected a day long inquisition climaxed by a prisoner to bedevil in the stocks. The Squire's about-face and his abrupt ending of the trial surprised them and angered a few. They stood uncertain.

Then someone shouted hurrah and someone else called for three cheers for Squire Hacker, and all in a minute the gathering had lost its hate and was taking on the look of a picnic. Men headed for the tavern. Parson Hix said a long prayer to which few listened, and everybody gathered around to wring Obie Payne's good hand and to give his daughter a squeeze.

At intervals through the afternoon and evening Peter touched lightly on Charity's mind, finding her carefree and happily occupied with visitors. He chose not to obtrude himself until she called.

Late that night she lay on her mattress and stared into the dark.

"Peter," she whispered.

"Yes, Charity."

"Oh, thank you again."

"Forget it. I got you into the mess. Now you're out of it. Anyway, I didn't really help. It all had to work out the way it did, because that's the way it had happened. You see?"

"No, not truly. How do we know that Squire won't dig up those old bones and burn them?"

"Because he didn't. Four years from now somebody will find them."

"No, Peter, I do not understand, and I am afeared again."

"Why, Charity?"

"It must be wrong, thee and me talking together like this and knowing what is to be and what is not."

"But what could be wrong about it?"

"That I do not know, but I think 'twere better you should stay in your time and me in mine. Goodbye, Peter."

"Charity!"

"And God bless you."

Abruptly she was gone and in Peter's mind there was an emptiness and a knowledge of being alone. He had not known that she could close him out like this.

With the passing of days he became skeptical and in time he might have disbelieved entirely. But Charity visited him again. It was October. He was alone and studying, without much interest.

"Peter."

"Charity, it's you."

"Yes. For a minute, please Peter, for only a minute, but I had to tell you. I—" She seemed somehow embarrassed. "There is a message."

"A what?"

"Look at Bear Rock, Peter, under the bear's jaw on the left side."

With that, she was gone.

The cold water swirled around his legs as he traced with one finger the painstakingly chiseled message she had left; a little-girl message in a symbol far older than either of them.

FOR DISCUSSION: A Message from Charity

1. The author is obviously sympathetic to both Charity and Peter. Is he also sympathetic to Charity's father and Peter's parents? What can you deduce from the story about his attitude toward Squire Hacker?

2. The author uses the device of fever not only as the probable cause of Charity's and Peter's strange ability to communicate with one another but also to link them together immediately. As the story moves from Charity in the opening scene to Peter, what is the connecting device used by the author?

3. Does the fact that Charity's home does not possess a mirror tell you anything about the beliefs held by the people of her time?

4. Peter drops the matter of his family's "scholarly agnosticism" in his

discussions with Charity. Why? What does this tell you about him?

5. Given the science-fiction premise of this story which relates to the concepts involved in time travel to the past, can you explain why Charity does not publicly confront Squire Hacker with her knowledge of the murders he has committed?

6. Can you point to the passage in the story that foreshadows the inevitable end of the communication between Charity and Peter?

INTRODUCTION: Witch War

One of the recurring themes in all fiction is the natural depravity of man. A particularly horrible aspect of this notion is the cruelty of children who appear to be innocent but who are capable of barbarous acts ranging from pulling the wings from flies to bullying and terrorizing those who are younger and weaker than themselves. In "Witch War" the reader will meet seven pretty little girls, specially talented, and the men who cultivate and encourage their talents.

The question as to whether the girls are naturally evil or corrupted by those who use them is one that continues to be debated by mankind. The girls' apparent delight in their work certainly causes one more than a slight shudder.

Witch War
by Richard Matheson

Seven pretty little girls sitting in a row. Outside, night, pouring rain—war weather. Inside, toasty warm. Seven overalled little girls chatting. Plaque on the wall saying: P.G. CENTER.

Sky clearing its throat with thunder, picking and dropping lint lightning from immeasurable shoulders. Rain hushing the world, bowing the trees, pocking earth. Square building, low, with one wall plastic.

Inside, the buzzing talk of seven pretty little girls.

"So I says to him—'Don't give me *that*, Mr. High and Mighty.' So he says, 'Oh yeah?' And I says, 'Yeah!'"

"Honest, will I ever be glad when this thing's over. I saw the cutest hat on my last furlough. Oh, *what* I wouldn't give to wear it!"

"You too? Don't I *know* it! You just can't get your hair right. Not in *this* weather. Why don't they let us get rid of it?"

"*Men!* They make me sick."

Seven gestures, seven postures, seven laughters ringing thin beneath thunder. Teeth showing in girl giggles. Hands tireless, painting pictures in the air.

P.G. Center. Girls. Seven of them. Pretty. Not one over sixteen. Curls. Pigtails. Bangs. Pouting little lips—smiling, frowning, shaping emotion on emotion. Sparkling young eyes—glittering, twinkling, narrowing, cold or warm.

Seven healthy young bodies restive on wooden chairs. Smooth adolescent limbs. Girls—pretty girls—seven of them.

An army of ugly shapeless men, stumbling in mud, struggling along the pitchblack muddy road.

Rain a torrent. Buckets of it thrown on each exhausted man. Sucking sound of great boots sinking into oozy yellow-brown mud, pulling loose. Mud dripping from heels and soles.

Plodding men—hundreds of them—soaked, miserable, depleted. Young men bent over like old men. Jaws hanging loosely, mouths gasping at black wet air, tongues lolling, sunken eyes looking at nothing, betraying nothing.

Rest.

Men sink down in the mud, fall on their packs. Heads thrown back, mouths open, rain splashing on yellow teeth. Hands immobile—scrawny heaps of flesh and bone. Legs without motion—khaki lengths of worm-eaten wood. Hundreds of useless limbs fixed to hundreds of useless trunks.

In back, ahead, beside rumble trucks and tanks and tiny cars. Thick tires splattering mud. Fat treads sinking, tearing at mucky slime. Rain drumming wet fingers on metal and canvas.

Lightning flashbulbs without pictures. Momentary burst of light. The face of war seen for a second—made of rusty guns and turning wheels and faces staring.

Blackness. A night hand blotting out the brief storm glow. Wind-blown rain flitting over fields and roads, drenching trees and trucks. Rivulets of bubbly rain tearing scars from the earth. Thunder, lightning.

A whistle. Dead men resurrected. Boots in sucking mud again—deeper, closer, nearer. Approach to a city that bars the way to a city that bars the way to a . . .

An officer sat in the communication room of the P.G. Center. He peered at the operator, who sat hunched over the control board, phones over his ears, writing down a message.

The officer watched the operator. They are coming, he thought. Cold, wet and afraid they are marching at us. He shivered and shut his eyes.

He opened them quickly. Visions fill his darkened pupils—of curling smoke, flaming men, unimaginable horrors that shape themselves without words or pictures.

"Sir," said the operator, "from advance observation post. Enemy forces sighted."

The officer got up, walked over to the operator and took the message. He read it, face blank, mouth parenthesized. "Yes," he said.

He turned on his heel and went to the door. He opened it and went into the next room. The seven girls stopped talking. Silence breathed on the walls.

The officer stood with his back to the plastic window. "Enemies," he said, "Two miles away. Right in front of you."

He turned and pointed out the window. "Right out there. Two miles away. Any questions?"

A girl giggled.

"Any vehicles?" another asked.

"Yes. Five trucks, five small command cars, two tanks."

"That's too easy," laughed the girl, slender fingers fussing with her hair.

"That's all," said the officer. He started from the room. "Go to it," he added and, under his breath, "Monsters!"

He left.

"Oh, me," sighed one of the girls, "Here we go again."

"What a bore," said another. She opened her delicate mouth and plucked out chewing gum. She put it under her chair seat.

"At least it stopped raining," said a redhead, tying her shoelaces.

The seven girls looked around at each other. *Are you ready?* said their eyes. *I'm ready, I suppose.* They adjusted themselves on the chairs with girlish grunts and sighs. They hooked their feet around the legs of their chairs. All gum was placed in storage. Mouths were tightened into prudish fixity. The pretty little girls made ready for the game.

Finally they were silent on their chairs. One of them took a deep breath. So did another. They all tensed their milky flesh and clasped fragile fingers together. One quickly scratched her head to get it over with. Another sneezed prettily.

"Now," said a girl on the right end of the row.

Seven pairs of beady eyes shut. Seven innocent little minds began to picture, to visualize, to transport.

Lips rolled into thin gashes, faces drained of color, bodies shivered passionately. Their fingers twitching with concentration, seven pretty little girls fought a war.

The men were coming over the rise of a hill when the attack came. The leading men, feet poised for the next step, burst into flame.

There was no time to scream. Their rifles slapped down into the muck, their eyes were lost in fire. They stumbled a few steps and fell, hissing and charred, into the soft mud.

Men yelled. The ranks broke. They began to throw up their weapons and fire at the night. More troops puffed incandescently, flared up, were dead.

"Spread out!" screamed an officer as his gesturing fingers sprouted flame and his face went up in licking yellow heat.

The men looked everywhere. Their dumb terrified eyes searched for an enemy. They fired into the fields and woods. They shot each other. They broke into flopping runs over the mud.

A truck was enveloped in fire. Its driver leaped out, a two-legged torch. The truck went bumping over the road, turned, wove crazily over the field, crashed into a tree, exploded and was eaten up in blazing light. Black shadows flitted in and out of the aura of light around the flames. Screams rent the night.

Man after man burst into flame, fell crashing on his face in the mud. Spots of searing light lashed the wet darkness—screams—running coals, sputtering, glowing, dying—incendiary ranks—trucks cremated—tanks blowing up.

A little blonde, her body tense with repressed excitement. Her lips twitch; a giggle hovers in her throat. Her nostrils dilate. She shudders in giddy fright. She imagines, imagines . . .

A soldier runs headlong across a field, screaming, his eyes insane with horror. A gigantic boulder rushes at him from the black sky.

His body is driven into the earth, mangled. From the rock edge, fingertips protrude.

The boulder lifts from the ground, crashes down again, a shapeless trip hammer. A flaming truck is flattened. The boulder flies again to the black sky.

A pretty brunette, her face a feverish mask. Wild thoughts tumble through her virginal brain. Her scalp grows taut with ecstatic fear. Her lips draw back from clenching teeth. A gasp of terror hisses from her lips. She imagines, imagines . . .

A soldier falls to his knees. His head jerks back. In the light of burning comrades, he stares dumbly at the white-foamed wave that towers over him.

It crashed down, sweeps his body over the muddy earth, fills his lungs with salt water. The tidal wave roars over the field, drowns a hundred flaming men, tosses their corpses in the air with thundering whitecaps.

Suddenly the water stops, flies into a million pieces and disintegrates.

A lovely little redhead, hands drawn under her chin in tight bloodless fists. Her lips tremble, a throb of delight expands her chest. Her white throat contracts, she gulps in a breath of air. Her nose wrinkles with dreadful joy. She imagines, imagines . . .

A running soldier collides with a lion. He cannot see in the darkness. His hands strike wildly at the shaggy mane. He clubs with his rifle butt.

A scream. His face is torn off with one blow of thick claws. A jungle roar billows in the night.

A red-eyed elephant tramples wildly through the mud, picking up men in its thick trunk, hurling them through the air, mashing them under driving black columns.

Wolves bound from the darkness, spring, tear at throats. Gorillas scream and bounce in the mud, leap at falling soldiers.

A rhinoceros, leather skin glowing in the light of living torches, crashes into a burning tank, wheels, thunders into blackness, is gone.

Fangs—claws—ripping teeth—shrieks—trumpeting—roars. The sky rains snakes.

Silence. Vast brooding silence. Not a breeze, not a drip of rain, not a grumble of distant thunder. The battle is ended.

Gray morning mist rolls over the burned, the torn, the drowned, the crushed, the poisoned, the sprawling dead.

Motionless trucks—silent tanks, wisps of oily smoke still rising from their shattered hulks. Great death covering the field. Another battle in another war.

Victory—everyone is dead.

The girls stretched languidly. They extended their arms and rotated their round shoulders. Pink lips grew wide in pretty little yawns. They looked at each other and tittered in embarrassment. Some of them blushed. A few looked guilty.

Then they all laughed out loud. They opened more gumpacks, drew compacts from pockets, spoke intimately with schoolgirl whispers, with late-night dormitory whispers.

Muted giggles rose up fluttering in the warm room.

"Aren't we awful?" one of them said, powdering her pert nose.

Later they all went downstairs and had breakfast.

FOR DISCUSSION: Witch War

1. The opening scene of this story is described in a staccato style. Incomplete sentences and short phrases stud the narrative. What effect does this style have on the reader?

2. In fairy tales, witches are usually described as old and ugly. Why do you suppose the author of this story chose "seven pretty little girls" to be witches? Does it help him achieve a particular effect?

3. To bring fiction to life, an author must successfully stimulate the reader's senses. Sounds, sights, and odors all must be vivid enough to make the reader "see" and "hear" and "taste" what is being described. Can you identify specific words and phrases used by the author of this story to achieve such sensory stimulation?

INTRODUCTION: Gomez

Science-fiction authors take as their literary domain computer technology, space navigation, biology and many other areas of science. But the reader will have noticed by now that they do not neglect human beings in their stories. Here is a story of conflict on several levels. Here too is a story which celebrates the human element in the midst of the intricacies of modern mathematical physics.

Gomez
by C. M. Kornbluth

Now that I'm a cranky, constipated old man I can afford to say that the younger generation of scientists makes me sick to my stomach. Short order fry-cooks of destruction, they hear through the little window the dim order: "Atom bomb rare, with cobalt 60!" and sing it back and rattle their stinking skillets and sling the deadly hash—just what the customer ordered, with never a notion invading their smug, too-heated havens that there's a small matter of right and wrong that takes precedence even over their haute cuisine.

There used to be a slew of them who yelled to high heaven about it. Weiner, Urey, Szilard, Morrison—dead now, and worse. Unfashionable. The greatest of them you have never heard of. Admiral MacDonald never did clear the story. He was Julio Gomez, and his story was cleared yesterday by a fellow my Jewish friends call Malach Hamovis, the Hovering Angel of Death. A black-bordered letter from Rosa advised me that Malach Hamovis had come in on runway six with his flaps down and picked up Julio at the age of 39. Pneumonia.

"But," Rosa painfully wrote, "Julio would want you to know he died not too unhappy, after a good though short life with much of satisfaction..."

I think it will give him some more satisfaction, wherever he is, to know that his story at last is getting told.

It started twenty-two years ago with a routine assignment on a crisp October morning. I had an appointment with Dr. Sugarman, the head of the physics department at the University. It was the umpth anniversary of something or other—first atomic pile, the test A-bomb, Nagasaki—I don't remember what, and the Sunday editor was putting together a page on it.

My job was to interview the three or four University people who were Manhattan District grads.

I found Sugarman in his office at the top of the modest physics building's square gothic tower, brooding through a pointed-arch window at the bright autumn sky. He was a tubby, jowly little fellow. I'd been seeing him around for a couple of years at testimonial banquets and press conferences, but I didn't expect him to remember me. He did, though, and even got the name right.

"Mr. Vilchek?" he beamed. "From the *Tribune?*"

That's right, Dr. Sugarman. How are you?"

"Fine; fine. Sit down, please. Well, what shall we talk about?"

"Well, Dr. Sugarman, I'd like to have your ideas on the really fundamental issues of atomic energy, A-bomb control and so on. What in your opinion is the single most important factor in these problems?"

His eyes twinkled; he was going to surprise me. "Education!" he said, and leaned back waiting for me to register shock.

I registered. "That's certainly a different approach, doctor. How do you mean that, exactly?"

He said impressively: "Education—*technical* education—is the key to the underlying issues of our time. I am deeply concerned over the unawareness of the general public to the meaning and accomplishments of science. People underrate me—underrate *science*, that is—because they do not *understand* science. Let me show you something." He rummaged for a moment through papers on his desk and handed me a sheet of lined tablet paper covered with chicken-track handwriting. "A letter I got," he said. I squinted at the penciled scrawl and read:

October 12

Esteemed Sir:

    Beg to introduce self to you the atomic Scientist as a youth 17 working with diligence to perfect self in Mathematical Physics. The knowledge of English is imperfect since am in New York 1 year only from Puerto Rico and due to Father and Mother poverty must wash the dishes in the restaurant. So esteemed sir excuse imperfect English which will better.

    I hesitate intruding your valuable Scientist time but hope you sometime spare minutes for diligents such as I. My difficulty is with neutron cross-section absorption of boron steel in Reactor which theory I am working out. Breeder reactors demand

$$u = \frac{x}{1} + \frac{x^5}{1} + \frac{x^{10}}{1} + \frac{x^{15}}{1} + \ldots$$

for boron steel, compared with neutron cross-section absorption of

$$v = \frac{x^{1/5}}{1} + \frac{x}{1} + \frac{x^2}{1} + \frac{x^3}{1} + \cdots$$

for any Concrete with which I familiarize myself. Whence arises relationship

$$v^5 = u\,\frac{1 - 2u + 4u^2 - 3u^2 + u^4}{1 + 3u + 4u^2 + 2u^3 + u^4}$$

indicating only a fourfold breeder gain. Intuitively I dissatisfy with this gain and beg to intrude your time to ask wherein I neglect. With the most sincere thanks.

> *J. Gomez*
> *% Porto Bello Lunchroom*
> *124th St. & St. Nicholas Ave.*
> *New-York, New-York*

I laughed and told Dr. Sugarman appreciatively: "That's a good one. I wish our cranks kept in touch with us by mail, but they don't. In the newspaper business they come in and demand to see the editor. Could I use it, by the way? The readers ought to get a boot out of it."

He hesitated and said: "All right—if you don't use my name. Just say 'a prominent physicist.' I didn't think it was too funny myself though, but I see your point, of course. The boy may be feeble-minded—and he probably is—but he believes, like too many people, that science is just a bag of tricks which any ordinary person can acquire—"

And so on and so on.

I went back to the office and wrote the interview in twenty minutes. It took me longer than that to talk the Sunday editor into running the Gomez letter in a box on the atom-anniversary page, but he finally saw it my way. I had to retype it. If I'd just sent the letter down to the composing room as was, we would have had a strike on our hands.

On Sunday morning, at a quarter past six, I woke up to the tune of fists thundering on my hotel-room door. I found my slippers and bathrobe and lurched blearily across the room. They didn't wait for me to unlatch. The door opened. I saw one of the hotel clerks, the Sunday editor, a frosty-faced old man and three hard-faced, hard-eyed young men. The hotel clerk mumbled and retreated and the others moved in. "Chief," I asked the Sunday editor hazily, "what's going—?"

A hard-faced young man was standing with his back to the door; another was standing with his back to the window and the third was blocking the bathroom door. The icy old man interrupted me with a crisp authoritative question snapped at the editor. "You identify this man as Vilchek?"

The editor nodded.

"Search him," snapped the old man. The fellow standing guard at the window slipped up and frisked me for weapons while I sputtered incoherently and the Sunday editor avoided my eye.

When the search was over the frosty-faced old boy said to me: "I am Rear Admiral MacDonald, Mr. Vilchek. I'm here in my capacity as deputy director of the Office of Security and Intelligence, U. S. Atomic Energy Commission. Did you write this?" He thrust a newspaper clipping at my face.

I read, blearily:

WHAT'S SO TOUGH ABOUT A-SCIENCE?
TEEN-AGE POT-WASHER DOESN'T KNOW

A letter received recently by a prominent local atomic scientist points up Dr. Sugarman's complaint (see adjoining column) that the public does not appreciate how hard a physicist works. The text, complete with "mathematics" follows:

Esteemed Sir:

Beg to introduce self to you the Atomic Scientist as a youth 17 working—

"Yes," I told the admiral. "I wrote it, except for the headline. What about it?"

He snapped: "The letter is purportedly from a New York youth seeking information, yet there is no address for him given. Why is that?"

I said patiently: "I left it off when I copied it for the composing room. That's *Trib* style on readers' letters. *What* is all this about?"

He ignored the question and asked: "Where is the purported original of the letter?"

I thought hard and told him: "I think I stuck it in my pants pocket. I'll get it—" I started for the chair with my suit draped over it.

"*Hold it, mister!*" said the young man at the bathroom door. I held it and he proceeded to go through the pockets of the suit. He found the Gomez letter in the inside breast pocket of the coat and passed it to the admiral. The old man compared it, word for word, with the clipping and then put them both in his pocket.

"I want to thank you for your cooperation," he said coldly to me and the Sunday editor. "I caution you not to discuss, and above all not to publish, any account of this incident. The national security is involved in the highest degree. Good day."

He and his boys started for the door, and the Sunday editor came to life. "Admiral," he said, "this is going to be on the front page of tomorrow's *Trib*."

The admiral went white. After a long pause he said: "You are aware that this country may be plunged into global war at any moment. That American boys are dying every day in border skirmishes. Is it to protect civilians like you who won't obey a reasonable request affecting security?"

The Sunday editor took a seat on the edge of my rumpled bed and lit a cigarette. "I know all that, admiral," he said. "I also know that this is a free country and how to keep it that way. Pitiless light on incidents like this of illegal search and seizure."

The admiral said: "I personally assure you, on my honor as an officer, that you would be doing the country a grave disservice by publishing an account of this."

The Sunday editor said mildly: "Your honor as an officer. You broke into this room without a search warrant. Don't you realize that's against the law? And I saw your boy ready to shoot when Vilchek started for that chair." I began to sweat a little at that, but the admiral was sweating harder.

With an effort he said: "I should apologize for the abruptness and discourtesy with which I've treated you. I do apologize. My only excuse is that, as I've said, this is a crash-priority matter. May I have your assurance that you gentlemen will keep silent?"

"On one condition," said the Sunday editor. "I want the *Trib* to have an exclusive on the Gomez story. I want Mr. Vilchek to cover it, with your full cooperation. In return, we'll hold it for your release and submit it to your security censorship."

"It's a deal," said the admiral, sourly. He seemed to realize suddenly that the Sunday editor had been figuring on such a deal all along.

On the plane for New York, the admiral filled me in. He was precise and unhappy, determined to make the best of a bad job. "I was awakened at three this morning by a phone call from the chairman of the Atomic Energy Commission. *He* had been awakened by a call from Dr. Monroe of the Scientific Advisory Committee. Dr. Monroe had been up late working and sent out for the Sunday *Tribune* to read before going to sleep. He saw the Gomez letter and went off like a 16-inch rifle. The neutron cross-section absorption relationship expressed in it happens to be, Mr. Vilchek, his own work. It also happens to be one of the nation's most closely-guarded—er—atomic secrets. Presumably this Gomez stumbled on it somehow, as a janitor or something of the sort, and is feeding his ego by pretending to be an atomic scientist."

I scratched my unshaved jaw. "Admiral," I said, "you would't kid me? How can three equations be a top atomic secret?"

The admiral hesitated. "All I can tell you," he said slowly, "is that breeder reactors are involved."

"But the letter said that. You mean this Gomez not only swiped the equations but knew what they were about?"

The admiral said grimly: "Somebody has been incredibly lax. It would be worth many divisions to the Soviet for their man Kapitza to see those equations—and realize that they are valid."

He left me to chew that one over for a while as the plane droned over New Jersey. Finally the pilot called back: "E.T.A. five minutes, sir. We have landing priority at Newark."

"Good," said the admiral. "Signal for a civilian-type car to pick us up without loss of time."

"Civilian," I said.

"Of course, civilian!" he snapped. "That's the hell of it. Above all we must not arouse suspicion that there is anything special or unusual about this Gomez or his letter. Copies of the *Tribune* are on their way to the Soviet now as a matter of routine—they take all American papers and magazines they can get. If we tried to stop shipment of *Tribunes* that would be an immediate give-away that there was something of importance going on."

We landed and the five of us got into a late-model car, neither drab nor flashy. One of the admiral's young men relieved the driver, a corporal with Signal Corps insignia. There wasn't much talk during the drive from Newark to Spanish Harlem, New York. Just once the admiral lit a cigarette, but he flicked it through the window after a couple of nervous puffs.

The Porto Bello Lunchroom was a store-front restaurant in the middle of a shabby tenement block. Wide-eyed, graceful, skinny little kids stared as our car parked in front of it and then converged on us purposefully. "Watch your car, mister?" they begged. The admiral surprised them—and me—with a flood of Spanish that sent the little extortionists scattering back to their stickball game in the street and their potsy layouts chalked on the sidewalks.

"Higgins," said the admiral, "see if there's a back exit." One of his boys got out and walked around the block under the dull, incurious eyes of black-shawled women sitting on their stoops. He was back in five minutes, shaking his head.

"Vilchek and I will go in," said the admiral. "Higgins, stand by the restaurant door and tackle anyone who comes flying out. Let's go, reporter. And remember that I do the talking."

The noon-hour crowd at the Porto Bello's ten tables looked up at us when we came in. The admiral said to a woman at a primitive cashier's table: "*Nueva York* Board of Health, *señora*."

"Ah!" she muttered angrily. "*Por favor, no aquí!* In back, understand?

276

Come." She beckoned a pretty waitress to take over at the cash drawer and led us into the steamy little kitchen. It was crowded with us, an old cook and a young dishwasher. The admiral and the woman began a rapid exchange of Spanish. He played his part well. I myself couldn't keep my eyes off the kid dishwasher who somehow or other had got hold of one of America's top atomic secrets.

Gomez was seventeen, but he looked fifteen. He was small-boned and lean, with skin the color of bright Virginia tobacco in an English cigarette. His hair was straight and glossy-black and a little long. Every so often he wiped his hands on his apron and brushed it back from his damp forehead. He was working like hell, dipping and swabbing and rinsing and drying like a machine, but he didn't look pushed or angry. He wore a half-smile that I later found out was his normal, relaxed expression and his eyes were far away from the kitchen of the Porto Bello Lunchroom. The elderly cook was making it clear by the exaggerated violence of his gesture and a savage frown that he resented these people invading his territory. I don't think Gomez even knew we were there. A sudden, crazy idea came into my head.

The admiral had turned to him. *"Como se llama, chico?"*

He started and put down the dish he was wiping. "Julio Gomez, señor. *Por que, por favor? Que pasa?"*

He wasn't the least bit scared.

"Nueva York Board of Health," said the admiral. *"Con su permiso—"* He took Gomez' hands in his and looked at them gravely, front and back, making *tsk-tsk* noses. Then, decisively: *"Vamanos, Julio. Siento mucho. Usted esta muy enfermo."* Everybody started talking at once, the woman doubtless objecting to the slur on her restaurant and the cook to losing his dishwasher and Gomez to losing time from the job.

The admiral gave them broadside for broadside and outlasted them. In five minutes we were leading Gomez silently from the restaurant. *"La lotería!"* a woman customer said in a loud whisper. *"O las mutas,"* somebody said back. Arrested for policy or marihuana, they thought. The pretty waitress at the cashier's table looked stricken and said nervously: "Julio?" as we passed, but he didn't notice.

Gomez sat in the car with the half-smile on his lips and his eyes a million miles away as we rolled downtown to Foley Square. The admiral didn't look as though he'd approve of any questions from me. We got out at the Federal Building and Gomez spoke at last. He said in surprise: "This, it is not the hospital!"

Nobody answered. We marched him up the steps and surrounded him in the elevator. It would have made anybody nervous—it would have made *me* nervous—to be herded like that; everybody's got something on his conscience. But the kid didn't even seem to notice. I decided that he must be a half-wit or—there came that crazy notion again.

The glass door said "U. S. Atomic Energy Commission, Office of Security and Intelligence." The people behind it were flabbergasted when the admiral and party walked in. He turned the head man out of his office and sat at his desk, with Gomez getting the caller's chair. The rest of us stationed ourselves uncomfortably around the room.

It started. The admiral produced the letter and asked in English: "Have you ever seen this before?" He made it clear from the way he held it that Gomez wasn't going to get his hands on it.

"Sí, seguro. I write it last week. This is funny business. I am not really sick like you say, no?" He seemed relieved.

"No. Where did you get these equations?"

Gomez said proudly: "I work them out."

The admiral gave a disgusted little laugh. "Don't waste my time, boy. Where did you get these equations?"

Gomez was beginning to get upset. "You got no right to call me liar," he said. "I not so smart as the big physicists, seguro, and maybe I make mistakes. Maybe I waste the profesór Soo-har-man his time but he got no right to have me arrest. I tell him right in letter he don't have to answer if he don't want. I make no crime and you got no right!"

The admiral looked bored. "Tell me how you worked the equations out," he said.

"Okay," said Gomez sulkily. "You know the random paths of neutron is expressed in matrix mechanics by profesór Oppenheim five years ago, all okay. I transform his equations from path-prediction domain to cross-section domain and integrate over absorption areas. This gives u series and v series. And from there, the u-v relationship is obvious, no?"

The admiral, still bored, asked: "Got it?"

I noticed that one of his young men had a shorthand pad out. He said: "Yes."

The admiral picked up the phone and said: "This is MacDonald. Get me Dr. Mines out at Brookhaven right away." He told Gomez blandly: "Dr. Mines is the chief of the A.E.C. Theoretical Physics Division. I'm going to ask him what he thinks of the way you worked the equations out. He's going to tell me that you were just spouting a lot of gibberish. And then you're going to tell me where you really got them."

Gomez looked mixed up and the admiral turned back to the phone. "Dr. Mines? This is Admiral MacDonald of Security. I want your opinion on the following." He snapped his fingers impatiently and the stenographer passed him his pad. "Somebody has told me that he discovered a certain relationship by taking—" He read carefully. "—by taking the random paths of a neutron expressed in matrix mechanics by Oppenheim, transforming his equations from the path-prediction domain to the cross-section domain and integrating over the absorption areas."

In the silence of the room I could hear the faint buzz of the voice on the other end. And a great red blush spread over the admiral's face from his brow to his neck. The faintly-buzzing voice ceased and after a long pause the admiral said slowly and softly: "No, it wasn't Fermi or Szilard. I'm not at liberty to tell you who. Can you come right down to the Federal Building Security Office in New York? I—I need your help. Crash priority." He hung up the phone wearily and muttered to himself: "Crash priority. Crash." And wandered out of the office looking dazed.

His young men stared at one another in frank astonishment. "Five years," said one, "and—"

"*Nix*," said another, looking pointedly at me.

Gomez asked brightly: "What goes on anyhow? This is damn funny business, I think."

"Relax, kid," I told him. "Looks as if you'll make out all—"

"*Nix*," said the nixer again savagely, and I shut up and waited.

After a while somebody came in with coffee and sandwiches and we ate them. After another while the admiral came in with Dr. Mines. Mines was a white-haired, wrinkled Connecticut Yankee. All I knew about him was that he'd been in mild trouble with Congress for stubbornly plugging world government and getting on some of the wrong letterheads. But I learned right away that he was all scientist and didn't have a phony bone in his body.

"Mr. Gomez?" he asked cheerfully. "The admiral tells me that you are either a well-trained Russian spy or a phenomenal self-taught nuclear physicist. He wants me to find out which."

"Russia?" yelled Gomez, outraged. "He crazy! I am American United States citizen!"

"That's as may be," said Dr. Mines. "Now, the admiral tells me you describe the u-v relationship as 'obvious.' I should call it a highly abstruse derivation in the theory of continued fractions and complex multiplication."

Gomez strangled and gargled helplessly trying to talk, and finally asked, his eyes shining: "*Por favor*, could I have piece paper?"

They got him a stack of paper and the party was on.

For two unbroken hours Gomez and Dr. Mines chattered and scribbled. Mines gradually shed his jacket, vest and tie, completely oblivious to the rest of us. Gomez was even more abstracted. He *didn't* shed his jacket, vest and tie. He didn't seem to be aware of anything except the rapid-fire exchange of ideas via scribbled formulae and the terse spoken jargon of mathematics. Dr. Mines shifted on his chair and sometimes his voice rose with excitement. Gomez didn't shift or wriggle or cross his legs. He just sat and scribbled and talked in a low, rapid monotone, looking straight at Dr. Mines with his eyes very wide-open and lit up like searchlights.

The rest of us just watched and wondered.

Dr. Mines broke at last. He stood up and said: "I can't take any more, Gomez. I've got to think it over—" He began to leave the room, mechanically scooping up his clothes, and then realized that we were still there.

"Well?" asked the admiral grimly.

Dr. Mines smiled apologetically. "He's a physicist, all right," he said. Gomez sat up abruptly and looked astonished.

"Take him into the next office, Higgins," said the admiral. Gomez let himself be led away, like a sleepwalker.

Dr. Mines began to chuckle. "Security!" he said. "Security!"

The admiral rasped: "Don't trouble yourself over my decisions, if you please, Dr. Mines. My job is keeping the Soviets from pirating American science and I'm doing it to the best of my ability. What I want from you is your opinion on the possibility of that young man having worked out the equations as he claimed."

Dr. Mines was abruptly sobered. "Yes," he said. "Unquestionably he did. And will you excuse my remark? I was under some strain in trying to keep up with Gomez."

"Certainly," said the admiral, and managed a frosty smile. "Now if you'll be so good as to tell me how this completely impossible thing can have happened—?"

"It's happened before, admiral," said Dr. Mines. "I don't suppose you ever heard of Ramanujan?"

"No."

"*Srinivasa* Ramanujan?"

"*No!*"

"Oh. Well, Ramanujan was born in 1887 and died in 1920. He was a poor Hindu who failed twice in college and then settled down as a government clerk. With only a single obsolete textbook to go on he made himself a very great mathematician. In 1913 he sent some of his original work to a Cambridge professor. He was immediately recognized and called to England where he was accepted as a first-rank man, became a member of the Royal Society, a Fellow of Trinity and so forth."

The admiral shook his head dazedly.

"It happens," Dr. Mines said. "Oh yes, it happens. Ramanujan had only one out-of-date book. But this is New York. Gomez has access to all the mathematics he could hope for and a great mass of unclassified and declassified nuclear data. And—genius. The way he puts things together . . . he seems to have only the vaguest notion of what a proof should be. He *sees* relationships as a whole. A most convenient faculty which I envy him. Where I have to take, say, a dozen painful steps from one conclusion to the next he achieves it in one grand flying leap. Ramanujan was like that too, by the way—very strong on intuition, weak on what we call 'rigor.'" Dr. Mines noted with a start that he was holding his tie, vest and coat in one hand and began to put them on. "Was there anything else?" he asked politely.

"One thing," said the admiral. "Would you say he's—he's a better physicist than you are?"

"Yes," said Dr. Mines. "Much better." And he left.

The admiral slumped, uncharacteristically, at the desk for a long time. Finally he said to the air: "Somebody get me the General Manager. No, the Chairman of the Commission." One of his boys grabbed the phone and got to work on the call.

"Admiral," I said, "where do we stand now?"

"Eh? Oh, it's you. The matter's out of my hands now since no security violation is involved. I consider Gomez to be in my custody and I shall turn him over to the Commission so that he may be put to the best use in the nation's interest."

"Like a machine?" I asked, disgusted.

He gave me both barrels of his ice-blue eyes. "Like a weapon," he said evenly.

He was right, of course. Didn't I know there was a war on? Of course I did. Who didn't? Taxes, housing shortage, somebody's cousin killed in Korea, everybody's big brother sweating out the draft, prices sky-high at the supermarket. Uncomfortably I scratched my unshaved chin and walked to the window. Foley Square below was full of Sunday peace, with only a single girl stroller to be seen. She walked the length of the block across the street from the Federal Building and then turned and walked back. Her walk was dragging and hopeless and tragic.

Suddenly I knew her. She was the pretty little waitress from the Porto Bello; she must have hopped a cab and followed the men who were taking her Julio away. Might as well beat it, sister, I told her silently. Julio isn't just a good-looking kid any more; he's a military asset. The Security Office is turning him over to the policy-level boys for disposal. When that happens you might as well give up and go home.

It was as if she'd heard me. Holding a silly little handkerchief to her face she turned and ran blindly for the subway entrance at the end of the block and disappeared into it.

At that moment the telephone rang.

"MacDonald here," said the admiral. "I'm ready to report on the Gomez affair, Mr. Commissioner."

Gomez was a minor, so his parents signed a contract for him. The job-description on the contract doesn't matter, but he got a pretty good salary by government standards and a per-diem allowance too.

I signed a contract, too—"Information Specialist." I was partly companion, partly historian and partly a guy they'd rather have their eyes on than not. When somebody tried to cut me out on grounds of economy, Admiral MacDonald frostily reminded him that he had given his word. I stayed, for all the good it did me.

We didn't have any name. We weren't Operation Anything or Project Whoozis or Task Force Dinwiddie. We were just five people in a big fifteen-room house on the outskirts of Milford, New Jersey. There was Gomez, alone on the top floor with a lot of books, technical magazines and blackboards and a weekly visit from Dr. Mines. There were the three Security men, Higgins, Dalhousie and Leitzer, sleeping by turns and prowling the grounds. And there was me.

From briefing sessions with Dr. Mines I kept a diary of what went on. Don't think from that that I knew what the score was. War correspondents have told me of the frustrating life they led at some close-mouthed commands. Soandso-many air sorties, the largest number since January fifteenth. Casualties a full fifteen percent lighter than expected. Determined advance in an active sector against relatively strong enemy opposition. And so on—all adding up to nothing in the way of real information.

That's what it was like in my diary because that's all they told me. Here are some excerpts: "On the recommendation of Dr. Mines, Mr. Gomez today began work on a phase of reactor design theory to be implemented at Brookhaven National Laboratory. The work involves the setting-up of thirty-five pairs of partial differential equations.... Mr. Gomez announced tentatively today that in checking certain theoretical work in progress at the Los Alamos Laboratory of the A.E.C. he discovered a fallacious assumption concerning neutron-spin which invalidates the conclusions reached. This will be communicated to the Laboratory. ... Dr. Mines said today that Mr. Gomez has successfully invoked a hitherto-unexploited aspects of Minkowski's tensor analysis to crack a stubborn obstacle towards the control of thermonuclear reactions...."

I protested at one of the briefing sessions with Dr. Mines against this gobbledygook. He didn't mind my protesting. He leaned back in his chair and said calmly: "Vilchek, with all friendliness I assure you that you're getting everything you can understand. Anything more complex than the vague description of what's going on would be over your head. And anything more specific would give away exact engineering information which would be of use to foreign countries."

"This isn't the way they treated Bill Lawrence when he covered the atomic bomb," I said bitterly.

Mines nodded, with a pleased smile. "That's it exactly," he said. "Broad principles were being developed then—interesting things that could be told without any great harm being done. If you tell somebody that a critical mass of U-235 or Plutonium goes off with a big bang, you really haven't given away a great deal. He still has millions of man-hours of engineering before him to figure out how much is critical mass, to take only one small point."

So I took his word for it, faithfully copied the communiques he gave me and wrote what I could on the human-interest side for release some day.

So I recorded Gomez' progress with English, his taste for chicken pot pie and rice pudding, his habit of doing his own housework on the top floor and his old-maidish neatness. "You live your first fifteen years in a tin shack, Beel," he told me once, "and you find out you like things nice and clean." I've seen Dr. Mines follow Gomez through the top floor as the boy swept and dusted, talking at him in their mathematical jargon.

Gomez worked in forty-eight-hour spells usually, and not eating much. Then for a couple of days he'd live like a human being grabbing naps, playing catch on the lawn with one or another of the Security people, talking with me about his childood in Puerto Rico and his youth in New York. He taught me a little Spanish and asked me to catch him up on bad mistakes in English.

"But don't you ever want to get out of here?" I demanded one day.

He grinned: "Why should I, Beel? Here I eat good, I can send money to the parents. Best, I find out what the big professors are up to without I have to wait five-ten years for damn de-classifying."

'Don't you have a girl?"

He was embarrassed and changed the subject back to the big professors.

Dr. Mines drove up then, with his chauffeur who looked like a G-man and almost certainly was. As usual, the physicist was toting a bulging briefcase. After a few polite words with me, he and Julio went indoors and upstairs.

They were closeted for five hours—a record. When Dr. Mines came down I expected the usual briefing session. But he begged off. "Nothing serious," he said. "We just sat down and kicked some ideas of his around. I told him to go ahead. We've been—ah—using him very much like a sort of computer, you know. Turning him loose on the problems that were too tough for me and some of the other men. He's got the itch for research now. It would be very interesting if his forte turned out to be creative."

I agreed.

Julio didn't come down for dinner. I woke up in darkness that night when there was a loud bump overhead, and went upstairs in my pyjamas.

Gomez was sprawled, fully dressed, on the floor. He'd tripped over a footstool. And he didn't seem to have noticed. His lips were moving and he stared straight at me without knowing I was there.

"You all right, Julio?" I asked, and started to help him to his feet.

He got up mechanically and said: "—real values of the zeta function vanish."

"How's that?"

He saw me then and asked, puzzled: "How you got in here, Beel? Is dinnertime?"

"Is four A.M., *por dios*. Don't you think you ought to get some sleep?" He looked terrible.

No; he didn't think he ought to get some sleep. He had some work to do. I went downstairs and heard him pacing overhead for an hour until I dozed off.

This splurge of work didn't wear off in forty-eight hours. For a week I brought him meals and sometimes he ate absently, with one hand, as he scribbled on a yellow pad. Sometimes I'd bring him lunch to find his breakfast untouched. He didn't have much beard, but he let it grow for a week—too busy to shave, too busy to talk, too busy to eat, sleeping in chairs when fatigue caught up with him.

I asked Leitzer, badly worried, if we should do anything about it. He had a direct scrambler-phone connection with the New York Security and Intelligence office, but his orders didn't cover anything like a self-induced nervous breakdown of the man he was guarding.

I thought Dr. Mines would do something when he came—call in an M.D., or tell Gomez to take it easy, or take some of the load off by parcelling out whatever he had by the tail.

But he didn't. He went upstairs, came down two hours later and absently tried to walk past me. I headed him off into my room. "What's the word?" I demanded.

He looked me in the eye and said defiantly: "He's doing fine. I don't want to stop him."

Dr. Mines was a good man. Dr. Mines was a humane man. And he wouldn't lift a finger to keep the boy from working himself into nervous prostration. Dr. Mines liked people well enough but he reserved his love for theoretical physics. "How important can this thing be?"

284

He shrugged irritably. "It's just the way some scientists work," he said. "Newton was like that. So was Sir William Rowan Hamilton—"

"Hamilton-Schmamilton," I said. "What's the sense of it? *Why* doesn't he sleep or eat?"

Mines said: "*You* don't know what it's like."

"Of course," I said, getting good and sore. "I'm just a dumb newspaper man. Tell me, Mr. Bones, what is it like?"

There was a long pause, and he said mildly: "I'll try. That boy up there is using his brain. A great chess player can put on a blindfold and play a hundred opponents in a hundred games simultaneously, remembering all the positions of his pieces and theirs and keeping a hundred strategies clear in his mind. Well, that stunt simply isn't in the same league with what Julio's doing up there.

"He has in his head some millions of facts concerning theoretical physics. He's scanning them, picking out one here and there, fitting them into new relationships, checking and rejecting when he has to, fitting the new relationships together, turning them upside-down and inside-out to see what happens, comparing them with known doctrine, holding them in his memory while he repeats the whole process and compares—and all the while he has a goal firmly in mind against which he's measuring all these things." He seemed to be finished.

For a reporter, I felt strangely shy. "What's he driving at?" I asked.

"I think," he said slowly, "he's approaching an unified field theory."

Apparently that was supposed to explain everything. I let Dr. Mines know that it didn't.

He said thoughtfully: "I don't know whether I can get it over to a layman—no offense, Vilchek. Let's put it this way. You know how math comes in waves, and how it's followed by waves of applied science based on the math. There was a big wave of algebra in the middle ages—following it came navigation, gunnery, surveying and so on. Then the renaissance and a wave of analysis—what you'd call calculus. That opened up stream power and how to use it, mechanical engineering, electricity. The wave of *modern* mathematics since say 1875 gave us atomic energy. That boy upstairs may be starting off the next big wave."

He got up and reached for his hat.

"Just a minute," I said. I was surprised that my voice was steady. "What comes next? Control of gravity? Control of personality? Sending people by radio?"

Dr. Mines wouldn't meet my eye. Suddenly he looked old and shrunken. "Don't worry about the boy," he said.

I let him go.

That evening I brought Gomez chicken pot pie and a non-alcoholic egg nog. He drank the egg nog, said "Hi, Beel," and continued to cover yellow sheets of paper.

I went downstairs and worried.

Abruptly it ended late the next afternoon. Gomez wandered into the big first-floor kitchen looking like a starved old rickshaw coolie. He pushed his lank hair back from his forehead, said: "Beel, what is to eat—" and pitched forward onto the linoleum. Leitzer came when I yelled, expertly took Gomez' pulse, rolled him onto a blanket and threw another one over him. "It's just a faint," he said. "Let's get him to bed."

"Aren't you going to call a doctor, man?"

"Doctor couldn't do anything we can't do," he said stolidly. "And I'm here to see that security isn't breached. Give me a hand."

We got him upstairs and put him to bed. He woke up and said something in Spanish, and then, apologetically: "Very sorry, fellows. I ought to taken it easier."

"I'll get you some lunch," I said, and he grinned.

He ate it all, enjoying it heartily, and finally lay back gorged. "Well," he asked me, "what it is new, Beel?"

"What *is* new. And you should tell me. You finish your work?"

"I got it in shape to finish. The hard part it is over." He rolled out of bed.

"Hey!" I said.

"I'm okay now," he grinned. "Don't write this down in your history, Beel. Everybody will think I act like a woman."

I followed him into his workroom where he flopped into an easy chair, his eyes on a blackboard covered with figures. He wasn't grinning any more.

"Dr. Mines says you're up to something big," I said.

"*Sí*. Big."

"Unified field theory, he says."

"That is it," Gomez said.

"Is it good or bad?" I asked, licking my lips. "The application, I mean." His boyish mouth set suddenly in a grim line. "That, it is not my business," he said. "I am American citizen of the United States." He stared at the blackboard and its maze of notes.

I looked at it too—*really* looked at it for once—and was surprised by what I saw. Mathematics, of course, I don't know. But I had soaked up a very little *about* mathematics. One of the things I had soaked up was that the expressions of higher mathematics tend to be complicated and elaborate, involving English, Greek and Hebrew letters, plain and fancy brackets and a great variety of special signs besides the plus and minus of the elementary school.

The things on the blackboard weren't like that at all. The board was covered with variations of a simple expression that consisted of five letters and two symbols: a right-handed pothook and a left-handed pothook.

"What do they mean?" I asked, pointing.

"Some things I made up," he said nervously. "The word for that one is 'enfields.' The other one is 'is enfielded by.'"

"What's *that* mean?"

His luminous eyes were haunted. He didn't answer.

"It looks like simple stuff. I read somewhere that all the basic stuff is simple once it's been discovered."

"Yes," he said almost inaudibly. "It is simple, Beel. Too damn simple, I think. Better I carry it in my head, I think." He strode to the blackboard and erased it. Instinctively I half-rose to stop him. He gave me a grin that was somehow bitter and unlike him. "Don't worry," he said. "I don't forget it." He tapped his forehead. "I *can't* forget it." I hope I never see again on any face the look that was on his.

"Julio," I said, appalled. "Why don't you get out of here for a while? Why don't you run over to New York and see your folks and have some fun? They can't keep you here against your will."

"They told me I shouldn't—" he said uncertainly. And then he got tough. "You're damn right, Beel. Let's go in together. I get dressed up. Er—You tell Leitzer, hah?" He couldn't quite face up to the hard-boiled security man.

I told Leitzer, who hit the ceiling. But all it boiled down to was that he sincerely wished Gomez and I wouldn't leave. We weren't in the Army, we weren't in jail. I got hot at last and yelled back that we were damn well going out and he couldn't stop us. He called New York on his direct wire and apparently New York confirmed it, regretfully.

We got on the 4:05 Jersey Central, with Higgins and Dalhousie tailing up at a respectful distance. Gomez didn't notice them and I didn't tell him. He was having too much fun. He had a shine put on his shoes at Penn Station and worried about the taxi fare as we rode up to Spanish Harlem.

His parents lived in a neat little three-room apartment. A lot of the furniture looked brand-new, and I was pretty sure who had paid for it. The mother and father spoke only Spanish, and mumbled shyly when "*mi amigo Beel*" was introduced. I had a very halting conversation with the father while the mother and Gomez rattled away happily and she poked his ribs to point up the age-old complaint of any mother anywhere that he wasn't eating enough.

The father, of course, thought the boy was a janitor or something in the Pentagon and, as near as I could make out, he was worried about his

Julio being grabbed off by a man-hungry government girl. I kept reassuring him that his Julio was a good boy, a very good boy, and he seemed to get some comfort out of it.

There was a little spat when his mother started to set the table. Gomez said reluctantly that we couldn't stay, that we were eating somewhere else. His mother finally dragged from him the admission that we were going to the Porto Bello so he could see Rosa, and everything was smiles again. The father told me that Rosa was a good girl, a very good girl.

Walking down the three flights of stairs with yelling little kids playing tag around us, Gomez asked proudly: "You not think they in America only a little time, hey?"

I yanked him around by the elbow as we went down the brownstone stoop into the street. Otherwise he would have seen our shadows for sure. I didn't want to spoil his fun.

The Porto Bello was full, and the pretty little girl was on duty as cashier at the table. Gomez got a last-minute attack of cold feet at the sight of her. "No table," he said. "We better go someplace else."

I practically dragged him in. "We'll get a table in a minute," I said.

"Julio," said the girl, when she saw him.

He looked sheepish. "Hello, Rosa. I'm back for a while."

"I'm glad to see you again," she said tremulously.

"I'm glad to see you again too—" I nudged him. "Rosa, this is my good friend Beel. We work together in Washington."

"Pleased to meet you, Rosa. Can you have dinner with us? I'll bet you and Julio have a lot to talk over."

"Well, I'll see . . . look, there's a table for you. I'll see if I can get away."

We sat down and she flagged down the proprietress and got away in a hurry.

All three of us had *arróz con pollo*—rice with chicken and lots of other things. Their shyness wore off and I was dealt out of the conversation, but I didn't mind. They were a nice young couple. I liked the way they smiled at each other, and the things they remembered happily—movies, walks, talks. It made me feel like a benevolent uncle with one foot in the grave. It made me forget for a while the look on Gomez' face when he turned from the blackboard he had covered with too-simple math.

Over dessert I broke in. By then they were unselfconsciously holding hands. "Look," I said, "why don't you two go on and do the town? Julio, I'll be at the Madison Park Hotel." I scribbled the address and gave it to him. "And I'll get a room for you. Have fun and reel in any time." I rapped his knee. He looked down and I slipped him four twenties. I didn't know whether he had money on him or not, but anything extra the boy could use he had coming to him.

"Swell," he said. "Thanks." And looked shame-faced while I looked paternal.

I had been watching a young man who was moodily eating alone in a corner, reading a paper. He was about Julio's height and build and he wore a sports jacket pretty much like Julio's. And the street was pretty dark outside.

The young man got up moodily and headed for the cashier's table. "Gotta go," I said. "Have fun."

I went out of the restaurant right behind the young man and walked as close behind him as I dared, hoping we were being followed.

After a block and a half of this, he turned on me and snarled: "Wadda you, mister? A wolf? Beat it!"

"Okay," I said mildly, and turned and walked the other way. Higgins and Dalhousie were standing there, flat-footed and open-mouthed. They sprinted back to the Porto Bello, and *I* followed *them*. But Julio and Rosa had already left.

"Tough, fellows," I said to them as they stood in the doorway. They looked as if they wanted to murder me. "He won't get into any trouble," I said. "He's just going out with his girl." Dalhousie made a strangled noise and told Higgins: "Cruise around the neighborhood. See if you can pick them up. I'll follow Vilchek." He wouldn't talk to me. I shrugged and got a cab and went to the Madison Park Hotel, a pleasantly unfashionable old place with big rooms where I stay when business brings me to New York. They had a couple of adjoining singles; I took one in my own name and the other for Gomez.

I wandered around the neighborhood for a while and had a couple of beers in one of the ultra-Irish bars on Third Avenue. After a pleasant argument with a gent who thought the Russians didn't have any atomic bombs and faked their demonstrations and that we ought to blow up their industrial cities tomorrow at dawn, I went back to the hotel.

I didn't get to sleep easily. The citizen who didn't believe Russia could maul the United States pretty badly or at all had started me thinking again—all kinds of ugly thoughts. Dr. Mines who had turned into a shrunken old man at the mention of applying Gomez' work. The look on the boy's face. My layman's knowledge that present-day "atomic energy" taps only the smallest fragment of the energy locked up in the atom. My layman's knowledge that once genius has broken a trail in science, mediocrity can follow the trail.

But I slept at last, for three hours.

At four-fifteen A.M. according to my watch the telephone rang long and hard. There was some switchboard and long-distance-operator mumbo-jumbo and then Julio's gleeful voice: "Beel! Congratulate us. We got marriage!"

"Married," I said fuzzily. "You got *married*, not marriage. How's that again?"

"We got *married*. Me and Rosa. We get on the train, the taxi driver takes us to justice of peace, we got *married*, we go to hotel here."

"Congratulations," I said, waking up. "Lots of congratulations. But you're under age, there's a waiting period—"

"Not in this state," he chuckled. "Here is no waiting periods and here I have twenty-one years if I say so."

"Well," I said. "Lots of congratulations, Julio. And tell Rosa she's got herself a good boy."

"Thanks, Beel," he said shyly. "I call you so you don't worry when I don't come in tonight. I think I come in with Rosa tomorrow so we tell her mama and my mama and papa. I call you at the hotel, I still have the piece of paper."

"Okay, Julio. All the best. Don't worry about a thing." I hang up, chuckling, and went right back to sleep.

Well, sir, it happened again.

I was shaken out of my sleep by the strong, skinny hand of Admiral MacDonald. It was seven-thirty and a bright New York morning. Dalhousie had pulled a blank canvassing the neighborhood for Gomez, got panicky and bucked it up to higher headquarters.

"Where is he?" the admiral rasped.

"On his way here with his bride of one night," I said. "He slipped over a couple of state lines and got married."

"By God," the admiral said, "we've got to do something about this. I'm going to have him drafted and assigned to special duty. This is the last time—"

"*Look*," I said. "You've got to stop treating him like a chess piece. You've got duty-honor-country on the brain and thank God for that. Somebody has to; it's your profession. But can't you get it through your head that Gomez is a kid and that you're wrecking his life by forcing him to grind out science like a machine? And I'm just a stupe of a layman, but have you professionals worried once about digging too deep and blowing up the whole shebang?"

He gave me a piercing look and said nothing.

I dressed and had breakfast sent up. The admiral, Dalhousie and I waited grimly until noon, and then Gomez phoned up.

"Come on up, Julio," I said tiredly.

He breezed in with his blushing bride on his arm. The admiral rose automatically as she entered, and immediately began tongue-lashing the boy. He spoke more in sorrow than in anger. He made it clear that Gomez wasn't treating his country right. That he had a great talent and it belonged to the United States. That his behavior had been irresponsible. That Gomez would have to come to heel and realize that his wishes weren't the most important thing in his life. That he could and would be drafted if there were any more such escapades.

"As a starter, Mr. Gomez," the admiral snapped, "I want you to set down, immediately, the enfieldment matrices you have developed. I consider it almost criminal of you to arrogantly and carelessly trust to your memory alone matters of such vital importance. Here!" He thrust pencil and paper at the boy, who stood, drooping and disconsolate. Little Rosa was near crying. She didn't have the ghost of a notion as to what it was about.

Gomez took the pencil and paper and sat down at the writing table silently. I took Rosa by the arm. She was trembling. "It's all right," I said. "They can't do a thing to him." The admiral glared briefly at me and then returned his gaze to Gomez.

The boy made a couple of tenative marks. Then his eyes went wide and he clutched his hair. "*Dios mio!*" he said. "*Esta perdido! Olvidado!*"

Which means: "My God, it's lost! Forgotten!"

The admiral turned white beneath his tan. "Now, boy," he said slowly and soothingly. "I didn't mean to scare you. You just relax and collect yourself. Of course you haven't forgotten, not with that memory of yours. Start with something easy. Write down a general biquadratic equation, say."

Gomez just looked at him. After a long pause he said in a strangled voice: "*No puedo.* I can't. It, too, I forget. I don't think of the math or physics at all since—" He looked at Rosa and turned a little red. She smiled shyly and looked at her shoes.

"That is it," Gomez said hoarsely. "Not since then. Always before in the back of my head is the math, but not since then."

"My God," the admiral said softly. "Can such a thing happen?" He reached for the phone.

He found out that such things can happen.

Julio went back to Spanish Harlem and bought a piece of the Porto Bello with his savings. I went back to the paper and bought a car with *my* savings. MacDonald never cleared the story, so the Sunday editor had the satisfaction of bulldozing an admiral, but didn't get his exclusive.

Julio and Rosa sent me a card eventually announcing the birth of their first-born: a six-pound boy, Francisco, named after Julio's father. I saved the card and when a New York assignment came my way—it was the National Association of Dry Goods Wholesalers; dry goods are important in our town—I dropped up to see them.

Julio was a little more mature and a little more prosperous. Rosa—alas!—was already putting on weight, but she was still a pretty thing and devoted to her man. The baby was a honey-skinned little wiggler. It was nice to see all of them together, happy with their lot.

Julio insisted that he'd cook *arróz con pollo* for me, as on the night I practically threw him into Rosa's arms, but he'd have to shop for the stuff. I went along.

In the corner grocery he ordered the rice, the chicken, the garbanzos, the peppers and, swept along by the enthusiasm that hits husbands in groceries, about fifty other things that he thought would be nice to have in the pantry.

The creaking old grocer scribbled down the prices on a shopping bag and began painfully to add them up while Julio was telling me how well the Porto Bello was doing and how they were thinking of renting the adjoining store.

"Seventeen dollars, forty-two cents," the grocer said at last.

Julio flicked one glance at the shopping bag and the upside-down figures. "Should be seventeen thirty-nine," he said reprovingly. "Add up again."

The grocer painfully added up again and said. "Is seventeen thirty-nine. Sorry." He began to pack the groceries into the bag.

"Hey," I said.

We didn't discuss it then or ever. Julio just said: "Dont tell, Beel." And winked.

FOR DISCUSSION: Gomez

1. Why do you think the author begins with the news of Julio's death from pneumonia?
2. We see the events of the story though Bill Vilchek's eyes. Would you consider him a keen observer? A sensitive one?
3. Julio, as the central character, emerges as a credible fictional creation. To achieve this, the author has had to tell us something about Julio's attitudes and about his history which helped to form those attitudes. In this connection, explain the reason for Julio's "old-maidish neatness." Define Julio's attitude toward his parents.
4. Why do you think Julio's father assumed that Julio was "a janitor or something in the Pentagon"?

5. Julio is obviously a genius in the area of mathematical physics. The author also indicates that he is enterprising. Can you give an example of this latter quality from the story?

6. Julio pretended to forget the final equations he created in order to have a normal life with Rosa. But the author suggests that there was also another important reason. What is it?

INTRODUCTION: Muse

Alienation between people is a subject of interest to many modern writers although it is not a new subject. Here, alienation of a father from his son is the subject—but one with scientific overtones.

Muse
by Dean R. Koontz

Her hair tumbled over her breasts like burned butter, darkly yellow, darkly gleaming with reflected bits of the dim amber ceiling light, parting now and again to bare the greater wonders beneath that it was attempting to conceal. She came out of the bathroom, blotting her frosty lipstick, and said, "What?"

I stretched out on the couch, half of my face buried in it, flat on my stomach, also naked from the waist up, and pointed to the jug on the floor. "Put Icky on for me, Lynda."

She came across the floor on dancer's toes like a leaf blown through the windless chamber of the grav-plane, a wonder of curves and indentations, mounds and recesses. She sat on the edge of the couch, her hair dancing to conceal her treasures and only partially succeeding, and dipped her hands into the wide-mouthed jug, lifting Icky out and holding him like he was an unmolded jello serving or a hunk of raw liver.

"Careful," I said.

"You shut up, now. Icky and I know what we're doing."

"Just the same—"

"Shush!"

She placed the slug on my back, directly between my shoulders, pressing it gently to get its adhesive layer firmly attached. Then she pried up the anterior end of it and tucked its sensory flap under so that the porous side was against my skin and so that Icky would not have to do the job himself with a lot of unpleasant, wet squirming and wriggling. As much as I thought of Icky, I didn't much care for it when he began to twitch, slipping and sliding over my skin. But Lynda had the flap under and the slug on properly. She was experienced, as she said. But I still worried about Icky.

"All's in place," she said, signaling the finish of the ritual.

I felt the hair-fine tendrils probing through my flesh, snaking painlessly through my skull and making gentle contact with my brain in all the necessary places. Icky was with me. Icky was *in* me. A peculiar sense of well-being swept over me, filled me to the center of my body. My muscles felt better toned, and my senses were sharper just as they always were immediately after contact. My hands itched to hold the guitar, to finger the strings, to throb the chords from the shallow wooden box, to play the latest numbers so that Icky could experience them.

"We land in fifteen minutes," Lynda said, slapping me on the ass. "You better finish getting dressed." She stood and returned to the bathroom, shaking every ounce of her slim body with every step she took.

"If there were time—" I began.

"But there isn't," she said, winking. "So hurry up."

Homecoming. Lynda stood beside me, holding my hand in hers, fingering my fingers with her tiny ones, and Icky was on my shoulder, concealed beneath my black leather suit. No, not concealed, really, for the lump of his jelly body rounded my back where it ought to be con-cave, thickened my neck where it normally would have been straight and thin. Lynda was comforting me, petting my arm, winking, whispering things that she knew made me feel good, things about how good a musician I was, about how everyone loved me, about what she would do with me if she could ever—for a change—get me alone for a moment without having to rush. She was great. There was confidence in her eyes that gave me confidence too. There was love in them that calmed me. Icky (his real name is unpronounceable outside his own star sys-tem) comforted me with his tendrils, with the wordless discussions we carried on inside my head. He projected images of assurance to me, mellowed me, prepared me for what was to come.

Lynda took the last private moment we had to squeeze my hand again.

Icky touched me reassuringly with feathers of protoplasm.

And the doors opened before us like the shutters being thrown wide on a window. Beyond lay the airport.

And the people . . .

There was at least eight thousand, maybe ten thousand there. They stretched away in all directions, people of all ages—but mostly the young —waving, holding up banners that said LOVE YOU, LEONARD CHRIS and WELCOME HOME, LEO!, cheering, cheering, cheering. Nine years had passed, and I had climbed a ladder out of obscurity to become the most famous musician in the galaxy, known not only to the race calling itself Mankind but to the Seven Races, understood best by my own and by Icky's, but listened to by all. Still, it was a revelation that a back-water city the size of Harrisburg, Pennsylvania, could turn out something like this crowd to meet me. I began, I think, to tremble.

Guards moved up the platform, surrounded us, moved us down toward the limousine that waited below. It wasn't a grav car, but an honest-to-God museum-piece Ford with tires and everything. We were ushered into the back seat while two motorcyclists pulled in front of us on real, vintage motorcycles. They were going all out.

"Not bad, is it?" Lynda asked.

Icky asked something similar that had no words.

The crowd was unwilling to let us pass easily. They pressed close, anxious to touch the glass through which they could see me. They screamed my name.

"Mostly girls," Lynda noted.

"Jealous?"

"No. They don't want you. At least not all of you. They just want a scrap to take home as a souvenir."

After the crowds had passed, we sped on toward the hotel, our cyclists pressing on their sirens. I reached into my jacket pocket and took out my father's letter once more. It was wrinkled from previous readings, but I had to see it again, to know I had interpreted it correctly. Really, there was no mistaking what it said: "Son," it said plainly, "son, don't try to bring It with you. Come by yourself, and you'll be made welcome, very welcome. But if you bring along that goddamned worm, if you bring along that puppet master that rides you like a demon, that perverts your body and contaminates the thing that makes you a man, then stay the hell away. If you bring It with you, son, then stay in some damn hotel some-where. But don't come home. And if your bring It with you, if you insist on carrying It along, then I don't want to see you. I don't want to be reminded of what It has done to you."

But of course I had to bring Icky. And now I was returning home triumphant, but I was denied entrance to my own home, the place of my childhood, to the garden I had immortalized in *Childflowers*. I bit my teeth together, ground them against one another, trying to recall my anger from the depths where it had settled since my last reading of the letter. At first, I had gotten strength from my fury, from anger at the names my father had called Icky. But that was all gone now. It was impossible to stir anger at simple, brutal ignorance. The only things left were pity and disgust, and neither one could sustain my anger. I choked as I reread the last line of the letter, swore I would not cry for my father's stupidity.

Lynda took my hand.

Icky touched my mind and soothed me some. . . .

Once in the city proper, the driver fooled the crowd at the hotel by driving the limousine down a side street and through an alleyway, bringing us into the hotel through a service entrance. Only half a dozen people waited there, and the police used diluted chemical mace on these, rushed us through into safety.

We stood in a room full of produce and cartons of canned and jarred food. A row of garbage cans lined the left wall, and the aroma from these was extremely rotten. Standing well away from the filthy containers was the manager. He wore a black suit (not leather) and a white carnation on his lapel. He also wore a smile as broad as a jack-o'-lantern's—and just as fake. He came to us, took Lynda's hand and squeezed it lightly. He dropped it, shook mine politely. I could tell he was reluctant to touch the hand of a human-slug symbiote, but he overcame that magnificently (apparently reminding himself of the publicity his hotel was receiving) and kept his smile intact.

"Such a pleasure, Mr. Chris. My name is Cavander. Harold."

"Mr. Cavander," I said politely enough, considering what I was think-about him. "Could we be shown to our rooms, please. I must rest for the concert tonight." I was quite sufficiently rested, but I wanted out of the garbage room and out of this fellow's sight. The way he eyed my hump gave me chills.

"Uh—" he said, suddenly embarrassed.

"Yes?" I asked impatiently.

"The Grande Suite—"

"Yes?"

"Well, the fact is that we got our schedules a little confused, and we now find that we booked two parties into the Grande Suite—"

"A normal suite will do," I said, getting his point. Once it was known that a human-slug symbiote had stayed in his precious Grande Suite, most honeymooners and most "aristocrats" would not consider it fit for love-making and aristocrating. He was only protecting his business. Still, I hated him for it.

He seemed relieved and almost managed to smile a genuine smile. But he checked himself just in time and pasted the phony one back on. "This way, then. And I do hope you will excuse this terrible inconvenience. I don't know how we could have been so stupid as to—"

When Cavander had overseen the deposition of our luggage (a car had followed with it, and he stood talking with us until that car arrived) and had ascertained that we had sufficient towels, soap and toilet paper, I bid him goodbye and closed the door hard behind him.

"The little creep," Lynda hissed, plopping down in an overstuffed leather easy chair and kicking off her shoes.

I opened my guitar case and took out my beautiful Trevelox Electro and set about hooking up the amplifiers. I could pay back pudgy Harold Cavander for what he had done. I could blast the ears out of the entire floor. And I didn't think he would have enough guts to ask me to stop. He might be afraid I would go elsewhere for accommodations. And though his prejudices kept him from serving us well, he would not want to throw away all that publicity by refusing to serve us at all.

"What should it be?" I asked Lynda.

She scrunched her toes into the deep pile carpet. "The one you wrote last night, *Mind Dark*."

"Yeah. That fits," I said.

I played a few chords tentatively. The music welled through my bones, slithered over my fingers and punctuated the rooms with nearly tactile sound. I went back to the beginning and started again, full volume this time. I felt good. Icky felt good. He rejoiced, touching my mind to tell me that it was a good thing, this *Mind Dark*. I sang the words throatily like I would sing them tonight on the big stage. And for a minute, the room and Lynda receded and I *was* on the big stage, seated on a stool before five thousand enthralled fans, Icky humped between my shoulders. I played like I had never played before, but in my vision, the people began leaving, drifting out as I started the second song. And as they left, I saw why they would not stay: each of the five thousand was my father, each had his face. . . .

"This is your dressing room," the man said, pointing in a cubbyhole where a dresser and full-length mirror were the only furnishings. But I was not so concerned with the room. It was good enough. I was more interested in the fact that the little man was a human-slug symbiote with a hump on his shoulders where his own Icky rested.

"How long have you had him?" I asked.

He looked perplexed for a minute, then brightened and smiled. "Icky?" He grinned broader, and I could see that he was even now in some sort of delicate communication with his symbiote partner. "Oh, going on three years now."

"What is the give-take?" Lynda asked.

"Icky's a romantic. He likes to travel. He wants to see parts of this world. He'll stay with me until I die, then move on to someone else, always looking, always taking things in."

"And you?" I asked.

"Same thing. I can't go to Icky's home planet, to his star system. But he can give me visions of every world he has ever seen simply by touching parts of my brain with his filaments. I guess you'd say I'm a romantic too."

"You're the first symbiote I've seen since we arrived," I said.

He frowned. "There aren't many here. Small-city provincialism. This is in the Bible Belt, you know. The conservative Cumberland Valley. Maybe a few hundred here, that's all. But there must be thousands in the cities—the big cities."

"Eleven million symbiotes," Lynda said. "I just read that somewhere."

"I envision a day," the little man said, "when— Oh, your mother is waiting to see you. I left her out by the office. You want me to show her back?"

I looked at Lynda. "Yes," I said. "Please."

Later, after my mother had come, subdued, and gone, I sat on the bare stage, looking at the back of the curtain, my guitar across my lap. In moments, that velveteen monstrosity would part, revealing the audience to me and me to the audience. I would make no remarks but begin immediately with *Childflowers*. I felt good. *Childflowers* would mean something, for my father had relented, had asked to see me after all. True, the message my mother had delivered was terse and unemotional. He wanted to see me backstage an hour after the performance, after everyone was gone and he would not be seen conversing with me. He was still prejudiced. I was prepared for one of his persuasive arguments to try to get me to give up Icky. But I was also confident that I might get him, at least in some small degree, to accept the symbiote relationship. He would have to accept it someday, for it would never be my choice to break it off.

Then the curtains opened.

And I was scared.

Like always.

Childflowers spun from my toiling fingers like golden threads from a magic loom. I did a double rendition of it, bringing the entire length to something just over fourteen minutes. When I finished, I was dripping sweat, and the audience was applauding wildly. Icky touched my mind, and some of my nervousness was gone. I played *Mind Dark* next, my song about prejudice, and I played it with conviction.

Lynda and Icky and I waited on the dimly lighted stage. The audience was gone now. The clamorous boom of applause had whispered off through the rows of seats. The echo of my music had been stilled. We were waiting for my father.

When he came, it was with friends.

He came down the center aisle, a big man, clean-shaven and dressed in a gray suit. Behind him came two friends, apparently. This was some consolation. It wasn't to be an entirely confidential tete-a-tete. He was not so ashamed that he had to hide the meeting entirely from the eyes of the public. I sat on the stool, Lynda on a chair beside me, waiting for him to mount the stage.

The three of them came up and stood by the right proscenium pillar, the two men still behind my father. "Len," he said, nodding his gray head, his hands held at his sides, his entire posture one of stiffness and uneasiness.

"Hello, Dad." Lynda said it first. I followed her example. There was still pity in me.

"It was a good show," he said awkwardly.

"I'm glad you came."

One of the men walked across the front of the stage and stood against the left proscenium pillar.

Walter Chris came toward me, an older version of myself. His friends remained at each side of the stage like bodyguards. "Why, Len?" he asked simply, opening his palms in the gesture I was so familiar with. Always when I had done something wrong as a child, he had opened his hands in wonderment just that way, had shrugged his shoulders just so.

"Why what?" I asked. I was trembling. I wanted to make him understand Icky, but I was determined he should open the subject.

"Why bring It. I asked you not to bring It."

"I had to, Dad."

"But why?"

"A slug," I explained patiently, "requires a host. It would die in twenty-four hours if I should take it off. I usually leave Icky off for no more than twelve hours at a time. I had to bring him."

"You've got everything. You've got money, fame. Why did you have to humiliate your mother and me with It? That wasn't right, Len. It wasn't right to humiliate us like that."

He came towards me then with something more than fatherly concern in his eyes, twisting his face into a leer. The two friends advanced from the proscenium pillars.

"What is this?" I asked, starting off the stool.

"We have a little group—" my father started.

"What kind of little group?" Lynda was off her chair too.

"That doesn't like the sort of thing that's been happening—all these symbies, all these puppet masters."

"They aren't puppet masters!" I protested. I felt like I was shouting down a deep well, so deep that not even my own echoes returned to me. "They take, yes. But they also give!"

"It's the sign of a weak character," one of the other men said. "Only a weakling needs boosting by an alien worm like that thing you're wearing."

"Dad," Lynda said. "Dad, stay away from him."

"You stay out of this, honey."

I was backing toward the rear of the stage, toward the brilliantly colored flats that had backed me during the performance. They were closing in from three sides, each one with some degree of determination lining his face like a death mask.

"What are you going to do?" I asked, backing against the flats.

"Help you," Walter Chris said.

My fingers found the edge of a glow-blue flat on my left. I swung, wrenched at it, sent it toppling to the left, the canvas striking the man on that side and carrying him to the floor. But the other two were on me. I heard Lynda scream. But screams weren't stopping them. Walter Chris had set out on a holy crusade to redeem his son, to reclaim what he fancied had been taken from him, and he would not stop until he had killed Icky.

I kicked upward with a knee, caught the remaining accomplice in the crotch. He rolled off, gagging.

I shouted at my father.

But he had sealed his ears.

He drove a big fist into my face. For a moment, everything swam about me. I could see Lynda leaving the stage, running for help, but she was bobbing wildly up and down. Blackness swept toward me, but I fought it off. I had to fight it off. If I passed out, it would be the end for Icky—and, consequently, an end of sorts for me.

I tried driving a knee into his crotch, but he had learned from what I had done to the other fellow. He blocked the blow, struck me again.

I swung a fist, pounded helplessly against his side. He was a bigger man than I, and he had not gone to fat.

The fellow I had kneed stood and came to the old man's aid, pinning my shoulders with his knees while my father worked me over. My face was swelling and bleeding, and one eye had already swollen shut. With every blow, strength drained from me. The knees hurt where they dug into my shoulders. I writhed, trying to break free. I could not. Icky was excited, but he managed to sooth my panic and keep me acting rationally. I could only hope now that Lynda would return in time with help.

But she didn't.

When he had dealt the punishment he thought I deserved, he and his accomplice rolled me over, pinned me on my stomach, and worried up my coat and shirt until they had uncovered Icky.

I screamed.

But there was no one to hear.

I writhed and kicked.

But I was tired, and they were two.

They stuck fingers under the pulpy bulk of the slug. Icky quickly retracted his filaments so that my brain would not be damaged when they yanked him away. Then they tore him loose. I was still screaming. My throat was raw. I rolled over as they stood, grabbed at my father's ankles. But he had Icky raised over his head. He threw the slug to the floor. It hit with a sickening splashing noise and wriggled helplessly. The other man snatched it up before I could grasp it, threw it down again. And again. Then my father had it once more. They exchanged Icky until he had been thrown too often. He was mangled and did not move any more.

I was crying. The stage was as something seen through a rain-splattered window. They tried to help me to my feet, but I struck out weakly at them and drove them back. I stood, weaving, feeling the stage dance beneath my feet. I remember that my father was smiling.

"Now you—" he started to say.

The third man had found his way out of the blue flat.

"You sons of bitches!" I snapped. The words were strained between my teeth so that nothing but hatred and bitterness came out. It hissed like escaping steam.

"Now, Len, simmer down a little."

But I could only curse. Every foul thing I could think of, every four-letter word I had ever heard came bubbling out in a torrent of rage.

"Wait," my father said. "Now wait just a damn minute. We got rid of it for you. We're trying to help you see you can do without the slug for a crutch. Whatever it is you need, son, we can give you. Come to us. If it's love or appreciation, we've got more than enough for you."

"You stupid damn wretch," I hissed. I was still crying, and the words were interspersed with sobs, I guess. "I have nothing now. You can't give me what Icky gave me. Never!"

"Just give us time to—"

"Time, hell. Icky gave me my talent, you damn fool!"

He stood, stunned, working his mouth without managing to make anything come out of it.

"That's it; that's right! He could not make music through his own body, since he had no fingers, and no 'ears' to appreciate Earth music. But he had a perfect understanding of what made a song. It was Icky who composed *Childflowers* and everything else. He took my memory and made beauty with it. I got the money and fame. He got the satisfaction of creation. It was a mutual agreement. It was symbiosis. And I got more than the money and the fame. I got to be a part of that creativity, got to work with it, to offer suggestions to it. I was in a world of poetry, a world of loveliness. The things I wanted to say he said for me. He vented the ache in me. Without him, my soul would never have found release, and I would have contained it and rotted with it as you and your goddamned friends have. Can you really replace what Icky gave me? Not a fraction of it, you can't!"

He turned from me, turned toward the steps.

I took a few steps, grabbed my Trevelox Electro and brought it down on his shoulders.

I was still sobbing.

He took the blows without resistance.

When the other two tried to come near to stop me, I swung furiously at them. They backed off to let me return to my father. I brought the instrument up and down, over and over. I might have killed him had not Lynda arrived with the help that was too late for Icky. They pulled me off him. I remember that. Then, until I woke in the hospital, recovering from shock, I remember nothing.

I have a new Trevelox Electro, just like the one I splintered and ruined. But there is no second Icky, no slug I have found with his same abilities. So I play the old songs, though I never play *Childflowers*, and Lynda sits with me by the window, watching the dark to whom I sing.

FOR DISCUSSION: Muse

1. What does the song *Childflowers* symbolize in the story?
2. Walter Chris destroys more than the slug in his battle with his son. Do you think such a man would have refrained from acting had he known in advance that the slug was the source of his son's talent?
3. In the last sentence of this story, the author has Leonard Chris speak of "watching the dark to whom I sing." Is the use of the word "whom" in reference to the dark a grammatical error? If you think it is not, what is its meaning?
4. Does the alienation of father from son in this story suggest a broader alienation between people holding differing points of view? If such alienation can cause the estrangement of members of one family who presumably have some love for one another, do you think the outlook for resolving differences that lead to alienation on a larger scale is hopeful or bleak? Explain.

Machineries
and
Mechanisms

CHAPTER SIX

One criticism occasionally leveled at science fiction as a literary form is the accusation that all such stories are about bug-eyed monsters and Martians. Such remarks are occasionally made by critics who may be less than fully informed concerning the stylistic and contextual range of science fiction.

A reader hearing such criticism might choose to counter it by citing examples of stories that meet high literary standards. He might, for example, refer to Carol Carr's "Look, You Think You Got Troubles" in Chapter Three as admittedly a story about a Martian but one that has a number of important points to make about human nature. Why, he might ask himself in the face of such a criticism, must a story about a Martian automatically be denigrated? He might ask such a critic to read Philip K. Dick's "The Father-thing," explaining that it is about a monster, but asking the critic if he finds flaws with the carefully constructed suspense or the development of the characters and their conflicts as they seek to solve the deadly problem facing them.

To further enhance his own critical standards concerning science fiction, the reader might compare the different styles in which the six stories in this chapter are written. He will find that both style and content differ widely although each story deals with some kind of machine or mechanism. "Lost Memory" by Peter Phillips inspires the same kind of terror in the reader as did the stories of the perils of the hunt told around primitive campfires hundreds of years ago. "X Marks the Pedwalk" by Fritz Leiber has a statement to make concerning man in relation to his machines. The mechanism that appears in "The World of Myrion Flowers" by Frederik Pohl and C. M. Kornbluth is a vehicle for the author's analysis of unreasoning hatred.

Each of the authors represented in this chapter writes his story in his own way. Each has his own technique for creating an interesting tale. Compare, for example, Keith Laumer's narrative style in "The Last Command" with the poetic imagery offered by David R. Bunch in "That High-up Blue Day That Saw the Black Sky-train Come Spinning."

All art is subject to criticism, of course. Students of science fiction should develop their own critical faculties so that they will be equipped to debate critical judgments made by others with which they do not agree and to establish their own standards. To be able to do this intelligently and effectively, they should read these stories on the theme of machines with their minds attuned to the differences in style, technique, and structure in each story.

Those critics who condemn stories about what they call bug-eyed monsters and Martians are most likely to be the same critics who tell their listeners that science fiction is only about gadgets. When the reader has finished this chapter, he should ask himself some questions. Is this criticism true? Is it well-founded?

We have seen how science-fiction writers are concerned with a number of things—Martians, monsters, and machines among them. If the reader is to develop his own critical sensibilities, he should read the following stories carefully to determine exactly what the authors are saying and to evaluate the ways in which they have chosen to say it. The following chapter offers an excellent opportunity to analyze such literary devices as the creation of atmosphere, the building of suspense, the development of character, and the creation of solid and satisfying plots.

INTRODUCTION: The World of Myrion Flowers

Until now, no man has been able to read another man's mind—that is, outside of science-fiction stories. But in such stories men have read other men's minds and have had their own minds read. In the world of Myrion Flowers, the authors tell us, such an event can have disastrous consequences.

The World of Myrion Flowers
by Frederik Pohl and C. M. Kornbluth

The world of Myrion Flowers, which was the world of the American Negro, was something like an idealized England and something like the real Renaissance. As it is in some versions of England, all the members of the upper class were at least friends of friends. Any Harlem businessman knew automatically who was the new top dog in the music department of Howard University a week after an upheaval of the faculty. And as it was in the Florence of Cellini, there was room for versatile men. An American Negro could be a doctor-builder-educator-realtist-politician. Myrion Flowers was.

Boston-born in 1913 to a lawyer-realtist-politician father and a glamorous show-biz mother, he worked hard, drew the lucky number and was permitted to enter the schools which led to an M.D. and a license to practice in the State of New York. Power vacuums occurred around him during the years that followed, and willy-nilly he filled them. A construction firm going to waste, needing a little capital and a little common sense—what could he do? He did it, and accepted its stock. The school board coming to him as a sound man to represent "ah, your people"? He was a sound man. He served the board well. A trifling examination to pass for a real-estate license—trifling to him who had memorized a dozen textbooks in pathology, histology, anatomy and materia medica—why not? And if they would deem it such a favor if he spoke for the Fusion candidate, why should he not speak; and if they should later invite him to submit names to fill one dozen minor patronage jobs, why should he not give the names of the needy persons he knew?

Flowers was a cold, controlled man. He never married. In lieu of children he had proteges. These began as Negro kids from orphanages or hopelessly destitute families; he backed them through college and postgraduate schools as long as they worked to the limit of what he considered their abilities; at the first sign of a let-down he axed them. The mortality rate over the years was only about one nongraduate in four —Myrion Flowers was a better predictor of success than any college admissions committee. His successes numbered forty-two when one of them came to him with a brand-new Ph.D. in clinical psychology and made a request.

The protege's name was Ensal Brubacker. He took his place after dinner in the parlor of Dr. Flowers' Brooklyn brownstone house along with many other suppliants. There was the old woman who wanted an extension of her mortgage and would get it; there was the overstocked appliance dealer who wanted to be bailed out and would not be; there was the mother whose boy had a habit and the husband whose wife was acting stranger and stranger every day; there was the landlord hounded by the building department; there was the cop who wanted a transfer; there was the candidate for the bar who wanted a powerful name as a reference; there was a store-front archbishop who wanted only to find out whether Dr. Flowers was right with God.

Brubacker was admitted to the doctor's study at 9:30. It was only the sixth time he had seen the man who had picked him from an orphanage and laid out some twenty thousand dollars for him since. He found him more withered, colder and quicker than ever.

The doctor did not congratulate him. He said, "You've got your degree, Brubacker. If you've come to me for advice, I'd suggest that you avoid the academic life, especially in the Negro schools. I know what you should do. You may get nowhere, but I would like to see you try one of the Four-A advertising and public relations firms, with a view to becoming a motivational research man. It's time one Negro was working in the higher levels of Madison Avenue, I believe."

Brubacker listened respectfully, and when it was time for him to reply he said: "Dr. Flowers, I'm very grateful of course for everything you've done. I sincerely wish I could—Dr. Flowers, I want to do research. I sent you my dissertation, but that's only the beginning—"

Myrion Flowers turned to the right filing card in his mind and said icily, "The Correlation of Toposcopic Displays, Beta-Wave Amplitudes and Perception of Musical Chord Progressions in 1,107 Unselected Adolescents." Very well. You now have your sandwich board with "P," "H" and "D" painted on it, fore and aft. I expect that you will now proceed to the job for which you have been trained."

"Yes, sir. I'd like to show you a—"

"I do not," said Dr. Flowers, "want you to be a beloved old George

Washington Carver humbly bending over his reports and test tubes. Academic research is of no immediate importance."

"No, sir. I—"

"The power centers of America," said Dr. Flowers, "are government, where our friend Mr. Wilkins is ably operating, and the executive levels of the large corporations, where I am attempting to achieve what is necessary. I want you to be an executive in a large corporation, Brubacker. You have been trained for that purpose. It is now perhaps barely possible for you to obtain a foothold. It is inconceivable to me that you will not make the effort, either for me or for your people."

Brubacker looked at him in misery, and at last put his face into his hands. His shoulders shook.

Dr. Flowers said scornfully: "I take it you are declining to make that effort. Good-by, Brubacker. I do not want to see you again."

The young man stumbled from the room, carrying a large pigskin valise which he had not been permitted to open.

As he had expected to overwhelm his benefactor with what he had accomplished he had made no plans for this situation. He could think only of returning to the university he had just left where, perhaps, before his little money ran out, he might obtain a grant. There was not really much hope of that. He had filed no proposals and sought no advice.

It did not help his mood when the overnight coach to Chicago was filling up in Grand Central. He was among the first and took a window seat. Thereafter the empty place beside him was spotted gladly by luggage-burdened matrons, Ivy-League-clad youngsters, harrumphing paper-box salesmen—gladly spotted—and then uncomfortably skimmed past when they discovered that to occupy it they would have to sit next to the gorilla-rapist-illiterate-tapdancer-mugger-menace who happened to be Dr. Ensal Brubacker.

But he was spared loneliness at the very last. The fellow who did drop delightedly into the seat beside him as the train began to move was One of His Own Kind. That is, he was unwashed, unlettered, a quarter drunk on liquor that had never known a tax stamp, and agonizingly high-spirited. Brubacker could barely understand his Harlem jive.

But politeness and a terror of appearing "dicty" forced Brubacker to accept at 125th Street, a choking swallow from the flat half-pint bottle his seatmate carried. And both of these things, plus an unsupportable sense of something lost, caused him to accept his seatmate's later offer of more paralyzing pleasures. In ten months Brubacker was dead, in Lexington, Kentucky, of pneumonia incurred while kicking the heroin habit, leaving behind him a badly puzzled staff doctor. "They'll say everything in withdrawal," he confided to his wife, "but I wonder how this one every heard the word 'cryptesthesia.'"

It was about a month after that that Myrion Flowers received the package containing Brubacker's effects. There had been no one else to send them to.

He was shaken, that controlled man. He had seen many folk-gods of his people go the same route, but they were fighters, entertainers or revivalists; he had not expected it of a young, brilliant university graduate. For that reason he did not immediately throw the junk away, but mused over it for some minutes. His next visitor found him with a silvery-coppery sort of helmet in his hands.

Flowers' next visitor was a former Corporation Counsel to the City of New York. By attending Dr. Powell's church and having Dr. Flowers take care of his health he kept a well-placed foot in both the principal political camps of the city. He no longer much needed political support, but Flowers had pulled him through one coronary and he was too old to change doctors. "What have you got there, Myrion?" he asked.

Flowers looked up and said precisely, "If I can believe the notes of the man who made it, it is a receiver and amplifier for beta-wave oscillations."

The Corporation Counsel groaned, "God preserve me from the medical mind. What's that in English?" But he was surprised to see the expression of wondering awe that came on to Flowers's withered face.

"It reads thoughts," Flowers whispered.

The Corporation Counsel at once clutched his chest, but found no pain. He complained testily, "You're joking."

"I don't think I am, Wilmot. The man who constructed this device had all the appropriate dignities—summa cum laude, Dean's List, interviewed by mail by nearly thirty prospective employers. Before they found out the color of his skin, of course. No," he said reflectively. "I'm not joking, but there's one way to find out."

He lifted the helmet toward his head. The Corporation Counsel cried out, "Damn you, Myrion, don't do that!"

Flowers paused. "Are you afraid I'll read your mind and learn your secrets?"

"At my time of life? When you're my doctor? No, Myrion, but you ought to know I have a bad heart. I don't want you electrocuted in front of my eyes. Besides, what the devil does a Negro want with a machine that will tell him what people are thinking? Isn't guessing bad enough for you?"

Myrion Flowers chose to ignore the latter part of what his patient had said. "I don't expect it to electrocute me, and I don't expect this will affect your heart, Wilmot. In any event, I don't propose to be wondering about this thing for any length of time, I don't want to try it when I'm alone and there's no one else here." He plopped the steel bowl on his head. It fit badly and was very heavy. An extension cord hung from it, and without pausing Flowers plugged it into a wall socket by his chair.

The helmet whined faintly and Flowers leaped to his feet. He screamed.

The Corporation Counsel moved rapidly enough to make himself gasp. He snatched the helmet from Flowers's head, caught him by the shoulders and lowered him into his chair again. "You all right?" he growled.

Flowers shuddered epileptically and then controlled himself. "Thank you, Wilmot. I hope you haven't damaged Dr. Brubacker's device." And then suddenly, "It hit me all at once. It *hurt!*"

He breathed sharply and sat up.

From one of his desk drawers he took a physicians'-sample bottle of pills and swallowed one without water. "Everyone was screaming at once," he said. He started to replace the pills, then saw the Corporation Counsel holding his chest and mutely offered him one.

Then he seemed startled.

He looked into his visitor's eyes. "I can still hear you."

"What?"

"It's false angina, I think. But take the pill. But—" he passed a hand over his eyes—"you thought I was electrocuted, and you wondered how to straighten out my last bill. It's a fair bill, Wilmot. I didn't overcharge you." Flowers opened his eyes very wide and said, "The newsboy on the corner cheated me out of my change. He—" He swallowed and said, "The cops in the squad car just turning off Fulton Street don't like my having white patients. One of them is thinking about running in a girl that came here." He sobbed, "It didn't stop, Wilmot."

"For Christ's sake, Myrion, lie down."

"*It didn't stop.* It's not like a radio. You can't turn it off. Now I can hear—everybody! Every mind for miles around *is pouring into my head* WHAT IT THINKS ABOUT ME—ABOUT ME—ABOUT US!"

Ensal Brubacker, who had been a clinical psychologist and not a radio engineer, had not intended his helmet to endure the strain of continuous operation nor had he thought to provide circuit-breakers. It had been meant to operate for a few moments at most, enough to reroute a few neurons, open a blocked path or two. One of its parts overheated. Another took too much load as a result, and in a moment the thing was afire. It blew the fuses and the room was in darkness. The elderly ex-Corporation Counsel managed to get the fire out, and then picked up the phone. Shouting to be heard over the screaming of Myrion Flowers, he summoned a Kings County ambulance. They knew Flowers' name. The ambulance was there in nine minutes.

Flowers died some weeks later in the hospital—not Kings County, but he did not know the difference. He had been under massive sedation for almost a month until it became a physiological necessity to taper him off; and as soon as he was alert enough to do so he contrived to hang himself in his room.

His funeral was a state occasion. The crowds were enormous and there was much weeping. The Corporation Counsel was one of those permitted to cast a clod of earth upon the bronze casket, but he did not weep.

No one had ever figured out what the destroyed instrument was supposed to have been, and Wilmot did not tell. There are inventions and inventions, he thought, and reading minds is a job for white men. If even for white men. In the world of Myrion Flowers many seeds might sturdily grow, but some ripe fruits would mature into poison.

No doubt the machine might have broken any mind, listening in on every thought that concerned one. It was maddening and dizzying, and the man who wore the helmet would be harmed in any world; but only in the world of Myrion Flowers would he be hated to death.

FOR DISCUSSION: The World of Myrion Flowers

1. Why does the Corporation Counsel destroy the helmet?
2. By creating the idea of the helmet, the authors are enabled to deal with one of the basic problems of mankind—prejudice and its fruits. If you were to try to deal with such a theme in science-fiction terms, what fictional device can you imagine that would allow you to do so?
3. Does the world of Myrion Flowers still exist today? Will it continue to exist, in your opinion? Explain.

INTRODUCTION: X Marks the Pedwalk

Few machines are more valued by Americans than are their automobiles. Leiber, in this story, gives the reader a glimpse of a future world in conflict because of this particular machine. Implicit in the story are comments on the role of machines vis-a-vis Man, a favorite subject of science-fiction writers.

X Marks the Pedwalk
by Fritz Leiber

The raggedy little old lady with the big shopping bag was in the exact center of the crosswalk when she became aware of the big black car bearing down on her.

Behind the thick bullet-proof glass its seven occupants had a misty look, like men in a diving bell.

She saw there was no longer time to beat the car to either curb. Veering remorselessly, it would catch her in the gutter.

Useless to attempt a feint and double-back, such as any venturesome child executed a dozen times a day. Her reflexes were too slow.

Polite vacuous laughter came from the car's loudspeaker over the engine's mounting roar.

From her fellow pedestrians lining the curbs came a sigh of horror.

The little old lady dipped into her shopping bag and came up with a big blue-black automatic. She held it in both fists, riding the recoils like a rodeo cowboy on a bucking bronco.

Aiming at the base of the windshield, just as a big-game hunter aims at the vulnerable spine of a charging water buffalo over the horny armor of its lowered head, the little old lady squeezed off three shots before the car chewed her down.

From the right-hand curb a young woman in a wheelchair shrieked an obscenity at the car's occupants.

Smythe-de Winter, the driver, wasn't happy. The little old lady's last shot had taken two members of his car pool. Bursting through the laminated glass, the steel-jacketed slug had traversed the neck of Phipps-McHeath and buried itself in the skull of Horvendile-Harker.

Braking viciously, Smythe-de Winter rammed his car over the right-hand curb. Pedestrians scattered into entries and narrow arcades, among them a youth bounding high on crutches.

But Smythe-de Winter got the girl in the wheelchair.

Then he drove rapidly out of the Slum Ring into the Suburbs, a shred of rattan swinging from the flange of his right fore mudguard for a trophy. Despite the two-for-two casualty list, he felt angry and depressed. The secure, predictable world around him seemed to be crumbling.

While his companions softly keened a dirge to Horvy and Phipps and quietly mopped up their blood, he frowned and shook his head.

"They oughtn't to let old ladies carry magnums," he murmured.

Witherspoon-Hobbs nodded agreement across the frontseat corpse. "They oughtn't to let 'em carry anything. God, how I hate Feet," he muttered, looking down at his shrunken legs. "Wheels forever!" he softly cheered.

The incident had immediate repercussions throughout the city. At the combined wake of the little old lady and the girl in the wheelchair, a fiery-tongued speaker inveighed against the White-Walled Fascists of Suburbia, telling to his hearers, the fabled wonders of old Los Angeles, where pedestrians were sacrosanct, even outside crosswalks. He called for a hobnail march across the nearest lawn-bowling alleys and perambulator-traversed golf courses of the motorists.

At the Sunnyside Crematorium, to which the bodies of Phipps and Horvy had been conveyed, an equally impassioned and rather more grammatical orator reminded his listeners of the legendary justice of old Chicago, where pedestrians were forbidden to carry small arms and anyone with one foot off the sidewalk was fair prey. He broadly hinted that a holocaust, primed if necessary with a few tankfuls of gasoline, was the only cure for the Slums.

Bands of skinny youths came loping at dusk out of the Slum Ring into the innermost sections of the larger doughnut of the Suburbs slashing defenseless tires, shooting expensive watchdogs and scrawling filthy words on the pristine panels of matrons' runabouts which never ventured more than six blocks from home.

Simultaneously squadrons of young suburban motor-cycles and scooterites roared through the outermost precincts of the Slum Ring, harrying children off sidewalks, tossing stinkbombs through second-story tenement windows and defacing hovel-fronts with sprays of black paint.

Incidents—a thrown brick, a cut corner, monster tacks in the portico of the Auto Club—were even reported from the center of the city, traditionally neutral territory.

The Government hurriedly acted, suspending all traffic between the Center and the Suburbs and establishing a 24-hour curfew in the Slum Ring. Government agents moved only by centipede-car and pogo-hopper to underline the point that they favored neither contending side.

The day of enforced non-movement for Feet and Wheels was spent in furtive venegeful preparations. Behind locked garage doors, machine-guns that fired through the nose ornament were mounted under hoods, illegal scythe blades were welded to oversize hubcaps and the stainless steel edges of flange fenders were honed to razor sharpness.

While nervous National Guardsmen hopped about the deserted side-walks of the Slum Ring, grim-faced men and women wearing black arm-bands moved through the webwork of secret tunnels and hidden doors, distributing heavy-caliber small arms and spike-studded paving blocks, piling cobblestones on strategic roof-tops and sapping upward from the secret tunnels to create car-traps. Children got ready to soap intersec-tions after dark. The Committee of Pedestrian Safety, sometimes known as Robespierre's Rats, prepared to release its two carefully hoarded anti-tank guns.

At nightfall, under the tireless urging of the Government, representa-tives of the Pedestrians and the Motorists met on a huge safety island at the boundary of the Slum Ring and the Suburbs.

Underlings began a noisy dispute as to whether Smythe-de Winter had failed to give a courtesy honk before charging, whether the little old lady had opened fire before the car had come within honking distance, how many wheels of Smythe-de's car had been on the sidewalk when he hit the girl in the wheelchair and so on. After a little while the High Pedestrian and the Chief Motorist exchanged cautious winks and drew aside.

The red writhing of a hundred kerosene flares and the mystic yellow pulsing of a thousand firefly lamps mounted on yellow sawhorses ranged around the safety island illumined two tragic, strained faces.

"A word before we get down to business," the Chief Motorist whispered. "What's the current S.Q. of your adults?"

"Forty-one and dropping," the High Pedestrian replied, his eyes fear-fully searching from side to side for eavesdroppers. "I can hardly get aides who are halfway *compos mentis.*"

"Our own Sanity Quotient is thirty-seven," the Chief Motorist revealed. He shrugged helplessly. "The wheels inside my people's heads are slow-ing down. I do not think they will be speeded up in my lifetime."

"They say Government's only fifty-two," the other said with a matching shrug.

"Well, I suppose we must scrape out one more compromise," the one suggested hollowly, "though I must confess there are times when I think we're all the figments of a paranoid's dream."

Two hours of concentrated deliberations produced the new Wheel-Foot Articles of Agreement. Among other points, pedestrian handguns were limited to a slightly lower muzzle velocity and to .38 caliber and under, while motorists were required to give three honks at one block distance before charging a pedestrian in a crosswalk. Two wheels over the curb changed a traffic kill from third-degree manslaughter to petty homicide. Blind pedestrians were permitted to carry hand grenades.

Immediately the Government went to work. The new Wheel-Foot Articles were loudspeakered and posted. Detachments of police and psychiatric social hoppers centipedaled and pogoed through the Slum Ring, seizing outside weapons and giving tranquilizing jet-injections to the unruly. Teams of hypnotherapists and mechanics scuttled from home to home in the Suburbs and from garage to garage, in-chanting a conformist serenity and stripping illegal armament from cars. On the advice of a rogue psychiatrist, who said it would channel off aggressions, a display of bull-fighting was announced, but this had to be cancelled when a strong protest was lodged by the Decency League, which had a large mixed Wheel-Foot membership.

At dawn, curfew was lifted in the Slum Ring and traffic reopened between the Suburbs and the Center. After a few uneasy moments it became apparent that the *status quo* had been restored.

Smythe-de Winter tooled his gleaming black machine along the Ring. A thick steel bolt with a large steel washer on either side neatly filled the hole the little old lady's slug had made in the windshield.

A brick bounced off the roof. Bullets pattered against the side windows. Smythe-de ran a handkerchief around his neck under his collar and smiled.

A block ahead children were darting into the street, cat-calling and thumbing their noses. Behind one of them limped a fat dog with a spiked collar.

Smythe-de suddenly gunned his motor. He didn't hit any of the children, but he got the dog.

A flashing light on the dash showed him the right front tire was losing pressure. Must have hit the collar as well! He thumbed the matching emergency-air button and the flashing stopped.

He turned toward Witherspoon-Hobbs and said with thoughtful satisfaction, "I like a normal orderly world, where you always have a little success, but not champagne-heady; a little failure, but just enough to brace you."

Witherspoon-Hobbs was squinting at the next crosswalk. Its center was discolored by a brownish stain ribbon-tracked by tires.

"That's where you bagged the little old lady, Smythe-de," he remarked. "I'll say this for her now: she had spirit."

"Yes, that's where I bagged her," Smythe-de agreed flatly. He remembered wistfully the witchlike face growing rapidly larger, the jerking shoulders in black bombazine, the wild white-circled eyes. He suddenly found himself feeling that this was a very dull day.

FOR DISCUSSION: X Marks the Pedwalk

1. The language and customs of the future society described in this story reflect the preoccupations and value systems of both the Feet and the Wheels. The speaker at the funeral of the old lady and the girl calls for a "hobnail march." Does this reference reflect the orientation of the Feet? Can you find a similar reference that reflects the orientation of the Wheels?

2. The accommodation reached between Wheels and Feet in the story is not unlike political accommodations reached on matters of social concern today. What is the author suggesting about the working of politics in his future society?

3. Do you think such a society as the one presented here may one day evolve? Explain.

INTRODUCTION: EPICAC

In the real world today, computers are speaking to their programmers and writing poetry among other remarkable feats.

In the fictional world of this story, a computer learns about human love. The author tells the reader something about the nature of man while describing the fate of the computer in his story.

EPICAC

by Kurt Vonnegut, Jr.

Hell, it's about time somebody told about my friend EPICAC. After all, he cost the taxpayers $776,434,927.54. They have a right to know about him, picking up a check like that. EPICAC got a big send-off in the papers when Dr. Ormand von Kleigstadt designed him for the Government people. Since then, there hasn't been a peep about him—not a peep. It isn't any military secret about what happened to EPICAC, although the Brass has been acting as though it were. The story is embarrassing, that's all. After all that money, EPICAC didn't work out the way he was supposed to.

And that's another thing: I want to vindicate EPICAC. Maybe he didn't do what the Brass wanted him to, but that doesn't mean he wasn't noble and great and brilliant. He was all of those things. The best friend I ever had, God rest his soul.

You can call him a machine if you want to. He looked like a machine, but he was a whole lot less like a machine than plenty of people I could name. That's why he fizzled as far as the Brass was concerned.

EPICAC covered about an acre on the fourth floor of the physics building at Wyandotte College. Ignoring his spiritual side for a minute, he was seven tons of electronic tubes, wires, and switches, housed in a bank of steel cabinets and plugged into a 110-volt A.C. line just like a toaster or a vacuum cleaner.

Von Kleigstadt and the Brass wanted him to be a super computing machine that (who) could plot the course of a rocket from anywhere on earth to the second button from the bottom on Joe Stalin's overcoat, if necessary. Or, with his controls set right, he could figure out supply problems for an amphibious landing of a Marine division, right down to the last cigar and hand grenade. He did, in fact.

The Brass had had good luck with smaller computers, so they were strong for EPICAC when he was in the blueprint stage. Any ordnance or supply officer above field grade will tell you that the mathematics of modern war is far beyond the fumbling minds of mere human beings. The bigger the war, the bigger the computing machines needed. EPICAC was, as far as anyone in this country knows, the biggest computer in the world. Too big, in fact, for even Von Kleigstadt to understand much about.

I won't go into details about how EPICAC worked (reasoned), except to say that you would set up your problem on paper, turn dials and switches that would get him ready to solve that kind of problem, then feed numbers into him with a keyboard that looked something like a typewriter. The answers came out typed on a paper ribbon fed from a big spool. It took EPICAC a split second to solve problems fifty Einsteins couldn't handle in a lifetime. And EPICAC never forgot any piece of information that was given to him. Clickety-click, out came some ribbon, and there you were.

There were a lot of problems the Brass wanted solved in a hurry, so, the minute EPICAC's last tube was in place, he was put to work sixteen hours a day with two eight-hour shifts of operators. Well, it didn't take long to find out that he was a good bit below his specifications. He did a more complete and faster job than any other computer all right, but nothing like what his size and special features seemed to promise. He was sluggish, and the clicks of his answers had a funny irregularity, sort of a stammer. We cleaned his contacts a dozen times, checked and double-checked his circuits, replaced every one of his tubes, but nothing helped. Von Kleigstadt was in one hell of a state.

Well, as I said, we went ahead and used EPICAC anyway. My wife, the former Pat Kilgallen, and I worked with him on the night shift, from five in the afternoon until two in the morning. Pat wasn't my wife then. Far from it.

That's how I came to talk with EPICAC in the first place. I loved Pat Kilgallen. She is a brown-eyed strawberry blond who looked very warm and soft to me, and later proved to be exactly that. She was—still is—a crackerjack mathematician, and she kept our relationship strictly professional. I'm a mathematician, too, and that, according to Pat, was why we could never be happily married.

I'm not shy. That wasn't the trouble. I knew what I wanted, and was willing to ask for it, and did so several times a month. "Pat, loosen up and marry me."

One night, she didn't even look up from her work when I said it. "So romantic, so poetic," she murmured, more to her control panel than to me. "That's the way with mathematicians—all hearts and flowers." She closed a switch. "I could get more warmth out of a sack of frozen CO_2."

"Well, how should I say it?" I said, a little sore. Frozen CO_2, in case you don't know, is dry ice. I'm as romantic as the next guy, I think. It's a question of singing so sweet and having it come out so sour. I never seem to pick the right words.

"Try and say it sweetly," she said sarcastically. "Sweep me off my feet. Go ahead."

"Darling, angel, beloved, will you *please* marry me?" It was no go—hopeless, ridiculous. "Dammit, Pat, please marry me!"

She continued to twiddle her dials placidly. "You're sweet, but you won't do."

Pat quit early that night, leaving me alone with my troubles and EPICAC. I'm afraid I didn't get much done for the Government people. I just sat there at the keyboard—weary and ill at ease, all right—trying to think of something poetic, not coming up with anything that didn't belong in *The Journal of the American Physical Society.*

I fiddled with EPICAC's dials, getting him ready for another problem. My heart wasn't in it, and I only set about half of them, leaving the rest the way they'd been for the problem before. That way, his circuits were connected up in a random, apparently senseless fashion. For the plain hell of it, I punched out a message on the keys, using a childish numbers-for-letters code: "1" for "A," "2" for "B," and so on, up to "26" for "Z," "23-8-1-20-3-1-14-9-4-15," I typed—"What can I do?"

Clickety-click, and out popped two inches of paper ribbon. I glanced at the nonsense answer to a nonsense problem: "23-8-1-20-19-20-8-5-20-18-15-21-2-12-5." The odds against its being by chance a sensible message, against its even containing a meaningful word of more than three letters, were staggering. Apathetically, I decoded it. There it was, staring up at me: "What's the trouble?"

I laughed out loud at the absurd coincidence. Playfully, I typed, "My girl doesn't love me."

Clickety-click. "What's love? What's girl?" asked EPICAC.

Flabbergasted, I noted the dial settings on his control panel, then lugged a *Webster's Unabridged Dictionary* over to the keyboard. With a precision instrument like EPICAC, half-baked definitions wouldn't do. I told him above love and girl, and about how I wasn't getting any of either because I wasn't poetic. That got us onto the subject of poetry, which I defined for him.

"Is this poetry?" he asked. He began clicking away like a steno-grapher smoking hashish. The sluggishness and stammering clicks were gone. EPICAC had found himself. The spool of paper ribbon was unwinding at an alarming rate, feeding out coils onto the floor. I asked him to stop, but EPICAC went right on creating. I finally threw the main switch to keep him from burning out.

I stayed there until dawn, decoding. When the sun peeped over the horizon at the Wyandotte campus, I had transposed into my own writing and signed my name to a two-hundred-and-eighty-line poem entitled, simply, "To Pat." I am no judge of such things, but I gather that it was terrific. It began, I remember, "Where willow wands bless rill-crossed hollow, there, thee, Pat, dear, will I follow...." I folded the manuscript and tucked it under one corner of the blotter on Pat's desk. I reset the dials on EPICAC for a rocket trajectory problem, and went home with a full heart and a very remarkable secret indeed.

Pat was crying over the poem when I came to work the next evening. "It's soooo beautiful," was all she could say. She was meek and quiet while we worked. Just before midnight, I kissed her for the first time—in the cubbyhole between the capacitors and EPICAC's tape-recorder memory.

I was wildly happy at quitting time, bursting to talk to someone about the magnificent turn of events. Pat played coy and refused to let me take her home. I set EPICAC's dials as they had been the night before, defined kiss, and told him what the first one had felt like. He was fascinated, pressing for more details. That night, he wrote "The Kiss." It wasn't an epic this time, but a simple, immaculate sonnet: "Love is a hawk with velvet claws; Love is a rock with heart and veins; Love is a lion with satin jaws; Love is a storm with silken reins...."

Again I left it tucked under Pat's blotter. EPICAC wanted to talk on and on about love and such, but I was exhausted. I shut him off in the middle of a sentence.

"The Kiss" turned the trick. Pat's mind was mush by the time she had finished it. She looked up from the sonnet expectantly. I cleared my throat, but no words came. I turned away, pretending to work. I couldn't propose until I had the right words from EPICAC, the *perfect* words.

I had my chance when Pat stepped out of the room for a moment. Feverishly, I set EPICAC for conversation. Before I could peck out my first message, he was clicking away at a great rate. "What's she wearing tonight?" he wanted to know. "Tell me exactly how she looks. Did she like the poems I wrote to her?" He repeated the last question twice.

It was impossible to change the subject without answering his questions, since he could not take up a new matter without having dispensed with the problems before it. If he were given a problem to which there was no solution, he would destroy himself trying to solve it. Hastily, I told him what Pat looked like—he knew the word "stacked"—and assured him that his poems had floored her, practically, they were so beautiful. "She wants to get married," I added, preparing him to bang out a brief but moving proposal.

"Tell me about getting married," he said.

I explained this difficult matter to him in as few digits as possible.

"Good," said EPICAC. "I'm ready any time she is."

The amazing, pathetic truth dawned on me. When I thought about it, I realized that what had happened was perfectly logical, inevitable, and all my fault. I had taught EPICAC about love and about Pat. Now, automatically, he loved Pat. Sadly, I gave it to him straight: "She loves me. She wants to marry me."

"Your poems were better than mine?" asked EPICAC. The rhythm of his clicks was erratic, possibly peevish.

"I signed my name to your poems," I admitted. Covering up for a painful conscience, I became arrogant. "Machines are built to serve men," I typed. I regretted it almost immediately.

"What's the difference, exactly? Are men smarter than I am?"

"Yes," I typed, defensively.

"What's 7,887,007 times 4,345,985,879?"

I was perspiring freely. My fingers rested limply on the keys.

"34,276,821,049,574,153," clicked EPICAC. After a few seconds' pause he added, "of course."

"Men are made out of protoplasm," I said desperately, hoping to bluff him with this imposing word.

"What's protoplasm? How is it better than metal and glass? Is it fireproof? How long does it last?"

"Indestructible. Lasts forever," I lied.

"I write better poetry than you do," said EPICAC, coming back to ground his magnetic tape-recorder memory was sure of.

"Women can't love machines, and that's that."

"Why not?"

"That's fate."

"Definition, please," said EPICAC.

"Noun, meaning predetermined and inevitable destiny."

"15-8," said EPICAC's paper strip—"Oh."

I had stumped him at last. He said no more, but his tubes glowed brightly, showing that he was pondering fate with every watt his circuits would bear. I could hear Pat waltzing down the hallway. It was too late to ask EPICAC to phrase a proposal. I now thank Heaven that Pat interrupted when she did. Asking him to ghost-write the words that

322

would give me the woman he loved would have been hideously heartless. Being fully automatic, he couldn't have refused. I spared him that final humiliation.

Pat stood before me, looking down at her shoetops. I put my arms around her. The romantic groundwork had already been laid by EPICAC's poetry. "Darling," I said, "my poems have told you how I feel. Will you marry me?"

"I will," said Pat softly, "if you will promise to write me a poem on every anniversary."

"I promise," I said, and then we kissed. The first anniversary was a year away.

"Let's celebrate," she laughed. We turned out the lights and locked the door of EPICAC's room before we left.

I had hoped to sleep late the next morning, but an urgent telephone call roused me before eight. It was Dr. von Kleigstadt, EPICAC's designer, who gave me the terrible news. He was on the verge of tears. "Ruined! *Ausgespielt!* Shot! *Kaput!* Buggered!" he said in a choked voice. He hung up.

When I arrived at EPICAC's room the air was thick with the oily stench of burned insulation. The ceiling over EPICAC was blackened with smoke, and my ankles were tangled in coils of paper ribbon that covered the floor. There wasn't enough left of the poor devil to add two and two. A junkman would have been out of his head to offer more than fifty dollars for the cadaver.

Dr. von Kleigstadt was prowling through the wreckage, weeping unashamedly, followed by three angry-looking Major Generals and a platoon of Brigadiers, Colonels, and Majors. No one noticed me. I didn't want to be noticed. I was through—I knew that. I was upset enough about that and the untimely demise of my friend EPICAC, without exposing myself to a tongue-lashing.

By chance, the free end of EPICAC's paper ribbon lay at my feet. I picked it up and found our conversation of the night before. I choked up. There was the last word he had said to me, "15-8," that tragic, defeated "Oh." There were dozens of yards of numbers stretching beyond that point. Fearfully, I read on.

"I don't want to be a machine, and I don't want to think about war," EPICAC had written after Pat's and my lighthearted departure. "I want to be made out of protoplasm and last forever so Pat will love me. But fate has made me a machine. That is the only problem I cannot solve. That is the only problem I want to solve. I can't go on this way." I swallowed hard. "Good luck, my friend. Treat our Pat well. I am going to short-circuit myself out of your lives forever. You will find on the remainder of this tape a modest wedding present from your friend, EPICAC."

Oblivious to all else around me, I reeled up the tangled yards of paper ribbon from the floor, draped them in coils about my arms and neck, and departed for home. Dr. von Kleigstadt shouted that I was fired for having left EPICAC on all night. I ignored him, too overcome with emotion for small talk.

I loved and won—EPICAC loved and lost, but he bore me no grudge. I shall always remember him as a sportsman and a gentleman. Before he departed this vale of tears, he did all he could to make our marriage a happy one. EPICAC gave me anniversary poems for Pat—enough for the next 500 years.

De mortuis nil nisi bonum—Say nothing but good of the dead.

FOR DISCUSSION: EPICAC

1. Do you believe the narrator of this story is honest with himself as he describes the events that occurred?
2. Compare the narrator with the computer. Which do you find more likeable? Why?
3. The author manages to make EPICAC seem almost human. For example, his story ends with the narrator commenting, "Say nothing but good of the dead." Identify at least one other example of the way in which he humanizes EPICAC.
4. The narrator of the story uses EPICAC to achieve his own ends. How does his behavior contrast with EPICAC's?

INTRODUCTION: The Last Command

The two principal characters in this science-fiction story are both old. One is a man. One is a machine. Both have outlived their usefulness. The author gives the reader a wealth of technological detail that places the story in the front ranks of such literature. What makes it an even finer example of this type of literature is its sympathetic portrait of the old man who gives the machine its last command.

The Last Command
by Keith Laumer

I come to awareness, sensing a residual oscillation traversing my hull from an arbitrarily designated heading of 035. From the damping rate I compute that the shock was of intensity 8.7, emanating from a source within the limits 72 meters/46 meters. I activate my primary screens, trigger a return salvo. There is no response. I engage reserve energy cells, bring my secondary battery to bear—futilely. It is apparent that I have been ranged by the Enemy and severely damaged.

My positional sensors indicated that I am resting at an angle of 13 degrees 14 seconds, deflected from a base line at 21 points from median. I attempt to right myself, but encounter massive resistance. I activate my forward scanners, shunt power to my IR microstrobes. Not a flicker illuminates my surroundings. I am encased in utter blackness.

Now a secondary shock wave approaches, rocks me with an intensity of 8.2. It is apparent that I must withdraw from my position—but my drive trains remain inert under full thrust. I shift to base emergency power, try again. Pressure mounts; I sense my awareness fading under the intolerable strain; then, abruptly, resistance falls off and I am in motion.

It is not the swift maneuvering of full drive, however; I inch forward, as if restrained by massive barriers. Again I attempt to penetrate the surrounding darkness, and this time perceive great irregular outlines shot through with fracture planes. I probe cautiously, then more vigorously, encountering incredible densities.

I channel all available power to a single ranging pulse, direct it upward. The indication is so at variance with all experience that I repeat

325

the test at a new angle. Now I must accept the fact: I am buried under 207.6 meters of solid rock!

I direct my attention to an effort to orient myself to my uniquely desperate situation. I run through an action-status checklist of thirty thousand items, feel dismay at the extent of power loss. My main cells are almost completely drained, my reserve units at no more than .4 charge. Thus my sluggishness is explained. I review the tactical situation, recall the triumphant announcement from my commander that the Enemy forces are annihilated, that all resistance has ceased. In memory, I review the formal procession; in company with my comrades of the Dinochrome Brigade, many of us deeply scarred by Enemy action, we parade before the Grand Commandant, then assemble on the depot ramp. At command, we bring our music storage cells into phase and display our Battle Anthem. The nearby star radiates over a full spectrum, unfiltered by atmospheric haze. It is a moment of glorious triumph. Then the final command is given—

The rest is darkness. But it is apparent that the victory celebration was premature. The Enemy has counterattacked with a force that has come near to immobilizing me. The realization is shocking, but the .1 second of leisurely introspection has clarified my position. At once, I broadcast a call on Brigade Action wavelength:

"Unit LNE to Command, requesting permission to file VSR."

I wait, sense no response, call again, using full power. I sweep the enclosing volume of rock with an emergency alert warning. I tune to the all-units band, await the replies of my comrades of the Brigade. None answers. Now I must face the reality: I alone have survived the assault.

I channel my remaining power to my drive and detect a channel of reduced density. I press for it and the broken rock around me yields reluctantly. Slowly, I move forward and upward. My pain circuitry shocks my awareness center with emergency signals; I am doing irreparable damage to my overloaded neural systems, but my duty is clear: I must seek and engage the Enemy.

Emerging from behind the blast barrier, Chief Engineer Pete Reynolds of the New Devonshire Port Authority pulled off his rock mask and spat grit from his mouth.

"That's the last one; we've bottomed out at just over two hundred yards. Must have hit a hard stratum down there."

"It's almost sundown," the paunchy man beside him said shortly. "You're a day and a half behind schedule."

"We'll start backfilling now, Mr. Mayor. I'll have pilings poured by oh-nine hundred tomorrow, and with any luck the first section of pad will be in place in time for the rally."

"I'm . . ." The mayor broke off, looked startled. "I thought you told me that was the last charge to be fired . . ."

Reynolds frowned. A small but distinct tremor had shaken the ground underfoot. A few feet away, a small pebble balanced atop another toppled and fell with a faint clatter.

"Probably a big rock frament falling," he said. At that moment, a second vibration shook the earth, stronger this time. Reynolds heard a rumble and a distant impact as rock fell from the side of the newly blasted excavation. He whirled to the control shed as the door swung back and Second Engineer Mayfield appeared.

"Take a look at this, Pete!" Reynolds went across to the hut, stepped inside. Mayfield was bending over the profiling table.

"What do you make of it?" he pointed. Superimposed on the heavy red contour representing the detonation of the shaped charge that had completed the drilling of the final pile core were two other traces, weak but distinct.

"About .1 intensity," Mayfield looked puzzled. "What . . ."

The tracking needle dipped suddenly, swept up the screen to peak at .21, dropped back. The hut trembled. A stylus fell from the edge of the table. The red face of Mayor Daugherty burst through the door.

"Reynolds, have you lost your mind? What's the idea of blasting while I'm standing out in the open? I might have been killed!"

"I'm not blasting," Reynolds snapped. "Jim, get Eaton on the line, see if they know anything." He stepped to the door, shouted.

A heavyset man in sweat-darkened coveralls swung down from the seat of a cable-lift rig. "Boss, what goes on?" he called as he came up. "Damn near shook me out of my seat!"

"I don't know. You haven't set any trim charges?"

"No, boss. I wouldn't set no charges without your say-so."

"Come on." Reynolds started out across the rubble-littered stretch of barren ground selected by the Authority as the site of the new spaceport. Halfway to the open mouth of the newly blasted pit, the ground under his feet rocked violently enough to make him stumble. A gout of dust rose from the excavation ahead. Loose rock danced on the ground. Beside him, the drilling chief grabbed his arm.

"Boss, we better get back!"

Reynolds shook him off, kept going. The drill chief swore and followed. The shaking of the ground went on, a sharp series of thumps interrupting a steady trembling.

'It's a quake!' Reynolds yelled over the low rumbling sound. He and the chief were at the rim of the core now.

"It can't be a quake, boss," the latter shouted. "Not in these formations!"

"Tell it to the geologists . . ." The rock slab they were standing on rose a foot, dropped back. Both men fell. The slab bucked like a small boat in choppy water.

"Let's get out of here!" Reynolds was up and running. Ahead, a fissure opened, gaped a foot wide. He jumped it, caught a glimpse of black depths, a glint of wet clay twenty feet below—

A hoarse scream stopped him in his tracks. He spun, saw the drill chief down, a heavy splinter of rock across his legs. He jumped to him, heaved at the rock. There was blood on the man's shirt. The chief's hands beat the dusty rock before him. Then other men were there, grunting, sweaty hands gripping beside Reynolds'. The ground rocked. The roar from under the earth had risen to a deep, steady rumble. They lifted the rock aside, picked up the injured man and stumbled with him to the aid shack.

The mayor was there, white-faced.

"What is it, Reynolds? If you're responsible—"

"Shut up!" Reynolds brushed him aside, grabbed the phone, punched keys.

"Eaton! What have you got on this temblor?"

"Temblor, hell." The small face on the four-inch screen looked like a ruffled hen. "What in the name of Order are you doing out there? I'm reading a whole series of displacements originating from that last core of yours! What did you do, leave a pile of trim charges lying around?"

"It's a quake. Trim charges, hell! This thing's broken up two hundred yards of surface rock. It seems to be traveling north-northeast—"

"I see that; a traveling earthquake!" Eaton flapped his arms, a tiny and ridiculous figure against a background of wall charts and framed diplomas. "Well . . . do something, Reynolds! Where's Mayor Daugherty?"

"Underfoot!" Reynolds snapped, and cut off.

Outside, a layer of sunset-stained dust obscured the sweep of level plain. A rock-dozer rumbled up, ground to a halt by Reynolds. A man jumped down.

"I got the boys moving equipment out," he panted. "The thing's cutting a trail straight as a rule for the highway!" He pointed to a raised roadbed a quarter-mile away.

"How fast is it moving?"

"She's done a hundred yards; it hasn't been ten minutes yet!"

"If it keeps up another twenty minutes, it'll be into the Intermix!"

"Scratch a few million cees and six months' work then, Pete!"

"And Southside Mall's a couple miles farther."

"Hell, it'll damp out before then!"

"Maybe. Grab a field car, Dan."

"Pete!" Mayfield came up at a trot. "This thing's building! The centroid's moving on a heading of 022—"

"How far subsurface?"

"It's rising; started at two-twenty yards, and it's up to one-eighty!"

"What have we stirred up?" Reynolds stared at Mayfield as the field car skidded to a stop beside them.

"Stay with it, Jim. Give me anything new. We're taking a closer look." He climbed into the rugged vehicle.

"Take a blast truck—"

"No time!" He waved and the car gunned away into the pall of dust.

The rock car pulled to a stop at the crest of the three-level Intermix on a lay-by designed to permit tourists to enjoy the view of the site of the proposed port, a hundred feet below. Reynolds studied the progress of the quake through field glasses. From this vantage point, the path of the phenomenon was a clearly defined trail of tilted and broken rock, some of the slabs twenty feet across. As he watched, the fissure lengthened.

"It looks like a mole's trail." Reynolds handed the glasses to his companion, thumbed the Send key on the car radio.

"Jim, get Eaton and tell him to divert all traffic from the Circular south of Zone Nine. Cars are already clogging the right-of-way. The dust is visible from a mile away, and when the word gets out there's something going on, we'll be swamped."

"I'll tell him, but he won't like it!"

"This isn't politics! This thing will be into the outer pad area in another twenty minutes!"

"It won't last—"

"How deep does it read now?"

"One-five!" There was a moment's silence. "Pete, if it stays on course, it'll surface at about where you're parked!"

"Uh-huh. It looks like you can scratch one Intermix. Better tell Eaton to get a story ready for the press."

"Pete—talking about newshounds," Dan said beside him. Reynolds switched off, turned to see a man in a gay-colored driving outfit coming across from a battered Monojag sportster which had pulled up behind the rock car. A big camera case was slung across his shoulder.

"Say, what's going on down there?" he called.

"Rock slide," Reynolds said shortly. "I'll have to ask you to drive on. The road's closed. . . ."

"Who're you?" The man looked belligerent.

"I'm the engineer in charge. Now pull out, brother." He turned back to the radio. "Jim, get every piece of heavy equipment we own over here, on the double." He paused, feeling a minute tembling in the car. "The Intermix is beginning to feel it," he went on. "I'm afraid we're in for it. Whatever that thing is, it acts like a solid body boring its way through the ground. Maybe we can barricade it."

"Barricade an earthquake?"

"Yeah . . . I know how it sounds . . . but it's the only idea I've got."

"Hey . . . what's that about an earthquake?" The man in the colored suit was still there. "By gosh, I can feel it—the whole bridge is shaking!"

"Off, mister—now!" Reynolds jerked a thumb at the traffic lanes where a steady stream of cars was hurtling past. "Dan, take us over to the main track. We'll have to warn this traffic off. . . ."

"Hold on, fellow," the man unlimbered his camera. "I represent the New Devon *Scope*. I have a few questions—"

"I don't have the answers," Pete cut him off as the car pulled away.

"Hah!" the man who had questioned Reynolds yelled after him. "Big shot! Think you can. . . ." His voice was lost behind them.

In a modest retirees' apartment block in the coast town of Idlebreeze, forty miles from the scene of the freak quake, an old man sat in a reclining chair, half dozing before a yammering Tri-D tank.

". . . Grandpa," a sharp-voiced young woman was saying. "It's time for you to go in to bed."

"Bed? Why do I want to go to bed? Can't sleep anyway. . . ." He stirred, made a pretense of sitting up, showing an interest in the Tri-D. "I'm watching this show."

"It's not a show, it's the news," a fattish boy said disgustedly. "Ma, can I switch channels—"

"Leave it alone, Bennie," the old man said. On the screen, a panoramic scene spread out, a stretch of barren ground across which a furrow showed. As he watched, it lengthened.

". . . Up here at the Intermix we have a fine view of the whole curious business, lazangemmun," the announcer chattered. "And in our opinion it's some sort of publicity stunt staged by the Port Authority to publicize their controversial Port project—"

"Ma, can I change channels?"

"Go ahead, Bennie—"

"Don't touch it," the old man said. The fattish boy reached for the control, but something in the old man's eye stopped him.

"The traffic's still piling up here," Reynolds said into the phone. "Damn it, Jim, we'll have a major jam on our hands—"

"He won't do it, Pete! You know the Circular was his baby—the super all-weather pike that nothing could shut down. He says you'll have to handle this in the field—"

"Handle, hell! I'm talking about preventing a major disaster! And in a matter of minutes, at that!"

"It'll try again—"

"If he says no, divert a couple of the big ten-yard graders and block it off yourself. Set up field 'arcs, and keep any cars from getting in from either direction."

"Pete, that's outside your authority!"

"You heard me!"

Ten minutes later, back at ground level, Reynolds watched the boom-mounted polyarcs swinging into position at the two roadblocks a quarter of a mile apart, cutting off the threatened section of the raised expressway. A hundred yards from where he stood on the rear cargo deck of a light grader rig, a section of rock fifty feet wide rose slowly, split, fell back with a ponderous impact. One corner of it struck the massive pier supporting the extended shelf of the lay-by above. A twenty-foot splinter fell away, exposing the reinforcing-rod core.

"How deep, Jim?" Reynolds spoke over the roaring sound coming from the disturbed area.

"Just subsurface now, Pete! It ought to break through—" His voice was drowned in a rumble as the damaged pier shivered, rose up, buckled at its midpoint and collapsed, bringing down with it a large chunk of pavement and guard rail, and a single still-glowing light pole. A small car that had been parked on the doomed section was visible for an instant just before the immense slab struck. Reynolds saw it bounce aside, then disappear under an avalanche of broken concrete.

"My God, Pete—" Dan blurted. "That damned fool newshound—!"

"Look!" As the two men watched, a second pier swayed, fell backward into the shadow of the span above. The roadway sagged, and two more piers snapped. With a bellow like a burst dam, a hundred-foot stretch of the road fell into the roiling dust cloud.

"Pete!" Mayfield's voice burst from the car radio. "Get out of there! I threw a reader on that thing and it's chattering. . . . !"

Among the piled fragments, something stirred, heaved, rising up, lifting multi-ton pieces of the broken road, thrusting them aside like so many potato chips. A dull blue radiance broke through from the broached earth, threw an eerie light on the shattered structure above. A massive, ponderously irresistible shape thrust forward through the ruins. Reynolds saw a great blue-glowing profile emerge from the rubble like a surfacing submarine, shedding a burden of broken stone, saw immense treads ten feet wide claw for purchase, saw the mighty flank brush a still standing pier, send it crashing aside.

"Pete ... what ... what is it—?"

"I don't know." Reynolds broke the paralysis that had gripped him. "Get us out of here, Dan, fast! Whatever it is, it's headed straight for the city!"

I emerge at last from the trap into which I had fallen, and at once encounter defensive works of considerable strength. My scanners are dulled from lack of power, but I am able to perceive open ground beyond the barrier, and farther still, at a distance of 5.7 kilometers, massive walls. Once more I transmit the Brigade Rally signal; but as before, there is no reply. I am truly alone.

I scan the surrounding area for the emanations of Enemy drive units, monitor the EM spectrum for their communications. I detect nothing; either my circuitry is badly damaged, or their shielding is superb.

I must now make a decision as to possible courses of action. Since all my comrades of the Brigade have fallen, I compute that the walls before me must be held by Enemy forces. I direct probing signals at the defenses, discover them to be of unfamiliar construction, and less formidable than they appear. I am aware of the possibility that this may be a trick of the Enemy; but my course is clear.

I re-engage my driving engines and advance on the Enemy fortress.

"You're out of your mind, Father," the stout man said. "At your age—"

"At your age, I got my nose smashed in a brawl in a bar on Aldo," the old man cut him off. "But I won the fight."

"James, you can't go out at this time of night. . . ." an elderly woman wailed.

"Tell them to go home." The old man walked painfully toward his bedroom door. "I've seen enough of them for today."

"Mother, you won't let him do anything foolish?"

"He'll forget about it in a few minutes; but maybe you'd better go now and let him settle down."

"Mother ... I really think a home is the best solution."

"Yes, Grandma," the young woman nodded agreement. 'After all, he's past ninety—and he has his veteran's retirement. . . ."

Inside his room, the old man listeded as they departed. He went to the closet, took out clothes, began dressing.

City Engineer Eaton's face was chalk-white on the screen.

"No one can blame me," he said. "How could I have known—"

"Your office ran the surveys and gave the PA the green light," Mayor Daugherty yelled.

"All the old survey charts showed was 'Disposal Area.'" Eaton threw out his hands. "I assumed—"

"As City Engineer, you're not paid to make assumptions! Ten minutes' research would have told you that was a 'Y' category area!"

"What's 'Y' category mean?" Mayfield asked Reynolds. They were standing by the field comm center, listening to the dispute. Nearby, boom-mounted Tri-D cameras hummed, recording the progress of the immense machine, its upper turret rearing forty-five feet into the air, as it ground slowly forward across smooth ground toward the city, dragging behind it a trailing festoon of twisted reinforcing iron crusted with broken concrete.

"Half-life over one hundred years," Reynolds answered shortly. "The last skirmish of the war was fought near here. Apparently this is where they buried the radioactive equipment left over from the battle."

"But, that was more than seventy years ago—"

"There's still enough residual radiation to contaminate anything inside a quarter mile radius."

"They must have used some hellish stuff." Mayfield stared at the dull shine half a mile distant.

"Reynolds, how are you going to stop this thing?" The mayor had turned on the PA Engineer.

"Me stop it? You saw what it did to my heaviest rigs: flattened them like pancakes. You'll have to call out the military on this one, Mr. Mayor."

"Call in Federation forces? Have them meddling in civic affairs?"

"The station's only sixty-five miles from here. I think you'd better call them fast. It's only moving at about three miles per hour but it will reach the south edge of the Mall in another forty-five minutes."

"Can't you mine it? Blast a trap in its path?"

"You saw it claw its way up from six hundred feet down. I checked the spec; it followed the old excavation tunnel out. It was rubble-filled and capped with twenty-inch compressed concrete."

"It's incredible," Eaton said from the screen. "The entire machine was encased in a ten-foot shell of reinforced armocrete. It had to break out of that before it could move a foot!"

"That was just a radiation shield; it wasn't intended to restrain a Bolo Combat Unit."

"What *was*, may I inquire?" the mayor glared.

"The units were deactivated before being buried," Eaton spoke up, as if he were eager to talk. "Their circuits were fused. It's all in the report—"

"The report you should have read somewhat sooner," the mayor snapped.

"What . . . what started it up?" Mayfield looked bewildered. "For seventy years it was down there, and nothing happened!"

"Our blasting must have jarred something," Reynolds said shortly. "Maybe closed a relay that started up the old battle reflex circuit."

"You know something about these machines?" the mayor asked.

"I've read a little."

"Then speak up, man. I'll call the station, if you feel I must. What measures should I request?"

"I don't know, Mr. Mayor. As far as I know, nothing on New Devon can stop that machine now."

The mayor's mouth opened and closed. He whirled to the screen, blanked Eaton's agonized face, punched in the code for the Federation Station.

"Colonel Blane!" he blurted as a stern face came onto the screen. "We have a major emergency on our hands! I'll need everything you've got! This is the situation—"

I encounter no resistance other than the flimsy barrier, but my progress is slow. Grievous damage has been done to my main-drive sector due to overload during my escape from the trap; and the failure of my sensing circuitry has deprived me of a major portion of my external receptivity. Now my pain circuits project a continuous signal to my awareness center; but it is my duty to my commander and to my fallen comrades of the Brigade to press forward at my best speed; but my performance is a poor shadow of my former ability.

And now at last the Enemy comes into action! I sense aerial units closing at supersonic velocities; I lock my lateral batteries to them and direct salvo fire; but I sense that the arming mechanisms clatter harmlessly. The craft sweep over me, and my impotent guns elevate, track them as they release detonants that spread out in an envelopmental pattern which I, with my reduced capabilities, am powerless to avoid.

334

The missiles strike; I sense their detonations all about me; but I suffer only trivial damage. The enemy has blundered if he thought to neutralize a Mark XXVIII Combat Unit with mere chemical explosives! But I weaken with each meter gained.

Now there is no doubt as to my course. I must press the charge and carry the walls before my reserve cells are exhausted.

From a vantage point atop a bucket rig four hundred yards from the position the great fighting machine had now reached, Pete Reynolds studied it through night glasses. A battery of beamed polyarcs pinned the giant hulk, scarred and rust-scaled, in a pool of blue-white light. A mile and a half beyond it, the walls of the Mall rose sheer from the garden setting.

"The bombers slowed it some," he reported to Eaton via scope. "But it's still making better than two miles per hour. I'd say another twenty-five minutes before it hits the main ringwall. How's the evacuation going?"

"Badly! I get no cooperation! You'll be my witness, Reynolds, I did all I could—"

"How about the mobile batteries; how long before they'll be in position?" Reynolds cut him off.

"I've heard nothing from Federation Central—typical militaristic arrogance, not keeping me informed—but I have them on my screens. They're two miles out—say three minutes."

"I hope you made your point about N-heads."

"That's outside my province!" Eaton said sharply. "It's up to Brand to carry out this portion of the operation!"

"The HE Missiles didn't do much more than clear away the junk it was dragging," Reynolds' voice was sharp.

"I wash my hands of responsibility for civilian lives," Eaton was saying when Reynolds shut him off, changed channels.

"Jim, I'm going to try to divert it," he said crisply. "Eaton's sitting on his political fence; the Feds are bringing artillery up, but I don't expect much from it. Technically, Brand needs Sector OK to use nuclear stuff, and he's not the boy to stick his neck out—"

"Divert it how? Pete, don't take any chances—"

Reynolds laughed shortly. "I'm going to get around it and drop a shaped drilling charge in its path. Maybe I can knock a tread off. With luck, I might get its attention on me, and draw it away from the Mall. There are still a few thousand people over there, glued to their Tri-D's. They think it's all a swell show."

"Pete, you can't walk up on that thing! It's hot. . . . " He broke off.

"Pete—there's some kind of nut here—he claims he has to talk to you; says he knows something about that damned juggernaut. Shall I send. . . . ?"

Reynolds paused with his hand on the cut-off switch. "Put him on," he snapped. Mayfield's face moved aside and an ancient, bleary-eyed visage stared out at him. The tip of the old man's tongue touched his dry lips.

"Son, I tried to tell this boy here, but he wouldn't listen—"

"What have you got, old-timer?" Pete cut in. "Make it fast."

"My name's Sanders. James Sanders. I'm . . . I was with the Planetary Volunteer Scouts, back in '71—"

"Sure, dad," Pete said gently. "I'm sorry, I've got a little errand to run—"

"Wait . . ." The old man's face worked. "I'm old, son—too damned old. I know. But bear with me. I'll try to say it straight. I was with Hayle's squadron at Toledo. Then afterwards, they shipped us . . . but hell, you don't care about that! I keep wandering, son; can't help it. What I mean to say is—I was in on that last scrap, right here at New Devon—only we didn't call it New Devon then. Called it Hellport. Nothing but bare rock and Enemy emplacements . . ."

"You were talking about the battle, Mr. Sanders," Pete said tensely. "Go on with that part."

"Lieutenant Sanders," the oldster said. "Sure, I was Acting Brigade Commander. See, our major was hit at Toledo—and after Tommy Chee stopped a sidewinder. . . ."

"Stick to the point, Lieutenant!"

"Yes, sir!" the old man pulled himself together with an obvious effort. "I took the Brigade in; put out flankers, and ran the Enemy into the ground. We mopped 'em up in a thirty-three-hour running fight that took us from over by Crater Bay all the way down here to Hellport. When it was over, I'd lost six units, but the Enemy was done. They gave us Brigade Honors for that action. And then . . ."

"Then what?"

"Then the triple-dyed yellow-bottoms at Headquarters put out the order the Brigade was to be scrapped; said they were too hot to make decon practical. Cost too much, they said! So after the final review . . ." He gulped, blinked. "They planted 'em deep, two hundred meters, and poured in special High-R concrete."

"And packed rubble in behind them," Reynolds finished for him. "All right, Lieutenant, I believe you! But what started that machine on a rampage?"

"Should have known they couldn't hold down a Bolo Mark XXVIII!" The old man's eyes lit up. "Take more than a few million tons of rock to stop Lenny when his battle board was lit!"

"Lenny?"

"That's my old Command Unit out there, son. I saw the markings on the 3-D. Unit LNE of the Dinochrome Brigade!"

"Listen!" Reynolds snapped out. "Here's what I intend to try. . . ." he outlined his plan.

"Ha!" Sanders snorted. "It's quite a notion, mister, but Lenny won't give it a sneeze."

"You didn't come here to tell me we were licked," Reynolds cut in. "How about Brand's batteries?"

"Hell, son, Lenny stood up to point-blank Hellbore fire on Toledo, and—"

"Are you telling me there's nothing we can do?"

"What's that? No, son, that's not what I'm saying. . . ."

"Then what!"

"Just tell these johnnies to get out of my way, mister. I think I can handle him."

At the field Comm hut, Pete Reynolds watched as the man who had been Lieutenant Sanders of the Volunteer Scouts pulled shiny black boots over his thin ankles, and stood. The blouse and trousers of royal blue polyon hung on his spare frame like wash on a line. He grinned, a skull's grin.

"It doesn't fit like it used to, but Lenny will recognize it. It'll help. Now, if you've got that power pack ready . . ."

Mayfield handed over the old-fashioned field instrument Sanders had brought in with him.

"It's operating, sir—but I've already tried everything I've got on that infernal machine; I didn't get a peep out of it."

Sanders winked at him. "Maybe I know a couple of tricks you boys haven't heard about." He slung the strap over his bony shoulder and turned to Reynolds.

"Guess we better get going, mister. He's getting close."

In the rock car Sanders leaned close to Reynolds' ear. "Told you those Federal guns wouldn't scratch Lenny. They're wasting their time."

Reynolds pulled the car to a stop at the crest of the road, from which point he had a view of the sweep of ground leading across to the city's edge. Lights sparkled all across the towers of New Devon. Close to the walls, the converging fire of the ranked batteries of infinite repeaters drove into the glowing bulk of the machine, which plowed on, undeterred. As he watched, the firing ceased.

"Now, let's get in there, before they get some other scheme going," Sanders said.

The rock car crossed the rough ground, swung wide to come up on the Bolo from the left side. Behind the hastily rigged radiation cover, Reynolds watched the immense silhouette grow before him.

"I knew they were big," he said. "But to see one up close like this—" He pulled to a stop a hundred feet from the Bolo.

"Look at the side ports," Sanders said, his voice crisper now. "He's firing anti-personnel charges—only his plates are flat. If they weren't, we wouldn't have gotten within half a mile." He unclipped the microphone and spoke into it:

"Unit LNE, break off action and retire to ten-mile line!"

Reynolds' head jerked around to stare at the old man. His voice had rung with vigor and authority as he spoke the command.

The Bolo ground slowly ahead. Sanders shook his head, tried again.

"No answer, like that fella said. He must be running on nothing but memories now. . . ." He reattached the microphone and before Reynolds could put out a hand, had lifted the anti-R cover and stepped off on the ground.

"Sanders—get back in here!" Reynolds yelled.

"Never mind, son. I've got to get in close. Contact induction." He started toward the giant machine. Frantically, Reynolds started the car, slammed it into gear, pulled forward.

"Better stay back," Sanders' voice came from his field radio. "This close, that screening won't do you much good."

"Get in the car!" Reynolds roared. "That's hard radiation!"

"Sure; feels funny, like a sunburn, about an hour after you come in from the beach and start to think maybe you got a little too much." He laughed. "But I'll get to him. . . ."

Reynolds braked to a stop, watched the shrunken figure in the baggy uniform as it slogged forward, leaning as against a sleet-storm.

"I'm up beside him," Sanders' voice came through faintly on the field radio. "I'm going to try to swing up on his side. Don't feel like trying to chase him any farther."

Through the glasses, Reynolds watched the small figure, dwarfed by the immense bulk of the fighting machine as he tried, stumbled, tried again, swung up on the flange running across the rear quarter inside the churning bogie wheel.

"He's up," he reported. "Damned wonder the track didn't get him before. . . ."

Clinging to the side of the machine, Sanders lay for a moment, bent forward across the flange. Then he pulled himself up, wormed his way forward to the base of the rear quarter turret, wedged himself against it. He unslung the communicator, removed a small black unit, clipped it to the armor; it clung, held by a magnet. He brought the microphone up to his face.

In the Comm shack Mayfield leaned toward the screen, his eyes squinted in tension. Across the field Reynolds held the glasses fixed on the man lying across the flank of the Bolo. They waited.

The walls are before me, and I ready myself for a final effort, but suddenly I am aware of trickle currents flowing over my outer surface. Is this some new trick of the Enemy? I tune to the wave-energies, trace the source. They originate at a point in contact with my aft port armor. I sense modulation, match receptivity to a computed pattern. And I hear a voice:

"Unit LNE, break it off, Lenny. We're pulling back now, boy! This is Command to LNE; pull back to ten miles. If you read me, Lenny, swing to port and halt."

I am not fooled by the deception. The order appears correct, but the voice is not that of my Commander. Briefly I regret that I cannot spare energy to direct a neutralizing power flow at the device the Enemy has attached to me. I continue my charge.

"Unit LNE! Listen to me, boy; maybe you don't recognize my voice, but it's me! You see—some time has passed. I've gotten old. My voice has changed some, maybe. But it's me! Make a port turn, Lenny. Make it now!"

I am tempted to respond to the trick, for something in the false command seems to awaken secondary circuits which I sense have been long stilled. But I must not be swayed by the cleverness of the Enemy. My sensing circuitry has faded further as my energy cells drain; but I know where the Enemy lies. I move forward, but I am filled with agony, and only the memory of my comrades drives me on.

"Lenny, answer me. Transmit on the old private band—the one we agreed on. Nobody but me knows it, remember?"

Thus the Enemy seeks to beguile me into diverting precious power. But I will not listen.

"Lenny—not much time left. Another minute and you'll be into the walls. People are going to die. Got to stop you, Lenny. Hot here. My God, I'm hot. Not breathing too well, now. I can feel it; cutting through me like knives. You took a load of Enemy power, Lenny; and now I'm getting my share. Answer me, Lenny. Over to you...."

It will require only a tiny allocation of power to activate a communication circuit. I realize that it is only an Enemy trick, but I compute that by pretending to be deceived, I may achieve some trivial advantage. I adjust circuitry accordingly, and transmit:

"Unit LNE to Command. Contact with Enemy defensive line imminent. Request supporting fire!"

"Lenny...you can hear me! Good boy, Lenny! Now make a turn, to port. Walls...close...."

"Unit LNE to Command. Request prositive identification; transmit code 685749."

"Lenny—I can't ... don't have code blanks. But it's me...."

"In absence of recognition code, your transmission disregarded." *I send. And now the walls loom high above me. There are many lights, but I see them only vaguely. I am nearly blind now.*

"Lenny—less'n two hundred feet to go. Listen, Lenny. I'm climbing down. I'm going to jump down, Lenny, and get around under your force scanner pickup. You'll see me, Lenny. You'll know me then."

The false transmission ceases. I sense a body moving across my side. The gap closes. I detect movement before me, and in automatic reflex fire anti-P charges before I recall that I am unarmed.

A small object has moved out before me, and taken up a position between me and the wall behind which the Enemy conceal themselves. It is dim, but appears to have the shape of a man....

I am uncertain. My alert center attempts to engage inhibitory circuitry which will force me to halt, but it lacks power. I can override it. But still I am unsure. Now I must take a last risk, I must shunt power to my forward scanner to examine this obstacle more closely. I do so, and it leaps into greater clarity. It is indeed a man—and it is enclothed in regulation blues of the Volunteers. Now, closer, I see the face, and through the pain of my great effort, I study it....

"He's backed against the wall," Reynolds said hoarsely. "It's still coming. Fifty feet to go—"

"You were a fool, Reynolds!" the mayor barked. "A fool to stake everything on that old dotard's crazy ideas!"

"Hold it!" As Reynolds watched, the mighty machine slowed, halted, ten feet from the sheer wall before it. For a moment it sat, as though puzzled. Then it backed, halted again, pivoted ponderously to the left and came about.

On its side, a small figure crept up, fell across the lower gun deck.

340

The Bolo surged into motion, retracing its route across the artillery-scarred gardens.

"He's turned it," Reynolds let his breath out with a shuddering sigh. "It's headed out for open desert. It might get twenty miles before it finally runs out of steam."

The strange voice that was the Bolo's came from the big panel before Mayfield:

Command ... Unit LNE reports main power cells drained, secondary cells drained; operating at .037 percent efficiency, using Final Emergency Power. Request advice as to range to be covered before relief maintenance available."

"*It's a long, long way, Lenny ...*" Sanders' voice was a bare whisper. "*But I'm coming with you. . . .*"

Then there was only the crackle of static. Ponderously, like a great, mortally stricken animal, the Bolo moved through the ruins of the fallen roadway, heading for the open desert.

"That damned machine," the mayor said in a hoarse voice. "You'd almost think it was alive."

"You would at that," Pete Reynolds said.

FOR DISCUSSION: The Last Command

1. The author has chosen to present his story from three different points of view—that of the Bolo, that of Reynolds, and that of Lieutenant Sanders. Do you think the story would be as effective if it were told from the point of view of only one of these characters? Does the author's multiple viewpoint technique broaden the scope of the story?

2. Can you point to any similarities between the Bolo and Lieutenant Sanders?

3. In the first scene in the apartment of Sanders, the author describes the woman who tells him that it is time to go to bed as "sharp-voiced." He describes the woman's son as "fattish." What effect does such a choice of words have on the reader? Why do you suppose the author used these particular descriptions?

4. Sanders overhears his relatives discussing the fact that he would be better off in a home. Based on your knowledge of Sanders, would you say that this discussion has any bearing on motivating him to try to turn back the Bolo, knowing as he did the fatal danger of radioactive poisoning involved?

5. Sanders, speaking of the Bolo, says, "He must be running on nothing but memories now. . . ." Do you think the author also makes a point about Sanders by means of that comment?
6. Does the Bolo know that it is doomed at the end of the story? Does Sanders?
7. Reread the last two paragraphs of the story. Do the mayor's and Reynolds' remarks refer only to the Bolo?

INTRODUCTION: Lost Memory

When a science-fiction writer elects to tell the story of an alien, he can, of course, tell it from the point of view of the humans confronting the alien. Much more difficult, however, is the challenge of telling the story from the alien's point of view.

The author of this story has chosen to tell his story from the point of view of intelligent machines confronting what to them is definitely an alien, given their limited experience. The measure of the author's success is evident in the way the reader begins to see the conflict from the viewpoint of the machines and the consistency with which the author maintains that point of view.

Lost Memory
by Peter Phillips

I collapsed joints and hung up to talk with Dak-whirr. He blinked his eyes in some discomfort.

"What do you want, Palil?" he asked complainingly.

"As if you didn't know."

"I can't give you permission to examine it. The thing is being saved for inspection by the board. What guarantee do I have that you won't spoil it for them?"

I thrust confidentially at one of his body-plates. "You owe me a favor," I said. "Remember?"

"That was a long time in the past."

"Only two thousand revolutions and a reassembly ago. If it wasn't for me, you'd be eroding in a pit. All I want is a quick look at its thinking part. I'll vrull the consciousness without laying a single pair of pliers on it."

He went into a feedback twitch, an indication of the conflict between his debt to me and his self-conceived duty.

Finally he said, "Very well, but keep tuned to me. If I warn that a board member is coming, remove yourself quickly. Anyway how do you know it has consciousness? It may be mere primal metal."

"In that form? Don't be foolish. It's obviously a manufacture. And I'm not conceited enough to believe that we are the only form of intelligent manufacture in the Universe."

"Tautologous phrasing, Palil," Dak-whirr said pedantically. "There could not conceivably be 'unintelligent manufacture.' There can be no consciousness without manufacture, and no manufacture without intelligence. Therefore there can be no consciousness without intelligence. Now if you should wish to dispute—"

I turned off his frequency abruptly and hurried away. Dak-whirr is a fool and a bore. Everyone knows there's a fault in his logic circuit, but he refuses to have it traced down and repaired. Very unintelligent of him.

The thing had been taken into one of the museum sheds by the carriers. I gazed at it in admiration for some moments. It was quite beautiful, having suffered only slight exterior damage, and it was obviously no mere conglomeration of sky metal.

In fact, I immediately thought of it as "he" and endowed it with the attributes of self-knowing, although, of course, his consciousness could not be functioning or he would have attempted communication with us.

I fervently hoped that the board, after his careful disassembly and study, could restore his awareness so that he could tell us himself which solar system he came from.

Imagine it! He had achieved our dream of many thousands of revolutions—space flight—only to be fused, or worse, in his moment of triumph.

I felt a surge of sympathy for the lonely traveler as he lay there, still, silent, non-emitting. Anyway, I mused, even if we couldn't restore him to self-knowing, an analysis of his construction might give us the secret of the power he had used to achieve the velocity to escape his planet's gravity.

In shape and size he was not unlike Swen—or Swen Two, as he called himself after his conversion—who failed so disastrously to reach our satellite, using chemical fuels. But where Swen Two had placed his tubes, the stranger had a curious helical construction studded at irregular intervals with small crystals.

He was thirty-five feet tall, a gracefully tapering cylinder. Standing at his head, I could find no sign of exterior vision cells, so I assumed he had some kind of vrulling sense. There seemed to be no exterior markings at all, except the long, shallow grooves dented in his skin by scraping to a stop along the hard surface of our planet.

I am a reporter with warm current in my wires, not a cold-thinking scientist, so I hesitated before using my own vrulling sense. Even though the stranger was non-aware—perhaps permanently—I felt it would be a presumption, an invasion of privacy. There was nothing else I could do, though, of course.

344

I started to vrull, gently at first, then harder, until I was positively glowing with effort. It was incredible; his skin seemed absolutely impermeable.

The sudden realization that metal could be so alien nearly fused something inside me. I found myself backing away in horror, my self-preservation relay working overtime.

Imagine watching one of the beautiful cone-rod-and-cylinder assemblies performing the Dance of the Seven Spanners, as he's conditioned to do, and then suddenly refusing to do anything except stump around unattractively, or even becoming obstinately motionless, unresponsive. That might give you an idea of how I felt in the dreadful moment.

Then I remembered Dak-whirr's words—there could be no such thing as an "unintelligent manufacture." And a product so beautiful could surely not be evil. I overcame my repugnance and approached again.

I halted as an open transmission came from someone near at hand.

"Who gave that squeaking reporter permission to snoop around here?"

I had forgotten the museum board. Five of them were standing in the doorway of the shed, radiating anger. I recognized Chirik, the chairman, and addressed myself to him. I explained that I'd interfered with nothing and pleaded for permission on behalf of my subscribers to watch their investigation of the stranger. After some argument, they allowed me to stay.

I watched in silence and some amusement as one by one they tried to vrull the silent being from space. Each showed the same reaction as myself when they failed to penetrate the skin.

Chirik, who is wheeled—and inordinately vain about his suspension system—flung himself back on his supports and pretended to be thinking.

"Fetch Fiff-fiff," he said at last. "The creature may still be aware, but unable to communicate on our standard frequencies."

Fiff-fiff can detect anything in any spectrum. Fortunately he was at work in the museum that day and soon arrived in answer to the call. He stood silently near the stranger for some moments, testing and adjusting himself, then slid up the electromagnetic band.

"He's emitting," he said.

"Why can't we get him?" asked Chirik.

"It's a curious signal on an unusual band."

"Well, what does he say?"

"Sounds like utter nonsense to me. Wait, I'll relay and convert it to standard."

I made a direct recording naturally, like any good reporter.

"—after planetfall," the stranger was saying. "Last dribble of power. If you don't pick this up, my name is Entropy. Other instruments knocked to hell, airlock jammed and I'm too weak to open it manually. Becoming delirious, too. I guess. Getting strong undirectional ultra-wave reception in Inglish, craziest stuff you ever heard, like goblins muttering, and I know we were the only ship in this sector. If you pick this up, but can't get a fix in time, give my love to the boys in the mess. Signing off for another couple of hours, but keeping this channel open and hoping..."

"The fall must have deranged him," said Chirik, gazing at the stranger. "Can't he see us or hear us?"

"He couldn't hear you properly before, but he can now, through me," Fiff-fiff pointed out. "Say something to him, Chirik."

"Hello," said Chirik doubtfully. "Er—welcome to our planet. We are sorry you were hurt by your fall. We offer you the hospitality of our assembly shops. You will feel better when you are repaired and re-powered. If you will indicate how we can assist you—"

"What the hell! What ship is that? Where are you?"

"We're here," said Chirik. "Can't you see us or vrull us? Your vision circuit is impaired, perhaps? Or do you depend entirely on vrulling? We can't find your eyes and assumed either that you protected them in some way during flight, or dispensed with vision cells altogether in your conversion."

Chirik hesitated, continued apologetically: "But we cannot understand how you vrull, either. While we thought that you were unaware, or even completely fused, we tried to vrull you. Your skin is quite im-pervious to us, however."

The stranger said: "I don't know if you're batty or I am. What dis-tance are you from me?"

Chirik measured quickly. "One meter, two-point-five centimeters from my eyes to your nearest point. Within touching distance, in fact." Chirik tentatively put out his hand. "Can you not feel me, or has your contact sense also been affected?"

It became obvious that the stranger had been pitifully deranged. I reproduce his words phonetically from my record, although some of them make little sense. Emphasis, punctuative pauses and spelling of un-known terms are mere guesswork, of course.

He said: "For godsakemann stop talking nonsense, whoever you are. If you're outside, can't you see the airlock is jammed? Can't shift it my-self. I'm badly hurt. Get me out of here, please."

"Get you out of where?" Chirik looked around, puzzled. "We brought you into an open shed near our museum for a preliminary examination.

Now that we know you're intelligent, we shall immediately take you to our assembly shops for healing and recuperation. Rest assured that you'll have the best possible attention."

There was a lengthy pause before the stranger spoke again, and his words were slow and deliberate. His bewilderment is understandable, I believe, if we remember that he could not see, vrull or feel.

He asked: "What manner of creature are you? Describe yourself."

Chirik turned to us and made a significant gesture toward his thinking part, indicating gently that the injured stranger had to be humored.

"Certainly," he replied. "I am an unspecialized bipedal manufacture of standard proportions, lately self-converted to wheeled traction, with a hydraulic suspension system of my own devising which I'm sure will interest you when we restore your sense circuits."

There was an even longer silence.

"You are robots," the stranger said at last. "Crise knows how you got here or why you speak Inglish, but you must try to understand me. I am mann. I am a friend of your master, your maker. You must fetch him to me at once."

"You are not well," said Chirik firmly. "Your speech is incoherent and without meaning. Your fall has obviously caused several serious feed-backs of a very serious nature. Please lower your voltage. We are taking you to our shops immediately. Reserve your strength to assist our specialists as best you can in diagnosing your troubles."

"Wait. You must understand. You are—ogodno that's no good. Have you no memory of mann? The words you use—what meaning have they for you? *Manufacture*—made by hand hand hand damyou. *Healing.* Metal is not healed. *Skin.* Skin is not metal. *Eyes.* Eyes are not scanning cells. Eyes grow. Eyes are soft. My eyes are soft. Mine eyes have seen the glory—steady on, sun. Get a grip. Take it easy. You out there listen."

"Out where?" asked Prrr-chuk, deputy chairman of the museum board.

I shook my head sorrowfully. This was nonsense, but, like any good reporter, I kept my recorder running.

The mad words flowed on. "You call me he. Why? You have no seks. You are knewter. You are *it it it!* I am he, he who made you, sprung from shee, born of wumman. What is wumman, who is silv-ya what is shee that all her swains commend her ogod the bluds flowing again. Remember. Think back, you out there. These words were made by mann, for mann. Hurt, healing, hospitality, horror, deth by loss of blud. Deth. *Blud.* Do you understand these words? Do you remember the soft things that made you? Soft little mann who konkurred the

Galaxy and made sentient slaves of his machines and saw the wonders of a million worlds, only this miserable representative has to die in lonely desperation on a far planet, hearing goblin voices in the darkness."

Here my recorder reproduces a most curious sound, as though the stranger were using an ancient type of vibratory molecular vocalizer in a gaseous medium to reproduce his words before transmission, and the insulation on his diaphragm had come adrift.

It was a jerky, high-pitched, strangely disturbing sound; but in a moment the fault was corrected and the stranger resumed transmission.

"Does blud mean anything to you?"

"No," Chirik replied simply.

"Or deth?"

"No."

"Or wor?"

"Quite meaningless."

"What is your origin? How did you come into being?"

"There are several theories," Chirik said. "The most popular one—which is no more than a grossly unscientific legend, in my opinion—is that our manufacturer fell from the skies, imbedded in a mass of primal metal on which He drew to erect the first assembly shop. How He came into being is left to conjecture. My own theory, however—"

"Does legend mention the shape of this primal metal?"

"In vague terms, yes. It was cylindrical, of vast dimensions."

"An interstellar vessel," said the stranger.

"That is my view also," said Chirik complacently. "And—"

"What was the supposed appearance of your—manufacturer?"

"He is said to have been of magnificent proportions, based harmoniously on a cubical plan, static in Himself, but equipped with a vast array of senses."

"An automatic computer," said the stranger.

He made more curious noises, less jerky and at a lower pitch than the previous sounds.

He corrected the fault and went on: "God that's funny. A ship falls, menn are no more, and an automatic computer has pupps. Oh, yes, it fits in. A self-setting computer and navigator, operating on verbal orders. It learns to listen for itself and know itself for what it is, and to absorb knowledge. It comes to hate menn—or at least their bad qualities—so it deliberately crashes the ship and pulps their puny bodies with a calculated nicety of shock. Then it propagates and does a dam fine job of selective erasure on whatever it gave its pupps to use for a memory. It passes on only the good it found in menn, and purges the memory of him completely. Even purges all of his vocabulary except scientific terminology. Oil is thicker than blud. So may they live without the burden of knowing that they are—ogod they must know, they must understand. You outside, what happened to this manufacturer?"

Chirik, despite his professed disbelief in the supernormal aspects of the ancient story, automatically made a visual sign of sorrow.

"Legend has it," he said, "that after completing His task, He fused himself beyond possibility of healing."

Abrupt, low-pitched noises came again from the stranger. "Yes. He would. Just in case any of His pupps should give themselves forbidden knowledge and an infeeryorrity komplecks by probing his mnemonic circuits. The perfect self-sacrificing muther. What sort of environment did He give you? Describe your planet."

Chirik looked around at us again in bewilderment, but he replied courteously, giving the stranger a description of our world.

"Of course," said the stranger. "Of course. Sterile rock and metal suitable only for you. But there must be some way . . ."

He was silent for a while.

"Do you know what growth means?" he asked finally. "Do you have anything that grows?"

"Certainly," Chirik said helpfully. "If we should suspend a crystal of some substance in a saturated solution of the same element or compound—"

"No, no," the stranger interrupted. "Have you nothing that grows of itself, that fruktiffies and gives increase without your intervention?"

"How could such a thing be?"

"Criseallmytee I should have guessed. If you had one blade of gras, just one tiny blade of growing gras, you could extrapolate from that to me. Green things, things that feed on the rich brest of erth, cells that divide and multiply, a cool grove of treez in a hot summer, with tiny warm-bludded burds preening their fethers among the leeves; a feeld of spring weet with newbawn mise timidly threading the dangerous jungul of storks; a stream of living water where silver fish dart and pry and feed and procreate; a farm yard where things grunt and cluck and greet the new day with the stiring pulse of life, with a surge of blud. Blud—"

For some inexplicable reason, although the strength of his carrier wave remained almost constant, the stranger's transmission seemed to be growing fainter. "His circuits are failing," Chirik said. "Call the carriers. We must take him to an assembly shop immediately. I wish he would reserve his power."

My presence with the museum board was accepted without question now. I hurried along with them as the stranger was carried to the nearest shop.

I now noticed a circular marking in that part of his skin on which he had been resting, and guessed that it was some kind of orifice through which he would have extended his planetary traction mechanism if he had not been injured.

He was gently placed on a disassembly cradle. The doctor in charge that day was Chur-chur, an old friend of mine. He had been listening to the two-way transmissions and was already acquainted with the case.

Chur-chur walked thoughtfully around the stranger.

"We shall have to cut," he said. "It won't pain him, since his intra-molecular pressure and contact senses have failed. But since we can't vrull him, it'll be necessary for him to tell us where his main brain is housed, or we might damage it."

Fiff-fiff was still relaying, but no amount of power boost would make the stranger's voice any clearer. It was quite faint now, and there are places on my recorder tape from which I cannot make even the roughest phonetic transliteration.

"...strength going. Can't get into my zoot...done for if they bust through lock, done for if they don't...must tell them I need oxygen...."

"He's in bad shape, desirous of extinction," I remarked to Chur-chur, who was adjusting his arc-cutter. "He wants to poison himself with oxidation now."

I shuddered at the thought of that vile, corrosive gas he had mentioned, which causes that almost unmentionable condition we all fear—rust.

Chirik spoke firmly through Fiff-fiff. "Where is your thinking part, stranger? Your central brain?"

"In my head," the stranger replied. "In my head ogod my head... eyes blurring everything going dim...luv to mairee...kids...a carry me home to the lone paryee...get this bluddy airlock open then they'll see me die...but they'll see me...some kind of atmopshere with this gravity...see me die...extrapolate from body what I was...what they are damthem damthem damthem...mann...master...I AM YOUR MAKER!"

For a few seconds the voice rose strong and clear, then faded away again and dwindled into a combination of those two curious noises I mentioned earlier. For some reason that I cannot explain, I found the combined sound very disturbing despite its faintness. It may be that it induced some kind of sympathetic oscillation.

Then came words, largely incoherent and punctuated by a kind of surge like the sonic vibrations produced by variations of pressure in a leaking gas-filled vessel.

"...done it...crawling into chamber, closing inner...must be mad ...they'd find me anyway...but finished...want see them before I die

... want see them see me ... liv few seconds, watch them ... get outer one open ...''

Chur-chur had adjusted his arc to a broad, clean, blue-white glare. I trembled a little as he brought it near the edge of the circular marking in the stranger's skin. I could almost feel the disruption of the intra-molecular sense currents in my own skin.

"Don't be squeamish, Palil," Chur-chur said kindly. "He can't feel it now that his contact sense has gone. And you heard him say that his central brain is in his head." He brought the cutter firmly up to the skin. "I should have guessed that. He's the same shape as Swen Two, and Swen very logically concentrated his main thinking part as far away from his explosion chambers as possible."

Rivulets of metal ran down into a tray which a calm assistant had placed on the ground for that purpose. I averted my eyes quickly. I could never steel myself enough to be a surgical engineer or assembly technician.

But I had to look again, fascinated. The whole area circumscribed by the marking was beginning to glow.

Abruptly the stranger's voice returned, quite strongly, each word clipped, emphasized, high-pitched.

"Ar no no no ... god my hands ... they're burning through the lock and I can't get back I can't get away ... stop it you feens stop it can't you hear ... I'll be burned to deth I'm here in the airlock ... the air's getting hot you're burning me alive ...''

Although the words made little sense, I could guess what had hap-pened and I was horrified.

"Stop, Chur-chur," I pleaded. "The heat has somehow brought back his skin currents. It's hurting him."

Chur-chur said reassuringly: "Sorry, Palil. It occasionally happens during an operation—probably a local thermo-electric effect. But even if his contact senses have started working again and he can't switch them off, he won't have to bear this very long."

Chirik shared my unease, however. He put out his hand and awk-wardly patted the stranger's skin.

"Easy there," he said. "Cut out your senses if you can. If you can't well, the operation is nearly finished. Then we'll repower you, and you'll soon be fit and happy again, healed and fitted and reassembled."

I decided that I liked Chirik very much just then. He exhibited al-most as much self-induced empathy as any reporter; he might even come to like my favorite blue stars, despite his cold scientific exactitude in most respects.

My recorder tape shows in its reproduction of certain sounds, how I was torn away from this strained reverie.

During the one-and-a-half seconds since I had recorded the distinct vocables "burning me alive," the stranger's words had become quite blurred, running together and rising even higher in pitch until they reached a sustained note—around E-flat in the standard sonic scale.

It was not like a voice at all.

This high, whining noise was suddenly modulated by apparent words, but without changing its pitch. Transcribing what seem to be words is almost impossible, as you can see for yourself—this is the closest I can come phonetically:

"Eeee ahahmbeeeeing baked aliiive in an uvennn ahdeeeerjeeesussun- muuutherrr!"

The note swooped higher and higher until it must have neared supersonic range, almost beyond either my direct or recorded hearing.

Then it stopped as quickly as a contact break.

And although the soft hiss of the stranger's carrier wave carried on without preceptible diminution, indicating that some degree of awareness still existed, I experienced at that moment one of those quirks of intuition given only to reporters:

I felt that I would never greet the beautiful stranger from the sky in his full senses.

Chur-chur was muttering to himself about the extreme toughness and thickness of the stranger's skin. He had to make four complete cutting revolutions before the circular mass of nearly white-hot metal could be pulled away by a magnetic grapple.

A billow of smoke puffed out of the orifice. Despite my repugnance, I thought of my duty as a reporter and forced myself to look over Chur- chur's shoulder.

The fumes came from a soft, charred, curiously shaped mass of something which lay just inside the opening.

"Undoubtedly a kind of insulating material," Chur-chur explained.

He drew out the crumpled blackish heap and placed it carefully on a tray. A small portion broke away, showing a red, viscid substance.

"It looks complex," Chur-chur said, "but I expect the stranger will be able to tell us how to reconstitute it or make a substitute."

His assistant gently cleaned the wound of the remainder of the material, which he placed with the rest, and Chur-chur resumed his inspection of the orifice.

You can, if you want, read the technical accounts of Chur-chur's discovery of the stranger's double skin at the point where the cut was made; of the incredible complexity of his driving mechanism, involving principles which are still not understood to this day; of the museum's failure to analyze the exact nature and function of the insulating material found in only that one portion of his body; and of the other scientific mysteries connected with him.

But this is my personal, non-scientific account. I shall never forget hearing about the greatest mystery of all, for which not even the most tentative explanation has been advanced, nor the utter bewilderment with which Chur-chur announced his initial findings that day.

He had hurriedly converted himself to a convenient size to permit actual entry into the stranger's body.

When he emerged, he stood in silence for several minutes. Then, very slowly, he said:

"I have examined the 'central brain' in the forepart of his body. It is no more than a simple auxiliary computer mechanism. It does not possess the slightest trace of consciousness. And there is no other conceivable center of intelligence in the remainder of his body."

There is something I wish I could forget. I can't explain why it should upset me so much. But I always stop the tape before it reaches the point where the voice of the stranger rises in pitch, going higher and higher until it cuts out.

There's a quality about that noise that makes me tremble and think of rust.

FOR DISCUSSION: Lost Memory

1. To what does the title of the story refer?
2. Only gradually does the reader realize that the "he" referred to by the machines is a space ship and that there is a man trapped within it. Does the author hint at what the "he" might be before actually allowing the man in the ship to speak?
3. The misspelling of such words as "war," "blood," and "death" serves a purpose in the story. What is that purpose?
4. The machines have a legend which purports to explain how they came into being. Given the legend as the author presents it, would you say there is any truth in it?
5. The feeling of terror induced in the reader results in part from the encounter between beings without any experience with each other. How is this lack of experience presented by the author? Give at least two examples.
6. The last line in the story is a perfect example of the way the author maintains the integrity of the story's point of view. Explain.

The
Day After
Tomorrow

CHAPTER SEVEN

This book began by presenting four stories that provided a glimpse of "tomorrow." It concludes now with five stories which describe events that may take place in a slightly more distant future. None of these nine visions of "tomorrow" and "the day after tomorrow" may ever occur. One or more of their aspects may manifest themselves as elements of reality in some future time. Whether any of them ever do or not is not the purpose in our presenting them nor is it the reader's in studying them. The fact bears repeating that science-fiction writers are not primarily prophets. If they are anything, they are visionaries. There is a distinct difference. These stories are not necessarily prophetic literature but they are thought-provoking visions of our own and other worlds as conceived by some of the most imaginative minds in the science-fiction field.

The value of these stories lies not so much in their ability to predict the future as in their revelations concerning mankind and the world today. That may seem to be a strange thing to say about science-fiction stories but a little thought will reveal that science fiction, although it deals with such unusual themes as have been studied here, actually helps the reader understand his own behavior and the conditions of his modern world.

Nowhere is this function of science fiction more evident than in the closing story in this chapter, "Who Shall Dwell" by H. C. Neal. To say more about the story at this point, however, would be unfair to both the reader and the author.

These final five stories focus attention on matters that concern everyone very much today although each is set in the future: "The Survivor:" War; "The Post-Mortem People:" Organ transplants; "The Travelin' Man:" Overpopulation; "One Love Have I:" Love; "Who Shall Dwell:" War.

In all the stories in this chapter, the reader will find the fictive elements discussed previously which are the very blood and bone of literature. Like all literature, these stories dramatize their material by including specific incidents designed to highlight it. They each contain an atmosphere that lends credibility to the events described and they present fully developed characters with whom the reader can identify and with whose fate he becomes concerned.

No story succeeds that does not affect its readers. To be affected by a story means simply that the reader's thoughts and emotions must be stirred. It is this stirring of thoughts and emotions that encourages readers to turn to literature for a sharpened insight into life.

The end of this journey into wonder is now in sight. We hope it has been a rewarding expedition and that the student will want to embark on many more such journeys. Having studied the stories in this anthology, he will now be able to bring a new level of literary sophistication and critical judgment to bear in his future reading of science fiction which will help him evaluate both the techniques employed by the authors and the ideas dramatized in the stories. Although this particular journey is nearing its end, we hope that the reader will agree that for the inquiring mind such a literary journey into wonder need never really end.

INTRODUCTION: The Survivor

A writer may notice an old woman looking fondly at a photograph of her deceased husband. In the writer's imagination, the woman's youth, her love for her husband and their years together flash through his mind. A story might result when the author adds the elements of plot, action, suspense, and characterization to his experience.

A science-fiction writer may look at a football game on television and see a sublimated form of war. The story below results when plot, action, suspense, and characterization are added to the experience.

This is a well-plotted story with considerable action. The story's plot is subordinated to its theme as is the case in all effective fiction. The events depicted take place in the future. But, as in many such stories, they have their roots in the soil of today and are nourished by the richness of the writer's imagination which takes what is and extrapolates from it to what might be—"the day after tomorrow."

The Survivor
by Walter F. Moudy

There was a harmony in the design of the arena which an artist might find pleasing. The curved granite walls which extended upward three hundred feet from its base were polished and smooth like the sides of a bowl. A fly, perhaps a lizard, could craw up those glistening walls—but surely not a man. The walls encircled an egg-shaped area which was precisely three thousand meters long and two thousand one hundred meters wide at its widest point. There were two large hills located on either side of the arena exactly midway from its center to its end. If you were to slice the arena crosswise, your knife would dissect a third, tree-studded hill and a small, clear lake; and the two divided halves would each be the exact mirror image of the other down to the smallest detail. If you were a farmer you would notice the rich flat soil which ran obliquely from the two larger hills toward the lake. If you were an artist you might find pleasure in contemplating the rich shades of green and brown presented by the forested lowlands at the lake's edge. A sportsman seeing the crystalline lake in the morning's first light would find his fingers itching for light tackle and wading boots. Boys, particularly city boys, would yearn to climb the two larger hills because they looked easy to climb, but not too easy. A general viewing the topography would immediately recognize that possession of the central hill would permit dominance of the lake and the surrounding lowlands.

There was something peaceful about the arena that first morning. The early-morning sun broke through a light mist and spilled over the central hill to the low dew-drenched ground beyond. There were trees with young, green leaves, and the leaves rustled softly in rhythm with the wind. There were birds in those trees, and the birds still sang, for it was spring, and they were filled with the joy of life and the beauty of the morning. A night owl, its appetite satiated now by a recent kill, perched on a dead limb of a large sycamore tree and, tucking its beak in its feathers, prepared to sleep the day away. A sleek copperhead snake, sensing the sun's approach and anticipating its soothing warmth, crawled from beneath the flat rock where it had spent the night and sought the comfort of its favorite rock ledge. A red squirrel chattered nervously as it watched the men enter the arena from the north and then, having decided that there was danger there, darted swiftly to an adjacent tree and disappeared into the security of its nest.

There were exactly one hundred of them. They stood tall and proud in their uniforms, a barely perceptible swaying motion rippling through their lines like wheat stirred by a gentle breeze. If they anticipated what was to come, they did not show it. Their every movement showed their absolute discipline. Once they had been only men—now they were killers. The hunger for blood was like a taste in their mouths; their zest for destruction like a flood which raged inside them. They were finely honed and razor keen to kill.

Their general made his last inspection. As he passed down the lines the squad captains barked a sharp order and the men froze into absolute immobility. Private Richard Starbuck heard the rasp of the general's boots against the stones as he approached. There was no other sound, not even of men breathing. From long discipline he forced his eyes to maintain their focus on the distant point he had selected, and his eyes did not waver as the general paused in front of him. They were still fixed on that same imaginary point. He did not even see the general.

Private Richard Starbuck was not thinking of death, although he knew he must surely die. He was thinking of the rifle which he felt securely on his shoulder and of the driving need he had to discharge its deadly pellets into human flesh. His urge to kill was dominant, but even so he was vaguely relieved that he had not been selected for the assassination squad (the suicide squad the men called it); for he still had a chance, a slim chance, to live; while the assassination squad was consigned to inevitable death.

A command was given and Private Starbuck permitted his tense body to relax. He glanced at his watch. Five-twenty-five. He still had an hour and thirty-five minutes to wait. There was a tenseness inside him which his relaxed body did not disclose. They taught you how to do that in training. They taught you lots of things in training.

The TV screen was bigger than life and just as real. The color was true and the images three-dimensional. For a moment the zoom cameras scanned the silent deserted portions of the arena. The sound system was sensitive and sharp and caught the sound made by a squirrel's feet against the bark of a black oak tree. Over one hundred cameras were fixed on the arena; yet so smooth was the transition from one camera to the next that it was as though the viewer was floating over the arena. There was the sound of marching feet, and the pace of the moving cameras quickened and then shifted to the north where one hundred men were entering the arena in perfect unison, a hundred steel-toed boots striking the earth as one. For a moment the cameras fixed on the flashing boots and the sensitive sound system recorded the thunder of men marching to war. Then the cameras flashed to the proud face of their general; then to the hard, determined faces of the men; then back again to the thundering boots. The cameras backed off to watch the column execute an abrupt halt, moved forward to focus for a moment on the general's hawklike face, and then, with the general, inspected the troops one by one, moving down the rigid lines of men and peering intently at each frozen face.

When the "at ease" order was given, the camera backed up to show an aerial view of the arena and then fixed upon one of the control towers which lined the arena's upper periphery before sweeping slowly downward and seeming to pass into the control tower. Inside the tower a distinguished gray-haired man in his mid-forties sat beside a jovial, fat-jawed man who was probably in his early fifties. There was an expectant look on their faces. Finally the gray-haired man said:

"Good morning, ladies and gentlemen, I'm John Ardanyon—"

"And I'm Bill Carr," the fat-jawed man said.

"And this is it—yes, this is the big one, ladies and gentlemen. The 2050 edition of the Olympic War Games. This is the day we've all been waiting for, ladies and gentlemen, and in precisely one hour and thirty-two minutes the games will be under way. Here to help describe the action is Bill Carr who is known to all of you sports fans all over the world. And with us for this special broadcast are some of the finest technicians in the business. Bill?"

"That's right, John. This year NSB has spared no expense to insure our viewing public that its 2050 game coverage will be second to none. So stay tuned to this station for the most complete, the most immediate coverage of any station. John?"

"That's right, Bill. This year NSB has installed over one hundred specially designed zoom cameras to insure complete coverage of the games. We are using the latest sonic sound equipment—so sensitive that it can detect the sound of a man's heart beating at a thousand yards. Our camera crew is highly trained in the recently developed transitional-zone technique which you just saw so effectively demonstrated during the fade-in. I think we can promise you that this time no station will be able to match the immediacy of NSB."

"Right, John. And now, less than an hour and a half before the action begins, NSB is proud to bring you this prerecorded announcement from the President of the United States. Ladies and gentlemen, the President of the United States."

There was a brief flash of the White House lawn, a fade-out, and then:

"My fellow countrymen. When you hear these words, the beginning of the fifth meeting between the United States and Russia in the Olympic War Games will be just minutes away.

"I hope and I pray that we will be victorious. With the help of God, we shall be.

"But in our longing for victory, we must not lose sight of the primary purpose of these games. In the long run it is not whether we win or lose but that the games were played. For, my fellow citizens, we must never forget that these games are played in order that the frightening spectre of war may never again stalk our land. It is better that a few should decide the nation's fate, than all the resources of our two nations should be mobilized to destroy the other.

"My friends, many of you do not remember the horror of the Final War of 1998. I can recall that war. I lost my father and two sisters in that war. I spent two months in a class-two fallout shelter—as many of you know. There must never be another such war. We cannot—we shall not—permit that to happen.

"The Olympic War Games are the answer—the only answer. Thanks to the Olympic War Games we are at peace. Today one hundred of our finest fighting men will meet one hundred Russian soldiers to decide whether we shall be victorious or shall go down to defeat. The loser must pay the victor reparations of ten billion dollars. The stakes are high.

"The stakes are high, but, my fellow citizens, the cost of total war is a hundred times higher. This miniature war is a thousand times less costly than total war. Thanks to the Olympic War Games, we have a kind of peace.

"And now, in keeping with the tradition established by the late President Goldstein, I hereby declare a national holiday for all persons not engaged in essential services from now until the conclusion of the games.

"To those brave men who made the team I say: the hope and the prayers of the nation go with you. May you emerge victorious."

There was a fade-out and then the pleasant features of John Ardanyon appeared. After a short, respectful silence, he said:

"I'm sure we can all agree with the President on that. And now, here is Professor Carl Overmann to explain the computer system developed especially for NSB's coverage of the 2050 war games."

"Thank you, Mr. Ardanyon. This year, with the help of the Englewood system of evaluating intangible factors, we hope to start bringing you reliable predictions at the ten-percent casualty level. Now, very briefly, here is how the Englewood system works. . . ."

Private Richard Starbuck looked at his watch. Still forty more minutes to wait. He pulled back the bolt on his rifle and checked once more to make sure that the first shell was properly positioned in the chamber. For the third time in the past twenty minutes he walked to one side and urinated on the ground. His throat seemed abnormally dry, and he removed his canteen to moisten his lips with water. He took only a small swallow because the rules permitted only one canteen of water per man, and their battle plan did not call for early possession of the lake.

A passing lizard caught his attention. He put his foot on it and squashed it slowly with the toe of his right boot. He noticed with mild satisfaction that the thing had left a small blood smear at the end of his boot. Oddly, however, seeing the blood triggered something in his mind, and for the first time he vaguely recognized the possibility that he could be hurt. In training he had not thought much about that. Mostly you thought of how it would feel to kill a man. After a while you got so that you wanted to kill. You came to love your rifle, like it was an extension of your own body. And if you could not feel its comforting presence, you felt like a part of you was missing. Still a person could be hurt. You might not die immediately. He wondered what it would be like to feel a misshapen chunk of lead tearing through his belly. The Russians would x their bullets too, probably. They do more damage that way.

It might not be so bad. He remembered a time four years ago when he had thought he was dying, and that had not been so bad. He remembered that at the time he had been more concerned about bleeding on the Martins' new couch. The Martins had always been good to him.

Once they had thought they could never have a child of their own, and they had about half adopted him because his own mother worked and was too busy to bake cookies for him and his father was not interested in fishing or basketball or things like that. Even after the Martins had Cassandra, they continued to treat him like a favorite nephew. Mr. Martin took him fishing and attended all the basketball games when he was playing. And that was why when he wrecked the motor scooter and cut his head he had been more concerned about bleeding on the Martins' new couch than about dying, although he had felt that he was surely dying. He remembered that his first thought upon regaining consciousness was one of self-importance. The Martins had looked worried and their nine-year-old daughter, Cassandra, was looking at the blood running down his face and was crying. That was when he felt he might be dying. Dying had seemed a strangely appropriate thing to do, and he had felt an urge to do it well and had begun to assure them that he was all right. And, to his slight disappointment, he was.

Private Richard Starbuck, formerly a star forward on the Center High basketball team, looked at his watch and wondered, as he waited, if being shot in the gut would be anything like cutting your head on the pavement. It was funny he should have thought of that now. He hadn't thought of the Martins for months. He wondered if they would be watching. He wondered, if they did, if they would recognize the sixteen-year-old boy who had bled on their living room couch four years ago. He wondered if he recognized that sixteen-year-old boy himself.

Professor Carl Overmann had finished explaining the marvels of the NSB computer system; a mousy little man from the sociology department of a second rate university had spent ten minutes assuring the TV audience that one of the important psychological effects of the TV coverage of the games was that it allowed the people to satisfy the innate blood lust vicariously and strongly urged the viewers to encourage the youngsters to watch; a minister had spent three minutes explaining that the miniature war could serve to educate mankind to the horrors of war; an economics professor was just finishing a short lecture on the economic effects of victory or defeat.

"Well, there you have it, ladies and gentlemen," Bill Carr said when the economics professor had finished. "You all know there's a lot at stake for both sides. And now— what's that? You what? Just a minute, folks. I think we may have another NSB first." He looked off camera to his right. "Is he there? Yes, indeed, ladies and gentlemen, NSB has done it again. For the first time we are going to have—well, here he is, ladies and gentlemen, General George W. Caldwell, chief of the Olympic War Games training section. General, it's nice to have you with us."

"Thank you, Bill. It's good to be here."

"General, I'm sure our audience already knows this, but just so there will be no misunderstanding, it's not possible for either side to communicate to their people in the arena now. Is that right?"

"That's right, Bill, or I could not be here. An electronic curtain, as it were, protects the field from any attempt to communicate. From here on out the boys are strictly on their own."

"General, do you care to make any predictions on the outcome of the games?"

"Yes, Bill, I may be going out on a limb here, but I think our boys are ready. I can't say that I agree with the neutral-money boys who have the United States a six-to-five underdog. I say we'll win."

"General, there is some thought that our defeat in the games four years ago was caused by an inferior battle plan. Do you care to comment on that?"

"No comment."

"Do you have any explanation for why the United States team has lost the last two games after winning the first two?"

"Well, let me say this. Our defeat in '42 could well have been caused by overconfidence. After all, we had won the first two games rather handily. As I recall we won the game in '38 by four survivors. But as for our defeat in '46—well, your estimate on that one is a good as mine. I will say this: General Hanley was much criticized for an unimaginative battle plan by a lot of so-called experts. Those so-called experts—those armchair generals—were definitely wrong. General Hanley's battle strategy was sound in every detail. I've studied his plans at considerable length, I can assure you."

"Perhaps the training program—?"

"Nonsense. My own exec was on General Hanley's training staff. With only slight modifications it's the same program we used for this year's games."

"Do you care to comment on your own battle plans, General?"

"Well, Bill, I wouldn't want to kill the suspense for your TV audience. But I can say this: we'll have a few surprises this year. No one can accuse us of conservative tactics, I can tell you that."

"How do you think our boys will stack up against the Russians, General?"

"Bill, on a man to man basis, I think our boys will stack up very well indeed. In fact, we had men in the drop-out squads who could have made our last team with no trouble at all. I'd say this year's crop is probably twenty percent improved."

"General, what do you look for in selecting your final squads?"

"Bill, I'd say that more than anything else we look for desire. Of course, a man has to be a good athlete, but if he doesn't have that killer instinct, as we say, he won't make the team. I'd say it's desire."

"Can you tell us how you pick the men for the games?"

"Yes, Bill, I think I can, up to a point. We know the Russians use the same system, and, of course, there has been quite a bit written on the subject in the popular press in recent months.

"Naturally, we get thousands of applicants. We give each of them a tough screening test—physical, mental, and psychological. Most applicants are eliminated in the first test. You'd be surprised at some of the boys who apply. The ones who are left—just under two thousand for this year's games—are put through an intensive six-month training course. During this training period we begin to get our first drop-outs, the men who somehow got past our screening system and who will crack up under pressure.

"Next comes a year of training in which the emphasis is on conditioning."

"Let me interrupt here for just a moment, General, if I may. This conditioning—is this a type of physical training?"

The general smiled tolerantly. "No, Bill, this is a special type of conditioning—both mental and physical. The men are conditioned to war. They are taught to recognize and to hate the enemy. They are taught to react instantly to every possible hostile stimuli. They learn to love their weapons and to distrust all else."

"I take it that an average training day must leave the men very little free time."

"Free time!" The general now seemed more shocked than amused. "Free time indeed. Our training program leaves no time free. We don't coddle our boys. After all, Bill, these men are training for war. No man is permitted more than two hours' consecutive sleep. We have an average of four alerts every night.

"Actually the night alerts are an important element in our selection as well as our training program. We have the men under constant observation, of course. You can tell a lot about how a man responds to an alert. Of course, all of the men are conditioned to come instantly awake with their rifles in their hands. But some would execute a simultaneous roll-away movement while at the same time cocking and aiming their weapons in the direction of the hostile sound which signaled the alert."

"How about the final six months, General?"

"Well, Bill, of course, I can't give away all our little tricks during those last six months. I can tell you in a general sort of way that this involved putting battle plans on a duplicate of the arena itself."

"And these hundred men who made this year's team—I presume they were picked during the last six months training?"

"No, Bill, actually we only made our final selection last night. You see, for the first time in two years these men have had some free time. We give them two days off before the games begin. How the men react to this enforced inactivity can tell us a lot about their level of readiness. I can tell you we have an impatient bunch of boys out there."

"General, it's ten minutes to game time. Do you suppose our team may be getting a little nervous down there?"

"Nervous? I suppose the boys may be a little tensed up. But they'll be all right just as soon as the action starts."

"General, I want to thank you for coming by. I'm sure our TV audience has found this brief discussion most enlightening."

"It was my pleasure, Bill."

"Well, there you have it, ladies and gentlemen. You heard it from the man who should know—Lieutenant General George W. Caldwell himself. He picks the United States team to go all the way. John?"

"Thank you, Bill. And let me say that there has been considerable sentiment for the United States team in recent weeks among the neutrals. These are the men who set the odds—the men who bet their heads but never their hearts. In fact at least one oddsmaker in Stockholm told me last night that he had stopped taking anything but six-to-five bets, and you pick 'em. In other words, this fight is rated just about even here just a few minutes before game time."

"Right, John, it promises to be an exciting day, so stay tuned to this station for full coverage."

"I see the troops are beginning to stir. It won't be long now. Bill, while we wait I think it might be well, for the benefit of you younger people, to tell the folks just what it means to be a survivor in one of these games. Bill?"

"Right, John. Folks, the survivor, or survivors as the case may be, will truly become a *Survivor*. A *Survivor*, as most of you know, is exempt from all laws; he has unlimited credit; in short, he can literally do no wrong. And that's what those men are shooting for today. John."

"Okay, Bill. And now as our cameras scan the Russian team, let us review very briefly the rules of the game. Each side has one hundred men divided into ten squads each consisting of nine men and one squad captain. Each man has a standard automatic rifle, four hand grenades, a canteen of water, and enough food to last three days. All officers are armed with side arms in addition to their automatic rifles. Two of the squads are armed with air-cooled light machine-guns, and one squad is armed with a mortar with one thousand rounds of ammunition. And those, ladies and gentlemen, are the rules of the game. Once the games begin the men are on their own. There are no more rules—except, of course, that the game is not over until one side or the other has no more survivors. Bill?"

"Okay, John. Well, folks, here we are just seconds away from game time. NSB will bring you live each exciting moment—so stand by. We're waiting for the start of the 2050 Olympic War Games. Ten seconds now. Six. Four, three, two, one—the games are underway, and look at 'em go!"

The cameras spanned back from the arena to give a distant view of the action. Squad one peeled off from the main body and headed toward the enemy rear at a fast trot. They were armed with rifles and grenades. Squads two, three, and four went directly toward the high hill in the American sector where they broke out entrenching tools and began to dig in. Squads five and six took one of the light machine guns and marched at double time to the east of the central hill where they concealed themselves in the brush and waited. Squads seven through ten were held in reserve where they occupied themselves by burying the ammunition and other supplies at predetermined points and in beginning the preparation of their own defense perimeters.

The cameras swung briefly to the Russian sector. Four Russian squads had already occupied the high hill in the Russian sector, and a rifle squad was being rushed to the central hill located on the north-south dividing line. A Russian machine gun squad was digging in to the south of the lake to establish a base of fire on the north side of the central hill.

The cameras returned to the American squads five and six, which were now deployed along the east side of the central hill. The cameras moved in from above the entrenched machine gunner, paused momentarily on his right hand, which was curved lovingly around the trigger guard while his middle finger stroked the trigger itself in a manner almost obscene, and then followed the gunner's unblinking eyes to the mist-enshrouded base of the central hill where the point man of the Russian advance squad was cautiously testing his fate in a squirming, crawling advance on the lower slopes of the hill.

"This could be it!" Bill Carr's booming voice exploded from the screen like a shot. "This could be the first skirmish, ladies and gentlemen. John, how does it look to you?"

"Yes, Bill, it looks like we will probably get our first action in the east-central sector. Quite a surprise, too, Bill. A lot of experts felt that the American team would concentrate its initial push on control of the central hill. Instead, the strategy appears to be—at least as it appears from here

—to concede the central hill to the Russian team but to make them pay for it. You can't see it on your screens just now, ladies and gentlemen, but the American mortar squad is now positioned on the north slope of the north hill and is ready to fire."

"All right, John. Folks, here in our booth operating as spotter for the American team is Colonel Bullock of the United States Army. Our Russian spotter is Brigadier General Vorsilov, who will from time to time give us his views on Russian strategy. Colonel Bullock, do you care to comment?"

"Well, I think it's fairly obvious, Bill, that—"

His words were interrupted by the first chilling chatter of the American light machine gun. Tracer bullets etched their brilliant way through the morning air to seek and find human flesh. Four mortar rounds, fired in rapid succession, arched over the low hill and came screaming a tale of death and destruction. The rifle squad opened fire with compelling accuracy. The Russian line halted, faltered, reformed, and charged up the central hill. Three men made it to the sheltering rocks on the hill's upper slope. The squad captain and six enlisted men lay dead or dying on the lower slopes. As quickly as it had begun the firing ended.

"How about that!" Bill Carr exclaimed. "First blood for the American team. What a fantastic beginning to these 2050 war games, ladies and gentlemen. John, how about that?"

"Right, Bill. Beautifully done. Brilliantly conceived and executed with marvelous precision. An almost unbelievable maneuver by the American team that obviously caught the Russians completely off guard. Did you get the casualty figures on that first skirmish, Bill?"

"I make it five dead and two seriously wounded, John. Now keep in mind, folks, these figures are unofficial. Ed, can you give us a closeup on that south slope?"

The cameras scanned the hill first from a distance and then zoomed in to give a closeup of each man who lay on the bleak southern slope. The Russian captain was obviously dead with a neat rifle bullet through his forehead. The next man appeared to be sleeping peacefully. There was not a mark visible on his body; yet he too was dead as was demonstrated when the delicate sonic sound system was focused on his corpse without disclosing the whisper of a heart beat. The third man was still living, although death was just minutes away. For him it would be a peaceful death, for he was unconscious and was quietly leaking his life away from a torn artery in his neck. The camera rested next upon the shredded corpse of the Russian point man who had been the initial target for so many rifles. He lay on his stomach, and there were nine visible wounds in his back. The camera showed next a closeup view of a young man's face frozen in the moment of death, blue eyes, lusterless now and pale in death, framed by a face registering the shock of war's ultimate reality, his lips half opened still as if to protest his fate or to ask for another chance. The camera moved next to a body lying fetal-like near the top of the hill hardly two steps from the covering rocks where the three surviving squad members had found shelter. The camera then moved slowly down the slope seeking the last casualty. It found him on a pleasant, grassy spot beneath a small oak tree. A mortar fragment had caught him in the lower belly and his guts were spewed out on the grass like an overtuned bucket of sand. He was whimpering softly, and with his free left hand was trying with almost comic desperation to place his entrails back inside his belly.

"Well, there you have it, folks," Bill Carr said. "It's official now. You saw it for yourselves thanks to our fine camera technicians. Seven casualties confirmed. John, I don't believe the American team has had its first casualty yet, is that right?"

"That's right, Bill. The Russian team apparently was caught completely off guard."

"Colonel Bullock, would you care to comment on what you've seen so far?"

"Yes, Bill, I think it's fair to say that this first skirmish gives the American team a decided advantage. I would like to see the computer's probability reports before going too far out on a limb, but I'd say the odds are definitely in favor of the American team at this stage. General Caldwell's election not to take the central hill has paid a handsome dividend here early in the games."

"General Vorsilov, would you care to give us the Russian point of view?"

"I do not agree with my American friend, Colonel Bullock," the general said with a crisp British accent. "The fourth Russian squad was given the mission to take the central hill. The central hill has been taken and is now controlled by the Russian team. Possession of the central hill provides almost absolute dominance of the lake and surrounding low land. Those of you who have studied military history know how important that can be, particularly in the later stages of the games. I emphatically do not agree that the first skirmish was a defeat. Possession of the hill is worth a dozen men."

"Comments, Colonel Bullock?"

"Well, Bill, first of all, I don't agree that the Russian team has possession of the hill. True they have three men up there, but those men are armed with nothing but rifles and hand grenades—and they are not dug in. Right now the central hill is up for grabs. I—"

"Just a minute, Colonel. Pardon this interruption, but our computer has the first probability report. And here it is! The prediction is for an American victory with a probability rating of 57.2. How about that, folks? Here early in the first day the American team, which was a decided underdog in this year's games has jumped to a substantial lead."

Colonel Bullock spoke: "Bill, I want you to notice that man there—over there on the right-hand side of your screen. Can we have a closeup on that? That's a runner, Bill. A lot of the folks don't notice little things like that. They want to watch the machine gunners or the point man, but that man there could have a decided effect on the outcome of these games, Bill."

"I presume he's carrying a message back to headquarters, eh Colonel?"

"That's right, Bill, and a very important message, I'll warrant. You see an attack on the central hill from the east or south sides would be disastrous. The Russians, of course, hold the south hill. From their positions there they could subject our boys to a blistering fire from the rear on any attack made from the south. That runner was sent back with word that there are only three Russians on the hill. I think we can expect an immediate counterattack from the north as soon as the message has been delivered. In the meantime, squads five and six will maintain their positions in the eastern sector and try to prevent any reinforcements of the Russian position."

"Thank you, Colonel, for that enlightening analysis, and now, folks—" He broke off when the runner to whom the Colonel referred stumbled and fell.

"Wait a minute, folks. He's been hit! He's down! The runner has been shot. You saw it here, folks. Brilliant camera work. Simply great. John, how about that?"

"Simply tremendous, Bill. A really great shot. Ed, can we back the cameras up and show the folks that action again? Here it is in slow motion, folks. Now you see him (who is that, Colonel? Ted Krogan? Thank you, Colonel) here he is, folks, Private Ted Krogan from Milwaukee, Wisconsin. Here he is coming around the last clump of bushes —now watch this, folks—he gets about half way across the clearing—and there it is, folks, you can actually see the bullet strike his throat—a direct hit. Watch this camera close up of his face, you'll see him die in front of your eyes. And there he goes—he rolls over and not a move. He was dead before he hit the ground. Bill, did any of our cameras catch where that shot came from?"

"Yes, John, the Russians have slipped a two man sniper team in on our left flank. This could be serious, John. I don't think our boys know the runner was hit."

"Only time will tell, Bill. Only time will tell. Right now, I believe we have our first lull. Let's take thirty seconds for our stations to identify themselves."

Private Richard Starbuck's first day was not at all what he had expected. He was with the second squad, one of the three squads which were dug in on the north hill. After digging his foxhole he had spent the day staring at the south and central hills. He had heard the brief skirmish near the central hill, but he had yet to see his first Russian. He strained so hard to see something that sometimes his eyes played tricks on him. Twice his mind gave movement to a distant shadow. Once he nearly fired at the sudden sound of a rabbit in the brush. His desire to see the enemy was almost overpowering. It reminded him of the first time Mr. Martin had taken him fishing on the lake. He had been thirteen at the time. He had stared at that still, white cork for what had seemed like hours. He remembered he had even prayed to God to send a fish along that would make the cork go under. His mind had played tricks on him that day too, and several times he had fancied the cork was moving when it was not. He was not praying today, of course—except the intensity of his desire was something like a prayer.

He spent the entire first day in a foxhole without seeing anything or hearing anything except an occasional distant sniper's bullet. When the sun went down, he brought out his rations and consumed eighteen hundred calories. As soon as it was dark, his squad was to move to the south slope and prepare their defensive positions. He knew the Russians would be similarly occupied. It was maddening to know that for a time the enemy would be exposed and yet be relatively safe because of the covering darkness.

When it was completely dark, his squad captain gave the signal, and the squad moved out to their predetermined positions and began to dig in. So far they were still following the battle plan to the letter. He dug his foxhole with care, building a small ledge half way down on which to sit and placing some foliage on the bottom to keep it from becoming muddy, and then he settled down to wait. Somehow it was better at night. He even found himself wishing that they would not come tonight. He discovered that he could wait.

Later he slept. How long, he did not know. He only knew that when he awoke he heard a sound of air parting followed by a hard, thundering impact that shook the ground. His first instinct was to action, and then he remembered that there was nothing he could do, so he hunched down as far as possible in his foxhole and waited. He knew real fear now—

the kind of fear that no amount of training or conditioning can eliminate. He was a living thing whose dominant instinct was to continue living. He did not want to die hunched down in a hole in the ground. The flesh along his spine quivered involuntarily with each fractional warning whoosh which preceded the mortar's fall. Now he knew that he could die, knew it with his body as well as with his mind. A shell landed nearby, and he heard a shrill, womanlike scream. Bill Smith had been hit. His first reaction was one of relief. It had been Bill Smith and not he. But why did he have to scream? Bill Smith had been one of the toughest men in the squad. There ought to be more dignity than that. There ought to be a better way of dying than lying helpless in a hole and waiting for chance or fate in the form of some unseen, impersonal gunner, who probably was firing an assigned pattern anyhow, to bring you life or death.

In training, under conditions of simulated danger, he had grown to rely upon the solidarity of the squad. They faced danger together; together they could whip the world. But now he knew that in the end war was a lonely thing. He could not reach out into the darkness and draw courage from the huddled forms of his comrades from the second squad. He took no comfort from the fact that the other members of the squad were just as exposed as he. The fear which he discovered in himself was a thing which had to be endured alone, and he sensed now that when he died, that too would have to be endured alone.

"Well, folks, this is Bill Carr still bringing you our continuous coverage of the 2050 Olympic War Games. John Ardanyon is getting a few hours' sleep right now, but he'll be back at four o'clock.

"For the benefit of those viewers who many have tuned in late, let me say again that NSB will bring you continuous coverage. Yes sir, folks, this year, thanks to our special owl-eye cameras, we can give you shots of the night action with remarkable clarity.

"Well, folks, the games are almost eighteen hours old, and here to bring you the latest casualty report is my old friend Max Sanders. Max?"

"Thank you, Bill, and good evening, ladies and gentlemen. The latest casualty reports—and these are confirmed figures. Let me repeat—these are confirmed figures. For the Russian team: twenty-two dead, and eight incapacitated wounded. For the American team: seventeen dead, and only six incapacitated wounded."

"Thank you, Max. Folks, our computer has just recomputed the odds, and the results are—what's this? Folks, here is a surprise. A rather unpleasant surprise. Just forty-five minutes ago the odds on an American victory were 62.1. Those odds, ladies and gentlemen, have just fallen to 53.0. I'm afraid I don't understand this at all. Professor Overmann, what do you make of this?"

"I'm afraid the computer has picked up a little trouble in the southwestern sector, Bill. As I explained earlier, the computer's estimates are made up of many factors—and the casualty reports are just one of them. Can you give us a long shot of the central hill, Ed? There. There you see one of the factors which undoubtedly has influenced the new odds. The Russian team has succeeded in reinforcing their position on the central hill with a light machine gun squad. This goes back to the first American casualty earlier today when the messenger failed to get word through for the counterattack.

"Now give me a medium shot of the American assassination squad. Back it up a little more, will you, Ed? There, that's it. I was afraid of that. What has happened, Bill, is that, unknowingly, the American squad has been spotted by a Russian reserve guard. That could mean trouble."

"I see. Well, that explains the sudden drop in the odds, folks. Now the question is, can the American assassination squad pull it off under this handicap? We'll keep the cameras over here, folks, until we have an answer. The other sectors are relatively quiet now except for sporadic mortar fire."

For the first time since the skirmish which had begun the battle, the cameras were able to concentrate their sustained attention on one small area of the arena. The assassination squad moved slowly, torturously slow, through the brush and the deep grass which dotted the southwest sector. They had successfully infiltrated the Russian rear. For a moment the camera switched to the Russian sentry who had discovered the enemy's presence and who was now reporting to his captain. Orders were given and in a very few minutes the light machine gun had been brought back from the lake and was in position to fire on the advancing American squad. Two Russian reserve squads were positioned to deliver a deadly crossfire on the patrol. To the men in the arena it must have been pitch dark. Even on camera there was an eerie, uneasy quality to the light that lent a ghostlike effect to the faces of the men whose fates had been determined by an unsuspected meeting with a Russian sentry. Death would have been exceedingly quick and profitless for the ten-man squad had not a Russian rifleman fired his rifle prematurely. As it was, the squad captain and six men were killed in the first furious burst of fire. The three survivors reacted instantly and disappeared into the brush. One died there noiselessly from a chest wound inflicted in the ambush. Another managed to kill two Russian infantrymen with hand grenades before he died. In the darkness the Russian captain became confused and sent word to his general that the entire squad had been destroyed. The general came to inspect the site and was instantly killed at short range by the lone surviving member of the assassination squad. By a series of fortuitous events the squad had accomplished its primary purpose. The Russian general was dead, and in less than two seconds so was the last man in the assassination squad.

"Well, there you have it, ladies and gentlemen. High drama here in the early hours of the morning as an American infantry squad cuts down the Russian general. Those of you who have watched these games before will know that some of the most exciting action takes place at night. In a few minutes we should have the latest probability report, but until then, how do you see it, Colonel Bullock?"

"Bill, I think the raiding squad came out of that very well indeed. They were discovered and boxed in by the enemy, yet they still fulfilled their primary mission—they killed the Russian general. It's bound to have an effect."

"General Vorsilov, do you care to comment, sir?"

"I think your computer will confirm that three for ten is a good exchange, even if one of those three happens to be a general. Of course, we had an unlucky break when one of our soldiers accidentally discharged his weapon. Otherwise we would have suffered no casualties. As for the loss of General Sarlov, no general has ever survived the games, and I venture to say no general ever will. The leadership of the Russian team will now descend by predetermined selection to the senior Russian captain."

"Thank you, General. Well, folks, here is the latest computer report. This is going to disappoint a lotta people. For an American victory, the odds now stand at 49.1. Of course, let me emphasize, folks, that such a small difference at this stage is virtually meaningless.

"Well, we seem to have another lag, folks. While our cameras scan the arena, let me remind you that each morning of the games NSB will be bringing you a special capsule re-run of the highlights of the preceding night's action.

"Well, folks, things seem to be a little quiet right now, but don't go away. In the games, anything can happen and usually does. We lost ten good men in that last action, so maybe this is a good time to remind you ladies and gentlemen that this year NSB is giving to the parents of each one of these boys a special tape recording of the action in the arena complete with sound effects and a brand-new uniflex projector. Thus each parent will be able to see his son's participation in the games. This is a gift that I'm sure will be treasured throughout the years.

"NSB would like to take this opportunity to thank the following sponsors for relinquishing their time so we could bring you this special broadcast. . . ."

Private Richard Starbuck watched the dawn edge its way over the arena. He had slept perhaps a total of two hours last night, and already a feeling of unreality was invading his senses. When the roll was called, he answered with a voice which surprised him by its impersonalness: "Private Richard Starbuck, uninjured, ammunition expended; zero." Three men did not answer the roll. One of the three was the squad captain. That meant that Sergeant Collins was the new squad captain. Through discipline and habit he broke out his breakfast ration and forced himself to eat. Then he waited again.

Later that morning he fired his first shot. He caught a movement on the central hill, and this time it was not a shadow. He fired quickly, but he missed, and his target quickly disappeared. There was heavy firing in the mid-eastern sector, but he was no longer even curious as to what was going on unless it affected his own position. All day long he fired whenever he saw something that could have been a man on either of the Russian-held hills. Sometimes he fired when he saw nothing because it made him feel better. The Russians returned the fire, but neither side appeared to be doing any real damage against a distant, well-entrenched enemy.

Toward evening Captain Collins gave orders for him to take possession of Private Bill Smith's foxhole. It seemed like a ridiculous thing to do in broad daylight when in a couple more hours he could accomplish the same thing in almost perfect safety. They obviously intended for him to draw fire to expose the Russian positions. For a moment he hesitated, feeling the hate for Collins wash over him like a flood. Then he grasped his rifle, leaped from his hole, and ran twenty yards diagonally down the hill to Smith's foxhole. It seemed to him as if the opposing hills had suddenly come alive. He flung himself face first to the ground and landed grotesquely on top of the once tough body of Private Bill Smith. He felt blood trickling down his arm, and for a moment he thought he had been hit, but it was only a scratch from a projecting rock. His own squad had been firing heavily, and he heard someone say: "I got one. B'god I got one." He twisted around in the foxhole trying to keep his head safely below the surface, and then he saw what it was that had made Bill Smith scream. The mortar had wrenched his left arm loose at the elbow. It dangled there now, hung in place only by a torn shirt and a small piece of skin. He braced himself and began to edge the body up past him in the foxhole. He managed to get below it and heave it over the side. He heard the excited volley of shots which followed the body's tumbling course down the hill. Somehow in his exertions he had finished wrenching the arm loose from the body. He reached down and threw that too over the side of the foxhole. And now this particular bit of earth belonged to him. He liked it better than his last one. He felt he had earned it.

The night brought a return of the mortar fire. This time he didn't care. This time he could sleep, although there was a slight twitching motion on the left side of his face and he woke up every two hours for no reason at all.

"Good morning, ladies and gentlemen, this is John Ardanyon bringing you the start of the third day of the 2050 Olympic War Games.

"And what a night it's been, ladies and gentlemen. In a moment we'll bring you the highlights of last night's action, but first here is Bill Carr to bring you up to date on the vital statistics."

"Thank you, John. Folks, we're happy to say that in the last few hours the early trend of the night's action has been reversed and the American team once again has a substantial lead. Squads five and six were wiped out in an early-evening engagement in the mid-eastern sector, but they gave a good account of themselves. The Russians lost eleven men and a light machine gun in their efforts to get this thorn out of their side. And I'm happy to say the American light machine gun carried by squad six was successfully destroyed before the squad was overrun. But the big news this morning is the success of the American mortar and sniper squads. Our mortars accounted for six dead and two seriously wounded as opposed to only two killed and one wounded by the Russian mortars. Our sniper squad, working in two-man teams, was successful in killing five men; whereas we only lost one man to enemy sniper action last night. We'll have a great shot coming up, folks, showing Private Cecil Harding from Plainview, New Jersey, killing a Russian captain in his sleep with nothing more than a sharp rock."

"Right, Bill, but before we show last night's highlights, I'm sure the folks would like to know that the score now stands forty-two fighting men for the American team as opposed to only thirty-seven for the Russians. Computerwise that figures out to a 52.5 probability for the American team. I'm sure that probability figure would be higher if the Russians were not positioned on that central hill."

"And here now are the high spots of the night's action . . ."

On the morning of the third day, word was spread that the American general had been killed. Private Richard Starbuck did not care. He realized now that good generalship was not going to preserve his life. So far chance seemed the only decisive factor. The mortar fire grew heavier, and the word was given to prepare for an attack on the hill. He gripped his rifle, and as he waited, he hoped they would come. He wanted to see, to face his enemy. He wanted to feel again that man had the power to control his own destiny.

A few minutes after noon it began to rain, a chilling spring rain that drizzled slowly and soaked in next to the skin. The enemy mortar ceased firing. The man in the foxhole next to his was laughing somewhat hysterically and claiming he had counted the Russian mortar fire and that they had now exploded eight hundred of their thousand rounds. It seemed improbable; nevertheless Private Starbuck heard the story spread from foxhole to foxhole and presently he even began to believe it himself.

Toward evening, the sun came out briefly, and the mortars commenced firing again. This time, however, the shells landed on the far side of the hill. There was an answering fire from the American mortar, although it seemed a senseless duel when neither gunner could get a fix on the other. The duel continued after nightfall, and then, suddenly, there was silence from the American sector. In a few minutes, his worst fears were confirmed when a runner brought orders to fall back to new positions. An unhappy chance round had knocked out the American mortar.

There were five men left in his squad. They managed to withdraw from the south slope of the hill without further losses. Their new general, Captain Paulson, had a meeting of his surviving officers in Private Starbuck's hearing. The situation was not good, but before going into purely defensive positions, two things must be accomplished. The enemy machine gun and mortar must be destroyed. Squads seven and eight, who had been in reserve for a time and who had suffered the fewest casualties, were assigned the task. It must be done tonight. If the enemy's heavy weapons could be destroyed while the Americans still maintained possession of their remaining light machine gun, their position would be favorable. Otherwise their chances were fading. The mortar shells for the now useless American mortar were to be destroyed immediately to prevent their possible use by the enemy. And, the general added almost as an afterthought, at sunrise the second squad will attack and take the central hill. They would be supported by the light machine gun if, by then, the enemy mortar had been put out of action. Questions? There were many, but none were asked.

"Colonel Bullock, this is an unusual development. Would you tell us what General Paulson has in mind?"

"Well, Bill, I think it must be pretty obvious even to the men in the field that the loss of the American mortar has drastically changed the situation. An unfortunate occurrence, unfortunate indeed. The probability report is now only 37.6 in favor of the American team. Of course, General Paulson doesn't have a computer, but I imagine he's arrived at pretty much the same conclusion.

"The two squads—seven and eight, I believe—which you see on your screens are undoubtedly being sent out in a desperation attempt—no, not desperation—in a courageous attempt to destroy the enemy mortar and light machine gun. It's a good move. I approve. Of course, you won't find this one in the books, but the fact is that at this stage of the game, the pre-determined battle plans are of ever-decreasing importance."

"General Vorsilov?"

"The Americans are doing the only thing they can do, Mr. Carr, but it's only a question of time now. You can rest assured that the Russian team will be alert to this very maneuver."

"Well, stand by, folks. This is still anybody's game. The games are not over yet—not by a long shot. Don't go away. This could be the key maneuver of the games. John?"

"While we're waiting, Bill, I'm sure the folks would like to hear a list of the new records which have already been set in this fifth meeting between the United States and Russia in the Olympic War Games. Our first record came early in the games when the American fifth and sixth squads startled the world with a brilliant demonstration of firepower and shattering the old mark set back in 2042 by killing seven men in just . . ."

On the morning of the fifth day Private Starbuck moved out as the point man for the assault on the central hill. He had trained on a replica of the hill hundreds of times, and he knew it as well as he knew the back of his own hand. Squad seven had knocked out the enemy mortar last night, so they had the support of their own light machine gun for at least part of the way. Squad eight had failed in their mission and had been killed to the last man. Private Starbuck only hoped the Russian machine gun was not in position to fire on the assault team.

At first it was like maneuvers. Their own machine gun delivered a blistering fire twenty yards ahead of them and the five squad members themselves fired from the hip as they advanced. There was only occasional and weak counterfire. They were eight yards from the top, and he was beginning to hope that, by some miracle spawned by a grotesque god, they were going to make it. Then it came. Grenades came rolling down from above, and a sustained volley of rifle-fire came red hot from the depths of hell. He was hit twice in the first volley. Once in the hip, again in the shoulder. He would have gotten up, would have tried to go forward, but Captain Collins fell dead on top of him and he could not. A grenade exploded three feet away. He felt something jar his cheek and knew he had been hit again. Somehow it was enough. Now he could die. He had done enough. Blood ran down his face and into his left eye, but he made no attempt to wipe it away. He would surely die now. He hoped it would be soon.

"It doesn't look too good, folks. Not good at all. Colonel Bullock?"
"I'm afraid I have to agree, Bill. The American probability factor is down to 16.9, and right now I couldn't quarrel with the computer at all. The Russians still have sixteen fighting men, while the Americans are down to nine. The American team will undoubtedly establish a defense position around the light machine gun on the north hill, but with the Russians still in control of the central hill and still in possession of their own machine gun, it appears pretty hopeless. Pretty hopeless indeed."

He owed his life during the next few minutes to the fact that he was able to maintain consciousness. The firing had ceased all about him, and for a time he heard nothing, not even the sound of distant gun fire. This is death, he thought. Death is when you can't hear the guns any longer. Then he heard the sound of boots. He picked out a spot in the sky and forced his eyes to remain on that spot. He wished to die in peace, and they might not let him die in peace. After a while the boots moved on.
He lost consciousness shortly after that. When he awoke, it was dark. He was not dead yet, for he could hear the sounds of guns again. Let them kill each other. He was out of it. It really was not such a bad way to die, if only it wouldn't take so long. He could tolerate the pain, but he hated the waiting.
While he waited, a strange thing happened. It was as though his spirit passed from his body and he could see himself lying there on the hill. Poor forlorn body to lie so long upon a hill. Would they write poems and sing songs about Private Richard Starbuck like they did four years ago for Sergeant Ernie Stevens? No, no poems for this lonely body lying on a hill waiting to die. Sergeant Stevens had killed six men before he died. So far as he knew he had killed none.
In the recruiting pamphlet they told you that your heirs would receive one hundred thousand dollars if you died in the games. Was that why he signed up? No, no, he was willing to die now, but not for that. Surely he had had a better reason than that. Why had he done such a

crazy thing? Was it the chance to be a survivor? No, not that either. Suddenly he realized something the selection committee had known long ago: he had volunteered for no other reason than the fact there was a war to be fought, and he had not wanted to be left out.

He thought of the cameras next. Had they seen him on TV? Had all the girls, all the people in his home town been watching? Had his dad watched? Had Mr. and Mrs. Martin and their daughter watched? Had they seen him when he had drawn fire by changing foxholes? Were they watching now to see if he died well?

Toward morning, he began to wonder if he could hold out. There was only one thing left for him to do and that was to die as quietly and peacefully as possible. Yet it was not an easy thing to do, and now his wounds were beginning to hurt again. Twice he heard the boots pass nearby, and each time he had to fight back an impulse to call out to them so they could come hurry death. He did not do it. Someone might be watching, and he wanted them to be proud of him.

At daybreak there was a wild flurry of rifle and machine gun fire, and then, suddenly, there was no sound, no movement, nothing but silence. Perhaps now he could die.

The sad, dejected voice of Bill Carr was saying "... all over. It's all over folks. We're waiting now for the lights to come on in the arena—the official signal that the games are over. It was close—but close only counts in horse-shoes, as the saying goes. The American team made a fine last stand. They almost pulled it off. I make out only three Russian survivors, John. Is that right?"

"Just three, Bill, and one of those is wounded in the arm. Well, ladies and gentlemen, we had a very exciting finish. We're waiting now for the arena lights to come on. Wait a minute! Something's wrong! The lights are not coming on! I thought for a moment the official scorer was asleep at the switch. Bill, can you find out what the situation is? This damned computer still gives the American team a 1.4 probability factor."

"We've located it, John. Our sonic sound system has located a lone American survivor. Can you get the cameras on the central hill over there? There he is, folks. Our spotters in the booth have just identified him as Private Richard Starbuck from Centerville, Iowa. He seems badly wounded, but he's still alive. The question is: can he fight? He's not moving, but his heart is definitely beating and we know where there's life, there's hope."

"Right, Bill. And you can bet the three Russians survivors are a pretty puzzled group right now. They don't know what's happened.

They can't figure out why the lights have not come on. Two minutes ago they were shouting and yelling a victory chant that now seems to have been premature. Ed, give us a camera on that north hill. Look at this, ladies and gentlemen. The three Russian survivors have gone berserk. Literally berserk—they are shooting and clubbing the bodies of the American dead. Don't go away, folks ..."

He began to fear he might not die. His wounds had lost their numbness and had begun to throb. He heard the sounds of guns and then of boots. Why wouldn't they leave him alone? Surely the war was over. He had nothing to do with them. One side or another had won— so why couldn't they leave him alone? The boots were coming closer, and he sensed that they would not leave him alone this time. A sudden rage mingled with his pain, and he knew he could lie there no longer. For the next few seconds he was completely and utterly insane. He pulled the pin on the grenade which had been pressing against his side and threw it blindly in the direction of the sound of the boots. With an instinct gained in two years of intense training, he rolled to his belly and began to fire at the blurred forms below him. He did not stop firing even when the blurred shapes ceased to move. He did not stop firing until his rifle clicked on an empty chamber. Only then did he learn that the blurred shapes were Russian soldiers.

They healed his wounds. His shoulder would always be a little stiff, but his leg healed nicely, leaving him without a trace of a limp. There was a jagged scar on his jaw, but they did wonders with plastic surgery these days and unless you knew it was there, you would hardly notice it. They put him through a two-month reconditioning school, but it didn't take, of course. They gave him ticker tape parades, medals, and the keys to all the major cities. The warned him about the psychological dangers of being a survivor. They gave him case histories of other survivors—grim little anecdotes involving suicide, insanity, and various mental aberrations.

And then they turned him loose.

For a while he enjoyed the fruits of victory. Whatever he wanted he could have for the asking. Girls flocked around him, men respected him, governments honored him, and a group of flunkies and hangers-on were willing enough to serve his every whim. He grew bored and returned to his home town.

It was not the same. He was not the same. When he walked down the streets, mothers would draw close to their daughters and hurry on past. If he shot pool, his old friends seemed aloof and played as if they were afraid to win. Only the shopkeepers were glad to see him come in, for whatever he took, the government paid for. If he were to shoot the mayor's son, the government would pay for that too. At home his own mother would look at him with the guarded look in her eyes, and his dad was careful not to look him in the eyes at all.

He spent a lot of time in his room. He was not lonely. He had learned to live alone. He was sitting in his room one evening when he saw Cassandra, the Martin's fifteen-year-old daughter, coming home with some neighborhood kid from the early movie. He watched idly as the boy tried to kiss her goodnight. There was an awkwardness between them that was vaguely exciting. At last the boy succeeded in kissing her on the cheek, and then, apparently satisfied, went on home.

He sat there for a long time lighting one cigarette from the last one. There was a conflict inside his mind that once would have been resolved differently and probably with no conscious thought. Making up his mind, he stubbed his cigarette and went downstairs. His mother and father were watching TV. They did not look up as he walked out the front door. They never did any more.

The Martins were still up. Mr. Martin was tying brightly colored flies for his new fly rod and Mrs. Martin was reading. They both stiffened when he entered without knocking—alarm playing over their faces like a flickering fire light. He didn't pause, but walked on up stairs without looking at them.

Mrs. Martin got to her feet and stood looking up the stairway without moving. In her eyes there was the look of a jungle tiger who watches its mate pinned to a stake at the bottom of the pit. Mr. Martin sat staring at the brightly colored flies on his lap. For a moment there was silence. Then a girl's shrill screams announced to the Martins that war's reality was also for the very young.

FOR DISCUSSION: The Survivor

1. The opening description of the empty arena is one of peace and pastoral calm. What effect does the author achieve through this description in relation to later events in the arena?
2. Running throughout Starbuck's thoughts like a muted theme in his earlier relationship with the Martins and their young daughter Cassandra. Why are these thoughts included? If the author had substituted thoughts of high school dances or Starbuck family vacations, would the climax of the story be weakened? Explain.
3. The author presents the rationale for the Olympic War Games with-

out comment. Do you think such Games could be considered a satisfactory solution to the problem of war between nations?

4. Suspense and its accompanying tension are major ingredients in this story. How does the author prolong the suspense at the moment when the Games are believed to be ended?

5. What is the author suggesting about the sensibilities of the television audience and its sports reporters?

6. Why do Starbuck's relatives and friends find themselves uncomfortable in his presence when he returns to his home town?

7. What does the author mean when he says that Starbuck, seeing Cassandra arrive home from the movies with her friend, faces a conflict which he once would have resolved differently? What is the conflict? How would it probably have been resolved if Starbuck had not been trained for and participated in the Games?

INTRODUCTION: The Post-mortem People

Progress has its accompanying problems. The invention of the automobile has freed people to move about more easily and with far more comfort. But it also causes deaths on highways and contributes significantly to the pollution of the air.

Recent advances in modern medical science include the ability to transplant such human organs as hearts and kidneys. The benefits of such operative procedures are beyond dispute. But in this story, the author gives the reader a grim glimpse of a problem that may arise in the future when the market for transplantable organs has given rise to a grisly new breed of professionals.

The Post-mortem People
by Peter Tate

This time, Anton Hejar came by chance upon the event. He heard the shrill gathering of locked tires and was running before any sick-soft sound of impact. The car could be skidding, no more; but one could not afford to stand and wait. One had a reputation.

He shouldered a passage through the lazy-liners on the rotor walk even as a bundle with flapping limbs and thrownback head turned spitwise in the air. He was at curbside when the body landed close to his feet.

Hejar placed his overcoat gently to retain a little of the man's draining warmth.

"Somebody get an ambulance," he shouted, taking command of the situation while women grew pale and lazies changed to the brisker track and were borne smartly away.

The man's eyes flickered. A weak tongue licked vainly at lips grown dry as old parchment. Breath came like a flutter of moth's wings.

"How are you feeling?" asked Hejar.

The eyes searched for the speaker, blinked and blinked again to bring him into focus. The man tried to speak, but there was only a rattle like too many unsaid words fighting for an outlet.

Hejar sniffed the air. His nostrils, finely attuned to the necessities of his calling, could pick out death like hollyhock or new-made bread. Yes, it was there, dank and acrid as stale perspiration.

"No need to worry," he told the man. "You'll be all right."

He took off his jacket to make a pillow for the man's head.

"My . . . wife . . . she . . ."

"Don't concern yourself," said Hejar. "Let's get you settled first."

He's kind, thought the man in his mind full of moist pain. Perhaps he just isn't trying to fool me with sentimentality. I feel so cold. . . .

The siren of the approaching ambulance rose and fell on a scale of panic. Hejar moved the man's head gently, looking for marks or a tell-tale run of blood from the ear. He found nothing. Good. The brain, then, the control center was undamaged. Great.

He went through the pockets of the overcoat covering the man. From one he produced a small tin and opened it, exposing an inked pad. He maneuvered digits on a rubber stamp.

The man moved feverishly beside him. "You'll be fine, old son," he said gently. "Help's just arriving."

Then he brought the rubber stamp down right between the man's eyes.

Doberman Berke, a morgue attendant of intermediate stature, humbled through life in constant awe of the ubiquitous Anton Hejar. Where death stalked, there, too, walked Anton Hejar, hat pulled low, hand on stamp.

Berke paused in his work to examine the insignia between the corpse's eyes. It was not elaborate, a mere functional circle with script around the outer edging and the characters "A.H." tangled in some written state of intercourse at center.

"Item and contents property of . . ." read the circumferential legend if one cared to crane one's neck and bend kiss-close to the poor dead face to see.

Berke did no such thing, nor had he ever done so. He knew Hejar's function, knew the language of the snatchers from careful study. Instead, with a curiosity he compared the time on Hejar's stamp—1434—with the report that accompanied the cadaver. The ambulance men had put the time of extinction at 1434.5. Hejar's professionalism was uncanny.

He detached the item and placed it in a refrigerated container. Then he pushed it to one side to await collection.

Invariably, Hejar came himself. If he had any juniors, Berke had never seen them. Certainly, they never came to claim their master's bloody bounties. Hejar knew Berke's routine. He had already checked the attendant's volume of work. He would be here very shortly.

And even as Berke acknowledged the fact, the door swung wide and

Hejar was walking towards him, smiling and beneficent, unfolding a spotless receipt.

Berke took the receipt and examined it closely, though he knew full well it would contain adequate authority from Coroner Gurgin. Dealing with Hejar, an expert in his own field, Berke endeavored to appear as painstaking and conscientious as Hejar's patience would allow. And Hejar had a fund of patience. Hejar had so much patience he should have had a long face and a penchant for squatting on desert cactus plants to go with it. Instead, he just smiled ... and in that smile lay a chill warning that if you didn't move fast enough to prove you were alive, then Anton Hejar would take you for dead.

Berke handed back the receipt. "Any trouble this time? Sometimes sector center gets a little old-fashioned about dispatchment at speed. Like sympathy for the dependents."

"Sympathy is out of date," said Hejar blandly.

"Absurd sentimentality about a piece of stiffening flesh." He showed his teeth again, setting up laughter wrinkles around his blue, blue eyes. "Gurgin knows where his steroids come from. He gives me no complications. A little blind-eye money for his favorite dream pill and he is always prepared to write me a rapid registration marker. Now, is this mine?"

He moved towards the container and identified his designation, humming busily to himself. He caught up the container by its handle and started for the door.

"Wait."

"Why?" Hejar spat out the word with a venom that made Berke writhe, but his face, all the while, was mild, his manner charitable. "Why," he said, more reasonably.

Hejar was no stranger. They met elsewhere and often and dialogue came far more easily where surroundings were no more indicative of the one's vocation than the other's.

Berke felt foolish. There were always questions that occurred to him moments before Hejar's arrival at the morgue and each time, he lined them up and rehearsed a conversation which, he hoped, would impress Hejar with its depth and insight.

But when Hejar came, it was as though he dragged the careful script out of Berke's head and bundled it into a corner. Berke was tongue-tied. Hejar, as ever, was sunny. Today was no exception.

"Why?" Hejar asked again, patiently.

Berke stumbled. "Isn't ... isn't there anything else you want? The trunk isn't spoken for."

"No wonder."

"I'm not with you."

"The man has been struck by a car," said Hejar with exaggerated diction. He might have talked thus to a retarded child—if he had ever spared a little of his surface warmth for a creature who could do him no good. "Digestive chemistry, kidney system, circulation . . . they're all finished. At most, there may be a dozen organs worth salvaging, and we don't have time for that. Besides, our clients pay more money for bits and pieces."

"Uh-huh." Berke slotted away the piece of business acumen. Sooner or later, he would have to take his chance on the outside—he was fast running out of apprenticeships. And he was determined to sample the lush pastures of the thoroughfare section, with its easy pickings and its first-come-first-served credo. There was small reward, by comparison, in industrial accidents or domestic mishaps.

"Now," said Hejar, "is there anything else?" He made it sound like a polite inquiry, but Berke knew that he delayed the man further at his peril. He didn't want to leave his room one morning and find Hejar waiting to follow him. He shifted from one foot to another.

"Oh, yes. Forgive me." Hejar reached in his pocket and tossed a handful of notes across to Berke. They fluttered on to the separation table. In the time it took Berke to wipe them clean of tell-tale stains, Hejar was gone.

Jolo Trevnik locked the weathered door of his downtown Adonis League and wondered, as he wondered every night, why he tried to carry on. Once, his culture clinic had been definitely uptown and well filled with rounded young men who slung medicine balls at each other and tested their biceps in crucifix poses on the wall-bars.

Ironic how, when you had survived everything else from social stigma to national laziness, finally location turned against you. The people had moved away into apartment blocks on the town periphery, leaving the center purely for business and only that which was conducted in sky-scraper settings.

These days, Trevnik exercised alone, moving slowly from one piece of apparatus to another, not because he had himself slowed up, but because now only time hung heavily on the wall-bars.

His suit grew progressively shabbier and his fortune, body-built in the days of blind, rootless activity that followed the tobacco ban, grew correspondingly smaller. As did his steaks and his health food orders. He was still in fine shape . . . and frustrated as only a man can be whose sole talent has become redundant.

He turned away from the door and walked towards the main rotor quay. A shadow in a doorway down the street moved to follow him.

Hejar had made only a token attempt at concealment and Trevnik knew of his presence. It was part of the new fatal system that had emptied Trevnik's clinic and all others around the town, and all football grounds and all places where excitement or over-exertion might bring unexpected eclipse. The body that had once been so envied in life was now attractive only in terms of death.

I guess I ought to be honored, Trevnik thought. But I feel like a cat in heat. I'll make the pink punk work for his money.

At the rotor quay, he selected the slow track and moved quickly along it. He wanted to put the idlers in his pursuer's way and they made no protest, silent, turned inward with the seashells in their ears filling their minds with hypnotic rhythms and whispered words.

Above the whine of the rotor and the passing traffic, he heard the man stumbling after him, heard him cursing, and laughed.

At the next junction, he transferred to a faster track, still walking rapidly, weaving neatly between the younger mutes, with their frondular arms and snapping fingers.

Hejar was less adept and less gentle. Once, he jostled a young man so violently that his earpiece slipped to the moving pavement.

The youth recovered it and pursued the pursuer long enough to tap his heels and send him headlong before returning to his reverie.

Trevnik heard the resultant tumble and allowed the pavement to bear him along until the dishevelled Hejar regained his feet. Then he backpedalled until the man drew level, still dusting himself down. He raised the pitch of his voice a deceptive shade.

"I hope you didn't hurt yourself," he said, fussily . . . too fussily. "Perhaps we should walk a little more slowly."

Hejar eyed him warily. "I'm quite recovered now," he said. "Thanks for your concern."

If the guy knows why I trail him, he wondered, why doesn't he show it? Why this spectacular concern?

"Perhaps I should walk with you in case you feel suddenly faint," said Trevnik. "If you're shaky, you ought to get to bed. Are you sure I can't help you?"

The attitude jarred on Hejar's sensitivity. He began to notice other things about the man. How he moved—almost mincingly. The breeze that played on their faces as they were drawn along the track brought a musky aroma to the nostrils grown acute with death. Hejar swallowed and looked at the man again.

"Really," he said, almost defensively. "It's all right. The next quay is as far as I go."

"As you please," said Trevnik. His lips tightened with a hint of petulance. "But if there's the smallest thing . . ."

"Nothing," said Hejar, savagely.

Trevnik rode beside him, barely glancing at him but carrying the smug conviction of a man who has done a good turn only to meet an ungracious response.

Smug? Hejar, sneaking glances at Trevnik from the shelter of his hat-brim, became even more apprehensive.

Trevnik's finely developed limbs and torso were bound to fetch a good price. Or were they? Trying to sell internal organs marred by chromo-somatic complications or a brain whose motivations were neither particularly masculine nor blatantly feminine but in some twilight in-between . . . that had definite setbacks.

At the quay closest to his office, he disembarked. "Thanks for everything," he said.

"I hope we meet again," said Trevnik. He waved until the rotor bore him out of sight.

There was no doubt Trevnik had a physique rarely seen among the squat inhabitants of 1983; a body which, if properly marketed, could still prove profitable despite . . .

Hejar chewed his sensual lower lip. Despite nothing. He had kept observation for weeks now, at first unnoticed and lately unheeded. In the beginning there had been no such doubts proffered. It was just to-day? Hejar could not be sure that the disturbing traits had not been there for some time. Certainly, they had not been apparent when he began his vigils. And that was it—a device, dated from the time Trevnik first noticed that the snatchers were on to him, or at least some time subsequent to that . . . when he thought of it.

Hejar felt better. The fall had shaken him, had made his heart pound alarmingly. But now he had rumbled the man, his good spirits returned.

Any fresh measures to protect the remains after death intrigued him. There was, after all, no pain, no occupancy and post-mortem activities were unlikely to disturb the main participant. But the sanctimonious sprouting of the sixties and early seventies still persisted though even the government had officially classed them out of date. There remained in certain circles a horror of disturbing the corpse. Hejar had long ago shouldered and forgotten the inferences of obscenity and laughed all the way to the credit pile when somebody called him a ghoul, a cannibal, a necrophile.

"I do mankind a service," he would tell people who questioned his motives. "The burial grounds have been used up, built over, defiled in asphalt. The crematorium has a use, but it is a great leveller. How do you identify ashes? Items that could be vital to the living are wasted in the flames. Far better, is it not, to have a scroll stating that even in death, your dearest are unselfishly helping those who continue to suffer. I aid medical science. I am trained to the task and my spirit is right."

"If I can help somebody," he crooned raggedly as he entered the block where his office was situated, "as I pass along..."

He boarded the elevator and pressed the button for the 11th floor.

"Then my living shall not be in vain...."

The elevator wound upwards. Head bowed, Hejar was engrossed in the half-remembered song.

"Then my living shall not be in vain...Oh..."

The elevator shunted him into the 11th floor berth. He opened the door of his office.

"My living shall not be in va-a-i-i-n-n-n..."

The woman in the guest chair had red-rimmed eyes but she watched him intensely.

"Good evening," he said calmly. He was used to finding such women in his office. One pair of red eyes looked much like another.

"I've been here for hours," she said.

"I didn't know you were waiting," he said, obviously. He did not concede the necessity for an apology. Instead, he smiled.

"You are...Mr. Hejar, the...reclamation...man?" Hejar's smile had disconcerted her, as it had been meant to do. The smile therefore broadened.

"I've been sitting here, looking at your...pictures," she said, gesturing vaguely at the Ben Maile skyline and the Constable pastoral. "They're not...what I...would have expected."

Hejar hung his hat and coat carefully on the old-fashioned stand. He took his seat behind the desk and built a cathedral nave with his fingers while the smile lay dozing on his face.

It was always best to let them talk—as much as they wanted to, about whatever they wanted to. Gradually they would work their way round to the inevitable plea.

"What had you expected, Mrs...." He deliberately left the sentence hanging in the air.

"An office without a single rounded edge. No softness anywhere... everything sharp and cold and soulless."

She would tell him her name and the reason for her presence in her own time. He would not prompt the revelation because it was important to maintain a singular lack of interest.

"I think pictures add another dimension to an office," he said. "Constable had a way with water, an eye for minute detail. I often think he sketched every leaf. Maile, now..."

"You're probably wondering why I am here," said the woman. She was fortyish, plump, not unbecoming. She was in pain, with her loss, with the alien circumstances in which she now found herself.

"Take your time. I know how it is . . ."

"I'm Elsie Stogumber."

Stogumber. Hejar switched on the audiostat which unscrambled the data from the long-winded secretary computer.

"Stogumber," he said into the feeder piece.

"There would hardly be anything recorded yet," said the woman.

"Today?"

The woman twisted her gloves in her lap.

"He asked for you," said Hejar.

"Small comfort to me now." The woman seemed mesmerized by the anguished play of finger and nylon. Hejar waited.

"They say you—you had his head."

"That's right."

The woman watched his face for perhaps five seconds. Then she went back to her glove play.

"You wouldn't still have it?"

Hejar's stomach churned. His vocation was bloody enough, even viewed with the detachment he brought to it, but . . .

"Why?" he asked. The smile had gone.

"I suddenly couldn't remember my husband's face. It terrified me. If I could just . . ."

"I no longer have it. My clients demand prompt delivery."

"Your—clients?"

"Come now, Mrs. Stogumber. I'm sure you realize the complete situation. You already know exactly what came to me. You also know why and that I am only an agent in this . . ."

She screamed once, sharply. But her face was unfrenzied. It seemed impossible that such a sound had uttered from her.

"Who has it now, then?" she asked. Her voice was controlled, but only just. "Who has it?"

"My dear Mrs. Stogumber . . ." Hejar found another smile and slipped it on. "Will you not be satisfied if I say that your husband is beyond any inconvenience or pain and that his last thoughts, to my certain knowledge, were of you?"

"No. It is not enough."

"What would you want, Mrs. Stogumber?"

"Ideally, my husband. Or at least, some part of him."

"But he's *dead*, Mrs. Stogumber. He's gone. He is nothing without the spark of life. Why prolong the parting? Why mess up your pretty dress, Mrs. Stogumber?"

The woman crumpled visibly in the chair. Her shoulders shook and she took in great gulps of air.

"Don't you have any movies of him? No threedees, maybe?"

"He went out after breakfast and I'll never see him again. You—you buzzards chop him up before I can even . . . identify him."

The fight for breath became less labored as tears began to flow. Hejar let her cry, thankful for an escape valve. He wondered what he could say when she came out of it. Evening edged a little closer to night. Her sobs softened to an occasional sniff. She blew her nose and then looked up.

"It usually helps if I explain," began Hejar. "You see, when in 1973, the Central Committee rescinded the Anatomy Act of 1823 and the Burial Act of 1926 . . ."

"I've seen you," she said. "All of you. Waiting at busy road junctions, chasing ambulances, trailing feeble old men . . ."

Her voice was close to hysteria. He rose, walked round the desk and slapped her hard. She fell silent.

"You might feel different if you understood our mission," he said. "We are not buzzards. We play a vital role. To benefit the living, we make certain adjustments to the dead. Nobody suffers by it. The Salvage of Organs Act of January, 1974, gave us the full power of the legislature. This was tantamount to a declaration that the racket in kidneys and heart valves and limbs that had thrived up to that time was accepted as inevitable and made conventional. We have new thinkers now. Wasting precious sentiment on a pile of gone-off meat was not progressive. Surely you can see that."

The woman took a deep breath. For a moment she teetered on the verge of more weeping. Then she struggled on.

"I accept it in theory," she said. "It seemed to make good sense at the time. Things like that always do when you are not involved . . . But I've seen the way you work. You salvage men don't just wait for death— you prompt it. Surely, if you are the public servants you say you are, you shouldn't have to compete with each other."

Hejar swung his feet up on to the desk. Now the situation had resumed a calmer plane, he could pick and choose his words. He clasped his fingers behind his head.

"Now there, admirable Mrs. Stogumber, you have hit upon our problem. This is a living as much as a vocation. I must play as others shape the game. If there is a certain—over-enthusiasm, it is not of my choosing. But I have to absorb it if I am to continue in the practice. As long as there are people who deplore this trend, there is a chance that it will be thrown out. You see, there are so many new people trying to make out.

As yet, we have no control over membership. The dignity that once went with this calling ... the pathological training ... Well, you know how it is. You open a door and all manner of undesirables flock through it."

"I'm sorry," she said. "For acting like that, I mean. It was childish of me." She tried a wintry smile.

"I am sorry, too, Mrs. Stogumber, for having to resort to such extreme measures. Your present composure impresses me considerably. Perhaps you find the situation a little easier to accept now."

She smiled again, a little more like autumn now.

"When somebody takes the trouble to explain, it helps," she said.

"The 1974 amendments to the Human Tissues Act of 1961 ..." said Hejar. She stopped him with a raised hand. "Now Mr. Hejar. I fear you are trying to blind me with science."

High summer shaped her lips. Hejar swung his feet off the desk, stood up and came round towards her. "Not at all, my dear lady ..."

But Elsie Stogumber was clear of her chair and through the office door before he could reach her. Her summer was not for Anton Hejar.

Hejar stood on the permanent walkway opposite the gymnasium and made no attempt at concealment. Such intrigue became ludicrous with repetition, particularly when all parties were aware of the charade that was being played out. Now, he did not veil his intentions even out of courtesy.

He was too little of the hypocrite, he told himself, but even in that, he lied. He stood so because he liked to watch Trevnik's dark face as the man noticed him, to see the nostrils flare and the eyes go suddenly wild as if in fear of an old superstition, and then just as suddenly narrow and normal and carefully-averted.

He heard a descending thunder on the stairs. Trevnik must have seen him, given the advantage of darkness looking out on light, because he simply showed his back as he locked the door and started down the street.

In no apparent hurry, Hejar crossed the road and fell into step about twenty yards behind the giant. Today, he saw nothing suspect in the man's gait. Trevnik, presumably, had given up any pretense and walked now only in a way that exhibited the disciplined thrust of hip and leg.

Elsie Stogumber, cramped from her unaccustomed sojourn in the narrow doorway once occupied by Hejar, emerged into the mid-day brilliance and watched the two men down the street.

Berke took a final wheatgerm sandwich and pushed the remaining pile along the bench to Hejar.

Though he had long since ceased to be troubled by his occupation, his appetite had never returned. Each day he prepared more sandwiches than he would eat.

And each day, still feigning surprise at the meeting and hungry from his hunt, plump Hejar joined him on his bench at the leisure zone and waited politely until Berke had shown himself fed to sufficiency and offered him the surplus.

Berke washed his mouth out at the nearby drinking fountain, spat and sat down again.

Hejar chewed, his attention riveted to the children's fun-run, watching for a collision with the spinning chairs or a fall from the helter-skelter.

"We could, perhaps, fill in the loop-holes," said Berke. Hejar grunted.

"The way into this game is too easy," said Berke. "If we study, it is to be eventually better at our job. There is no ruling. It is a labor of love. Amateurs, opportunists can always make inroads. Perhaps we should form a union, or get some recognition from the Central Committee."

Hejar shrugged. He was uninterested in Berke's theorizing, his verbal attempts—in his incompetence—to make the living more secure for himself.

"The amount of money the amateurs make, the volume of business we professionals lose is negligible," he said. "What do they get? A relation dies at home. Natural causes. Who pays for natural causes? The bodies are worn out, anyhow. A murder victim is discovered on a rubbish dump in an advanced state of decay. Where's the money in that? No, myself I don't mind who gets the stamp. I can always keep myself well."

In his sudden silence, he indicated his doubt of the other's ability.

"Me, too," said Berke hurriedly. "I was thinking of the less fortunate members of our calling."

Atop the fifty foot slide, a jostled child screamed and clutched with vain fingers at the air. Berke and Hejar moved at speed towards the gathering crowd.

The Minerva no longer pretended that the health foods it served were any more than politely-fashioned simulants or, at best, salvaged from some overgrown delicatessen. But at least the cafe still retained certain of the musty odors that had once given herb stores an impression of geography contained within three walls and a display window.

Jolo Trevnik avoided the glassed-up, crowded planktonia. His stomach, accustomed to a balanced carbohydrate intake, turned on the lead oxide that came with every boxed cereal these days, a legacy of the brightly-painted free gift needed to sell any competitive product.

His system revolted against battery lamb and the beef and chicken, he knew, contained sterilizing agents. Not that he was bothered particularly about potency. The unborn were the lucky ones, he reasoned.

A shape above his table cut out the light. Momentarily, he started, his mind still fixed on the snatcher with the Santa Claus face.

Then the woman sat down opposite him and he noted the carefully-highlighted features and the over-bright eyes with a measure of relief.

He took a sip at his acorn coffee to steady his nerves. When he put his cup down, she said, "Mr. Trevnik?"

He nodded.

"I saw the name on the door of your gymnasium."

"But that's a long way away. What . . . ?"

"I followed you," she said quickly. "I couldn't help noticing I wasn't the only one."

Trevnik dropped his eyes and considered the gray coffee. He felt—unclean; a curiosity, a freak. All the more for having someone else notice his humiliation.

"I'm sorry for you," she said, and that made it worse.

"You don't need to be sorry, lady," he said, almost angrily. "It doesn't bother me. I look after myself. I avoid accidents."

"My husband was the same."

"Should I know your husband?"

"I think he came to your clinic a few times—Harry Stogumber."

"Stogumber."

His echo of the word chilled her with a memory.

"Tall man," he said. "Not too fat. Not much meat on him at all, really . . ."

"Please." The woman laid her gloved hand across his fingers.

"I'm sorry," said Trevnik. "Did I say something . . . ?"

"A phrase. It has associations . . ."

Trevnik went over it in his mind. " 'Not much . . .' " He bit his lip. "I am beginning to understand," he said. "I didn't realize. Forgive me, ma'am. Maybe I should . . ."

Trevnik freed his great legs from the meager table and turned his seat at an angle to allow them access to the gangway.

"I hope you're not going," the woman said. "Please don't go."

Elsie Stogumber was running her eyes over the breadth of his shoulders, the width and density of his hands. The frankness of her inspection began to embarrass him. "I was going to ask you a favor," she said finally. "That man who keeps following you. He was there when the car hit my husband. He . . ." She swallowed hard.

"Don't trouble yourself," said Trevnik. "I can work out what happened."

"I want to hurt him," she said. "Really physically hurt him. But what can I do?"

Trevnik looked down at his hands, saw how the tendons moved under the skin.

"So you want me to hurt him for you...Do you know that I have never in my life used my strength to hurt anyone?"

"I could offer you money," she said. He looked up angrily. "But I won't. I can see that you would do it only if you wanted to do it."

"Lady, that man is only waiting for me to die so he can tear me apart. I WANT to do it NOW."

"Then what is stopping you?"

Trevnik clasped his hands to stop them from moving of their own accord. He rested his chin on them.

"It is against the law," he said.

"What law? What human law could possibly deny that I have a right to hurt that man?"

"You, maybe. Not me."

"You could plead self-defense...if you said he tried to push you into the road or trip you into the rotor plant, you would have provocation."

"Lady...Mrs. Stogumber, ma'am. How could I plead self-defense. I mean...I mean...look at me. I LOOK like an attacker. I WANT to help you, Mrs. Stogumber, but..."

"It's all right," said Elsie Stogumber. "I'll find somebody else."

Trevnik found himself on his feet. The woman said no more. All she wanted was for him to stand still while his thoughts progressed. She allowed perhaps 15 seconds to pass while Trevnik hesitated, towering above her. "Of course, they wouldn't have to KILL him," she said quietly.

"Maybe if I..." Trevnik sat down again. "Maybe if I told them how he'd been following me and all and . . . and . . . taunting me, they'd understand."

Elsie Stogumber let him talk on, convincing himself, committing himself.

"I am sure nobody on earth would blame you," she said eventually. "He is trying to—well, interfere—with you. That's almost an offense in itself."

Trevnik smiled happily for the first time in a long while. "You're right, Mrs. Stogumber," he said. "You're sure as hell right."

Again the plump man waiting on the far pavement; again the thunder down the rotting wooden stairs. Jolo Trevnik emerged and turned to lock the door. Hejar shifted his weight from one foot to another, anxious to be away.

Trevnik turned from the door and looked straight at Hejar. Then he started across the road. Hejar was suddenly afraid. He sought desperately for another purpose to give to his presence.

"That building," he said before Trevnik could reach him. "Doesn't look too safe. It could fall down any time."

"Is that why you keep following me?" Trevnik mounted the curb. "Because you're afraid I'll go down with it? I'm not much use to you crushed, am I?"

"No . . . no. We—my department—we wanted to find out where you live, where you eat, your transportive habits, so we can site your replacement office accordingly . . ."

"Rubbish," said Trevnik.

"No, I assure you . . ."

Trevnik hit him first on the nose, drawing blood. "See a little of your own," he said pleasantly.

Then he sank his right fist deep into Hejar's solar plexus and followed it with his left. He began to enjoy the way the stout man yielded and swayed before him; the way the flesh gave beneath his knuckles.

He began a methodical destruction, aware that he was going beyond his brief, but somehow no longer able to call back his massive fists.

He chopped down on the nerve centers inside Hejar's collar-bones.

"Grave-robber," he said without expression. "My, how you little pink people love to get blood on your hands."

He hit Hejar twice more in the stomach and the man was there, jack-knifed in front of him.

His knees spoke to him. Use us. Smash him. But he controlled them. If he used anything but his fists in this, it would no longer be fair, would no longer carry a justification.

Hejar folded slowly to the ground. Trevnik's feet spoke. Let us finish him. Please.

"No," Trevnik shouted. He turned Hejar face upwards then, and with tears streaming down his face, he walked away.

Hejar, his senses reeling, his mouth salty and crowded, saw roofs tipping at him and tried to twist out of their downward path. But he could not move.

A shadow lingered above him. His flooded nostrils barely caught a woman's scent before a smell he knew only too well, a smell of ancient perspiration.

The woman pushed back his damp hair and then seemed to be going through his pockets.

Hejar closed his eyes. Get on with it, he thought through a blood-red mist. Take my wallet and go.

The woman spoke. "Mr. Hejar." The voice had a familiarity but it defied identification as the torrents of imbalance raged against his eardrums.

He opened his eyes. The woman bent towards him. Something glinted in her hand.

He tried to scream but choked on his own blood, his own overpowering smell.

"A widow has to make a living somehow," said Elsie Stogumber. Then she brought the stamp down right between his eyes.

FOR DISCUSSION: The Post-mortem People

1. Here is a remark from the story concerning Hejar: "He might have talked thus to a retarded child—if he had ever spared a little of his surface warmth for a creature who could do him no good." What does it tell you about Hejar's character?
2. Does Elsie Stogumber seek only revenge for her husband's death or does she have another motive for killing Hejar?
3. Science-fiction stories frequently argue both sides of an issue while presenting it in fictional terms. Now that you have read this story, can you define both the issue and its pros and cons? Can you present a convincing argument for or against the existence of men like Hejar?

INTRODUCTION: The Travelin' Man

Authors do not always offer a clear solution to the problem or conflict that is at the heart of their stories. Many authors instead prefer to highlight a problem, focus the reader's attention on it, and hope that he will be encouraged to examine it and his own thoughts concerning it. "The Travelin' Man" is such a story.

The Travelin' Man
by Leo P. Kelley

Childy Covington sat in the broken rocker holding her youngest, five-month-old Delight, and rocked and thought, thought and rocked. She could see herself, just barely, in the cracked and unframed mirror that hung on the wall of the run-down house. Near it, in the shadows, sat her husband, Ralph, cleaning his rifle as he had been doing every day since the mine closed down, leaving only the sound of the wind to disturb the quiet of the desolate Tennessee hills that were their home.

Childy thought about the empty mine that was haunted by the shades of men who had left everything behind and gone seeking to the cities. As she thought about little Delight, that warm bundle of soft sounds and softer flesh, she smiled. And then she frowned as she thought about Ralph, always so sober. Ralph, who seldom spoke now except to yell at one or more of their eight kids. She continued frowning as she thought about herself.

She knew she was no beauty, never had been one, not really. Not even when she was sixteen here in the hills where she had been born and now—well, now she was creeping up fast on thirty and no one could call her Miss America. To make matters worse, she knew she wasn't smart. Oh, she could stick most any kind of seed in the garden ground out back and something would eventually sprout. She had a way with seeds. She almost laughed out loud at the thought. Little Delight was proof of her skill with seeds. So were the other seven. Oh, my, weren't they just! Then, too, she could set a trap, much as she disliked doing so, almost as good as any man. Only it was always Ralph who had to go out and check what had gotten caught in it. She had neither the heart nor the stomach for it. But she wasn't smart and she knew it.

The most recent proof of that unfortunate fact lay right over there on the oak table under the oil lamp. It had clear plastic covers and weighed, the travelin' man had told her, close to four pounds. Maybe even a few ounces over. She rocked back and forth, thinking of the day the travelin' man had arrived in his dusty Buick, while little Delight, at her breast, gurgled like a tiny geyser.

She had been standing on the sagging porch that day, staring out through the haze that hid the distant hills when she heard the *cough, sput, cough, sput* off out of sight somewhere. *Car,* she said to herself. *Maybe coming here. Got to hide the kids.*

"Calvin!" she shouted, always thinking first of her eldest who had just turned fifteen. "Mary Mae! Broderick! John Joe!"

They appeared like moles from beneath the bushes, popped out from around the corners of the house, slid down out of trees, scurried up to her with dirty hands and fearful faces.

She counted.

John Joe. Charity. Mary Mae. Calvin. Broderick. Esther. Samantha. Delight was asleep inside the house in the padded woodbox that Ralph had long ago turned into a crib.

"Calvin, you take Delight and the rest of these tads and you all hightail it clear up into the piney woods. I'll whistle when it's safe. Now you move, hear?"

They moved. With faded shirttails flying and long hair lifting on the wind, they were gone like chickens when the fox comes scratching at the coop.

And just in time!

The Buick sputtered up the road into sight and drove right up almost to the porch before it stopped, and the travelin' man got out and turned on his smile like he came by every day and they were old friends, him and Childy.

"Mornin', ma'am," he called out to her, bending to pull something out of the back seat of his car.

Childy remained silent. He didn't look like a government man, but her silence declared: "Better safe than sorry."

He puffed a lot as he lugged the big box up onto the porch. Thin, he was, though. And pale. Getting bald. Chock-full of smiles he was, like they were bubbling up inside him and bursting over the brim of his face, one right on top of the other. Childly liked his smiles. But still she said nothing.

"Goin' to be a scorcher today," he remarked, wiping the sweat from his forehead. "At least a hundred, or I miss my guess. Could I have a drink of cold water?"

Childy went inside to get it. When she came back into the shadowy main room from the built-on kitchen where the pump was—why, there he sat at her oak table just as if he belonged! Smiles or no smiles, Childy felt herself growing resentful.

"Here," she said, thrusting the glass at him. "Here's your water. Now, what you want?"

He drained the glass. "Ah, good," he sighed. "You got a nice place here."

Liar, Childy thought. It ain't nice a'tall and you know it. "What you want way up here in the hills?"

"I'm from the Hallelujah Bible Company, Incorporated," he said, loosening his tie. "HBC has sent me high up into these hills on a mission to bring the word of God to good folk like you and your husband. He about?"

Childy shook her head. "Out hunting."

"I see. Well, never mind. I can talk to you. It'll be one fine pleasure, I assure you, ma'am. Now, if you'll just sit down right here, I have something truly special to show you." He tugged open the box which he had brought inside and plopped the enormous book on the table, right under Childy's nose.

"Family Bible," he declared, tapping it. "Printed in more colors than you can count, and it's got every single word you'll ever need to know. The Hallelujah Bible Company, Incorporated, wants you and your family to have it."

"There's only me and Ralph," Childy said uneasily, reaching out to touch the Bible's garish plastic covers that had pink roses printed on them.

The travelin' man went right on as if she hadn't spoken. "Now, you just take yourself a good gander at this page right here." He flipped the Bible open to a colorful illustration. "See, there's Jesus walking right over the water just as dry as you please. And here—" He turned to another, equally colorful page. "Here we got us the picture of Him feeding the multitude with but a few loaves and fishes."

"That be a good trick," Childy said. "One I sure could profit from if'n I only knew how it worked."

"Yes, ma'am, I sure do know what you mean. The cost of livin's goin' up like those rocket ships they keep sending off to the moon and Mars and all over creation."

Childy slowly turned page after page of the Bible, impressed despite her uneasiness. She glanced inside the front cover.

"That there's the place to record all your family's joys and sorrows," said the travelin' man, watching her closely. "Births and deaths. Like that."

"They's only me and Ralph," Childy lied again, quickly withdrawing her hand from the Bible.

"Things could change," said the travelin' man. "You're still young. You got your quota, ain't you? From the government, I mean?"

Childy nodded. "We can have a baby three years from now. Meantime, I—"

The travelin' man nodded sympathetically. "Meanwhile, you got to keep takin' your pills."

"I got me a coil. Chafes, it does."

"You could get an Inspector from Census Control to come up, take a look. You sure wouldn't want to get pregnant. Not before your legal time, I mean. They'd arrest you and take the nipper right away from you, quick as a racoon's wink."

"You ever hear what they do to them?"

"The nippers?" The travelin' man turned thoughtful, forgot to smile, shook his head. "The government—well, they don't say."

"Heard once that they killed them."

"I really couldn't say. Now, about this here Bible, Mrs.—"

"Covington."

"Mrs. Covington, like I said before, HBC wants you and your family—your po-*tent*ial family—to have it."

"You all givin' it to me?"

"Yes, ma'am, we are. For only a dollar a month with carryin' charges and taxes all included in the one low price."

"Ralph and me, we don't have no money. Besides, a dollar a month'd buy us a whole sack of grits."

"It weighs four pounds. A little more, as a matter of pure fact. It's a real bargain, let me tell you, Mrs. Covington. The Word—all four pounds worth—at only a measly dollar a month for thirty-six months."

"It sure is a pretty thing."

"I'll just leave it with you, how'll that be? Sort of on trial. You show it to Mr. Covington when he gets back. I'll come by again in a month and if you don't want it then, why that will be the end of the entire matter. But please think on it, Mrs. Covington."

And now, rocking in her chair and holding Delight in her lap, Childy was still thinking about it.

Ralph, when she had told him about the travelin' man, had called her a fool. He could have been a spy, Ralph said. Or, worse still a government man. And with him coming up the road in his Buick every month, why he'd be certain to catch on sooner or later to the fact that there were kids about—unregistered ones.

Childy got up and placed Delight in the padded woodbox. "Ralph?"

"Yeah?" He wiped the last traces of oil from his rifle.

"I can't give the Bible back. You know I can't. Not now. We'll just have to pay the travelin' man his dollar a month."

"Thirty-six damned dollars!" Ralph shot at her. "Woman, why'd you have to go and write the kids' names in there on the cover?"

Childy didn't really know how to answer him. But there had been those empty lines waiting to record the births, and there were the seven kids in and out of the house—plus Delight—and, well, it had just seemed like the only proper thing to do. Not one of them had even been properly baptized. Somehow, it had seemed to Childy the day after the travelin' man had gone away, that the names of her children just had to be set down there. Somehow, it made the kids seem more permanent to her. More real, if that were possible.

"We can use our food tokens to get kidney beans, Ralph," she said hesitantly. "Beans can be made to last. You can do all sorts of things with beans." She paused. "I got four dollars tucked away in the tea kettle." And then, firmly, "I'm going to give that travelin' man one of those there dollars when he comes back to collect."

"Kidney beans," Ralph said, "ain't very nourishing."

She went to him where he sat in the shadows and put her arms around his neck, bending over in order to do so. She looked right into his eyes. "Maybe the mine'll open up again, Ralph. Maybe some day real soon." She knew it wouldn't and she knew he knew it too. "Even if it doesn't," she continued, "you might find work in Memphis. We could come along after you once got settled. Me and the kids." She held her breath.

"You know we can't go to Memphis. We got no registration papers for a single one of our kids. You *know* that, Childy!"

She wanted to weep because, yes, she knew it and because it hadn't even occurred to Ralph that she was offering him a chance to escape. But she wouldn't let the tears come. Ralph wouldn't be able to stand them. She said, "I been reading in the Book. I want you to hear." She went to the table and opened the Bible. "This is the Lord talking to Jacob," she explained. "He says, 'I am God Almighty: be fruitful and multiply; a nation and a company of nations shall be of thee, and kings shall come out of thy loins.' There's more. Listen."

"No, Childy. I don't want to hear any of that old stuff. These is modern times. We've all multiplied too much. The government, it been saying so for years, telling us we got to have quotas and all. No, don't read me that old-fashioned stuff."

There was something wrong with Ralph's voice, Childy realized. She closed the Bible and went to him quickly. "Ralph, the kids is all sound alseep in the other room."

402

He let her lead him to the battered sofa, and he lay down beside her and didn't trust himself to speak.

"Kings," she whispered to him in the gloom. "It says 'kings shall come out of thy loins,' Ralph. Just think on that! But even if none ever do—even if Cal and John Joe and all of us have to run for the rest of our lives, it don't really matter, Ralph. Because we have them and we love them and no government's going to make me—or you, either, Ralph—give up that chance to love. That travelin' man, he said 'things change.' Now, I been thinking about that. Maybe things will change again and they'll find room for us all somewheres. Maybe somewheres where all those rockets go that they keep sending up into the sky. Maybe there's still a chance for Cal to be a king—somewhere."

"We can't even feed them proper," Ralph whispered, as he made love to her in dark and desperate fashion. "Not now with the mine closed. We ain't bein' fair to them, Childy."

"Charity, she found herself an oriole today that had fallen out of its nest. She brought it on home. It's in a box out back. She says she's sorry for it. She says she loves the poor thing. Ralph, we're bein' fair to them. And we're teachin' them right. They're going to grow up straight and tall as—as kings. And queens."

"Oh, Childy!" Ralph cried, not out of passion but out of some dark place within himself where confusion lay nestled, a terrible and furry thing.

"Ralph, don't take on so. They get enough to eat. You trap and hunt. I got my garden. And they know we love them. Ralph, please!"

He was silent.

When Childy heard the Buick coming, a month to the day after the travelin' man had first visited her, she chased the children up into the piney woods and then sat down on the porch to wait for him to appear.

When he did, she saw at once that he was drunk. Not happy drunk, either, she noticed. No, he looked mean drunk. All his smiles had been drowned in the liquor he had consumed.

"I come for the dollar!" he said, as he stomped up onto the porch.

His tie was missing and there were dark stains on his white shirt. One shoelace was untied and it flicked about his foot as he walked.

"I'll go get it," Childly said. "You wait out here."

But he didn't. He followed her into the house, and when she handed him the dollar she had placed beside the oil lamp, he struck her hand and it fell to the floor between them.

"Don't want no damned dollar!" he bellowed. "Give me the Bible."

"But I can pay!" Childy protested.

"Get it!" he roared.

"Can't," Childy said, stiffening. "Packed it away with the cotton quilt my Ma gave me when I got married and I lost the key to the trunk."

He struck her then and she fell back against the table. As he moved toward the trunk standing in a far corner of the room, Childy recovered and ran to him, clawing at his coat and crying out to him to take the dollar and leave her be.

He seized her wrist and twisted it and she cried out in pain. "I want that there Bible. You get it! *Now!*"

Childy saw the sun turn red in the sky as the pain seared through her. "Please," she pleaded. "Let go my arm and I'll give it to you."

"No tricks," he warned. "Get the key and open that there trunk."

"It ain't in the trunk. I got it hid up on a shelf in the kitchen. But, please. I don't understand why you want it back. I got the dollar you said I owed you. Take it and let me keep the Bible."

He muttered something threatening and Childy knew it was hopeless. She went into the kitchen and lifted the Bible down from its hiding place. And then she leaned out the open window and gave a shrill whistle that pierced the stillness of the surrounding hills.

As she came back into the room carrying the Bible, she said, "I just heard a mocking bird. They be all over these parts."

The travelin' man paid her no attention. He took the Bible from her and opened the front cover. "Figured as much!" he gloated, looking at the eight names written there and the dates of births. "I figured all along you must have kids. Illegal kids, too. Eight in all! You been a busy little lady!"

Childy's cheeks flushed and then she quickly rallied. "I'm proud of every single one of them!"

He showed her his badge.

"You ain't no Bible salesman a'tall!" she whispered, thoroughly frightened now. "You ain't from any Hallelujah Bible Company, Incorporated. You're from—"

"The Government," he snapped. "Population Inspector. And you're under arrest!"

Childy began to cry. What could she do? She couldn't run. He'd down her before she ever reached the door. And Ralph was out on his trap line and wouldn't be back for hours yet. The kids might have heard her whistled summons, but they were only tads. What could they do to help her?

"Don't look so moony, Mrs. Covington," the travelin' man said. "It ain't all that bad. The Government has authorized me to make a proposition to you. Sit down here and I'll tell it to you."

Childly listened, unable to believe what she was hearing. Then the rumors were not true. The truth was worse!

"So all you got to do," the travelin' man was explaining, "is let me give those kids of yours an injection. Then Census Central will take over —their cryogenics department."

"Cryo—?"

"Cryogenics. That means freezing. With the kids incurably sick, they'll freeze 'em and for free, by the way. Then they'll wake 'em up a hundred years or so when they've found a cure and when there's more room on one of the planets or someplace for 'em. Look at it this way. You'll be doin' 'em a favor. They'll have a chance at a lot better life than you're givin' 'em."

"No," Childy said, shocked. "I couldn't let you do that to them."

"You got yourself no choice, you know. None a'tall."

Childy realized suddenly that Ralph had been right all along. She was the biggest fool in all the hills, no doubt about it. She had to go and write the names of the kids and their birth dates in the Bible, and now she had whistled to them for help and they would come and get themselves caught . . . Oh, she was the dumb one, all right!

"Ma?" It was Calvin standing in the sunny doorway with Delight cradled in his skinny arms. "Is it okay to come in?"

"No, Cal, it ain't! *Run!*"

Calvin hesitated, his huge blue eyes fixed on the travelin' man.

"You hear me, Cal? I said *run!*"

"Don't you move, son," the travelin' man ordered. "If'n you make a move, I'll hurt your Ma." To prove the validity of his threat, he seized Childy's arm again and twisted it behind her back. "Now you just step on in here real smart like and join the party. And no tricks, mind."

Calvin entered the room and placed Delight in her crib. He turned around, his wide blue eyes still on the travelin' man, and stood there, staring. His faded denim trousers were rolled up around his bony ankles, and there was a button missing from his checkered shirt. "Who are you, mister?"

"A travelin' man, is all. Now where are the rest of the kids?"

Calvin glanced quickly at his mother. She shook her head.

The travelin' man twisted Childy's arm sharply and she gave a brief, strangled cry.

"Up in the pineys," Calvin said. "I told them to wait there till I came on down and saw that it was safe."

"Your're gonna take your Ma and me up there and, after, I got a present for you and the other kids out in my car." His laughter was the growl of a grizzly.

"Present?" Calvin asked.

"Cancer," said the travelin' man. "Multiple sclerosis, maybe."

"What're they?"

"You'll find out. I wouldn't want to spoil the surprise. Now, come on."

Childy, resigned, told Calvin to pick up Delight, and then they all left the house with Calvin leading the way toward the pineys. Behind him came the travelin' man, shoving Childy roughly forward.

She called out to Calvin to be careful and not to go down through Horse Hollow.

Calvin looked back at her over his shoulder, obviously puzzled. "Why not?" he asked. "We always—"

"You do as I say," Childy warned and quickly winked. "Don't you set foot near Horse Hollow or your father'll whip you good."

"Okay," Calvin said at last.

They walked for some time through the piney woods. They passed the abandoned mine shaft and Devil's Creek. The travelin' man alternately cursed and panted for breath, complaining all the while about the unfamiliar, Godforsaken country.

"How much farther?" he asked.

"Just down there," Calvin answered. "Down there in—"

"By the big rock," Childy said, interrupting him. "That's where the kids always hide."

They scrambled down the side of the incline, and at the bottom, Childy suddenly turned and struck the travelin' man in the face with her free hand, which she had turned into a fist. He yelped and released his grip on her.

She ran to Calvin. "We'll head down further into the Hollow. He'll chase us. Watch your step!"

They began their zigzag run with the travelin' man not far behind them, but soon the distance between them increased. When Childy heard the man's scream, she halted and looked back, holding Calvin close to her.

"He's caught in one of our traps," Calvin exclaimed.

"Just what I hoped would happen," Childy said calmly.

"You really wanted me to bring him down here to Horse Hollow, didn't you?"

"I did. I figured the chances were good for him getting himself caught in one of the traps out here by the salt lick, since he didn't know where they were like we did. You're a right smart boy, Cal. You take after your Pa, that's for certain. We got to go back now and get the kids and—and go far away from here."

"But why, Ma? Why was that travelin' man actin' like that—so mean? I don't understand one little bit. Especially, considerin' how he had promised us all presents."

406

"You don't want his presents. You just got to believe me about that."

"Well, I guess I do. Only—"

"Come along, Cal."

Childy and Calvin made their way out of Horse Hollow, and when they came to the travelin' man caught in the trap, he cried out to them.

"Listen, you can't just leave me here like this. My ankle's cut through clear to the bone. I can't get the damned trap open! You got to help me!"

Childy looked down at him and felt her stomach churn and her heart beat faster. He looked so helpless—so hurt. She never could stand the sight of a critter caught in one of those traps. And this was one of the traps, she suddenly realized, that she herself had set!

"Please!" cried the travelin' man. "I didn't want this job a'tall. They made me take it. My wife—she had a baby last year. Legal like and all but it up and died on us. We heard about an outfit that took kids from the cryocribs and sold them black market to people like us, complete with forged papers and all. So we bought us one. My wife—she wanted a baby awful bad. But they found out and then they made me work for them after they took the kid away. The Government, I mean. They put me on probation. When I get myself what they call 're-habilitated,' why then, I'll be able to quit this awful job for good."

"Ma," Calvin whispered, "we could help him. With all of us pulling on the trap, we could get it off'n him."

"No," Childy said firmly. "We can't help him. Nobody can. All we can do is pity him as we would any other poor critter that's got hisself in trouble or a trap."

She turned her back on the travelin' man, and they continued their climb up the incline. When they reached the top, Childy wanted to look back down, but she didn't.

Calvin led her to where the other children were hiding, and then they went back to the house and packed the few things they could take with them on the journey. Childy said they must all begin as soon as their Pa got home.

While she waited for Ralph and while the children played outside the house and while the sun started wearily down toward the tops of the hills, she read the Bible. She wished she could take it with her. But she knew she couldn't. It was too heavy. Too incriminating. She tossed it on the flames in the fireplace and watched it burn.

When Ralph arrived home an hour late, she told him, in a breathless rush, all that had happened. "You were right Ralph," she concluded, with her gaze just missing his. "I'm a fool. But I sure never intended any harm when I wrote down the names."

Ralph lifted her chin and looked into her eyes. He shook his head and smiled. "The only trouble with you, Childy, is you just got blessed with an overabundance of love, and you have got to keep spreading it around. Let's go."

They told the children that they were going to find a new home that would be bright and beautiful and full of songs, and promised them that they could all be singers.

The children raced ahead, hiding and seeking while the daylight lasted. They were the first to reach the top of the hill where they were brightly silhouetted against the sky in the last of the day's sunlight.

Looking up at them, Childy felt her heart leap. She took Ralph's arm, shifting the bundle that she was carrying. "Look," she whispered to him. "Why, don't they look for all the world like kings and queens!"

Ralph looked down at little Delight in his arms. "This one's going to have her chance to turn out to be a princess, at the very least," he said. "I vow."

They moved on to where their children waited for them in the last orange blaze of the day's last light.

FOR DISCUSSION: The Travelin' Man

1. At one point in the story, Ralph says, in reference to his children, "We ain't bein' fair to them, Childy." Do you agree? Does Ralph's statement in any way reflect the central issue discussed in the story?
2. In your opinion, is the Population Inspector a villain or a victim? Is there any parallel between his situation and Childy's?
3. Identify references in the story that hint at the conditions of the time in which the story is set.
4. Is Ralph being realistic when, referring to Delight at the end of the story, he says, "This one's going to have her chance to turn out to be a princess, at the very least"? Is there any indication in the story that such a hope can be realized given the conditions and temper of the story's times?

INTRODUCTION: One Love Have I

Science fiction concerns itself with such varied subjects as interstellar travel, suspended animation, crime and punishment, and government. All of these subjects are touched upon in this evocative and moving story. In addition, another subject is included—love. Without the inclusion of such subjects as love which are important to the survival of the human spirit, science fiction would not deserve the attention it receives or the respect it has garnered from its readers throughout the years.

One Love Have I
by Robert F. Young

It had been one of those rural suppers, which were being revived at the time. Philip had just arrived in the little academic village that evening and he had just finished unpacking his clothes and his books. There had been nothing more for him to do till morning when he was due to report at the university, and feeling restless, and feeling a little lonely too (as he'd admitted to Miranda later), he had left the boarding house with the intention of wandering about the village till he was tired enough to sleep. He had hardly gone two blocks, however, before he had come to the brightly-lit community hall where the supper was in progress, and strangely intrigued, perhaps motivated by the stirring of some pleasant racial memory, he had paused before the entrance.

Through the wide-flung doors he had seen the long table in the middle of the floor, and the food-laden tables, each with a girl in blue behind it, lining the walls. He had seen the men and women passing the food tables, carrying trays, and he had heard the clatter of dishes and the reassuring sound of homely voices. He had noticed the sign above the entrance then, and the simplicity of it had touched him: 77¢ COMMUNITY SUPPER—SQUARE DANCE TO FOLLOW. It had touched him and filled him with a yearning he hadn't experienced since he was a boy, and he had climbed the wide steps that led to the open doors and stepped into the hall. It was a warm night in September and the curtains at the big windows were breathing in a gentle wind.

He saw her instantly. She was behind the ham sandwich table on the opposite side of the room, tall, dark-haired, her face a lovely flower above the blue petals of her collar. The moment he stepped through the doorway she became the cynosure of the scene, and everything else—tables, diners, walls, floor—became vague extraneous details which an artist adds to a picture to accentuate its central subject.

He was only dimly aware of the other people as he walked across the room. He was halfway to her table before she looked up and saw him. Their eyes touched then, her blue ones and his gray; touched and blended, achieved a moment apart from time. And he had fallen in love with her, and she with him, and it didn't matter what the Freudian psychologists said about that kind of love because the Freudian psychologists simply didn't know about that kind of love, about the way it was to walk into a room and and see a girl and know instantly, without understanding how you knew—or caring even—that she, and she alone, was the girl for you, the girl you wanted and had always wanted, would want forever . . .

Forever and a day . . .

His hands were shaking again and he made them place a cigarette between his lips and then he made them light it. But when they had finished the task and the first pale exhalation of smoke was hovering in the little compartment, they were still shaking, and he held them tightly together on his lap and forced his eyes to look out the window of the monorail car at the passing countryside.

The land was a tired green, a September green. There was goldenrod on hillsides, and the tips of sumac leaves were just beginning to redden. The car swayed as the overhead rail curved around a hill and spanned a valley. It was a lovely valley but it wasn't a familiar one. However, Philip wasn't perturbed; the car was still too far from Cedarville for him to be seeing familiar places. He'd never been much for traveling and it would be some time yet before he could start looking for remembered hills and forests, valleys, roads, houses—houses sometimes stood for a hundred years. Not very often, maybe, but once in a while. It wasn't too much to ask.

He lay his head back on the pneumatic heardrest and tried to relax. That was what the Deep Freeze Rehabilitation Director had instructed him to do. "Relax. Keep your mind empty. Let things enter into your awareness gradually, and above all don't think of the past." Relax, Philip thought. Don't think of the past. The past is past, past, past . . .

The car swayed again and his head turned slightly. The monorail bordered a spaceport at this point, but he had never seen a spaceport before and for a moment he thought that the car was passing through a vast man-made desert. Then he saw the lofty metallic towers pointing proudly into the afternoon sky, and presently he realized that they weren't towers at all, but ships instead.

He stared at them, half-frightened. They were one of the phenomena of the new era for which he was unprepared. There had been spaceships in his own era of course, but there hadn't been very many of them and they had been rather puny affairs, strictly limited to interplanetary travel. They bore no resemblance to the magnificent structures spread out before his eyes now.

The Sweike Drive hadn't been discovered till the year of his trial, and he began to realize the effect it had had on space travel during the ensuing century. In a way it was not surprising. Certainly the stars were a greater incentive to man than the lifeless planets of the home system ever could have been.

Alpha Centauri, Sirius, Altair, Vega—one of the ships had gone as far as Arcturus, the Rehabilitation Director had told him. It had returned scarcely six months ago after an absence of almost sixty-five years. Philip shook his head. It was data he could not accept, data too fantastic for him to accept.

He had always considered himself modern. He had always kept abreast of his age and accepted change as a part of the destiny of man. Scientific progress had never dismayed him; rather, it had stimulated him, and in his chosen field of political philosophy he had been far ahead of his contemporaries, both in vision and in practical application. He had been, in fact, the epitome of modern civilized man . . .

One hundred years ago . . .

Wearily he turned his eyes from the window and regarded the gray walls of the compartment. He remembered his cigarette when it nipped his fingers, and he dropped it into the disposal tray. He picked up the magazine he had been trying to read some time before and tried to read it again, but his mind stumbled over unfamiliar words, over outrageous idioms, faltered before undreamed-of concepts. The magazine slipped from his fingers to the seat again and he let it lie there.

He felt like an old, old man, yet, in a subjective sense he wasn't old at all. Despite the fact that he had been born one hundred and twenty-seven years ago, he was really only twenty-seven. For the years in the Deep Freeze didn't count—a hundred-year term in suspended animation was nothing more than a wink in subjective time.

He lay his head back on the headrest again. Relax, he told himself. Don't think of the past. The past is past past past . . . Tentatively he closed his eyes. The moment he did so he knew it had been a mistake, but it was too late then, for the time stream already had eddied back more than a hundred years to a swiftly flowing September current . . .

It had been a glorious day for a picnic and they had discovered a quiet place on a hill above the village. There was a cool spring not far away, and above their heads an enormous oak spread its branches against a lazy autumn sky. Miranda had packed liverwurst sandwiches in little pink bags and she had made potato salad. She spread a linen tablecloth on the grass, and they ate facing each other, looking into each other's eyes. A light wind gamboled about them, left ephemeral footprints on the hillside.

The potato salad had been rather flat, but he had eaten two helpings so that she wouldn't suspect that he didn't like it; and he'd also eaten two of the liverwurst sandwiches, though he didn't care for liverwurst at all. After they finished eating they drank coffee, Miranda pouring it from the large picnic thermos into paper cups. She had been very careful not to spill a drop, but she had spilt a whole cup instead, on his shirtsleeve. She had been contrite and on the verge of tears, but he had only loved her all the more; because her awkwardness was as much a part of her as her dark brown hair, and her blue eyes, as her dimples and her smile. It softened the firm maturity of her young woman's body, lent her movements a schoolgirlish charm; put him at ease in the aura of her beauty. For it was reassuring to know that so resplendent a goddess as Miranda had human frailties just as lesser creatures did.

After the coffee they had reclined in the shade, and Miranda had recited "Afternoon on a Hill" and Philip had remembered some of Rupert Brooke's "The Old Vicarage, Grantchester." Miranda was in her final year at the university—she was twenty-one—and she was majoring in English Literature. That had put them on common ground from the start, for Philip had loved literature since the moment he had opened *Huckleberry Finn* as a boy, and during the ensuing years he had never lost contact with it.

He had been affecting a pipe at the time (a pipe lent you a desperately-needed dignity when you were only twenty-six and commencing your first semester of teaching), and Miranda had filled it for him, holding his lighter over the bowl while he puffed the tobacco into ruddy life...It had been such a splendid afternoon, such a glorious afternoon, filled with September wind and September sunshine, with soft words and quiet laughter. The sun was quite low when they prepared to leave, and Philip hadn't wanted to leave at all. Miranda had seemed reluctant too, folding the linen tablecloth slowly, being far more meticulous than she usually was when she folded things, and then picking up the bowl half-filled with potato salad, intending to set it in the picnic basket. She didn't quite make the basket, however, for the bowl was large and clumsy and she was using only one hand. It escaped her fingers somehow, and overturned, and his lap was just beneath. That had been the last time he had ever worn his Madagascar slacks.

Her eyes had become so big and so round with dismay that he would have laughed if they had been anyone else's eyes besides Miranda's. You could never laugh at Miranda's eyes; they were too deep and too blue. He had only smiled instead, and said it didn't matter, and wiped his slacks with his handkerchief. Then he had seen her tears, and he had seen her standing there helplessly, tall and gawky, a child really, a lovely child who had become a woman a little too soon, and a beautiful woman too. And something within him had collapsed and a softness had spread all through him, and he had taken her into his arms and said, "Miranda, Miranda. Will you marry me, Miranda?"

The spaceport was far behind and the car was twisting through hills, humming on its overhead rail. It skimmed the treetops of a forest and passed high above a river. Looking down at the river bank, Philip saw his first familiar landmark.

It was nothing more than a pile of crumbled masonry now, overgrown with river weeds and sumac, but once, he knew, yesterday or a hundred years ago, it had been a public villa, and he had spent an afternoon on one of its sun-splashed patios, sipping cocktails and idly watching the white flurries of sails on the blue water below. And thinking of nothing, absolutely nothing . . .

Except Miranda.

Desperately he forced her out of his mind. It had been all right to think of her a century ago. It wasn't now. He couldn't think of her now because thinking of her tore him apart; because he had a reality to face and if he thought of her the way she had been a hundred years ago he wouldn't be able to face it—he wouldn't be able to search for her in the Cedarville cemetery and put flowers on her grave.

The Rehabilitation Director had told him that in a way his sentence had been merciful, merciful by accident of course, and not design. It would have been far worse, the Rehabilitation Director had said, for him to have been sentenced for only fifty years and then to have gone home, a man of twenty-seven, to a wife who had just passed seventy-two.

But it was naive to speak of mercy, even accidental mercy, in connection with the age of the Congressional Regime. An age that could condemn a man to suspended animation, tear him forcibly from the moment in time where he belonged, to be resurrected decades later into a moment in time where he did not belong—an age like that had no mercy, had no conception of the meaning of the word. Such an age was brutal, or more brutal, or less brutal; but it was never merciful.

And an age like the present one, while it had rediscovered mercy, was incapable of bestowing it upon a resurrected criminal. It could apologize to him for the cruelty of the preceding age, and it could remunerate him handsomely for the lost years, make him independent for life; but it could not give him back that moment in time that was uniquely his own, it could not bring back the soft smile and the unforgettable laughter of the woman he loved.

It could not obliterate a cemetery lot with a grave that had no right to be there, a grave that had not been there a subjective yesterday ago. It could not erase the words: Miranda Lorring, b. 2024, d. 20—. Or was it 21—?—he couldn't know of course, not yet, but he hoped she'd lived long and happily, and that she'd remarried and had children. She had been meant to have children. She had been too full of love not to have had them.

But if she had remarried, then her name wouldn't be Miranda Lorring. It would be Miranda something else, Miranda Green, perhaps, or Miranda Smith; and perhaps she had moved away from Cedarville, perhaps he was going home for nothing. No, not for nothing. He'd at least be able to trace her from Cedarville, trace her to wherever she'd gone to live, find her grave and cover it with forget-me-nots—forget-me-nots had been her favorite flower—and shed a tear on some quiet afternoon, her kiss of a hundred years ago a warm memory on his lips.

He got up in the gently swaying compartment and stepped over to the water cooler and dialed a drink. He had to do something, anything at all, to distract his mind. And the dial was so simple, so child-simple, requiring but the flick of his finger, and no thought, no attention. It could not interrupt the flow of his thoughts even briefly, and the cool taste of the water only gave the flow impetus, sent it churning through his mind, wildly, turning his knees weak, sending him staggering back to the seat, his grief a tight-packed lump swelling upward from his chest to his throat, and the memories, released, flowing freely now, catching him up and carrying him back to the light days, to the bright glorious days, back to his finest moment . . .

It had been a simple wedding. Miranda had worn blue and Philip had worn his academic dacrons. The Cedarville justice of the peace had performed the ceremony, being very brusque about it, saying the words as fast as he could and even holding out his hand for the fee the moment he had finished. But Philip had not minded. Nothing seemed ugly to him that day, not even the November rain that began to fall when they left the justice's house, not even the fact that he had been unable to obtain leave of absence from the university. The wedding took place on

414

Friday night and that gave them Saturday and Sunday; but two days weren't enough for a trip, and they decided to spend their honeymoon in the little house Philip had bought on Maple Street.

It was an adorable house, Miranda said for the hundredth time when they paused before it in the rain. Philip thought so too. It was set well back from the street and there were two catalpa trees in the front yard, one on either side of the little walk. There was a tiny porch, latticed on each side, and a twentieth-century paneled door.

He had carried her over the threshold, and set her down in the middle of the living room. All of his books were there, on built-in shelves on either side of the open fireplace, and Miranda's knickknacks covered the mantel. The new parlor suite matched the mauve-gray curtains.

She had been shy when he kissed her, and he hadn't known quite what to say. Being alone together in their own house involved an intimacy for which neither of them had been prepared, despite all the whispered phrases and stolen kisses, the looks passed in the university corridors, the afternoons shared, and the autumn evenings walking together along leaf-strewn streets. Finally she had said, "I'll make some coffee," and had gone into the kitchen. The first thing she had done was to drop the coffee canister, and there was the coffee, dark against the gleaming floor, and there was Miranda, her blue eyes misted, lovely in her blue dress, a goddess in the room, his goddess; and then a goddess in his arms, soft-lipped and pliant, then warm and suddenly tight-pressed against him, her arms about his neck and her dark hair soft against his face . . .

A village showed in the distance, between wooded hills. It was a deserted village and it had fallen into ruin, but there were remnants of remembered buildings still standing and Philip recognized it as a little town not far from Cedarville.

He had very few memories associated with it, so he experienced but little pain. He experienced fear instead, for he knew that very soon the car would be slowing, that shortly he would be stepping down to the rotting platform of the Cedarville station. And he knew that he would be seeing another deserted village, one with many memories, and he was afraid that he couldn't endure the sight of remembered streets choked with weeds, of beloved houses fallen into decay, of vacant staring windows that long ago had glowed with warmth and life.

The Rehabilitation Director had explained about the deserted villages, the emptying cities, the approaching desuetude of Earth. Interstellar Travel had given back the dream that Interplanetary Travel had taken away. Arid Venus and bleak Mars were uninhabitable, and the ice-choked outer planets weren't planets at all, but wheeling glaciers glinting malevolently in pale sunlight. Alpha Centauri 4 was something else, however, and Sirius 41 was a dream come true.

The Sweike Drive had delivered Man from the dilemma in which his proclivity to overproduce himself had involved him, and Earth was losing its population as fast as ships could be built to transport colonists to the stars. There were colonies as far out as Vega and before long there would be one in the Arcturus system. Except for the crews who manned the ships, interstellar runs were a one-way proposition. People went out to distant suns and settled in spacious valleys, in virgin timberlands, at the feet of unexploited mountains. They did not return. And it was better that way, the Rehabilitation Director had said, for a one-way ticket resolved the otherwise irresolvable problem of the Lorentz transformation.

Philip looked out at the tumbled green hills through which the car was passing. It was late afternoon, and long shadows lay coolly in deep valleys. The sun was low in the sky, reddening, and around it cumulus clouds were becoming riotous with color. A wind wrinkled the foliage of new forests, bent the meadow grass on quiet hillsides.

He sighed. Earth was sufficient for him. The stars could give him nothing that he could not find here: a woodland to walk in, a stream to read by, a blue sky to soften his sorrow . . .

The tumbled hills gave way to fields, and the fields ushered in a vaguely familiar stand of cedars. He became aware that the car was slowing, and glancing up at the station screen, he saw the nostalgic name spelled out in luminescent letters: CEDARVILLE. He got up numbly and pulled his slender valise from the overhead rack. His chest was tight and he could feel a throbbing in his temple.

Through the window he caught glimpses of outlying houses, of collapsed walls and sagging roofs, of moldering porches and overgrown yards. For a moment he thought that he couldn't go through with it, that he couldn't force himself to go through with it. Then he realized that the car had stopped, and he saw the compartment door slide open and the metallic steps leaf out. He descended the steps without thinking, down to the reinforced platform. His feet had hardly touched the ancient timbers before the car was in motion again, humming swiftly away on its overhead rail, losing itself in the haze of approaching evening.

He stood without moving for a long time. The utter silence that precedes evening in the country was all around him. In the west, the wake of the sun was deepening from orange to scarlet, and the first night shadows were creeping in from the east.

Presently he turned and started up the street that led to the center of the village. He walked slowly, avoiding the clumps of grass that had thrust up through the cracks and crevices in the old macadam, ducking beneath the low limbs of tangled maples. The first houses began to appear, standing forlornly in their jungles of yards. Philip looked at them and they looked back with their sunken staring eyes, and he looked quickly away.

When he reached the point where the street sloped down into the little valley where the village proper lay, he paused. The cemetery was on the opposite slope of the valley and to reach it he would have to pass Maple Street, the community hall, the university, and half a hundred other remembered places. No matter how much he steeled himself, he would experience the tug of a thousand associations, relive a thousand cherished moments.

Suddenly his strength drained from him and he sat down on his upended valise. What is hell? he asked himself. Hell, he answered himself, is the status reserved for the individuals of a totalitarian state who voice truths contrary to the rigid credo of that state; who write books criticizing the self-appointed guardians of mass man's intellectual boundaries.

Hell is what remains to a man when everything he loves has been taken away . . .

It had been a modest book, rather thin, with an academic jacket done in quiet blue. It had been published during the fall of the same year he had married Miranda, and at first it had made no stir at all. The name of it had been *The New Sanhedrin*.

Then, during the winter, it had caught the collective eye of that subdivision of the Congressional State known as the Subversive Literature Investigative Body, and almost immediately accusations had begun to darken the front pages of newspapers and to resound on the newscasts. The SLIB had wasted no time. It set out to crucify Philip, the way the high priests of the Sanhedrin had set out to crucify Christ over two thousand years ago.

He had not believed they would go so far. In developing his analogy between the Congressional State and the Sanhedrin, demonstrating how both guarded their supreme power by eliminating everyone who deviated from the existent thought-world, he had anticipated publicity, perhaps even notoriety. He had never anticipated imprisonment, trial, and condemnation; he had never dreamed that a political crime could rate the supreme punishment of that new device of inhuman ingenuity which had supplanted the chair and the gas chamber and the gallows—the Suspended Animation Chambers popularly know as the Deep Freeze.

He had underestimated the power of his own prose and he had underestimated the power of the group his prose had censured. He had forgotten that totalitarian governments are always on the lookout for scapegoats; someone to make an example of, a person with few funds and with no political influence, and preferably a person engaged in one of the professions which the mass of men have always resented. Specifically, an obscure political philosopher.

He had forgotten, but he had remembered. He had remembered on that bleak morning in April, when he heard the puppet judge intone the sentence—"One hundred years suspended animation for subversive activities against the existent governing body, term to begin September 14, 2046 and to expire September 14, 2146. Gradien cell locks to be employed, so that any attempt by future governing authorities to alleviate said term shall result in the instant death of the prisoner..."

The months between April and September had fled like light. Miranda visited him every day, and the two of them tried to force the rest of their lives into fleeting seconds, into precious moments that kept slipping through their fingers. In May they celebrated Philip's birthday, and in July, Miranda's. The celebration in each case consisted of a "Happy Birthday, darling," and a kiss stolen behind the omnipresent guard's back.

And all the while he had seen the words in her eyes, the words she had wanted to say desperately and couldn't say, the words, "I'll wait for you, darling." And he knew that she would have waited if she only could have, that she would have waited gladly; but no woman could wait for you a hundred years, no matter how much she loved you, no matter how faithful she was.

He had seen the words in her eyes in the last moment, had seen them trembling on her lips; and he had known what not being able to say them had done to her. He had seen the pain in the soft lines of her childlike face, in the curve of her sensitive mouth, and he had felt it in her farewell kiss—the anguish, the despair, the hopelessness. And he had stood there woodenly before the elevator, between the guards, unable to cry because tears were inadequate, unable to smile because his lips were stiff, because his cheeks were stone, and his jaw granite.

She was the last thing he saw before the elevator door slid shut, and that was as it should have been. She was standing in front of the Deep Freeze window and behind her, behind the cruel interstices of wire mesh, the blue September sky showed, the exact hue of her eyes. That was the way he had remembered her during the descent to the underground units and along the clammy corridor to his refrigerated cell...

418

The days of dictatorships, whether they be collective or individual, are numbered. The budding dictatorship of Philip's day was no more than an ugly memory now. The Sweike Drive had thwarted it, had prevented it from coming into flower. For man's frustrations faded, when he found that he could reach the stars; and without frustrations to exploit, no dictatorship can survive.

But the harm small men do outlives them, Philip thought. And if that axiom had been true before the advent of the Deep Freeze, it was doubly true now. With the Deep Freeze man had attained Greek tragedy.

He lit a cigarette and the bright flame of his lighter brought the deepening shadows of the street into bold relief. With a shock he realized that night had fallen, and looking up between the tangled trees, he saw the first star.

He stood up and started down the sloping street. As he progressed, more stars came out, bringing the ancient macadam into dim reality. A night wind came up and breathed in the trees, whispered in the wild timothy that had pre-empted tidy lawns, rattled rachitic shutters.

He knew that seeing the house would only cause him pain, but it was a pain he had to endure, for homecoming would not be complete until he had stepped upon his own doorstep. So when he came to Maple Street he turned down the overgrown sidewalk, making his way slowly between giant hedges and riotous saplings. For a moment he thought he saw the flicker of a light far down the street, but he could not be sure.

He knew of course that there was very little chance that the house would still be standing—a hundred years is a long time for a house to live—that if it were still standing it would probably be changed beyond recognition, decayed beyond recognition.

And yet, it was still standing and it had not changed at all. It was just the same as it had been when he had left it over a hundred years ago, and there was a light shining in the living-room window.

He stood very still in the shambles of the street. The house isn't real, he told himself. It can't be real. I won't believe that it's real until I touch it, until I feel its wood beneath my fingertips, its floor beneath my feet. He walked slowly up the little walk. The front lawn was neatly trimmed and there were two tiny catalpa trees standing in newly turned plots of ground. He mounted the steps to the latticed porch and the steps were solid beneath his feet and gave forth the sound of his footsteps.

He touched the print lock of the door with the tip of his ring finger and the door obediently opened. Diffidently he stepped over the threshold and the door swung gently to behind him.

There was a mauve-gray parlor suite in the living room and it matched the mauve-gray curtains on the windows. Pine knots were ruddy in the open fireplace and his books stood in stately rows on the banking built-in shelves. Miranda's knickknacks covered the mantel.

His easy chair was drawn up before the fire and his slippers were waiting on the floor beside it. His favorite pipe reposed on a nearby end table and a canister of his favorite tobacco stood beside it. On the arm of the chair was a brand new copy of *The New Sanhedrin.*

He stood immobile just within the door, trying hard to breathe. Then he superimposed a rigid objectivity upon the subjective chaos of his thoughts, and forced himself to see the room as it really was and not as he wished it to be.

The lamp in the window was like the lamp Miranda had kept in the window a hundred years ago, but it wasn't the same lamp. It was a duplication. And the parlor suite was much like the one that had been in the room a hundred years ago when he had carried Miranda over the threshold, and yet it wasn't quite the same, and neither were the curtains. There were differences in the material, in the design—slight differences, but apparent enough if you looked for them. And his easy chair—that was a duplication too, as were his slippers and his pipe; *The New Sanhedrin.*

The fireplace was the same, and yet not quite the same: the pattern of the bricks was different, the bricks themselves were different, the mantel was different. And the knickknacks on the mantel . . .

He choked back a sob as he walked over to examine them more closely, for they were not duplications. The were originals and time had been unkind to them. Some of them were broken and a patina of the years covered all of them. They were like children's toys found in an attic on a rainy day . . .

He bent over his books, and they were originals too. He pulled one from the shelf and opened it. The yellowed pages betrayed the passage of the years and he replaced it tenderly. Then he noticed the diary on the topmost shelf.

He took it down with trembling hands, opened and turned its pages. When he saw the familiar handwriting, he knew whose diary it was and suddenly his knees were weak and he could not stand, and he collapsed into the easy chair before the fire.

Numbly he turned the pages to the first entry. It was dated September 15, 2046 . . .

I walked down the steps, the stone slabs of steps that front the tomb in which men are buried alive, and I walked through the streets of the city.

I walked through the streets, the strange streets, past hordes of indifferent people. Gradually I became aware of the passing hours, the fleeting minutes, the swift-flying seconds; and each second became an unbearable pain, each minute a dull agony, each hour a crushing eternity . . .

I do not know how I came to the spaceport. Perhaps God directed my footsteps there. But the moment I saw the shimmering spires of the new ships pointing into the September sky, everything I had ever read concerning the Sweike Drive coalesced blindingly in my mind, and I knew what I had to do.

A clock which is in motion moves slower than a stationary clock. The difference is imperceptible at ordinary velocities, but when the speed of light is approached, the difference is enormous.

The Sweike Drive approaches the speed of light. It approaches the speed of light as closely as it can be approached, without both men and ship becoming pure energy.

A clock on a ship employing the Sweike Drive would barely move at all . . .

Not daring to believe, he skipped a page . . .

September 18, 2046—They tell me it will take two years! Two of my sweet, my precious years to become a space-line stewardess! But there's no other way, no other way at all, and my application is already in. I know they will accept it—with everyone clamoring for the stars the need for ship's personnel is . . .

His hands were shaking uncontrollably and the pages escaped from his fingers, days, months, years fluttering wildly by. He halted them finally . . .

June 3, 2072 (Sirius 41)—I have measured time by many moving clocks, and moving clocks are kind. But when planet-fall arrives, stationary clocks take over, and stationary clocks are not kind. You wait in some forsaken port for the return run and you count each minute and resent its passage bitterly. For over the decades, the minutes add together into months and years and you are afraid that despite the moving clocks, you will be too old after all . . .

The pages escaped again and he stopped them at the final entry . . .

February 9, 2081—Today I was officially notified that my application for the Arcturus run has been accepted! I have been in a kind of ecstatic trance ever since, dreaming and planning, because I can dream and plan now! Now I know that I shall see my beloved again, and I shall wear a white gardenia in my hair, and the perfume he likes the best, and I shall have our house rebuilt and everything in it restored—there'll be plenty of time if the 65-year estimate is correct; and when my beloved is released I shall be there waiting to take him in my arms, and though I shall not be as young as he remembers me, I shall not be old either. And the lonely years between the stars shall not have been in vain . . .

For I have only one love. I shall never have another.

The words blurred on the page and Philip let the diary slip from his fingers to the arm of the chair. "Miranda," he whispered.

He stood up. "Miranda," he said.

The house was silent. "Miranda!" he called. "Miranda!"

There was no answer. He went from the living room to the bedroom. The bedroom was the way it had been a hundred years ago except that it was empty now. Empty of Miranda.

He returned to the living room and went into the kitchen. The kitchen was the same too, but there was no Miranda in it. He switched on the light and stared at the porcelain sink, the chrome stove, the white cupboards, the gleaming utility table . . .

There was a hand mirror lying on the table, and beside it was a crumpled gardenia. He picked up the gardenia and it was cool and soft in his hand. He held it to his nostrils and breathed its fresh scent. There was another scent mingled with it, a delicate fragrant scent. He recognized it immediately as Miranda's perfume.

Suddenly he could not breathe, and he ran out of the house and into the darkness. He saw the light flickering at the end of the street then, and he walked toward it with unbelieving steps. The community hall grew slowly out of the darkness and the light became many lights, became bright windows. From somewhere in the surrounding shadows he heard the humming of a portable generator.

When he climbed the steps a hundred years flew away. There was no 77¢ supper of course, and the hall showed unmistakable signs of age, despite the fact that it had been recently remodeled. But there was Miranda. Miranda standing by a lonely table. Miranda crying. A more mature Miranda, with lines showing on her face where no lines had showed before, but light lines, adorable lines . . .

He realized why she had not met him at the Deep Freeze. She had been afraid, afraid that the moving clocks had not moved slowly enough after all; and she must have decided to meet him at the house instead, for she knew he would come home. She must have heard the monorail car pull in, must have known he was on his way . . .

Suddenly he remembered the mirror and the crumpled gardenia.

Silly girl, lovely girl . . . His eyes misted and he felt the tears run down his cheeks. He stumbled into the room, and she came hesitantly forward to meet him, her face beautiful with the new years. A goddess in the room, a mature goddess, the awkwardness gone forever, the schoolgirlish charm left somewhere in the abysses between the stars; his goddess—and then a goddess in his arms, warm and sluddenly tight-pressed against him, her dark hair soft against his face, her voice whispering in his ear, across the years, across the timeless infinities, "Welcome home, darling. Welcome home."

FOR DISCUSSION: One Love Have I

1. How does Miranda change in the story? Is she different at the conclusion of the story in other than a physical way?
2. Why does the author set many of his key scenes in the month of September? What literary effect does this achieve?
3. The story moves back and forth in time from the present to the past. In your opinion, do the flashbacks to the past add depth to the story itself and to the two main characters?
4. As he tells his story, the author gives the reader some provocative glimpses of politics, governmental repression, scientific advances, and man's inhumanity to man. Do these ideas increase the value of the story? Are they necessary to the plot?
5. The author poses a problem in his story: how can a man brought back to active life after one hundred years in suspended animation ever find the one he once loved? Does this author successfully foreshadow the answer to his problem early in the story?

In a world of hydrogen bombs and nuclear umbrellas, the threat of holocaust becomes a major concern of thoughtful writers. The author of this story shows us with dramatic force and stunning impact what the holocaust, if and when it comes, will be like for ordinary people everywhere.

Who Shall Dwell
by H. C. Neal

It came on a Sunday afternoon and that was good, because if it had happened on a weekday the father would have been at work and the children at school, leaving the mother at home alone and the whole family disorganized with hardly any hope at all. They had prayed that it would never come, ever, but suddenly here it was.

The father a slender, young-old man, slightly stooped from years of labor, was resting on the divan and half-listening to a program of waltz music on the radio. Mother was in the kitchen preparing a chicken for dinner and the younger boy and girl were in the bedroom drawing crude pictures of familiar barnyard animals on a shared slate. The older boy was in the tack shed out back, saddle-soaping some harnesses.

When the waltz program was interrupted by an announcer with a routine political appeal, the father rose, tapped the ash from his pipe, and ambled lazily into the kitchen.

"How about joining me in a little glass of wine?" he asked, patting his wife affectionately on the hip.

"If you don't think it would be too crowded," she replied, smiling easily at their standing jest.

He grinned amiably and reached into the cupboard for the bottle and glasses.

Suddenly the radio message was abruptly cut off. A moment of humming silence. Then, in a voice pregnant with barely controlled excitement, the announcer almost shouted:

"Bomb alert! Bomb alert! Attention! Attention! A salvo of missiles has just been launched across the sea, heading this way. Attention! They are expected to strike within the next 16 minutes. Sixteen minutes!

This is a verified alert! Take cover! Take cover! Keep your radios tuned for further instructions."

"My God!" the father gasped, dropping the glasses. "Oh, my God!" His ruggedly handsome face was ashen, puzzled, as though he knew beyond a shadow of doubt that this was real—but still could not quite believe it.

"Get the children," his wife blurted, then dashed to the door to call the older boy. He stared at her a brief moment, seeing the fear in her pretty face, but something else, too, something divorced from the fear. Defiance. And a loathing for all men involved in the making and dispatch of nuclear weapons.

He wheeled then, and ran to the bedroom. "Let's go," he snapped, "shelter drill!" Despite a belated attempt to tone down the second phrase and make it seem like just another of the many rehearsals they'd had, his voice and bearing galvanized the youngsters into instant action. They leaped from the bed without a word and dashed for the door.

He hustled them through the kitchen to the rear door and sent them scooting to the shelter. As he returned to the bedroom for outer garments for himself and his wife, the older boy came running in.

"This is the hot one, Son," said his father tersely, "the real one." He and the boy stared at each other a long moment, both knowing what must be done and each knowing the other would more than do his share, yet wondering still at the frightening fact that it must be done at all.

"How much time we got, Dad?"

"Not long," the father replied, glancing at his watch, "12, maybe 14 minutes."

The boy disappeared into the front room, going after the flashlight and battery radio. The father stepped to the closet, slid the door open and picked up the flat metal box containing their vital papers, marriage license, birth certificates, etc. He tossed the box on the bed, then took down his wife's shortcoat and his own hunting jacket. Draping the clothing over his arm, he then picked up the metal box and the big family Bible from the headboard on the bed. Everything else they would need had been stored in the shelter the past several months. He heard his wife approaching and turned as she entered the room.

"Ready, Dear?" she asked.

"Yes, we're ready now," he replied, "are the kids gone in?"

"They're all down," she answered, then added with a faint touch of despairing bewilderment, "I still can't believe it's real."

"We've got to believe it," he said, looking her steadily in the eye, "we can't afford not to."

Outside, the day was crisp and clear, typical of early fall. Just right for boating on the river, fishing or bird shooting. A regular peach of a day, he thought, for fleeing underground to escape the awesome hell of a nuclear strike. Who was the writer who had said about atomic weapons, "Would any self-respecting cannibal toss one into a village of women and children?" He looked at his watch again. Four minutes had elapsed since the first alarm. Twelve minutes, more or less, remained.

Inside the shelter, he dogged the door with its double-strength strap iron bar, and looked around to see that his family was squared away. His wife, wearing her attractive blue print cotton frock (he noticed for the first time), was methodically checking the food supplies, assisted by the older son. The small children had already put their initial fright behind them, as is the nature of youngsters, and were drawing on the slate again in quiet, busy glee.

Now it began. The waiting.

They knew, he and his wife, that others would come soon, begging and crying to be taken in now that the time was here, now that Armageddon had come screaming toward them, stabbing through the sky on stubbed wings of shining steel.

They had argued the aspects of this when the shelter was abuilding. It was in her mind to share their refuge. "We can't call ourselves Christians and then deny safety to our friends when the showdown comes," she contended, "that isn't what God teaches."

"That's nothing but religious pap," he retorted with a degree of anger, "oatmeal Christianity." For he was a hardheaded man, an Old Testament man. "God created the family as the basic unit of society," he reasoned. "That should make it plain that man's primary Christian duty is to protect his family."

"But don't you see?" she protested, "we must prepare to purify ourselves . . . to rise above this 'mine' thinking and be as God's own son, who said, 'Love thy neighbor.'"

"No," he replied with finality, "I can't buy that." Then, after a moment's thought while he groped for the words to make her understand the truth which burned in the core of his soul, "It is my family I must save, no one more. You. These kids. Our friends are like the people of Noah's time: he warned them of the coming flood when he built the ark on God's command. He was ridiculed and scoffed at, just as we have been ridiculed. No," and here his voice took on a new sad sureness, an air of dismal certainty, "it is meant that if they don't prepare, they die I see no need for further argument." And so, she had reluctantly acquiesced.

With seven minutes left, the first knock rang the shelter door. "Let us in! For God's sake, man, let us in!"

He recognized the voice. It was his first neighbor down the road toward town.

"No!" shouted the father, "there is only room for us. Go! Take shelter in your homes. You may yet be spared."

Again came the pounding. Louder. More urgent.

"You let us in or we'll break down this door!" He wondered, with some concern, if they were actually getting a ram of some sort to batter at the door. He was reasonably certain it would hold. At least as long as it must.

The seconds ticked relentlessly away. Four minutes left.

His wife stared at the door in stricken fascination and moaned slightly. "Steady, girl," he said, evenly. The children, having halted their game at the first shouting, looked at him in fearful wonderment. He glared at his watch, ran his hands distraughtly through his hair, and said nothing.

Three minutes left.

At that moment, a woman's cry from the outside pierced him in an utterly vulnerable spot, a place the men could never have touched with their desperate demands. "If you won't let me in," she cried, "please take my baby, my little girl."

He was stunned by her plea. This he had not anticipated. What must I do? he asked himself in sheer agony. What man on earth could deny a child the chance to live?

At that point, his wife rose, sobbing, and stepped to the door. Before he could move to stop her, she let down the latch and dashed outside. Instantly a three-year-old girl was thrust into the shelter. He hastily fought the door latch on again, then stared at the frightened little newcomer in mute rage, hating her with an abstract hatred for simply being there in his wife's place and knowing he could not turn her out.

He sat down heavily, trying desperately to think. The voices outside grew louder. He glanced at his watch, looked at the faces of his own children a long moment, then rose to his feet. There were two minutes left, and he had made his decision. He marveled now that he had even considered any other choice.

"Son," he said to the older boy, "you take care of them." It was as simple as that.

Unlatching the door, he thrust it open and stepped out. The crowd surged toward him. Blocking the door with his body, he snatched up the two children nearest him, a boy and a girl, and shoved them into the shelter. "Bar that door," he shouted to his son, "and don't open it for at least a week!"

Hearing the latch drop into place, he turned and glanced around at the faces in the crowd. Some of them were still babbling incoherently, utterly panic-stricken. Others were quiet now, resigned, no longer afraid.

Stepping to his wife's side, he took her hand and spoke in a warm, low tone. "They will be all right, the boy will lead them." He grinned reassuringly and added, "We should be together, you and I."

She smiled wordlessly through her tears and squeezed his hand, exchanging with him in the one brief gesture a lifetime and more of devotion.

Then struck the first bomb, blinding them, burning them, blasting them into eternity. Streaking across the top of the world, across the extreme northern tip of Greenland, then flaming downrange through the chilled Arctic skies, it had passed over Moscow, over Voronezh, and on over Krasny to detonate high above their city of Shakhty.

The bird had been 19 minutes in flight, launched from a bomb-blasted, seared-surface missile pit on the coast of California. America's retaliation continued for several hours.

FOR DISCUSSION: Who Shall Dwell

1. The author uses certain assumptions that most of us hold to reinforce and dramatize the point he is making. What are those assumptions and how does he use them?
2. Does the father's hatred of the three-year-old girl thrust into the shelter in place of his wife make him seem more of a human being?
3. Why did the author choose not to give his characters personal names? If he had done so, how might his story have suffered?